REAL ESTATE

Jane DeLynn

**POSEIDON
PRESS**
NEW YORK
LONDON
TORONTO
SYDNEY
TOKYO

This book is a work of fiction. Names, characters, places and incidents are either the product of the author's imagination or are used fictitiously. Any resemblance to actual events or locales or persons, living or dead, is entirely coincidental.

Copyright © 1988 by Jane DeLynn
All rights reserved
including the right of reproduction
in whole or in part in any form
Published by Poseidon Press
A Division of Simon & Schuster Inc.
Simon & Schuster Building
Rockefeller Center
1230 Avenue of the Americas
New York, New York 10020

POSEIDON PRESS is a registered trademark of Simon & Schuster Inc.

Designed by Karolina Harris
Manufactured in the United States of America

10 9 8 7 6 5 4 3 2 1

Library of Congress Cataloging-in-Publication Data

DeLynn, Jane.

  Real estate.

  I. Title.
PS3554.E4465R43   1988   813'.54   87-29299
ISBN 0-671-54424-1

For my friends who helped me with this book: Cathy, Jaime and Bill, Rachel, George and Lone, Susanna and Neil, Eileen, Roger, Bonnie, David, Rose, Johnny, Michael, and Michael—

My dear friend Tim—

My parents—

Butterscotch, Jackie, Katharyn, Isabelle, and—yes—John.

With thanks to my editor, Ann Patty, and my agent, Jane Rotrosen Berkey.

ONE

1 New York stories are about homes: renting them, buying them, renovating them, being evicted from them. Due to the exigencies of the real estate market it seemed crazy to Lorraine and David to move away from their rent-controlled apartment on Riverside Drive to spend almost two hundred thousand dollars (a fortune—so it seemed at the time) on a new (i.e., old) place that was neither larger, had better views, more direct sunlight, nor was in a more prestigious neighborhood; on the other hand, after more than fifteen years of marriage, all of them in the same 2500 square feet of space, they had begun to get bored. They had put off their grandiose plans for renovation until that moment (surely not distant in time) when their own building would co-op itself; then, as that date, beset by endless legal hassles and delays, continued to recede, they decided to go ahead and renovate before the title was officially in their name. Almost certainly it would be soon; in any case they were not going to move; the risk was negligible; why wait? They hired an architect and contractors and moved into a sublet on nearby West End Avenue, from which David (a lawyer) and Lorraine (fashion coordinator for a New York department store) could easily supervise the renovation.

Often during this temporary displacement they congratulated themselves on their wise decision. The investment would be repaid when they sold the apartment, and with the money they were saving by not putting down a down payment Lorraine could quit her job and establish the sportswear manufacturing firm she had always wanted to run. It would be a difficult six months or so—but then, they would have so much more to look forward to when they were back into their new, old home, with a new business and a new, old marriage.

Fatigued, courtesy of the fashion business, by the constant progression of color and style, Lorraine ordered everything—walls, floor, kitchen and bathroom tiles, piano—to be done over in white. Lately the world was so full of noise and visual stimuli, she was finding herself unable to think. Moldings were removed, beams bared, as she tried to make the apartment into the objective correlative for a sought inner emptiness—as well as a replication of the empty undecorated lofts of Soho and Tribeca she would surely have moved into did she not have an obligation to educate and otherwise raise her daughter in a more domestic environment than could be found south of Houston Street.

After slightly more than a year's time the contractors (already over budget) had done as much as they were going to do without recourse on David's part to either further payment or the law, so, no longer willing to postpone the move, Lorraine and David and Judy and Jack (the dog) and Jezebel (the cat) moved back into their new, old, still-unfinished apartment. Almost all the furniture was gone—donated, loaned, sold, or abandoned on the street for the garbage trucks to remove. Cartons full of books, papers, and old toys Judy retained sentimental attachments toward were stuffed in the maid's room behind the kitchen, to be disposed of on some future, more leisured occasion. The first night, sitting on the bare, pickled white floor, they all—even Judy and Jack—had a little champagne. When David got drunk and knocked over the second bottle, they opened a third. He staggered onto the platform bed the contractors had built (but left unpainted) in the master bedroom, then rolled over and started snoring. Lorraine chalked this up to alcohol and the stress of moving and determined not to let it bother her, but after a week of standing for meals at the kitchen counter (as yet they did not have stools) with David persistently passing out on the bed after dinner (there was no couch) a terrible emptiness overcame her.

Despite a year of nails, hammers, plaster, paint, she was

still the same person. Her husband was still her husband, her child her child, her dog her dog. Such gloom she had not experienced since her postpartum depression. Then David began to come home later and later, sometimes not till 1 or 2 A.M., saying he had to work late at the office. On the rare occasions when he tried to roll on top of her she pushed him and his increasingly overweight body and alcoholic breath over to the other side of their king-sized bed. Sick of the empty rooms and the housekeeper Aurelia's cooking and her mother's glumness, Judy began to go to her friends' houses after school every day, often staying there through dinner as Lorraine took advantage of her absence to work late herself. Sometimes she became so immersed in her work that, not looking at her watch until maybe ten, she would pick up Judy at a friend's house so late that the friend might already have been sent off to bed. The cold stares of Judy's friends' parents didn't bother Lorraine; in her depression she scarcely noticed them. Within six months, the only true beneficiary of the renovated apartment was Aurelia, who had constant access to TV sets, the microwave, the white piano. On this she played island tunes her mother had crooned to her. Once Lorraine had come home and heard her singing: "My island home / She calls to me / Every night I hear the breeze / Brushing through the bamboo trees / In the morning I awake / In this strange land / To my mistake."

The fact that Aurelia was in the apartment far more than anyone else drove Lorraine crazy. Often she thought of firing her. Her slowness, her insolence, her uncanny ability at picking out rotten pears, onions, tomatoes, the huge amounts of salt she put in the food she prepared for Judy—there were more than enough reasons. On the other hand, Lorraine would immediately have to replace her with someone else (no doubt equally lazy and insolent, but without the capacity to sing such haunting melodies) to clean the floors and do the laundry, shop and make at least the occasional dinner for Judy and herself and eventually even David—at that future undetermined time when everything in her life would fall into place.

Two years later this time still had not come.

At a gallery opening one night a man bumped into Lorraine, jostling the wine glass she was holding. A red stain appeared on her white dress. "I'm sorry," the man said, turning around.

"It's dumb to drink red wine at parties, isn't it?" she replied.

He followed her into the bathroom. It was a small room. Leaning against the cold of the sink, Lorraine became aware that the younger man's head, as he kneeled on the floor trying to rub away the wine stain, was very near her crotch. Was it merely this thought that created a feeling of warmth down there, or was it the young man himself?

Perhaps it was Jack's thoughts that had crept into her brain. He too had become aware of the possibilities in this apparently wealthy, well-dressed, somewhat older woman. She was different in most ways from the kind of women he usually dated. The "well-dressed" he liked, but the "older" somewhat bothered him; on the other hand, he was sick of his life. He used the wine spill as an excuse to offer to buy her dinner. Something told him to choose a better restaurant than he ordinarily would have. He ordered an expensive red burgundy. ("Can't ruin the dress more than it already is," said Lorraine.) Over dinner they discussed art, swimming, mice, Guaymas—a Mexican beach town they discovered they had both been to in the late '70s. It had never become chic; this, perversely, pleased them. They fantasized they had seen each other there; this story was so often repeated in the myth they created of their relationship that eventually it achieved the status of true memory. When they got outside on the street both were slightly drunk.

"Can I take you home?" asked Jack.

"No," said Lorraine. Jack's face fell—had he wasted almost half of his weekly take-home salary on her? "Actually, I'm still living with my husband," said Lorraine.

"Oh," said Jack. She had neglected to mention this over dinner. He looked down at her hand; she was not wearing a ring.

"I suppose you have children?" asked Jack.

"One. And a dog. Oddly enough, with your name. And a cat. And a housekeeper who hates me."

"Why?"

"Why does she hate me?" asked Lorraine.

"Why don't you get another housekeeper?"

"Judy likes her," said Lorraine. "That's my daughter." Pause. "She hates me too."

"I guess you can't get another daughter," said Jack.

"Or another husband." She looked quite openly at Jack as she said this. So it was in his lap, after all. Almost too easily. He was not sure he liked this; his fantasy about her had not had time to build. In the cab to his place she put her hand in his. Jack had not tried to seduce anyone in a cab for so long it made him feel even younger. There was something about the whole evening that seemed out of another place and time —relevant not to the kind of person he had ever been, but to the kind that at one time he had thought he was supposed to be. He felt like a child pretending to be a grown-up. Although their age difference was less than six years, this initial feeling of Jack's never left him. Always Lorraine was the mature one, always Jack the bumbling teenager. He reminded himself he was an adult, a thirty-five-year-old artist.

The more he tried to cheer himself up, the more he felt removed from what he was supposed to be doing in the taxi: putting his lips next to this strange woman's, moving his tongue out of his mouth and into hers, moving his hand up her stockinged leg.

At last they reached the building on Third Street off Second Avenue where Jack had lived in five small dark rooms ever since moving to Manhattan following his graduation from Pratt. During his tenure there the neighborhood had undergone a series of revivals and deliquescences, most of which seemed to have a close correlation with hairstyle: long-haired hippies, blue-haired punkettes, crewcut New Wavers.

"I haven't been down here since the Fillmore closed," said Lorraine. "Do you remember that?"

"Of course. Now it's the Saint. For a while it was a gay disco, but" (Jack shrugged) "AIDS. Over there is Night Birds, and up a street or two the Kiev and 103 Second Avenue."

"I don't know them," said Lorraine. "Are they nice?"

"I'm sick of them," said Jack. "Them, the neighborhood, my apartment. It was a temporary sublet fourteen years ago. But it always took a little bit more than I could afford to be able to move. Unless my career takes a big upswing, I'll probably be here until I die."

"Maybe it will go co-op," suggested Lorraine. "God knows, I'm hoping mine will."

"Even if I had the money for the down payment, I probably couldn't get a mortgage. Then, since it's a sublet, I don't think I have any legal rights. Every once in a while the original tenant threatens to move back."

"You should see a lawyer."

"I know."

This was not a sexy conversation. They climbed the rest of the stairs in silence. Jack felt his ears get hot as he opened the door. He could not remember whether he had brought the garbage downstairs, or left it tied up in a huge green bag behind the door. He took her coat, acting as if he were going to hang it up someplace, but the hall closet was still crowded with the previous tenant's clothing and records, so he took it inside and threw it on his bed. Then he went into his little kitchen and began opening drawers. "Wine, beer, cognac?" he asked.

"Cognac," said Lorraine, not so much because she wanted it as to maintain a sense of occasion. The expensive dinner had naturally created an expectation in her of a Soho or Tribeca loft. When the taxi had gone east on Fourteenth to turn down Second a certain sparkle had gone out of her. This was not very prosperous. She began to feel nervous. Through her thin stockings the nubby material on the couch irritated her, and she kept shifting positions. Jack, noticing this, worried that she was bored. He poured cognac into two wine glasses and brought these out to her. "Mmm," said Lorraine, as she took a sip. She leaned her head back against the couch and shut her eyes.

"Would you like some music?" asked Jack.

"Sure."

"What do you like?"

"You pick it. Something nice."

Carrying his glass, Jack walked over to the painted wooden box in which he kept his records. He knelt down and began to flip through them. An acute feeling of embarrassment washed over him. Almost all the records were old—relics from the late '60s or early '70s, plus a few obviously more recent records such as the Talking Heads or Brian Eno. What had he listened to in the last five years? He had no idea what someone her age would think nice. Mozart? Early Beatles albums? Linda Ronstadt? Everything seemed wrong.

"I don't care. Anything," said Lorraine. In desperation, Jack decided on Billie Holiday. Not exactly an imaginative choice, but surely it was safe; she was before *both* their times. He sat back down next to Lorraine on the couch. He landed a little too near her. He moved back a little. Then he realized this would look unfriendly, so he moved forward again. This awkwardness appealed to Lorraine. She could peer through his dark, slightly curly hair into his head as if it were a window. She decided it was okay he didn't have any money—especially as he had demonstrated his willingness to spend what little he had on her. Maybe she would even like him better for it. The new benignness of her attitude began to relax him. He began to be able to look at her, instead of at the objects in the room he knew far too well. Her skin was not great, but the structure of her bones was beautiful. She had a long neck. Her eyes were blue. They reeked of sadness, but perhaps that was merely the lines around them. He felt she wanted him to rescue her from something, and he felt obligated to do so—if only because he had already come this far. With a feeling of fatigue rather than expectation, he began to do what he supposed she wanted him to do.

After they were done, they lay a long time in silence. Jack felt like moving Lorraine's weight off him, but he was worried about appearing unfriendly. "God, that was *great*," said Lorraine. Was it? Jack hadn't realized. He patted Lorraine's head as it lay on his breastbone, hurting him, while he listened to the needle's repetitive hush over the grooves at the end of the record. He thought about getting up and flipping it over, but somehow it did not seem appropriate that he be noticing this. Instead, he cleared his throat.

As if on cue, Lorraine looked at her watch. She rolled off him and in one motion sat up on the bed. "A mother's work is never done," she said. She stood up and picked up her stained dress. "I'll have them dye it black," she said.

" 'Them'?" asked Jack.

"My girls. In the cutting room."

Jack winced at the "girls," though in another way it thrilled him. "What's the name of your firm again?" he asked.

"Q Design. You haven't heard of us, have you?"

Jack hadn't, though sometimes he read *Details*. When Jack was young and in art school the last thing any of his classmates would have thought it necessary to be aware of was pop culture (except that segment of it glamorized by Andy Warhol—and they had had contempt even for that), but of course this was no longer the case. Indeed, the line between "fashion" and "art"—once so great—had now almost dissolved. Jack did not like or approve of this, but so as not to appear out of it, he spent much of his time reading magazines, attending art shows and dance concerts and performances, taking advantage of free invitations to Area and Palladium—things that in themselves would not have interested him.

"I don't think so," he admitted.

"Why would you have?" asked Lorraine. "Overpriced sportswear for rich women."

"Well. . . ." Jack explained how he tried to keep up with current styles—not to copy but to know about them. This struck Lorraine as slightly pathetic, and compensated for the inferior feeling she, as a businesswoman, always experienced —to her chagrin—around artists.

Most of his life Jack had had a kind of instinctive revulsion against the business world and those who earned their living in it, but in the past few years, with the re-emergence of money as an accepted avant-garde goal, these people had acquired a respect they had hitherto lacked in his eyes. Then, he liked the idea of dating someone with money, someone whom he would not only not have to pay for (at least once he got to know her better), but who would, perhaps, even pay for him. And, if he were going to date somebody in business, what was more interesting, more "now" than fashion? He got dressed and walked Lorraine downstairs to a taxi. He felt like an imposter as she shoved her lips against his in a passionate goodbye. "Don't take this personally, but I love you," she said.

Naturally Jack assumed that Lorraine's spontaneity and intensity were her normal character, not some odd aberration called up by the evening. He walked upstairs to his apartment feeling as if he had been with a foreigner whose physical gestures and facial expressions possessed an iconography unknown to him. He had been paying attention to the stereo as they made love, while she had been thinking it was great. Jack could have felt flattered by this, but he did not. As usual, he decided it was his coldness that had been at fault. Because of this he felt a huge compassion for her, though he was certain it would never turn into love.

The next morning she called him from the office. She had gotten up, seen her daughter off to school, read *Women's Wear Daily*, and gone over some budgets, all while Jack was still nursing his morning coffee. "You lazy artists," she said. "How I envy you."

"Nothing but cocaine and absinthe," said Jack.

"All I use is coffee. What a dull life."

"Money. Yawn," said Jack.

By the end of this conversation, all the elements in their relationship had congealed: Jack's "lazy artistry," Lorraine's "spontaneity," Jack's pretended (albeit real) envy and jocular (albeit real) contempt for Lorraine's uptown life, Lorraine's pseudo-envy of Jack's bohemian (as Lorraine called it) existence. It was okay with Jack—he liked being treated as if life were less serious than it was.

"By the way, I told David I had to work this weekend, so he's going alone with Judy to Vermont, which means you and I can play."

Play: how Jack hated that word. "He won't mind?"

"He won't know."

"I mean, he won't mind that you're not going?"

"Are you kidding? He'll probably dump Judy at the

Strausses', and find some excuse to come back to New York
and see Cecilia."

"Cecilia?"

"His girlfriend."

"Oh." Her degree of cool almost repelled him.

Friday night Jack arrived at Lorraine's apartment with an
overnight bag containing a clean shirt, underwear, a sketch
pad, and pastels. He worried a little about this too-public
acknowledgment of their relationship, but if Lorraine was
not concerned, why should he be?

Nobody answered the bell, though he pushed it a number
of times. He could hear the elevator man behind him shifting
his feet. "I don't understand," said Jack. "I just spoke to her."
In desperation he banged on the door. "Lorraine!" he shouted.
"Lorraine!"

A scratching sound could be heard against the metal door,
then a high-pitched whine and heavy breathing. Through the
door he heard the sound of heels against the floor, and the
unlatching of the door. Behind him the elevator door closed.

"I was worried," said Jack. "How come you didn't answer
the bell?"

"It's broken. Didn't the elevator man tell you?"

"No."

"Bastard! Did I tell you he hates me?"

"Him too?" The way she looked at Jack made him feel, for
a moment, that she considered him part of this not-so-select
company of enemies; then she moved aside to let him in.
Immediately, a panting face with a cold black nose and a body
of longish, straggly hair that went every which way was rubbing up against him. Jack squatted down. "*You* must be
Jack," said Jack, an exaggerated amount of enthusiasm and
delight in his voice. He put his hands behind the dog's ears
and scratched. Jack yelped with happiness. When Jack (the
man) stood up, Jack (the dog) rushed away and in a moment
came back with a plastic toy hanging out of his mouth.

"He wants you to throw it," said Lorraine. Jack threw it.
The dog bounded away, then came back with it in his mouth.

"You're in for it now," said Lorraine. Jack threw it a few more times. "Okay. *Enough*," said Lorraine. She pointed to a spot on the floor. Jack lay down on the floor, head on his paws, slobbering with happiness, then almost immediately jumped up to follow them from room to room as Lorraine showed Jack around her apartment.

It gave him a shock—though one quite different from what his had given her. In an old prewar fifteen-story apartment building on Riverside Drive (really fourteen stories, since in those days they superstitiously did not number the thirteenth floor), was an apartment that looked as much like a loft as what was once an eight-room apartment could look.

Of course Jack had not known the original layout. But he knew what apartments were like in luxury buildings on the Upper West Side of New York City—bumpy walls, layers of paint gently detaching themselves from the ceilings, chipped baseboards, moldings whose relief patterns were slowly being obscured by accumulations of enamel, long dark halls that wandered between rooms, parquet floors whose wax you could scrape up with your fingernails, windows whose warped sashes stuck in their frames, which could be forced open or closed only by jamming the bottom of one's palm against the swollen sash. But here were white pickled floors, smooth uncracked white walls, huge picture windows or smaller (but still large) ones that swiveled, a gigantic bathroom with a separate little area for a whirlpool and shower—as large and empty as any downtown loft, and as impersonal. He couldn't tell whether he liked or hated it. Certainly the high-tech toys—whirlpool, Cuisinart, electric espresso maker, computer—appealed to him. The only ordinary room was the maid's room, behind the kitchen. Tiny, with moldings and crumbling plaster walls and ceiling, it looked out on the air shaft. Jack could not enter it, for it was stuffed halfway to the ceiling with cartons, broken chairs, busted dolls and rocking horses, kids' record players, old chairs, piles of randomly ordered volumes of the old *Encyclopedia Brittanica*. This was the only room in the apartment that resembled any Jack had ever lived in.

"We fought with the contractors before they got around to renovating this room," Lorraine explained apologetically. Like a rotting tooth in a mouth full of caps the room always embarrassed her—both because of its old-fashioned styling and what it revealed of a hidden pack-rat sensibility.

"There's more furniture here than in the rest of the house put together," said Jack.

"I should call up the Salvation Army and have done with it."

"You could salvage a few chairs for the living room."

"*Not* my style," said Lorraine emphatically. "I just haven't gotten around to sorting this junk out. We really should re-paint it. But I guess I should leave it in case the case ever comes to trial. Something which I have great doubts will ever happen."

"What case?"

"We're suing the contractors, or maybe it's them suing us, I'm not sure."

"Don't you know?"

"David says they are. But you never know."

"What do you mean?"

"He's not—how does he put it?—'enslaved' by the necessity of telling the truth."

In Lorraine's bedroom there was a huge closet filled with David's Armani suits and Cerutti shirts, his Sulka ties and Gucci shoes. It was the wardrobe of a fag, but Jack had seen his photograph, and it was not the photo of a fag.

"Have you ever considered getting a divorce?"

"Sure. You want to lend me five thousand dollars for a retainer?"

"Ha ha," said Jack. "You're not broke, are you?" he asked, in mock (but real) concern. Was nothing in life the way it appeared?

"Oh no, just because Con Ed is supposed to shut me off Monday, and my firm owes the union back payments for three months, and I'm overdrawn a hundred" (by which he assumed she meant thousand) "on my account, oh no, what makes you think I'm broke?" Nonetheless, the way she said this made Jack feel secure. All his life he had dated women who didn't know where their next rent check was coming from, who sometimes didn't own a single color TV—let alone three or four, he'd lost count going through the rooms. On the rare occasions he had gone out with professional women, he had been astonished by the predictability of their domiciles (framed posters on the wall passing for "art," tedious chrome lamps), the banality of their ambitions, their refusal to help pay for dinner. To rack up large business debts seemed—glamorous.

As Lorraine prepared, with much ado, a simple Italian dish involving veal and various new (porcini mushrooms, radicchio, sun-dried tomatoes) and oddly colored (purple broccoli, white asparagus, yellow eggplant, red pasta) foods he had not heard of three years ago, Jack played with the remote control unit of the 25-inch Sony, flipping happily from HBO to MTV to ESPN; he couldn't get cable in his building. After dinner they rolled this living-room TV—the one with the VCR— into the bedroom, and put on *PeeWee Herman's Big Adventure*. Enchanted by the vast array of remote controls by the bed, Jack accidentally flipped on Lorraine's bedroom TV. During the lulls in *PeeWee Herman* he kept flipping the other dial. Images and sounds bombarded each other without cease, like acid trips Jack had taken in the old days. Then Lorraine turned down the sound and crawled on top of him.

Jack had trouble concentrating. The venetian blind was broken; the streetlamp shone in almost level to the second-floor window. He could feel its light behind his closed eyes, and pretended it was a full moon. He kept fantasizing what it would be like to climb into that whirlpool in the huge bathroom when they were done, and smoke a joint. He wondered what images were chasing each other across the TVs; at times he sneaked open his lids to peek.

"Do you love me, Jack?" Lorraine asked afterward.

"Those words make me nervous," said Jack.

"Tell me when you do," she said.

She began kissing him. As she did this the words she had requested he speak paraded through his head. Did this mean they were true, or was he just testing them out? How could he tell, when due to strange physical surroundings he felt so little like himself?

Finally it was time to climb into the giant bathtub. As it filled they washed themselves briefly in the shower, then (since one of the things the contractors had neglected to build was a little tile step leading into the bath) they hoisted themselves up on the tile edge of the elevated tub. The cold of the tile against his ass warm from the shower made him shiver. The water was slightly green from wildflower bath oil beads. Carefully Jack lowered himself into the hot water. "Oww," he said, and hopped from foot to foot until the cold water he began pouring in cooled it off. Lorraine pulled up the blinds. The water vapor on the black window surrounded the streetlight with a misty glow. With his hand Jack rubbed a spot through which he could see the park. When it clouded over he picked up a joint from an ashtray he had carefully placed on the side of the tub. After taking a hit he leaned back with a deep exhalation of contentment. Then he flipped the whirlpool switch on. Lorraine immediately leaned forward and shut it off.

"Why did you do that?" Jack said.

"It's broken," said Lorraine. "Didn't I tell you, nothing in this house works?"

Like an attack of indigestion, disappointment flashed through Jack. "Can't you get it fixed?"

"I spose. The pipes were put in the wrong place, by the window, without insulation. They froze and cracked, and when we replaced them, something went wrong with the whirlpool. But there are so many other things I should do first. Please, let's not talk about my apartment." She took a hit of the joint. From the way she inhaled he could tell she wasn't used to smoking very much. Could he love someone who didn't know how to smoke a joint? God, I'm superficial, he thought.

The phone in the bedroom rang. There was a phone on the tile wall of the bathroom but Lorraine didn't pick it up. "Broken, of course," she said.

"No machine?" asked Jack.

"The housekeeper dropped it. Did I tell you she hates me?"

"Yes."

They sat there, listening to it ring. It stopped, then shortly after started again.

"I could bring the one in the bedroom in here," said Jack.

"Don't bother," said Lorraine. "I'll call Judy before I go to sleep."

"How do you know it's her?"

"She hates me when I'm around, but misses me when I'm away. That's what it's like to be thirteen years old."

"I don't remember," said Jack.

"You will."

"Jack! You old thing!" said Jack, for the dog was forlornly trying to stand on his hind two legs on the wet and slippery tile floor of the shower, his paws up on the tile edge of the tub, demanding to be petted.

"He misses David, I guess," said Lorraine. "A man of the house."

Saturday Jack discovered other peculiar things about the apartment: the broken dishwasher; the fridge that wouldn't make ice; a kitchen sink (from the old pantry) that wouldn't run cold water; an icemaker (in another fridge) that flooded; the hall closet with a wooden (rather than a chrome) hanger rod that had collapsed, leaving coats piled on top of each other on the floor; inexplicable electrical outlets that used direct current; an illegal food disposal with a smell that neither Comet nor bleach could make disappear; a dryer that scorched; a phone that tended to disconnect in the middle of conversations. . . .

"I don't understand why you don't get these fixed," Jack told Lorraine.

"Jack, please, I can't talk about it."

It was inexplicable, but no more inexplicable than Jack being here with Lorraine in what on the open market would be at the minimum a $750,000 co-op while her husband and daughter were off in another state, no more inexplicable than a child born with an arm coming out of its head, or a high school athlete being paralyzed from a policeman's stray bullet; so Jack, chewing on a bagel and lox from Zabar's in bed as he gazed out upon a park where children were rolled in strollers, where teenagers slung up basketballs into round, basketless rims, beyond which a mile and a half across an ice-blue river a pier was burning in another state, sending beautiful clouds of dark gray smoke into the blue air, let it go.

Saturday night, while Lorraine and Jack were drinking Absolut in the kitchen, a key turned in the lock, and the man with the wardrobe of a fag came into the kitchen. Jack, happily prancing and leaping, followed him. "David!" said Lorraine.

"That's me," said David. He rather ostentatiously scratched behind Jack's ears, graciously permitting himself to be licked, then stuck out his still-salivy hand and introduced himself to Jack. "Don't mind if I have a drink, do you?" asked David, pouring some vodka.

"It's not my house," said Jack.

"You could have fooled me," said David.

"Jack's an artist. We might be commissioning him to do something for our showroom. Where's Judy?" answered Lorraine, not skipping a beat.

"In Vermont with the Strausses. They'll drive her back tomorrow."

"I don't suppose you want to join us for dinner," said Lorraine.

"I don't suppose." David flashed an odd look of triumph at Lorraine, downed his vodka, poured another, then walked out of the kitchen. In a few seconds they heard the TV. In the glass of the kitchen cabinets Jack saw David reflected: in front of the TV set, watching the end of a football game. Saturday. College. In a few minutes he came back for his third vodka.

"You better slow down," said Lorraine.

"Oh yeah, Lorraine? Why should I slow down? Can you give me" (he faced Jack) "one good reason why I should slow down?"

"You won't be good company for Cecilia." Lorraine said evenly.

"Oh. 'I won't be good company for Cecilia.' And what's that to you?"

"Skip it," she said disgustedly.

"I don't want to skip it."

"Well I do." She got up and went to the sink. Without thinking, David threw the empty glass against the wall. He stared at her, not knowing what to do. Then he tore off a huge amount of Bounty and bent down to pick up the glass.

"Last time he got so angry he put his fist through the wall," Lorraine told Jack. "You'd have thought his architect buddies would have known David well enough to know he couldn't get by with paper walls. But no, they were so busy theorizing about 'dynamic thrust' and 'negative spaces' they couldn't pay attention to such mundane things as supervising contractors."

"I'll have you know, those architects got written up in the home section of the *Times* a few months ago," David told Jack.

"With the amount of coke they stuck up their noses they ought to be! That's where our money went to" (Lorraine turned to Jack) "up their noses."

"At least some people know how to have fun," sneered David.

"Some people like the nose, and some people prefer other organs," said Lorraine.

David picked up the phone and dialed. "Hon," he said, "it's me. I'm just picking up some stuff at home and then I'll be right over." He hung up.

"Cute, David, very cute," said Lorraine.

"Would you believe, this is the same lady who used to beg me to stick my dick up her asshole? Good luck, fella," David said, punching Jack's arm. "You seem like a nice enough guy. Maybe you'll outlast the others." He punched Jack's arm again. Jack jumped up. He wondered whether he should punch him. Of course he didn't. A few seconds later they heard the door close. Then Lorraine bolted the door and turned off the TV.

"Sorry about that," said Lorraine. She poured herself some more vodka.

"Don't you want me to do something?" asked Jack.

"Like what?" She opened the fridge and got out some cheese.

"I don't know." Jack watched his fist open and shut. "It just doesn't seem right to . . . let him say stuff like that to you."

"Don't get melodramatic. He weighs fifty pounds more than you. He works out, he's strong. It's his house."

"But—"

"Believe me, it's not worth it. He won't remember a thing he said in the morning."

Jack sat down. "I still think it's wrong."

"Don't be silly. It's stupid to let it spoil our evening." She poured him some more vodka, and Jack tried to cheer up. But he found it difficult. Even more than the incident, Lorraine's composure disturbed him. But he felt he didn't know her well enough to tell her this. And what could he say—that she should develop more scruples, act shocked, *be* shocked? Until this moment, he had not considered those conventional qualities—rather, responses—ones he admired. But the absence of these conventions and responses in her bothered him. Unless this was how married people talked to each other all the time?

On the other hand, in some perverse way the incident also turned him on, and he enjoyed sex that night with Lorraine more than he ever had before.

"I'm having an affair," Lorraine told David the next week as he was reading the sports pages.

"Umm," said David, turning the page.

"Did you hear me, David? I said I'm having an affair. I'm in love."

"That putz Jack, I suppose?"

"I thought you said you liked him."

"Gimme a break." He continued holding the newspaper, as if he were really reading it. It was suddenly very quiet. He heard the kitchen clock tick, the water (from the washer he kept forgetting to change) drip, as a huge, irrational anger (for he did not at all love Lorraine) surged up in him.

"Is that all you're going to say?"

"I refuse to concede to your desires for hysterical reactions. You make your bed, you lie in it. At least we don't have to go through any more crap about Cecilia."

Lorraine's stomach clenched and bile rose within her, leaving a sour taste in her mouth. She felt like punching him, but that would have put her on his level. And yet, in a weird way, she found herself respecting his lack of sentimentality; in anything but name, their marriage had been over for a long time.

"You *schmuck*," she said.

"You want a scene, but you're not going to get one." David smiled. He got up and left the room, made a phone call, dumped some clothes in a Gucci overnight bag, and shortly afterward left the house.

"Life is dumb," Lorraine told Jack the next night, over an expensive dinner at a new *nouvelle* Italian restaurant she assured Jack she would charge to her company—something she did more and more frequently, and which Jack felt he should feel more upset about than he did. "I love you, David loves Cecilia, and yet he's stuck sleeping with me most nights, while you're all alone in that tiny little apartment."

"How do you know I sleep alone?" asked Jack. Out of both laziness and AIDS he tended to be monogamous, yet the assertion of this as a principle always bothered him.

"I *know*. But that's not important. If we love each other, that's what counts. You do love me, Jack, don't you?"

He didn't say yes, he didn't say no. In his mind that held him unaccountable for all that followed. "What are you really saying?" asked Jack.

"Cause if you do, we might as well move in together. It would save all this running around and hiding out from Judy."

"But we hardly know each other!"

"You've always told me you like people better when you first know them. What's the point of waiting around two years until you find out you don't really like me?"

It seemed unfair for Lorraine to call him on each careless

remark. She drummed her pale lavender nails against the wine glass. "If you don't love me, just say so. I'll understand."

Would she? "What about Judy?" Jack asked, instead. "Wouldn't this upset her?"

Lorraine took his hand. "Jack, you've got to realize, *nothing* makes an adolescent happy—at least not until they start fucking. Come on, tell me the real problem."

"The whirlpool," said Jack. "It's broken."

"Be serious."

"There's no place for me to work."

"There will be."

"Where?"

"Wherever you want. The living room, the back room, whatever your little heart desires. Paint looking out the window, your view's right there for you. What could be easier?"

Indeed, what *could* be easier? No more stairs to climb, no more nights to toss around in bed alone, no more telephone numbers to request at parties. "Wouldn't you mind me messing up the living room?" asked Jack.

"No. After all, it's your *work*. And it'll be a wonderful influence on Judy, you saw those paintings she did last year. Without somebody to force her—"

"She's more self-conscious now," said Jack, "that's all. The older people are, the harder it is for them to paint." Comments about youthful talent never ceased to irritate him.

"Look, you've told me yourself how you've reached some kind of impasse, and were worried maybe your studio had 'gone dead' on you." Jack had told her this, more than once —with the half-conscious purpose of creating a proposition such as this. But now that it was here, it made him nervous.

"Are you sure it's not some trick to acquire some furniture?" Jack joked. "I know how much you love my old couch."

"We *have* had some fun on it," said Lorraine, almost wistfully. She took his hand and kissed his knuckles. She knew that her compulsive desire to get things settled had an unfortunate habit of destroying them. But in her hatred of muddle she could not help herself. The unarticulated and ambiguous disgusted her the same way old furniture and linoleum floors did. And yet what had she ended up with?—broken appliances, a failed tub, useless pipes and electrical lines . . .

As she kissed his knuckles a wave of electricity went through Jack, stronger and somehow purer than when she did other, more intimate things. The expensive restaurant and good wine had already made him giddy. Why shouldn't life be easy and spontaneous, instead of hashed out endlessly over intense discussions? So he said yes. The recklessness was part of the attraction. All his life he'd had a notion of his personality and character that now seemed the very thing that had constrained him. Who had told him what those things were, that he had to obey the limited definition of a person they gave him?

Jack's mind had wandered when Lorraine talked about Judy, so he was unprepared when he met her for the first time at her favorite restaurant, Anita's Chili Parlor. Subconsciously he had been expecting a somewhat larger version of the scruffy five- and six-year-old kids of his friends; instead, she had the haircut and clothing of a model, the tastes of someone who read *Interview* or *Details*. She had just turned thirteen.

"So you're the guy Lorraine's been fucking," Judy said, eying Jack from crotch to toe. "She said you were very good-looking . . ." She let the sentence die with the very clear implication that her mother had misled her.

"Judy. *Please*. She's showing off for you," Lorraine told Jack. "She never talks like this."

"*Really*, Mother. Only you could think that saying 'fucking' is showing off. I don't know what you think we talk like in school. You'd think someone involved in fashion would be more cool, wouldn't you?" she asked Jack.

"I don't know," said Jack. "It's probably such a strain to be trendy, they slip back into their old-fashioned habits as soon as they leave the office."

Judy stopped the waiter. "We'll have three margaritas."

"*Two* margaritas," Lorraine corrected her.

"*Three*," Judy repeated. Almost immediately the waiter brought back three glasses.

"Don't you realize this is a thirteen-year-old?" Lorraine asked him.

"We have a nonalcoholic version for the children," he said.

"Tsk." Judy put the glass down with disgust.

"What is *with* you today, young lady?" asked Lorraine. "He'll never believe all those nice things I said about you."

"One, gimme a break. Two, who gives a shit. Three, you are like . . . like . . . totally sicko."

"Judy. Stop it. I mean it."

"*Mother.*" She rolled her eyes, then grabbed Lorraine's drink and took a few sips. Lorraine watched her for a moment, then grabbed it out of her hand. "Honestly, I've never seen her act this way," she told Jack.

"What's the matter, you're scared Jack's gonna stop liking you?" Judy gave Jack a mean little stare. Jack, having almost no current knowledge of adolescents, didn't know what to do, so he followed an old instinct and stuck out his tongue.

It was the right decision. Judy laughed, then Lorraine did too. "*Two* kids," she said. "Okay." The evening became fun, as Judy tried to show off in more civilized ways by asking Jack his opinion of every movie, rock, and rock video star she could think of. When dinner was over they went to Judy's current favorite movie, *The Breakfast Club*, which she had seen only twice. Later they had to stop at the Paper House for Judy to look at the bracelets and toys.

"Does all this" (by which Lorraine meant to indicate not so much the store as the whole night) "make you want to change your mind?" she asked Jack, only half-humorously.

"Change his mind about *what?*" asked Judy.

"About moving in with us, when Daddy moves in with Cecilia," said Lorraine, with a perhaps too-effortful casualness.

Judy looked at her in surprise, then her face turned red. She ran out of the store.

"Hey!" said the storekeeper, for Judy had a bracelet over her arm.

"That's all right, I'll pay," said Lorraine. "David said he

told her," Lorraine said to Jack as they hurried out. Jack rolled his eyes in disbelief.

They looked up and down the street for Judy. Lorraine, increasingly frantic, was about to hail a taxi for the few blocks home, when Jack spied Judy inside a clothing store several doors away, holding up shirts in front of a mirror. As soon as Jack and Lorraine entered the store Judy went to the cash register and dropped the shirts on the counter. "My mother will take care of it," she told the man, then walked out.

"We will *not*," Lorraine told the man. "I'm sorry." She followed Judy into the street. Judy looked through her as she swung around a NO PARKING sign pole. "Look," said Lorraine. "Your father said—"

"*Shut up!*" yelled Judy.

Lorraine knew she was being blackmailed, but (feeling her moral position at the moment to be weak) she let it go. In silence they began to walk home, Judy lagging behind them kicking stones and twirling herself around parking meters. As soon as they got into the apartment, she went into her room and slammed the door. A few seconds later they could hear Madonna blaring loudly.

"I'll never trust that man again," said Lorraine. "He *swore* he told her. He insisted that it be him who told her."

"How could you possibly trust him?" asked Jack. "After the things he says to you?"

"I don't know. He *is* my husband."

"But—"

"Jack, you've never been married. You just don't know. Honestly, he's not that bad."

"Come *on*. He messed up my whole relationship—*your* whole relationship—with Judy."

"Poo." Lorraine let out a soft breath of air between her lips. "Believe me, she'll get over it."

"I think I better go," said Jack. He went to Judy's room and banged on the door, on the outside of which a DO NOT DISTURB sign had been posted.

" 'Do not disturb' means *do not disturb!*" Judy shouted from behind the closed door.

"It's Jack," he said.

Scissors in hand, she threw open the door. "What *is* it?" she demanded querulously.

"I'm leaving," said Jack. "I just wanted to say goodbye."

"Don't go on *my* account," she said with false sophistication in a terrible English accent. She moved back so that he could enter the room. Jack did not know precisely what he had expected, but surely it was something other than for Judy to be happily engaged in littering the floor with cut-up fan mags.

"You like movie stars?" he asked.

"Yeah. What do you think, I'm a dork?"

"Are you kidding? I've never met anybody your age as sophisticated as you."

"Really?" A grin of pleasure made her largish lips open around her large, straight teeth.

"Would I kid you?" asked Jack. He picked up a mag, dropped it, sighed.

"What's the matter? You guys have a fight?"

"Not exactly."

A knock was heard on the partially opened door, then Lorraine walked in. "Do you mind?"

"Mind *what*? You walking in my room uninvited, or you fucking Jack?"

"Judy, I wish you wouldn't talk—"

"You are *so* outmoded," said Judy. "The whole world could be collapsing and all you'd be thinking about is whether I'm talking politely or not."

"No, Judy, that's not what I would be thinking about. Do you feel like the whole world is collapsing?" She put her arm around her.

Judy pushed her away. "Stop acting so corny, Mother. I don't care if you fuck the entire police force, so long as you leave me out of it."

"You'd better start watching your language," said Lorraine. "Or—" She stopped. More than anyone, she knew how inconsistent and hopeless her punishments were.

"Or *what*, Mother?" Judy sneered. "Just tell me one thing. If *fucking* is such a disgusting thing, then how come you do it? As far as normal people are concerned, that's a *lot* worse than talking about it!"

"Judy!"

"Lighten up, Mother, wouldja? I'm practically the only virgin in the whole school."

"Are you beginning to remember thirteen?" Lorraine asked Jack.

"Things were different then," he replied.

"Yeah? In what way?" asked Judy.

"Well." Jack blushed. "One day I had this wet dream, and I didn't know what it was. I thought I was urinating in my sleep."

" 'Wet dream.' I always thought those words were so beautiful," said Lorraine.

"God, you guys are *so-o* gross," said Judy.

As Jack packed the clothing and paints and records and books that were absolutely necessary for him to bring to Lorraine's (he was holding onto his sublet both for possible investment purposes and as a safety valve for their relationship), he asked himself if he were making a huge mistake. Very likely he was. On the other hand, looking around his small, dark, dingy apartment, it could not help but occur to him that the rest of his life had been a huge mistake too.

2

"Of course you can stay here," David's girlfriend Cecilia had told him when he called her following his conversation with Lorraine. For almost a year they had been seeing each other. They told each other they loved each other. But a strange thing happened almost as soon as David moved in. The source of their problem— Lorraine (rather, what they had always perceived as the source of their problem)—removed, it turned out there was nothing there. Sexual desire evaporated; they began to have trouble making conversation. Soon Cecilia became a stranger to David, as impenetrably obdurate as his own wife, as boring as a table. He'd look at her and think: why did I go to all this trouble? She'd look at him and think: what could have made me think that I loved him? In short, the exchange of one body and residence for another became almost superfluous, a huge amount of trouble over nothing. As they became objects for each other instead of subjects they began to quarrel—a quarrel in which the word "Michael"— the name of Cecilia's previous lover, who had left her for an older, divorced woman—began to be heard more and more frequently. David, for his part, began to think about Lorraine —not as a piece of furniture, but as a living, breathing human being. He might walk along the street having an argument in his head with her—usually about money, sometimes about movies. He had not done this in perhaps twenty years. Of course, he could not be sure whether he missed her, or merely the established pattern of their arguing. Cecilia wondered what she had done to make Michael leave her—for an older woman, no less. The quirkiness of this choice—which she had experienced only indirectly, as a consequence—nonetheless soon came to dominate her memories of him. She resented it immensely, while in a weird way also admiring it.

Soon David decided what he missed wasn't Lorraine, but his old apartment. Cecilia had a one-bedroom in one of those huge white brick buildings that had been constructed on the East Side in the middle 1960s. Low ceilings, tiny bedroom, efficiency kitchen with counter space so small the cutting board had to be put away right after it was used—actually, this turned out not to be so great a problem as he would have supposed, as the lack of a decent ventilating system (the kitchen had no window) and Cecilia's paucity of kitchen utensils made it impossible to whip up anything more elaborate than an English and scrambled eggs. For all her faults, Lorraine was a good—if not especially spontaneous—cook. For all the faults of the former kitchen (so inefficiently planned you had to carry the dirty dishes from the sink that had the garbage disposal almost fifteen feet around the island block to the dishwasher) you could cook, eat, iron, and wash clothing in it. Looking at Cecilia's flat white latex walls in the morning, he would remember his own semi-gloss white walls—and the steel-blue river in the windows beyond them. In retrospect, the broken bathtub, the lowered ceilings where the architects had neglected to run wiring for overhead lighting, the broken, illegal garbage disposal, seemed unimportant, subjects of comedy rather than tragedy.

With these stories he amused Cecilia's friends, but not Cecilia. "Everybody knows you're only here because you're too lazy to find your own apartment," she would state matter-of-factly. In his protestation David did not try to sound totally convincing. His unhappiness with Cecilia's apartment somehow balanced out his being too old for her; each of them had something significant, irreconcilable, to complain about in the other.

Living with a twenty-nine-year-old woman—one who had yet to start a family—made David self-conscious. Cecilia's friends were her age and had interests, not that David couldn't share but, on the contrary, that he had shared for so many years that it was hard to continue to maintain enthusiasm for them: restaurants, clubs, wine. Other times they seemed like old people, in their obsession with security, money, disease. Soon he found himself looking in the mirror, not out of vanity, but fear. His hairline was receding; the hair that he did have was thinner.

He bought a tube of hair-coloring goo, which he hid amongst his undershirts. He couldn't decide if it would damage his ego worse to use it or to watch his hair go gray. One night he came home and found it sitting on his pillow.

"They left it as free samples at the club," he explained lamely.

"Really creepy, David," said Cecilia.

"It's creepy to go through people's drawers," he said.

"I was trying to find Michael's watch."

"It's *your* watch. Michael gave it to you."

"I know." She started to cry. It was impossible to tell if she actually loved Michael, or if her ego had been hurt that he had abandoned her for another woman—not just any other woman, but an *older* other woman. David had been through similar scenes more than once before. He repeated once again that this was not very "feminist" of her, and fell asleep.

Cecilia pounded him with a pillow. With reluctance he dragged himself from the realm of great happiness to the real, latex-walled world. From a distance he heard her say that "it" wasn't working out, that she wasn't happy, that although (of course) she'd like to continue seeing him, he'd better find someplace else to live, at least until they were clearer about what was happening between them.

"Who's not clear?" he asked. "I'm clear." He tried to be friendly, but weariness seeped out of his voice as he longed for his dream.

"No you're not," said Cecilia. "And I'm not either."

"But Cecilia, I've just finished schlepping my stuff here."

"How romantic," she said sarcastically.

This was true, but nonetheless unfair; had they ever, genuinely, been romantic? David knew it was because he was too old for her, too world-weary, that the symmetry of him as an older man (to balance Michael's having an older female lover) had gone stale. But Cecilia pretended it was because he had fallen asleep when she had been trying to express her emotions. "I've got to be with someone who can relate to my emotional life," she said. "For all his faults Mich—"

"Cecilia, let's face it. People's emotional lives are *boring*."

"Excepting yours. We should all curl up on the edge of our seats."

"That's why I never talk about it. I don't even like to *think* about it. I mean, if it's boring to you, just think how boring it is to me!"

"David, you talk about it *all the time*."

"Do I?" He felt queasy. Yet he didn't necessarily believe her.

"You ruined that pigeon dinner talking about it."

"*What* pigeon dinner?"

"In green pepper sauce, with the little orange hoojies with it. You know, turnips. What's the point of eating at expensive restaurants, if you can't even remember the meal?"

"Parsnips."

"Yeah. What was the name of that place?"

For some reason, in his profound fatigue, David got an erection. He reached out to her, but she pushed him away.

"You can stay until you find a new apartment. As long as it doesn't take forever."

"What makes you think it won't?"

Again he reached out, but she got up and went into the bathroom. In the mirror that hung on the back of the door—now half open—he could see her reflected. She was a stranger washing her face, plucking her eyebrows, putting on lipstick to go out to dinner with him—a dinner he would pay for.

She was attractive, yes, but not in a way that he was especially attracted to.

He wondered what bothered him more—the breakup, or the necessity of having to find a new apartment. He thought it was wrong of Cecilia—almost un-American—to change the rules of the game in the middle. But could he tell her that the fact that they had never really loved each other hadn't been a bar to their relationship before, so why should it be so now? What relationship had it ever been a bar to? What could it even mean to be in love at the age of forty-six? Surely she did not expect him to think about her constantly, as he had about a girl whose name he had forgotten in a high school homeroom, thirty years ago, before she was even born.

After an unpleasant lunch with his partners, during which they argued about the purchase of certain air rights, David told the receptionist he was leaving for the day. He headed uptown in a cab, glancing dishearteningly at the real estate section. The realtor was snotty, as if David were morally at fault because he had to search for an apartment, rather than being a real man and throwing his wife's lover (and maybe his wife) out on the street. "Nice going! This yo-yo gets to live in a seven-hundred-fifty-thousand-dollar apartment, while you got to chintz it out in some crummy one-bedroom."

"Seven hundred fifty *if* it goes co-op," said David. "At the moment . . ."

"Tough spot, buddy." The realtor whistled. "What if the wife seeks a divorce? Because of the kid she'll get to keep the apartment, buy it for a cheap insider price when it goes co-op, and you probably won't get a penny back for all that money you sunk in there fixing it up. You can't get a second mortgage on the increased equity, you can't—"

"Oh," groaned David. He was feeling more and more sorry for himself. How had his comfortable existence—a wife, kid, mistress on the side—gone so awry? What terrible things had he done, that he should be punished this way?

"You want to option the insider rights to me, you can," added the realtor.

"I don't want to go into it," said David. "It's too upsetting."

The realtor spun in his revolving chair, as if there were something interesting out the window. Then he turned back to David, leaned forward, clasped his hairy hands on his desk. "Tell you what. Bad enough you don't get to live in your own place. At least get the bozo to pay *your* rent, while you pay *his*."

"He can't," said David. "He's poor. A starving artist."

"A gigolo, you mean."

"*Not* a gigolo." It was wretched to have to defend Jack.

"He's also got this place in the East Village that he has to pay rent on. He can't sublet it because it's already a sublet, and the landlord would like nothing more than an excuse to evict him, which from his point of view would be disastrous since it might also go co-op. Anyway, he'll need it for when he and Lorraine break up."

"*If* they break up. So *you* buy his rights to buy *his* place, and make yourself a nice investment."

"And put cash in his pocket? You got to be kidding!"

"Most of it will come back to you—that is your wife—as rent."

"But if the place doesn't go co-op, or they decide he's not legally a tenant and he's not permitted to buy—then I end up giving him ten or fifteen thousand for nothing."

"If he were smart he'd make a deal with the landlord, get his stuff out, give up his rights, and try to make a go of it with your wife."

"Believe me, sooner or later she'll get sick of him."

"Tell me, why does she want to live with such a bum?"

"*Women,*" said David. He raised his eyebrows, shrugged—possibly at the interjection, possibly at the self-consciousness he felt raising his eyebrows. "He's okay, really. After all, it's not *his* fault he can't make a decent living in this society." Of course, David would have taken the opposite point of view with anyone but the realtor.

"Whose fault is it? The jigaboos? Just joking." Not wishing to get into a political discussion, David didn't respond. "That's okay, buddy. My wife had a midlife crisis of her own a couple years ago, decided she was a dyke."

He paused. David felt obligated to ask him what had happened. He was sure the realtor had told the story many times.

"She told her best friend she was in love with her. The best friend wasn't a dyke, but you know women, they'll try anything—just to be able to talk about it. It wasn't so hot, but they joined a discussion group so as to have some nice witnesses for their story, one of the women hit on her—before you know she's living with this bulldyke on the Lower East Side. The Lower East Side—ha! Believe me, if you knew my wife, the original Zabar's queen, you'd know what a joke that

is! But she got furious whenever I laughed at her, so I decided
to cool it. You understand she wasn't 'in love' with this
woman, but was just living with her until she 'worked
through' her feelings. What a crock! Of course, what with
prices the way they've been, she wasn't able to find a place
of her own, and after a while she moved back home."

"Were you very angry?" asked David.

The broker shook his head. "I stopped getting angry a couple years ago. Lucky thing. I read the other day that it's bad
for your health. Increases the risk of heart attacks and can-
cer."

"I thought it was just the opposite. That represssing it was
bad."

"Nope. That's what they used to think. But they did a
new study, and everything they thought before was absolutely wrong! Look, I got a place for you on Columbus and
Sixty-seventh—new building, thirtieth floor, ten sixty for
a bedroom and semi-kitchen, swimming pool on the
roof."

"That's too much, I told you. I'm not made of money."

"Okay, you want to chintz it out? Here's something came
in this morning. Ninety-second between Broadway and Am-
sterdam. Seven seventy-five for a 'small' one-bedroom with
efficiency kitchen. I hate to tell you what they mean when
they tell you out front it's small. Your dog won't have room
to take a fart. On the other hand, you get bored, you walk to
the SRO next door and buy some ups, downs, whatever does
it for you." He handed David the keys.

"Lorraine's got the dog," said David. The thought sent him
into a sulk, though he hardly could have brought Jack to
Cecilia's. He walked up Broadway to Ninety-second Street,
turned right a few buildings up the block, climbed up three
flights of stairs. A short time later he was back at the realtor's. He threw the keys down on the realtor's desk.

"No luck?" asked the realtor.

"Every time I used the closet I would've had to move the
bed."

"Get a futon!" chuckled the realtor.

David grabbed him by the collar. "Don't fuck with me. I

work out. See?" He rolled up his sleeves to show his muscles, then smiled, to show he was joking.

"Nice," said the realtor. "But you ain't the only boy who belongs to a health club." He put down the *Times*, stood up, rolled up his sleeves. What had looked like fat turned out to be muscle. "I can bench press two fifty. How about you?"

David was surprised and impressed by the muscles. He pulled up his shirt, tightened his stomach muscles, and told the realtor to punch him in the stomach. At first the realtor refused, then he did it too softly; then, when David pressed him, did it hard enough to double David over. The realtor brought him water, then coffee. David mixed the powdered vegetable coffee whitener and the powdered coffee diet sweetener with a cheap stainless spoon that looked as if it had been stolen from a luncheonette. The sun hit the dust on the windows so he could see the specks clearly. This reminded him of college. For a while he gazed at them, happy the way he had been happy in college, though at the time he had not recognized that state as happiness. No, he had thought of it as boredom. Tears filled his eyes at the thought of this younger, more naive self.

"You wait six months or so, I got a nice cheap condo for you in Alphabet City," said the realtor. "I'm developing it myself."

"Alphabet City? What's that?" asked David.

"Boy, buddy, do you got a lot to learn."

The next morning David was at the realtor's by nine, in hope of catching the new listings as they came in. "W 70s garden duplex, 1 bed, $1295" and "60s W—Lux 1 bed, d/m, laundry, $1350" cost too much. "80s lg 1 br din alc $895" was a dark tenement with linoleum floors, "50s W large newly ren 1 br $800" was above a souvlaki stand on Columbus Circle, "stunning 3½ huge terrace, skyline view $895" was in Staten Island, "E 90s large studio with alcove, bright, hi ceilings" was Ninety-ninth Street between Fifth and Madison—the beginning of East Harlem—and "90s WEA $800 1 bed d/m," he found in the midst of a bidding war to buy the support of the super. At $1500 and counting, David, who didn't have that much cash with him, left.

"A one-time expense, you should have bribed the super," said the realtor, without sympathy.

"That's illegal!"

"Mr. Clean are you?"

"I'm going crazy!"

"They read the papers but they don't believe it," said the realtor. "Here's one in a new building. Twelve ninety-five with a health club in the basement."

"I got a health club I like, thanks."

"Doorman and an eight-by-ten sleeping alcove. That's bigger than some living rooms."

"But not than my parking space."

After leaving the realtor's, David decided he'd better take an exercise break at his health club before returning to the office. He got undressed and went upstairs to the running machines. After five minutes he went to the weight room. He did a quick Nautilus circuit, then put four fifty-pound weights and two twenty-five-pound weights on the bar and tried to lift. It didn't move. When he took twenty-five off each side he could raise it off the floor for half a second, but he felt a terrible pain go through the left side of his back. He sat down on the floor and decided that it wasn't a heart attack but a muscle pull. He heard the disco music for an aerobics class and walked in during the warm-ups. He was at least ten years older than anybody else in the class. His heart was revved from the Nautilus and weights but after ten minutes of high kicks, jumping, and running in place his face was red, his heart was pounding, sweat was running down his legs. He hated to quit but, to give himself a chance to catch his breath, he kept stopping to retie his shoelaces, or massage his calves, or do Achilles-heel stretches against the wall. Sometimes, ostensibly to massage his neck muscles, but really to check his pulse, he put his hand on his neck below his ear. He counted twenty-eight beats in ten seconds. Expecting to die any second, he left the room. He sat down against the wall

counting his pulse till it was down to 110. He thought of
returning to the aerobics class but when he stood up he felt
dizzy. Maybe he wasn't dying, just sugar short. He walked to
the cafeteria, reflexively feeling his shorts for money. But of
course he was in his gym shorts, which had no pocket. His
wallet was downstairs in his locker. To get it he would have
to go down three flights of stairs, ask the attendant to open
his locker, get the money, come back upstairs. This required
a level of blood sugar he didn't have.

"I don't feel well," he told the Moroccan who worked behind the counter. "I need fruit juice. I'll bring you the money
later." He spoke slowly, distinctly, convincingly, the way
anybody could with a gun in their hand.

The Moroccan gave him an apple-strawberry soda. David
sipped it, listening to the claps of the aerobics class doing
jumping jacks. When he was done he went downstairs to the
"spa" area, where he changed into a bathing suit, took a
shower and a little steam before heading toward the pool.

It was almost empty at this time of day. After a few slow
laps of breast- and backstroke he went into the whirlpool. A
young woman sat with a towel wrapped around her head,
reading a book. It was the expensive kind of paperback, with
a shiny cover that wouldn't get ruined if it fell in the water.
The paper might get wet, and dry in odd patterns, but it
wouldn't crumple and disintegrate like the cheaper ones
would. "Hi," said David. She glanced at him for a second
with a look that dismissed rather than acknowledged him,
then returned to her reading. Leaning over at an angle David
saw the title: *S/Z*, by Roland Barthes. He felt embarrassed,
then angry: what the hell was so repugnant about him that
she couldn't even say hello to him?

"Barthes, huh?" he said in a loud voice. "I never heard of
this one, but I read *The Sotweed Factor*. Well, some of it
anyway. Is it good?"

"You're thinking of John Barth," she replied, without lifting her head from the page.

"Something the matter with me, you can't even look at
me?" asked David. The woman continued reading. He
walked over next to her.

"You're in my light," she said. David looked up, to where the lights lay recessed on little cylinders set into the plastic panels of the ceiling, then down, to the gray cast by his swollen shadow over the book. He felt like ripping it out of her hands.

"You're not so greatlooking yourself, you know," he said. "I felt sorry for you, that's all." In revenge he walked around the whirlpool, trying out different jets, on occasion bumping into her, but when she continued to refuse to bite he lay back in a corner, coccyx against one jet, legs up on the tile bench against another, and fell into a pleasant trance. When you came right down to it, it was more interesting watching somebody read a book, than reading one oneself. Was it more interesting to watch someone else eat, sleep, look at the tube, listen to records, even make love, than to do these things oneself?

But even as he sat there basking in this pleasure, it began to dissipate, until soon it was gone entirely. Soon he would be living alone, with no one to watch cook, read, listen to TV, yell at him. He thought of what it would be like to have a heart attack—not here in the club where people at least knew CPR and could get an ambulance in minutes, but alone in his apartment at three o'clock in the morning, unsure whether it was indigestion, muscle pull, anxiety attack, or the real McCoy—or two (or three) of the above. You could take a Valium and wait to see what happened—whether within twenty-two minutes you began to calm down and breathe normally or felt your left arm start to go numb.

He felt hot, dizzy, ill. No doubt it was because he'd spent too much time in the whirlpool, but it might, just might, be a heart attack—either the one he'd worried about earlier or a new one.

He yearned to cool off in the pool, but the lifeguard sat with his feet up on a chair, engrossed in a book. Think of the meaning of the word—"engrossed"—as David had his heart attack, and drowned.

Later that afternoon, David realized he had forgotten to give the Moroccan money for the apple-strawberry soda.

•

During the next few days David's list of permissible residential areas expanded beyond the East and West Sides south of Ninety-sixth Street and north of Central Park South to include the Village, Waterside, Kips Bay, Gramercy Park— even Chelsea. The very inaccessibility of the area might turn out to be a blessing in disguise, if he could park his car on the street overnight, and use the money he saved on rent as an excuse to garage his car uptown during the day.

Once the car entered the picture Brooklyn, which he had hitherto ruled out, became a serious possibility. The Heights were almost as bad as Manhattan, but on the other side of Atlantic Avenue, in Cobble Hill, there were rumors a person could find a home for something less than half one's after-tax income. David drove there on a Sunday with Cecilia, diligently crisscrossing the streets in his 1985 silver-gray Cadillac, a car that had begun to embarrass him. On occasion, while making a turn, they would spot the walled fortresses of downtown Manhattan surrounded by their giant moats— the East and Hudson rivers, New York Bay.

"I didn't know places like this existed in New York," said Cecilia in surprise. There was block after block of attached and semi-attached houses, well kept up, with little lawns in back (and sometimes front), on streets of low population density where kids played football, moving to the side of the road when cars drove past. Dried leaves of red, brown, and gold crackled underfoot when they stepped out of the car, a smell that reminded David of high school football. All he ever got to play was special teams. In private driveways or parking lots of schools and churches they saw basketball hoops, usually without the basket, or at most with bits of string hanging down from them, into which live human beings were tossing round orange balls.

"You could barbecue out back," said David. "Put in swings for the kids. Plant rose gardens. Drive to work. Watch people read the Barth Brothers. Not such a bad life."

" 'Barth Brothers,' that's pretty funny," said Cecilia.

"Like Washington, or Philly," said David.

"I don't know Philly," said Cecilia.

"You've never been to the Barnes Collection?" asked David. "We should go one Sunday."

"Never *heard* of it!" Cecilia said with odd smugness.

"Lorraine always wanted to go there, but we never did." All of a sudden David felt bad about this. He pulled the car over to the side of the road. Tears piled up in his eyes, like football players on top of a running back.

"I'm sorry. I'm immature," he said.

"I know." Cecilia gave him a Kleenex and patted his hand. "You still love her."

"No more than you love Michael." They were silent awhile. As much to rescue the moment as from anything else David said: "I love you, Cecilia. I want to marry you after I work out my divorce."

"How sweet! But I want a family."

"Me *too!*"

"You've already got one."

"One kid, that's nothing." Like a chimp, he pounded his chest.

"But you're thirteen years older than me! Even if you got a divorce and we got married *tomorrow*, you'd be practically *fifty* by the time you could teach him to play baseball."

"So what? Look at Ted Kennedy. He plays touch football with his kids and grandkids."

"I don't think that's such a hot example. His wife's an alcoholic and he murdered his mistress."

"Believe me, Cecilia, I may be 46, but in my soul I'm a kid. *I'm just a kid.*" He took her by the shoulders and made her face him. Out of the corner of the car mirror he could see in the orangish late afternoon light he looked okay. A little lined, a little too much "there," but okay.

"Forty-*six?*" Her voice went up in surprise at the end. "You told me you were forty-*two*."

"Over forty it gets mixed up." David blushed. She gave him a look.

"I don't mean to be cynical, David, but isn't all this just because you happen to like this neighborhood? What if it had been raining, and kids hadn't been out playing basketball and stuff?"

"Don't be silly." What she was saying was partially true, but not entirely. "But even if it were true, what would it matter because there's always a reason for something—and there's worse reasons than a neighborhood where you can grow your own tomatoes," he said, no doubt too defensively, for he heard the whine in his voice.

"To tell you the truth, I think I'd rather grow my tomatoes in Bridgehampton."

"*Jesus.*" Tears began to form inside his eyes, partly at the conventionality of the preference, partly for his loss, partly because of male menopause. Lorraine or Cecilia, Cecilia or Lorraine—nice women, either of which a man would be lucky to have. Stay with one, go back to the other, start a new family, be content with the old; it hardly mattered, did it, which of these pleasant possibilities would come true?

As long as at least one of them did, that is.

The unfairness of it made his tears turn to sobbing.

In the graying light, somewhat misinterpreting this sobbing, Cecilia liked him again. Rather, for a moment she saw him as herself—or, perhaps, herself as him.

"Listen, David, when we had that conversation the other night, I didn't mean you had to move out right *away.* I just meant—oh, you know. You can wait a bit, if you want." She put her arm on his arm. "Does that help?"

Did it help? Does a chicken have lips? David felt like a gleaming building on a moat, a shiny new jet plane. An erection, long awaited, tightened his pants.

David's tongue in Cecilia's mouth as they kissed reminded her, by way of contrast, of Michael's, whose mouth, unlike David's, did not remind her of a dog's.

3

The realtor did not know why he had lied to David. His wife had not come back to him, but was still living with the woman she had moved in with on the Lower East Side—a fat woman with salt-and-pepper hair who had been the leader of his wife's therapy group. Her fatness wreaked greater havoc with the realtor's ego than her sex. He had not expected to miss his wife, but he had. Perhaps he just missed being able to vent his anger at her. After David left for the health club he went outside and hopped in a cab, ordering it to go to East Third Street, between First and Second avenues.

When his wife, Rena, had first moved there, a line of huge Harley-Davidsons had been almost constantly parked outside her door. This had discouraged real estate values, and Marion, his wife's lover, had suggested they buy the building. In the realtor's spitefulness he had refused, a decision that had already cost him maybe half a million dollars in profit. Sometimes it occurred to him that it wasn't the situation with his wife that disturbed him as much as the loss of the money.

Their apartment—rather, the two adjoining apartments that they had combined—looked out on the graveyard of an old church. Five rooms (seven if you counted rooms they had combined into larger ones) to the tune of four fifty a month —it was enough to make a man sick. God knows what he could have co-oped them for. Of course you had to climb four flights, the walls were crumbling, and wind whistled through the windows. Nonetheless, his wife compared this apartment —favorably—to the much newer one they used to live in uptown, and repeatedly said how happy she was to be here in the East Village, where the buildings were short, and pleasantly run down, and the people were "just people." In the summer she sat on the fire escape looking out over the garden, as she corrected spelling, grammatical, and typing errors in cookbooks, carpentry books, sailboat books. Sometimes she left stale bread for the birds. The gray pigeons would sit on the windowsill, pecking crumbs. If she had not known what horrible birds they were—dirty, germ-carrying,—she would not have been able to tell, merely by looking at them. But they were large fat birds who pushed the sparrows away. In the winter she sat in front of the closed windows insulated with plastic sheets that blurred the graveyard, the building, the falling snow.

There was no intercom, and the downstairs door wasn't locked. The realtor climbed four flights and knocked on the door. His wife seemed surprised to see him—not pleasantly so.

"It's been a while," he said.

"I suppose." She stood blocking the door.

"Aren't you going to invite me in?"

She moved aside. The living room was empty, but the bedroom door was closed. He sat down on the couch.

"Is Marion home?" he asked.

"No." He waited for her to ask if he wanted coffee. Instead, she began leafing idly through the *Post*.

"What do you read that rag for?" he asked.

"The prose. Did you come here for a reason, or just to annoy me?"

There was no reason. To fill the blank, he mentioned the possibility of starting divorce proceedings.

"All right," said his wife. "If that's what you want."

This was not what he wanted. He began to go into all the reasons why this was a bad idea at this time.

"Either way is fine with me," she said. "I certainly don't intend to get married again."

"Marion doesn't want to make a lifetime commitment, huh?" He got up, went to the fridge, searching for goodies. "You don't mind if I help myself?"

"Is that a question or a statement?"

"You're not acting like you're very happy to see me."

"I don't like surprises."

"I was in the neighborhood. The Chinks are driving me crazy on that Avenue B building."

"Next time call. Anyway, I was just about to sit down to work, so—" She stood up, went to the table by the window, picked up her manuscript.

"I'm trying to get together some investors. There's this J-51 tax break for construction in underdeveloped neighborhoods, if you want to come in on it."

"Are you joking? We don't have the money. We've got to save something in case this place goes co-op."

"Maybe we can work something out. Legally you're still my wife."

"Actually, Marion and I have been discussing buying someplace on Long Island—"

"Dykesville," the realtor sneered.

"The North Shore, *fucker*," his wife said with bitterness.

"Of course, that may not work out."

"What do you mean?"

"You know, things don't always work out."

"Even so, I don't see how it's any of your business."

"I don't know why it's not. You're family—all the family I have."

"Stop acting so pathetic. It gives me the creeps."

"It *is* pathetic. I'm pathetic. How do you think a guy feels when his wife leaves him for a fat pig with no dick?"

"I don't want to hear this. Marion's always gone out of her way to be nice to you."

"Fat people *have* to go out of their way to be nice, because they take up so much room."

"That's enough."

"You're goddam right it's enough!" He punched the wall. You couldn't do it to a new building without busting into the next apartment. It made him so happy he punched it again. "Fuck it, I think I broke my fucking arm."

His wife had never seen him behave like this. It frightened her, because here was a man she had lived with half her life, and look what she hadn't known. Maybe Marion had hidden sides too, which she would find out in the years to come.

Maybe she would never find out about them. Which was
better? "You're acting crazy," she said.

"Too much coffee. Male menopause." He lay on the sofa,
rubbing his fist.

"You're asking for trouble to drink that stuff at your age. If
you've got to have it, drink decaf."

"I'm not dead yet, like you and your stupid girlfriend."

"Ed, this is *not* you."

"It *is* me, you stupid cunt. Don't you know anything?" He
got off the sofa and began kicking the wall. "I should have
bought this fucking place. Then I could have thrown you
out!"

"I mean it, I've had enough."

"Oh yeah? How much is enough? Eight inches? Nine
inches? A foot and a half? Where's your fucking dildo?" He
went into the bedroom and began opening drawers, throwing
nylon underpants, stockings, wool socks up in the air.

Rena stood in the doorway. "Maybe you won't listen to
me. But you're in real trouble if Marion walks in. *Real* trouble."

"Yeah, she could sit on me and squash me to death! Ha
ha."

"You're sick."

"You're the one who sticks your nose up that fat pig and
I'm sick! That's a joke! God, how can you stand to look
at her?" He picked up a photograph of Marion from the
mantel over the fireplace (plasticked-over for insulation) and
smashed it on the floor.

"Get out this minute before I call the cops!" Rena went to
the door and opened it.

"Wash our laundry in public. Nice."

"I'm not kidding. *Get out.*"

"Make me.

"You don't believe me, okay, I'm gonna call the cops." She
let the door close.

The realtor ripped the phone out of the wall. "Try it," he
sneered. He sat down on the couch.

His wife looked at him as if he were a roach. "Okay. *I'll*

leave." She grabbed a jacket from an old wooden coat tree by the door and walked out.

"Jesus! Can't you take a joke?" he shouted after her.

The realtor sat there for a while, to see if this was a bluff. But no, he listened to her clomp down the stairs, then the front door open and close.

He felt like torching the apartment. Instead he went back into the bedroom and sat down on the bed. It was an old double bed with a headboard—carved oak—the kind you could have gotten upstate years ago for a song. Now, stripped and refinished, on Hudson Street, it would have cost you a ransom.

He lay down on the old blue-and-white quilt. The smell of it was familiar. Not nice, just familiar. He took a tiny glass bottle with a black screw-on top out of his pocket, poured some white powder out on a plate on the night table, mashed it into a couple of lines, rolled up a century bill, and snorted. He had been carrying this particular bottle around for two months. It was supposed to be a lucky talisman. Not using the powder made an armor around his body; he walked down the street thinking how much stronger he was than everybody else. Now he had pleasure in surrendering his strength. He spent a long time chopping the remainder of the coke into little pieces, then he snorted that too.

Instantly he felt better. Not different, just more energized, as if his real self had returned slightly larger than life. Chuckling at his foresightedness, he rinsed the bottle out in case the cops really did come. He began laughing. He could not have predicted his life. This seemed good. "Yeah, man, hot shit!" He walked around the apartment, banging his good fist into his bad hand. But he could stand the pain. He felt strong, like a building, lean and mean. Underneath this was an incredible kindness. Every minute of every day, he did not kill somebody. He was a strong man, right? A good man. He was a crazy man who controlled his craziness—a safe bet for president. He would never push a button. Never never never.

There was a noise at the kitchen window by the fire escape. A Puerto Rican was pushing up the window. Then he stuck a leg in. It was broad daylight. The realtor got a knife. The

Puerto Rican was holding a toy poodle. He put the dog down. The dog ran toward the realtor in the kitchen, sniffed him, lay down on his paws. He was a ridiculous attack dog. "One more step and I'll kill you," the realtor told the Puerto Rican.

"You nuts, man? I'm the super. I'm just bringing back the dog."

"What dog?"

"Eliza. Marion's dog. Are you crazy?"

"You're crazy. You stole her dog."

"No, man, I borrow her for my nephew."

"What for?"

"He likes to play with the dog."

"Maybe you're lying, maybe you're not."

"Look at the collar." The realtor looked at the metal plate dangling from the collar. His wife's phone number was engraved on it, and the words "My name is Eliza. I am allergic to flea medicine."

"I didn't know they had a dog."

"A friend gave it to them. Hey man, who are *you?*"

"What business is it of yours?"

"What the fuck you think?" The Puerto Rican put his hand in his pocket. Maybe he had a knife in there. Maybe not.

"My wife lives here. My ex-wife. I mean, she's still my wife."

"Your wife ran out on you, for a wo-man?" The Puerto Rican dragged out the last into two words: *woo* and *man.*

"Hard to believe, ain't it?"

"Chicks are weird. They always got a story. Hey, you want a hit?"

"Why not? I'd give you some of my coke, but it's gone." The realtor took out the empty bottle and waved it in the air.

"Sokay." The Puerto Rican slipped out a joint from a pack of Marlboros and lit it with a Cadillac-logoed lighter. He smoked nearly half the joint, then handed it to the realtor.

"Good" (suck) "stuff" (suck), said the realtor. He coughed; tears were in his eyes.

"You know something, man? You look unhappy."

"No, I'm real happy. I did up all this coke a few minutes ago."

"I know. But behind that happiness I see unhappiness."

"Yeah, but that's true for everybody." The realtor blushed. He was embarrassed, as he always was when people pretended to care about his insides. Then *he* had to pretend to care about *their* insides.

"So what? You're *you*, and that means your unhappiness is more important to you than anybody else's unhappiness."

"You mean my unhappiness is more important to me than mine is to you?" the realtor asked.

"Sure. You don't want to lie. That's not interesting."

"But your unhappiness is just as important to you as mine is to me?"

"Whatchoo think?" They sat in silence awhile. The realtor was conscious of trying to look like he smoked dope with Third World people all the time, but uncool white thoughts kept running through his mind: like, is this fucker gonna rob me? He began humming. The Puerto Rican turned on the radio. Latin rhythms blared out. He had always considered them a bit trashy. But now, they sounded great. Feeling self-conscious, he nonetheless began snapping his fingers.

"You want to do some coke?" the Puerto Rican asked.

"Sure."

The Puerto Rican's coke was much stronger than his. The realtor lay down, not because he was sleepy, but to smell the bed better. The dog jumped on the bed too. They smelled it together. For a fraction of a second he was a dog, he had a dog's brain. Because he was worried he was going to bark, he scratched the dog's ears. The dog rolled over on its back and spread apart its legs. It was like a human getting a massage. Only most humans didn't wear little collars around their necks. Rather, they wore collars but only for decoration. The realtor scratched Eliza for a long time, longer than he had ever done it for any of his own dogs. Usually he was too lazy. He wondered why he hadn't. It was no more boring than anything else. Come to think of it, his wife had never given him a massage either.

"Leashes are pretty weird," said the realtor. "Whew." He whistled through his teeth.

"You're telling me."

"They're degrading. Like owning slaves."

"I'd never have a dog in this city. My aunt lives in Jersey City. She has a dog. It's okay there."

"She own or she rent?"

"I don't know. She don't got much bread so I guess she rents."

"That don't mean nothing in Jersey," said the realtor, imitating what he imagined to be the Puerto Rican's language patterns. "There's special deals for rehabilitating the inner city. The government guarantees the loan."

"Nah, I don't think so."

"Yeah."

"I don't think so."

"I *know*. But you got to tell me where she lives."

"Jersey City, like I told ya."

"I'm not deaf. That ain't enough. Does she live in the inner city or what?"

"What's that?"

"The *inner city*, where the . . . uh, you know live."

"No, man, I don't know whatchoo mean." The Puerto Rican put his hand in his pocket.

"Let's not beat around the bush. She live in a nice area or with the, uh" (the realtor was about to say "niggers" or "spics") "dregs?"

"My aunt's no dreg."

"I don't mean that. I love your aunt. You know what I mean."

"Whatchoo mean you love my aunt? You don't know her."

"The fuck I don't. I know lots of chicks. What's her name?"

"Luisa Hernandez."

The realtor pretended to comb a vast memory. "She fucks goats, right?" In a flash the Puerto Rican had his switchblade open and extended.

"Man, that's not funny."

"Okay, so I got a lousy sense of humor. Is that a reason to kill me?"

The Puerto Rican flipped the knife in the air a few times like a baton, then put it away.

"Look here. I'm just trying to help you. Promise me you'll

tell her. *Low-cost government loans.* She'll thank you a lot
for that sometime, maybe even leave you her house, as a kind
of thanks."

The Puerto Rican looked at him strangely. "She's twenty-
seven, she ain't gonna die for a long time."

"Knock on wood. You never know."

The realtor knocked on an end table. The sound that came
out of the wood was a song. He had never heard it before, but
he also knew, as soon as he heard it, that it had always been
there. He had gone through life like a deaf, blind man. "You
know the woman who lives with Marion?" he asked.

"Sure, man, your wife."

"How do you know she's my wife?" The realtor sat up,
angry.

"Relax, man, you told me."

"You want to know something really interesting?"

"What?"

"I don't find her sexy."

"Shoo. That's why you split up. Everybody's happier now."

"Not me, fuck it."

"But you don't like her any more."

"I *never* liked her. Even when I married her I didn't find
her sexy. I mean, I thought she *could* be sexy, I mean, she
could have *been* sexy, but not to *me.*" He pounded his chest.

"Sure you did, man. You just forget. Otherwise you
wouldn't have married her."

"Gimme a break! We were dating. She let me *shtup* her.
These things happen, it's not hard to understand. But what *is*
hard to understand is, what was I doing going out with her in
the first place?"

"Cause you dug her."

"Nope! I remember very clearly this sentence kept running
through my head: 'I am not attracted to this woman.' You
see, we met on a blind date. Some friends of mine invited us
for dinner, for the purpose of meeting each other. Maybe *you
people* do that too?"

"Shoo. We're just like you."

"No shit!" The realtor was surprised. "Now I had heard
about her for months, how hot she was and everything, that

I thought my instincts were wrong, so I asked her out. I end up spending twenty years fucking somebody I'm not even attracted to, then she walks out on me! On top of that—she tells me she's never been physically attracted to *me*—that she never in all those years had an orgasm. What *is* this shit?"

"I think you've had too much coke. Why don't you lie down?"

"Don't talk to me like I'm an asshole. Just cause my wife's a dyke doesn't mean I'm an asshole."

"I know."

"You *don't* know. You offered me a little coke because you wanted to see what kind of asshole I'd act like if you gave me some coke. But I'm not. Do you understand?"

"Sure. Now I got to get back to my nephew."

"What are you, some faggot who picks kids off of the streets?"

"Man, you got to relax. My sister went with her husband to Paris on business. So I said I'd take the kid till they got back. Now we got to drive to the airport and pick them up."

"I didn't know spics were interested in Paris. That blows my mind."

"I got to go now. Catch you later."

"Yeah? Like *when?* Don't bullshit me."

After the Puerto Rican had gone, Eliza began to whimper. The realtor petted her, then turned on the radio. He was hungry from the grass, but not hungry because of the coke. He tried to figure out which sensation was more prominent. But they were both there in equal quantities: hungry, not hungry. Not eating took less effort. But he was nervous and needed to do something, so he opened a cabinet and pulled down a box of spaghetti.

He crunched on the dry spaghetti, imagining the wetness of it being cooked, the taste of the oil, tomato, garlic, basil. He imagined a world where Puerto Ricans had a thing about Paris. Maybe they liked London too. Maybe what every dark-skinned person wanted most in the depths of his soul was to turn into some white asshole with heavy bones, pale blotchy skin, facial hair, a knobby dick, layers of fat around the middle. Maybe the contempt he had always felt coming from them to him was an illusion, maybe they liked Schoenberg better than reggae, wanted to dance badly, out of rhythm and breath, wearing clothes that hung on their bodies as if on a hanger, pants that didn't outline crotch and ass. Could that be their secret ambition, the way his used to be to wear patent leather shoes and grease back his hair with Tres Flores? *Quién sabe!*

He started to jerk off, then decided no, he'll go down to Delancey Street and do some business. But first he'll buy himself a condom. Between VD, hepatitis, herpes, and AIDS, lately sex was more dangerous than getting on the subway.

"Condoms," he told the woman in the drugstore.

"What kind would you like?"

"The best. Money is no object. I think it's crazy to be chintzy when you're gonna get laid."

"I agree with you completely," said the woman. "The best *and* most expensive are made of sheepskin."

"That's what I want." He took out his wallet.

"Are you absolutely sure you want sheepskin on your penis?" she asked.

"Yeah, is something the matter with it? They haven't found some kind of carcinogen in it, have they?"

"Not that I know of. But if man got syphilis from fucking sheep, don't you think it's odd that men now use sheep to keep from getting syphilis?"

"It's . . . symmetrical," replied the realtor.

"I think it's weird, if we can send a man to the moon, that we can't make a decent synthetic condom. Not that I care, of course," she giggled.

"Well, it's not a priority."

"Why isn't it? Do you know how many millions of men get laid each night?"

"Less than you think, I bet."

"Are you gay?" she asked suspiciously.

"Are you kidding? Why would I come in here to buy a condom if I was a faggot?"

"You name it. AIDS. Herpes. Hepatitis B. Cuts down on the risk."

"Nothing could be further from the truth. I made a spur-of-the-moment decison to go down to Delancey Street to find myself a prostitute."

"They have transvestites on West Street that look just like women," the woman said coyly.

"I told you. That's not my ticket. You really think I look like a faggot?" The realtor felt immeasurably flattered. He looked in the mirror.

"You're not impotent, are you?"

"No!"

"Are you very kinky?"

"No more so than the ordinary guy."

"That's too bad."

"Why?"

"Because if you were very kinky, I might have let you go home with me."

She rang up the condoms and gave him his change. To his disgust the realtor found he had a hard-on, even though he hadn't found her even remotely attractive more than five sentences before. She was overweight and badly dressed, her lipstick a disgusting shade of pink, her hair a funny straw color from being dyed too many times. She had a little mustache. Of course, what really excited him was her disgustingness, the thought that he could get it up for someone this ugly.

4

The first few weeks in the apartment Jack treated almost as a vacation—rising with Lorraine, helping Judy off to school, reading *The New York Times* as he dawdled over a leisurely breakfast of smoked salmon and chubs long after Lorraine had left for work. Twice a week he taught; the rest of the time he was free to draw, paint, read, or merely watch the changing colors of the sky out the window as the housekeeper, Aurelia, changed the sheets and vacuumed. At first her presence amused and gratified him, then, perhaps because he was not yet painting, it began to annoy him. It was pleasant having his clothes washed and ironed, but unpleasant having them scorched. It was nice to be able to leave dishes in the sink, but unnerving to have her always there when he made lunch or went for snacks. Until this constant witness he had not realized how often during the course of the day he would drift into the kitchen, sometimes to grab a cookie, sometimes to pour coffee, sometimes just to wander over to the cupboard, check over the food, and walk away. At first he tried to talk to her, in much the same vein as he would to anyone else, though much more slowly and with attention to the careful pronunciation of each syllable—mentioning a movie he had seen the night before, or a crazy little incident he'd witnessed on the street, or a short appraisal of how he was feeling or how his work was progressing that day—but she never gave him any response except, on occasion, a nod. Thinking maybe she didn't speak English well enough or have enough money to go to the movies, he began to ask her questions about herself and her family—where she came from, how many kids she had—but as she always answered even these

monosyllabically, eventually he stopped. He became convinced she hated him. She almost never bought the foods he
put down on the general shopping list, unless he spoke to her
just before she went out about one special item, and gave her
the money to pay for it. Even so, she would find some way to
make a mistake: flavored oatmeal instead of plain, the wrong
brand or flavor ice cream, rotten fruit. Worse yet, she kept
the TV on from morning to evening. When he'd ask her to
turn it down she would do so, but then in a quarter of an
hour he'd find himself hearing it again.

"If you'd watch what you're ironing instead of the TV,
maybe you wouldn't burn my shirts," Jack finally said.

"Maybe I wouldn't, and maybe I would."

Exchanges such as this embarrassed Jack, made him think
of little children in Africa shrinking up into what looks like
pocketbooks. He was scared of her; her undisguised contempt
for him shamed him. She brought out all the guilt—and
hatred—he has ever felt against all those people who served
him, badly, in his life—cab drivers, waiters, repairmen, subway token sellers—especially when those people had skins
that were darker than his. What were the reasons she could
have for hating him? Jack could count at least six: (1) his
interference with her TV-watching, (2) his interference with
the sense of ownership and autonomy she must have felt
(however falsely) when she had the apartment to herself all
day, (3) her reduced opportunity to goof off due to his presence, (4) the possibility that the substitution of him for David
created more mess to be cleaned up (dishes, clothing, rags)
without (5) any augmentation of her salary, and, finally, (6)
his race. She could even be angry (7) because she was young
and he's never made a pass at her (though this was unlikely);
albeit in the Victorian era they would not have been allowed
unchaperoned in a room together. His anger at this presumed
hatred of him and how she evinced it via the nonperformance
of her duties was countered by a noblesse oblige that tells
him it was not her fault, that she was probably brought up in
poverty, now lives in a strange, cold country far from family
and friends—feelings that themselves have become undercut
by a sense of guilt concerning even this noblesse oblige: was

not lowering one's standards of expected manners and behavior for the benefit of another but a more subtle form of insult, a refusal to deal in total seriousness with that person? This, in turn, became mixed up with his feelings about affirmative actions and quotas, complicated by the fact that he was Jewish: a race stigmatized by the use of quotas, and one that certain segments of the black community periodically attacked. For these reasons he kept postponing talking about Aurelia to Lorraine—and thus his anger grew, further fueled by his belief that he wasted far more time and emotion thinking about Aurelia than she did in thinking about him.

Once Jack had spent a sufficient amount of time in Lorraine's apartment to become physically comfortable there, he began to try to work. After breakfast he would carry a second or third cup of coffee out to the coffee table in front of the couch facing the window and, pastel or oil crayon or pencil in hand, would try to draw the progression of sun across the floor, or the changing patterns of the clouds across the sky and water. A "Perceptual Realist," this view seemed expressly made for him: trees, water, a sky whose diffuseness was only enhanced by the jagged interruption of a building in the forefront of the canvas. Yet something was missing. Or, perhaps, it was too perfect. He would forget he was drawing, and sit there, forgotten pencil still in his hand, staring out the window, rejoicing in the good fortune that had led him to this house. When he thought about Lorraine and his life with her, it was always this image of himself that he saw. It occurred to him that during his years in the East Village he had learned to shut off that part of his mind that would have reacted to the ugliness of decaying buildings, streets without trees, people sheltered under newspapers, until, gradually, he had so constricted what he would allow himself to see that his perceptual mechanism had gone partially dead. Was this repression of the visual sense the reason why city dwellers became so overconscious of personality, conversation, and sex? Now, surrounded by wide clean streets and well-kept old buildings of elegant proportions, a park where kids played basketball, he almost felt as if he were regaining the use of a lost sense.

Nonetheless, he soon discovered, to his intense disappointment, that the dissatisfactions that had plagued him the past
year about his work had not vanished. His drawings were
dead, uninspired, mere lines and patterns. Inevitably, after an
hour or two, frustrated by his lack of productivity, he would
slip on his old brown bomber jacket and snap his fingers for
Jack the dog. Together they would walk down to the Seventy-
ninth Street Boat Basin. It was November, and usually the air
was cold, the ground hard. But on sunny days, leaves crackling underfoot, sun burning his face and the water, he felt
more at peace with himself than he had since a child. At the
heart of his feelings was a peaceful melancholy—as if the
exciting (but somewhat sleazy) era of his life was over, and
he were getting ready to settle down into a tranquil middle
age. For the first time, this prospect didn't appall him. It
promised, in fact, a respite from frustrated desires—personal
and professional. He would have liked to put this new-found
wisdom in his work, but of course painting was not about
wisdom, but about—paint. His work needed a change, but
what? He felt like a child wondering what he was going to do
when he grew up. He wondered how he had the nerve to get
up in front of a group of undergraduates and talk about painting, when in his heart he knew he knew—absolutely nothing. He told himself that everybody felt this way (at least
from time to time); sometimes he even believed it.

He liked to sit in front of the boat basin, warm sun glinting
on his cold face, turning orange and red as it sank toward
New Jersey and purple night, as pinpricks of yellow dotted
the increasingly invisible hillside, some static, some moving
up and down, disappearing for a while, then reappearing as
the road twisted back into view. He wondered what it would
be like to live on a boat on the water, a kind of hobo, no roots
except to a frail vehicle with an inordinate dependence on
the weather. No doubt it would be cold and damp, unbearably
windy; no doubt, also, there were visual secrets to be learned
only by weeks of cold and lonely afternoons spent staring at
the steel-gray water and sky—unless this was merely an illusion, created by the lonely to justify their loneliness. . . .

There was a painter on one of these boats who would sit

on deck with his pad and pencil, feet up on a railing. Once the man caught Jack looking at him and waved. Jack waved back. He thought of shouting that he, too, was an artist. But the predictability of the exchange—the forced appreciation of almost certainly bad work—stopped him, and he decided to keep the details of the man's existence in the realm of the possible rather than the actual. This way he could wave to him occasionally, and speculate pleasantly about him. It was better—and safer—than knowing him.

Other times he felt his thoughts about sunlight, water, and age were banal, that he was conventional—not in a new and unusual and subtle way (as he liked to think) but in an old-fashioned and uninteresting way. He would stare at the shifting colors in the river and think how lucky Monet had been, to have lived at a time when the world offered so much more to discover. He knew that, until he progressed beyond this feeling, his work would be, at best, mediocre.

The strategic approach would have been to reorder his mind, but the tactical approach—creating a proper studio space in which to work—seemed less all-encompassing and simpler. Privacy, a better physical organization of space: perhaps that was all that was needed. Of course, the uncomfortableness of his work area could be merely an excuse and not a reason, but how was he to know until he tried to remedy it? The space where he worked had views and sunlight, but it was in sight of delivery boys, Aurelia as she worked in the kitchen, and Judy when she came home. The back room was dark and filled with junk. He could go downtown to paint in his old apartment, but it took almost an hour to get there, and what was the point of having started a new life, if it only meant to return to the very aspects of what had failed him in the old?

Other times he thought perhaps the problem was that he thought of where he lived as "Lorraine's apartment," and not his own. He was afraid of messing "her" floors, "her" coffee table, "her" couch. The coffee table on which he drew was too low in relation to the couch for him to be able to lean on it without placing undue weight on his elbows, which caused them to ache. If he sat on the floor he got cold; cushions

tended to collapse at unpredictable moments; kneeling hurt
his knees; plus, from there there was such an acute angle
with the window that all you could see was the sky. In a rage
one day he found a dark red enamel table and an aluminum
beach chair with green and white plastic cross-straps hidden
in the back room. He went to the carpet store, bought an
eight-by-ten remnant of bright green indoor-outdoor carpeting, placed it under the table and beach chair, then he got out
his paints. He hadn't held a brush in his hand for a while;
like the touch of a few remembered lovers (not necessarily
ones he had especially liked), it gave him the chills.

"I don't think Mommy's going to like that," Judy an-
nounced when she came home from school. (She also said,
after looking at his paintings, that Saralee's sister—who went
to Music and Art—could do much better.)

"What's wrong with it? It's strong, it's sturdy, it's *honest*,"
he said, shaking the table, pointing at the carpet.

"Well, for one thing, it's not *white*. You know how
Mommy is about *white*." She dragged the phone into her
room and, with suddenly supernatural hearing powers, he
heard every word of a tedious conversation about a boy in her
class who might or might not have put his hand on Ellen's
breast. He wanted to tell her how unimportant, what a time-
waster sex was, that she'd be better off staring out the window.

"*Jesus Christ!*" said Lorraine, when she came home. She
dumped her briefcase on the floor and stared at the living
room.

"It's just temporary," Jack assured her. "Just until we figure out a decent way to arrange my studio. It's nice to have a
little color in the living room, for a change.

"Very nice, if you happen to enjoy having your living room
look like a Christmas tree." She walked out of the room. He
followed her to the bathroom, where she was trying to get
the shower nozzle to shoot across approximately four feet of
space into the whirlpool tub that now not only did not whirl
but whose pipes refused to release water. The plumber had
told Lorraine that to get it fixed she would have to rip out
(and of course replace) an entire wall, which meant the whole

bathroom should really be redone, as the original job was so sloppy as not to be worth repairing. Since Lorraine could not afford to do this, she had decided to do nothing. Intellectually speaking, Jack approved, but his heart sank at the thought that he might not be able to take a bath in his own (rather Lorraine's) bathroom for the next couple of years.

"Just where am I supposed to work?" he asked.

"I don't know, Jack, don't ask me."

"You're the one who gets upset—"

"Okay. In the maid's room."

"The maid's room is smaller than the walk-in closet in your bedroom, and it smells from the garbage out the back door."

"Leave me alone." She lay back in the eight inches of water she had been able to get in the tub and shut her eyes. The shower cap covered her hair and ears as if she were in surgery, or dead; for a dangerous second Jack felt sorry for her. "You're using me, Jack, aren't you. That's why you went out with me, so you could move into this apartment, isn't it?"

"Don't be silly. I love you."

"You love my house. Actually, you don't even love my house, you just love the rooms that look out on the river." This was not entirely true, but it was truer than Jack would have liked to admit. "Frankly, I'm surprised you haven't come right out with it, and asked Judy to move into the maid's room, so you can paint in her room. Or maybe you'd prefer that *I* move into the maid's room, so you could turn the bedroom into a painting studio?" Jack would have preferred this arrangement to the current one, though of course he couldn't say so: especially as, most of the time in bed one's eyes were closed. "Or maybe I should move downtown to the East Village with Judy so you can have the whole apartment to yourself. I mean, one day you might decide you have to be a sculptor, and bring in a crane."

"Lorraine, even if I told you I'd be willing to work in the maid's room you wouldn't let me—because you could never bring yourself to throw away the junk in there."

"That's true." She sighed.

"So? What am I supposed to do?"

"Are you really sure you want to be a painter?" She started

to cry. The idea of cleaning out the back room—throwing out
the last remains of her previous life—upset her in a way she
could not have predicted. She had begun to think of that
room as the objective correlative of her unconscious, where
all the junk of her life could express itself without threat to
the rest of her life. She too had her fantasy about the apartment. It involved sitting on the couch and looking, not at a
table full of paints or some half-painted canvases, but at
white walls, floors, ceilings, even sky. She did not want
chairs, rugs, paintings, or even a human being obstructing
the view—however much she may have loved that human
being all those other moments when she was not sitting
alone on the couch. It might sound trivial, but she needed
that, she felt, quite as much as Jack needed his views and
privacy.

"Don't be ridiculous," said Jack. "You said, before I moved
here, I could paint anywhere I liked."

"That's true." She sighed. "Okay, if that's what you really
want, I'll clean out the back room. But you've got to give me
a little time."

"Of course."

"To get used to it, I mean."

"Sure. Thanks." He tried not to let his irritation come
through in his voice, but of course it did. In turn, this made
Lorraine angry.

"Is something the matter?" she asked.

"No."

"Then why do you sound like that?"

"Like what?"

"Like you're angry I don't get out of the bath this minute
to execute your every whim."

"Why does it always come down to a question of power
with you?" asked Jack.

"That's what I'd like to ask you, Jack. As if it's not enough
that I let you finagle yourself into my house—"

" 'Finagle myself into your house'?" Jack was astonished.
"You begged me to come live with you."

" 'Begged you to come live with me'? Are you crazy?" Lorraine felt equally astonished. "I felt sorry for you in that pathetic little apartment of yours. . . ."

Jack *was* pathetic, though perhaps no more so than everybody else. But he'd be damned if he'd admit even this watered-down version of her statement to Lorraine, for she'd only end up using it against him. He stalked out of the room into the living room, where Judy lay with her head on the pillow next to the blasting stereo. He felt he did not possess the moral authority to order Judy to turn it off at this moment, so he went to the back of the apartment, beyond the pantry to the maid's room, and cleared a little space for himself amidst the boxes. There in the dark, behind his closed and dreamy eyes, a room began to materialize. An attic room with sloping ceilings that met at the top, a dormer window that was more a mysterious passage to another world than an ordinary window. This was the room he had slept in when he was young, when the woman who meant most to Jack in all the world was his mother: once a child in a big white hat standing by the railing of a ship (from her earliest photograph), now an old woman who was beginning to have trouble remembering things. Jack used to stand on a chair to climb to that window, a tower at the top of a castle. He would lie there for hours, watching the clouds move like a moving picture through the frame of the window. He had first learned to sound out those strange things called "words" as he sat up there after school; ever since, he had loved to read by a window in the dying afternoon light. It was there, too, that he had first brought his crayons and learned to create the world. Then the day came when he became too big to sit in the window comfortably. When his sister went off to college he was given her downstairs room. Soon after that, his father had died and they had sold the house. For some reason, lying on Lorraine's bed sometimes reminded Jack of that window and that room. Was this—and not sex—the reason he was here? Or were they perhaps the same, a feeling of being, at last—again—home?

Jack awoke when light hit his eyes. This was the light in the hall that became visible when Lorraine opened the door.

She came and stood next to him, so that it was easy to lean
his head against her stomach. "Look, we'll clean up this
room," she said. "I should have thrown out this junk ages
ago anyway. I just needed a good excuse."

"Thanks," said Jack. Still, he could not make himself
sound grateful.

"You don't sound enthusiastic," said Lorraine.

"Are you sure you don't mind?"

"Mind? I do billions of things I don't want to every day.
Starting with getting out of bed in the morning. Just tell me
what you want."

What *did* he want? Jack thought of the smallness, the darkness, the smell of the maid's room. He thought of the agora-
phobia of the living room, the insecurity of painting in front
of a window, exposed to everybody's eyes. "Another floor,"
he said.

"Jesus Christ!" Lorraine left the room. Jack sat there, listening to the fridge open and close, the faucets go on and off,
as she started to make dinner.

What was the matter with him? As usual, being put upon
gave him an obscure satisfaction. Once again he had found
yet another way for life to remain intractable to his dreams.

"I really think the problem is Aurelia," said Jack during
dinner. "The TV is driving me crazy. She won't pay attention
to me when I tell her to turn it down."

"She *is* a problem." Lorraine sighed. "I'd fire her, but then
I'd just have to find somebody else. And Judy likes her."

"Says *who?*" said Judy.

"Don't you? I thought you did."

"She's all right, I guess," said Judy, mushing around her
potatoes. "But . . . I don't like her messing around my room."

"That's what she's paid to do," said Lorraine.

"That book you gave me says people my age are entitled to
their privacy."

"I'm all for it. Of course, you could clean up after yourself,
you know. Like me and my sisters did when we were your
age."

Judy rolled her eyes. "Like, I am *so* impressed."

"We weren't just responsible for our rooms, but we had to set the table and clear it, stack the dishes, then we'd rotate washing and drying and putting things away."

"*Yawn*. There were five of you, and one of me."

"Yes, but we had a whole lot more dishes to wash. And *no* dishwashers. In any case, all I'm asking you to do, on the nights Aurelia isn't here, is to put the dishes in the dishwasher. And if you find that too much trouble, maybe *I'll* start finding it too much trouble to give you your allowance."

"Mother! That is *so* unfair! Jenny doesn't have to do dishes! Saralee doesn't have to do dishes!" She jumped up and ran out of the room.

"That's what comes from sending your kids to a ritzy private school where everybody's got a ton of money." Jack rolled his eyes: Lorraine always talked as if she were a pauper. Per usual, the conversation had gotten diverted from his problem to hers, theirs. This was always true about families.

"You didn't answer my question," said Jack. "Will you tell Aurelia she can't play the TV while I'm working?"

"*You* tell her, Jack, you're not a baby."

"I don't pay her salary, so she won't listen to me."

"Maybe there's a moral there, Jack."

"Lorraine, I can't *afford* to pay for a housekeeper. Do you think if I lived on my own, I would have a housekeeper?"

Lorraine got up and began clearing away the dishes. "I don't know. Leave me alone. I'm so tired."

Looking at her face, he could see, she *was*. She started to cry. Jack felt irritation at this blackmail, rather than pity. But because he wanted to be thought of—and to think of himself —as a moral, caring human being, he put his arm around her and led her to the couch. There, she resumed the monologue she had commenced soon after entering the apartment.

". . . postpone the meeting with Bergdorf's until three. Once the line was frozen there would be nothing I could do, and Chase was having their meeting at two. So I asked Tony to accept a bill of credit.

" 'Lorraine,' he said, 'you're really getting into it'—I love this guy, he's always telling me to go out of business.

" 'Tony,' I told him, 'we got problems, but *you* got problems *too*. Who the hell is going to buy knits and merino from you when they can get it in Italy twelve hundred lire to the dollar? And who the hell is going to buy me if they can get something with an Italian name for practically the same price?'

" 'Fucking A,' says Tony, 'pardon my French. They talk patriotism but when it comes to supporting the American worker they'd rather put him on welfare.' I knew this would get him going. Allison comes into my office to tell me Saks wants to send someone over to pick out stuff for the ad, and Raggedy Andy wants to drop by to ask Marianne some stuff for his column, but Marianne doesn't want to talk to him because he ignored our last show. Attitude! I tell Allison to try and write up a little something in case we can't talk sense into Marianne, but Allison's meeting with Macy's California in five minutes, so it's up to me, meanwhile Macy's is going to be here any minute. I get a phone call from Bob H, he wants me to send him over some figures so maybe he can make a case for me. I wanted to send Bob but Bob was in the back helping Marianne pick the clothes for Dallas. Do you realize two months ago he was a salesman at Parachute? Meanwhile Tony's on the other line wanting to call back later. . . ."

Jack's mind wandered, as it always did when Lorraine talked about her business. Too many Tonys, too many Bobs, too many cry-wolfs.

". . . meanwhile the buyers are spending all their money in Europe. Not that I blame them, if I were a buyer I'd be doing the same thing. People don't give a damn about good design any more. All they care about is the label."

Here, at last, was an opening. "It's the same with art," Jack interrupted. "Remember that opening I took you to last week, I used to be friends with that guy in Pratt. He used to do minimal-type drawings kind of in the Dorothea Rockbourne mode, but more image-like, then several years ago, when post-pseudo-cubism was just getting hot, he decided to totally change his style, so he dropped his old dealer and switched to Gracie Mansion, and now . . ." Jack was halfway through his story before he looked down and saw that Lorraine had fallen asleep. He woke her up and told her she should go lie down in the bedroom. "I will," she said, but instead of getting up, she rolled over to the other side, opened her mouth slightly, and began to snore. Jack nudged her to make her stop, but, after a few seconds, she started again. This was a habit that used to bother him as much as anything in the world, but, living with Lorraine, he had come to accept it. At times his maturity cheered him; at other times it depressed him, as a symbol of the compromises age had wrought upon him.

He tried to wake Lorraine again, then gave up and went into the kitchen. He looked at the clock: 9:45. He drank the last of the red wine out of the bottle. He brought the dishes from the table into the kitchen, placed them in the sink with the garbage disposal, and filled the sink with warm, soapy water. He sat there for a while watching the bubbles dissolve, then he went into Judy's room. 10:02. She was lying on her stomach, writing something in a book. She looked up as the door creaked open. "Who asked you to come in?" she asked, closing the book. It was small and pale blue: her diary.

"Nobody," said Jack. He felt a rage, that he had done *her* dishes as she lay there, and now he didn't even have her friendliness as a reward. He left the room. He sat back down on the couch next to Lorraine. He put his hand on her back. Out the window he stared, at the blackness that was the river, New Jersey, the sky. A terrible depression came over him, as it often did at night when he was alone—or with one or several other people—in an apartment, instead of being at some opening or party or dance place surrounded by millions of chic-looking people. Not that he liked chic people—or discos—or even art openings: unless the artist were not too successful, and Jack was surrounded by friends. And yet, when he was alone, it always seemed as if there was no one there, and this scared him.

Jack the dog started whimpering. At Jack's feet, he was sleeping too, a bad dream. Jack rubbed his ears as he looked out the window. He did it rhythmically, without thinking. Perhaps only due to the coincidence of names, he felt very close to Jack. Somehow they had the same status in the house. The only pets he had spent much time with previously were cats that had belonged to his girlfriends. His bachelor status had seemed to preclude the responsibility of being home at predictable enough hours to feed and take care of an animal with the excremental exigencies of a dog.

"Do you know how long you've been scratching that dog's ears?" asked Lorraine.

Jack's heart pounded. "How long have you been watching me?" he replied. He felt as if he'd been caught doing something dirty.

"Am I crazy, or is it odd that you're lying there touching that animal instead of me?" She reached over the couch, snapped her fingers. Immediately Jack stood up, staggered over to her hand, flopped down again, and began licking it. "You see, he still loves me best," she said.

"There's no contest," said Jack, though he felt hurt.

"Isn't it? You don't love me, Jack, do you?"

"Don't be silly. Of course I do."

"If you're here just because you wanted to live in a different place and couldn't afford to do it by yourself, that's all right. I never would have had the guts to get rid of David on my own, in a weird way I sometimes think I used you. . . ."

This information, although in a sense deflating to Jack's vanity, nonetheless, in a moral sense, relieved him of the terrible guilt he often felt.

"Not that I don't love you, I do, even if half the time I'm too tired to talk to you . . . I just wish you'd have the guts for once to tell me the truth, and tell me to my face you don't love me."

Sitting in the dark, looking out the black square (the window), Jack felt as if he and Lorraine were alone on a silver spaceship, condemned to wander among the stars forever. At moments like this he liked her best.

"Even if it were true, why would you want to know something like that?" Jack asked. Lorraine took his head between her hands, and kissed him on the lips. He felt just like a child. He liked it.

"Ooooh. *Gross*," said Judy, who had come out of her room. Lorraine sat up.

"Judy, dearest," said Lorraine, not sure how much such talk was preadolescent echolalia caused by confusion over nascent sexual feelings and how much a symptom of genuine neurosis, "there is nothing gross about a display of affection between two people who are genuinely fond of each other."

"I'm not your dearest, *Jack* is."

"No, dearest, you're my dearest, come here. Don't you know there isn't *anything* in the world I wouldn't do for you?" Lorraine pulled the reluctant Judy to her and kissed her. Judy stood like a board and rolled her eyes to the ceiling to show how unnecessary all this was. Jack acts pretty much the same way, Lorraine realized. Finally, Judy pushed her away.

"Look, Mom, can I go out on a double date with Saralee Saturday night?" she asked. "Please, pretty please, say yes and I'll do anything you want." Lorraine looked at Jack. "Actually it's not Saturday night. It's Saturday afternoon. Around six."

"That's *night*," said Lorraine. "No, I don't think so."

"*No!* Why not? You just said you'd do *anything* for me."

" 'Do anything' is not the same as 'let you do anything.' Frankly, I think you're a little too young to start dating boys. Especially at night. Maybe next year—"

"Next year everybody'll have a boyfriend but me! It's so *stupid.* I can go to the movies with Saralee, but not with Saralee and two boys! That makes a *lot* of sense! So what you're telling me is next time I have to lie."

"That's *not* what I'm telling you," said Lorraine.

"Yes, it is!"

"Thirteen is coming back, nice and strong," said Jack.

"Shut up, Jack!"

"Don't talk that way to Jack," said Lorraine.

"Don't talk that way to me," he echoed.

"God, I can't believe this. It's not *fair.* Saralee's two months younger than I am and her mother doesn't think she's too young."

"Saralee's mother obviously has different ideas than I do. Which doesn't mean that I'm necessarily right, and she's necessarily wrong, or that—"

"But we've already arranged it!" Judy's face got red, as if she were on the verge of tears.

"Whose fault is that?"

"Yours!"

"*Mine?*"

"Yeah, you said we could."

"I *did!* When? I don't re—"

"You *did!* I asked you about it last week when Saralee was here for dinner."

"That's funny. Maybe I did, but I don't remember."

"Whose fault is that? If you weren't so involved in your business and could pay a little attention to the rest of the world . . ."

"I really don't recall any of this, Judy, but if you say you told me, I guess you must have. I'll think about it, and let you know tomorrow."

"Mom!"

"By the way, did you clear off the table?" she asked.

"Not exactly."

"*I* did it," said Jack.

"Judy was supposed to."

Judy pouted, then threw a big smile. "Mom, you'll really think about it?"

"Only if you do the dishes."

"Blackmail, Mother. *Honestly.*"

"Did you walk Jack this afternoon?"

"*Mo-ther*, I have a paper due tomorrow!"

"Honestly, Judy, I cannot fathom your attitude. How would you feel if you were totally dependent on other people to take care of all your needs, people whom you loved terribly much, and then, when you were desperate to go to the bathroom, they couldn't be bothered to take you? Do you think I made you lie in bed screaming for me to take you to the bathroom in the middle of the night when you were young and just starting to be toilet-trained? I certainly did not!"

"Gimme a break!" Judy rolled her eyes.

"I will *not* give you a break. You were the one who wanted the dog. Remember?"

Judy pretended she didn't remember. She went over to the

TV and flipped it on. Jack, hearing his name, brought over the leash, dropped it in front of Lorraine. When he saw that Lorraine wasn't going to do anything with it he ran to the couch and rummaged under it for an old bone. Lorraine picked up the bone and threw it. Jack ran to the bone, picked it up, started to bring it back to her, then stopped. "Jack, come on, bring me the bone," said Lorraine. Jack started toward her, stopped, went back to the chair leg under which the bone had been thrown, then he deposited it there. "Jack, come on, bring me the bone." But he just stood there, stupidly, looking at her.

Judy picked up the bone and threw it. "Come on Jack, bring me the bone." Jack picked the bone up in his mouth, brought it back to Judy. He rolled on his back to have his stomach scratched. Lorraine felt humiliated. Who paid for Jack's food —she or Judy? Who walked Jack most of the time—she or Judy? Who picked Jack out of a dog pound to give him a happy life—she or Judy?

Judy was clearly pleased. "What can I say, Mom?" she asked. "You don't know how to empower people. "Empower" was a new word she had recently learned at a school workshop to improve student productivity and well-being; she had used it constantly for the past week.

"I may not be able to 'empower' you to do the dishes, or clean up your room," Lorraine said. "But I can assure you that if you don't have that room thoroughly straightened out by Friday evening, you certainly won't go to the movies with Saralee and those boys Saturday night."

" 'Might makes right,' " Judy replied sarcastically.

" 'Might' has nothing to do with it. It is right that you do the dishes—being as you are young, and apparently have nothing to do except listen to music and television—and I am older, less energetic, and work a ten-hour day."

"What about Jack? All he does is sit and stare out the window. Anyway, why don't you get the dishwasher fixed already?"

"One, I'm so busy paying for your school and *allowance* I don't have the money. Two, in any case there'd still be pots and serving bowls to do. Three, what Jack does or does not do is none of your business."

"I don't know why Aurelia can't do the dishes. What're we paying her for anyway?"

"Maybe I don't like Aurelia hanging around while I eat. Maybe I don't want to pay her cab fare home to Brooklyn every evening."

"Great! So I should skip my homework to do the dishes."

"I don't know, Judy." Lorraine shook her head wearily. "You have to learn how to budget your time so you get your work done before supper."

"Usually I *do*. But it's not *fair* to penalize me for doing my homework on time."

On and on it went—a fugue Jack already knew inside and out, backward, forward, sideways, transposed. It started with "duty," then moved to "justice," at last to "goodness"— either natural or acquired.

Jack stood up, picked up the leash, whistled for the dog. "*I'll* do it," he said.

"Should I keep you company?" asked Lorraine.

"*Power*," sneered Judy. "You really don't mind walking the dog after all."

5

Jack the dog is excited. Saliva pours out of his mouth as he scratches with his paws against the metal door, his tail waving its motley assortment of colors: tan, gold, white, brown, even bits of red and black. Saliva dripping, hind legs dancing to maintain balance as he leans up against the door, his mongrel energy and good nature, the near-neurosis of his terrier sensitivity, manifests itself. He's proud of his energy, his intelligence, even his neurosis. As a dog he must perform on command, but he's not really a slave. Voluntarily he's embraced his learning, his obedience. And his occasional disobedience too—for at times odd stirrings of rebellion fill his heart. Usually when a stick is thrown he runs after it, grabs it with his teeth, sticks it in his mouth, and starts trotting happily back to his master. But sometimes, he finds himself stopping halfway back, puzzled, the absurdity of this action suddenly overwhelming him. What's he doing with a huge piece of dead wood sticking out of his mouth—a piece of wood he fetches to his master only so that his master can throw it to him again, so that he can fetch it once again and bring it to his master? So he stops and pants, saliva dripping over the stick; always there is saliva, dripping out of his mouth, onto the floor, the rug, the bed . . . . What should he do? It's dumb to carry the stick, but dumb, perhaps—a form of overreaction—to refuse to carry it—for, after all, wasn't the stick thrown not for the master's enjoyment, but for his own? Worse, if he drops the stick, won't this show that it was pointless to have carried it this far, pointless, perhaps, to have played this game all the hundreds of times he and his master have played it in the past? Are they then both fools, he and his master? And after such knowledge, what forgiveness? And yet, each time he carries the stick, doesn't this only increase the sum total of his foolishness? The paralysis itself adds to his self-consciousness, until it reaches the point where he would be glad to forget the whole thing: bring the stick back to where it had been thrown, run back to where he had been before his master called him to her—but the stick was thrown, Lorraine or the Girl or the Man With His Name stands there expectant: who, after all, can reverse time? So, stick in mouth, tail wagging, saliva dripping, nose in air, Jack stands there, seemingly ignoring the shouting of his name.

Jack resolves the situation by dancing away with the stick, dropping it on the floor—not where it was originally thrown (for he desires to conceal the workings of his mind from his master), but partway there; intensionality may be ascribed or not, according to her whim. Although she thinks he is dumber than he is, he doesn't choose to disabuse her of her erroneous belief; first, because the demonstration of her lack of intuition would embarrass her; second, because his initial concealment of his intelligence, which contributed to her faulty perception, is something, now as then, he desires to maintain, for reasons unclear to him, but which are in fact similar to the impulses of servants before their masters.

Empty-mouthed, he runs back to Lorraine. She says, "Get the stick, Jack, get the stick." In themselves these sounds have no meaning to him, because he is a dog. It is hard for a dog to learn English. He can remember only a few words: "no," "walk," "leash," and of course his name, "Jack." Sometimes "food" sounds familiar and he runs for his food dish. Sometimes when he goes to his dish before food is put in the dish his master pets him. Sometimes, however, when he goes to the door to get his leash, because he thinks the meaningful sound his master uttered was the word for "leash," Lorraine irritatedly says "no"; Jack shamefacedly drops the leash out of his mouth, and curls up on the floor, lowering his head and shutting his eyes, like a timid girl of nineteen. He doesn't want to be seen for a while; he's shy. If other people are looking at him at moments like this, he becomes self-con-

scious and performs odd, uncharacteristic gestures—jumping
up on the couch or running up and down the apartment barking and wagging his tail, or standing on his hind legs so he
can put his paws on the windowsill—all to distract them
from the essential foolishness of himself. That is, he makes
a fool of himself so they'll laugh at him for what he chooses
to be laughed at for, instead of the shameful unarticulated
fact that he mistook the word "dish" for "leash."

"Stick," now, is another nervous-making word. Sometimes
Jack correctly anticipates the throwing of the stick, going so
far as to fetch it out of the closet; other times the sound must
be repeated many times for him to be able to understand
what Lorraine or the others are saying; sometimes, despite
the repetitions, he fails entirely, and grabs his leash or runs
into the kitchen and stands beside the food bowl. Sometimes
the meaning of the sound comes to him immediately—he
feels he knows everything there is in the world to know;
other times he must piece it out slowly, by elimination,
trying to remember if the reason he has to pee is that he has
not been walked recently, or because it is one of those spring
days when a dog's body is on fire.

But now it is not a spring day. It is a fall evening. Jack is
going out for a walk with the Man With His Name. This
coincidence is a constant puzzle to him, whose secret meaning he is forever trying to discern. Is the man named after
him? Was he, perhaps, named after the man? Are most men
named "Jack," with "David" the exception? Is this a sadistic
teasing on Lorraine's part or a loving reference? Is this other
Jack meant to be his special friend, or is Jack meant to sup-
plant Jack in Lorraine's affections? So far both seem to be
true. Lorraine is certainly more enthusiastic about the new
man than she is about the old dog, but, perhaps to compen-
sate, the new man takes Jack on long, intimate walks in the
afternoon, and at night, when Lorraine used to cursorily walk
him down to the mailbox on the corner, she and Jack and
Jack usually circumnavigate the block, sometimes even
meander together down to the park.

Now, hearing the word "walk," Jack runs to the door, grabs
with his teeth the leash that is hanging over the doorknob,

and trots back to Jack, tail waving proudly, leash in mouth. Jack fastens the leash on Jack's collar, opens the door, rings for the elevator. But as they're about to leave Lorraine joins them, making a deal of it as if she were doing Jack a favor— as if Jack (the dog) were not a sufficiently interesting companion for an evening walk. (If Jack—the dog—were not a sufficiently interesting companion, why did she buy a dog for a pet in the first place; why is a dog called "man's best friend"?) In the elevator Lorraine takes the leash. When they get downstairs Jack leaps out of the elevator but Lorraine pulls him back. Slowly the doorman moves toward the door. In an undignified way, Jack is on his hind legs, pawing at the sight of the street through the glass. He doesn't want to do this, but he can't help himself. Finally the door is opened, and Jack pulls Lorraine onto the street. The Man With His Name ambles behind.

The smells are pungent on the street because it has not rained in some time, and Jack runs from tire to lamp post to building to tire in delight, at first not even pausing to pee. The smell of urine and dog crap is everywhere, though the halcyon days when there were dark mounds of wonderful smells all over the streets are pretty much gone. Now owners stick little pieces of paper under their dogs—even Lorraine, who is lazy, does this—at least in the daytime. It embarrasses Jack, at times even prevents him from going. When he smells urine he lifts his right hind leg and squirts a little urine out of his penis onto the spot where he smelled urine—in this case a fire hydrant—so that any other dog who passes the fire hydrant will know that he, Jack, peed there first. Sometimes it crosses his mind that there is some other purpose—some deeper, more primeval meaning to his desire to pee not lots in one place, but small amounts in lots of places—such a strong, deep desire that he often finds himself lifting his hind leg when there's nothing left in his penis to squirt, though always he tries to squiggle out a few last drops. He can neither help nor explain himself, but something uncontrollable comes over him when he passes a fire hydrant or tire imbued with the smell of doggy effluence; in some ways he feels it connects him to the men he passes lying on the sidewalk in smelly old clothes, empty bottles emanating a delightfully strong smell lying on the ground next to them, the same smell that emanates from their noses or mouths when they exhale, and also from their skin as they sleep (a smell he has noticed on more than one occasion on Lorraine, and numerous times on the Man Who Went Away); plus there are other smells too, of a more acrid quality, coming out of their mouths and, seemingly, their entire bodies. The smell from the bottle is not the smell that attracts him, but he understands their pull toward it; they are the men who are driven by their noses. Most humans are not like that, only a few raise their hind legs to pee, but Jack does not assume this is due to human lack of smell-recognition ability, but because human civilization has progressed to the point where forepaws have been abolished as tools of locomotion. No, humans walk on their hind legs or rest in immobile worship in their large, motorized four-wheeled vehicles whose gas farts are to humans what dog urine is to dogs. Humans worshipped these vehicles by stopping on the street as they passed; to challenge this authority entailed a good risk of being struck down on the spot. Motor fart smell made Jack nauseous, but humans loved it; it hung over the city like the buildings overhead. The human desire for urine smell was more private; even when they peed in public they did it in an enclosed space, little glass booths on street corners where people dropped coins in machines in order to talk to themselves. Usually, however, they preferred urinating in the little tiled rooms in their homes, doors shut even to Jack. The injustice of this astonished Jack: did humans not forever avail themselves of the opportunity of watching him (and other dogs) as they did their business in the street? Not only that, they shoved coarse sheets of paper under him in order to remind him of the early days, when he was little, stuck in the house, and struck on the nose and backside when he did his business anywhere except on a piece of newspaper in the bathroom. First they forced him to do his business on the paper; then they forbade him to do it on the paper, and dragged him outside to do it on the bare street; and now, though he's still on the street, it's back to the newspaper. Just think what

would happen to the young members of the human species if
they were treated in such contradictory and schizophrenic-
making fashion! But of course, because they are his masters
he has to accept this, as he has to accept their being able to
watch him as he pees although he is unable to watch them
as they pee, as he has to accept the fact that it is forbidden
for him to lie on some chairs, and not on others. (Worse yet,
Jezebel, the cat, can lie anywhere—even on the bed!)

In many ways the world is complicated beyond his understanding. There is much to remember: which chairs he may
and may not jump on, which people he can jump up and put
his paws on and which others not, when he can run up and
down the apartment and when he must lie still—all on the
whim of a master who has evinced almost no interest in
Jack's preferences: whether he's hungry or tired or in the
mood for a walk, or whether he'd rather lie under a bed chewing an old shoe, dreaming of former times. If Lorraine had
created their relationship in a way that articulated its sado-
masochistic qualities, perhaps Jack would have been able to
respond more quickly and correctly—accepting, even rejoicing, in the arbitrariness of her decisions as a way of bringing
out the eroticism latent in their relationship—but instead,
there was always the tacit understanding that what was being
done was being done for Jack's "own good." Jack knows this
is a lie. Not speaking English he couldn't contradict this, save
in the grossest manner: biting Lorraine, peeing in the house,
refusing to eat.

In the spring, wildness overtakes him. It is then he drags
Lorraine and Judy all over the park. He lifts his hind leg so
high to pee that Lorraine and the other dog owners joke how
they wished they could do leg lifts like that in the gym. "Leg
lifts like that in the gym"—Jack does not understand these
sounds. But he understands they are laughing at him as he
pees. He understands that they are watching him while he
pees while he cannot watch them as they pee. He understands that they are the people who have separated him from
his great love—the beautiful Irish setter he met after leaving
the butcher's (where Lorraine had gotten him some fresh
bones) a long-ago fall afternoon—hair that glowed like sun-

sets he leaps up on his hind legs to watch from out the window in the late afternoon. On the way home he had taken quick strides quickly, almost dragging Lorraine, hardly able to wait until they got back to the apartment so he could hide the bones in his favorite places, sharpen his teeth on them in leisure, chew them up into small pieces. Then a sudden sharp yet subtle smell assaulted him, a smell of urine but also of something else, something both familiar and somehow new —as if he'd encountered it previously only in his dreams. Of an instant he forgot totally about the dog bones; he changed directions to follow this smell, so oblivious to the world around him that it came as a shock to be stopped by the pull of the leash around his neck. He thought it insignificant, and yanked against it; when Lorraine yanked back he dug his heels in against the pavement for leverage and pulled against her with all his might. He kept his eyes focused on the setter —until she disappeared around the corner of a building. And she—as she was dragged out of sight around that terrible corner: first her head, then her shoulders, then her drooping tail—she had stared at him too. Jack had yelped and moaned, a terrible hole in the center of his body, as if he could eat forever and not begin to fill it up. He knew he would remember this feeling —both the joy and the devastation—until . . . he knew not what. All the way home he had resisted the leash; then he crawled under the bed and refused to eat dinner. He could not believe Lorraine, his master, whom he had cherished and protected and obeyed from the time he had been so brutally torn from his mother, could be so callous to his feelings: did he not lie down at her feet when she cried, and lift up his head to be petted, and lick her hand, and bring her his hidden bones—all the things he could think of to comfort her in her hour of need? But now, in the hour of *his* need, she deserted him, as oblivious or indifferent to his feelings as if he were a stranger she had just met. (But even a stranger should have been able to divine what he and the Irish setter were experiencing!) Jack felt sick every time he passed that corner. He remembered lying down on the pavement, whimpering, stretching his head out on his crossed paws. First Lorraine had laughed, then she had gotten angry.

People on the street were sneering at her, thinking she was an owner who was controlled by her dog, rather than the other way around. She began to pull with all her might on Jack's leash. At a certain point he ceased resisting and let her drag his belly and legs along the rough bumpy pavement. This hurt but he didn't care, he almost welcomed it; she could have thrown him under the wheels of the motorized vehicles humans worshipped and had him executed for insubordination and he wouldn't have cared—anything to put him out of the consciousness of his loss. Humans had feelings, they assumed that even nonspeaking tiny humans of a very young age had feelings (why else would they rush to console them when they cried?), so why did they assume that a dog—so loving, so faithful, so malleable to training, to whom they entrusted the safety of their homes and selves—did not have feelings too? Why did they expect dogs to love only humans and not members of their own species? Dogs did not expect humans to love only dogs; how would a human feel if he or she were sentenced to spend their entire life with dogs? But it was assumed as a matter of course that if a master was sick a dog was unhappy, if a master died a dog's heart would be broken. Such things had been known to happen—jungle birds often became enamored of elephants, pigeons developed inordinate passions for particular limestone statues—yet how rarely was it spoken of when the passion went the other way: a dog dies and the master has a heart attack; the blind person loses desire to travel around the city, and falls into a terrible depression? When they got home Lorraine put the bones in the cold box instead of offering Jack any. Hours later she relented, but he was too angry, too hurt, too sad to have any appetite. Of what did these bones remind him, other than of the setter whom his heart had yearned after? To this day he had not seen or smelled her again.

The memories of how other animals on the street had reacted to him that afternoon contributed to this bitter memory. The Lhasa apso, the Akita, two toy poodles, a cat on a harness—all had stared at him in incomprehension. Jack crooned and barked and whimpered to convey to them the complexities of his emotions, but all they seemed to see was a dog hopelessly engaged in insubordination. In their eyes he saw himself reflected as his own eyes on thoughtless occasions had reflected them: pathetic, stupid, stubborn. He felt alienated, unconnected to the general canine life and emotions. He became conscious of his long, straggly hair, and felt hopelessly inferior to an Afghan who passed, nose in air, with hair so elegant what master would not love to run a hand through it? Throughout his life Jack had struggled to overcome his envy of dogs with long, smooth, silky hair. His own was thick and scraggly, a magnet to grass and dirt and insects and twigs. When he had first come to live with Lorraine and the Man Who Went Away they had combed his hair weekly with a strong wire brush, but as the years passed they had begun to neglect him. For nearly a year he had not been bathed. It almost broke his heart—not so much the lack of bathing itself (he liked his smell), but the indifference behind the lack. He had never ceased loving them—even the man who had moved away. It cut him to the quick when he saw their eyes look enviously at huskies and setters and hounds —neater, cleaner, more sophisticated-looking dogs than he. He did not exactly blame them but still it hurt. Jack tried to have manners but he could not help himself: when he was hungry he dove into the food dish in a way that nearly always resulted in food spilling onto the floor; when he was thirsty he lapped up water in such haste drops fell everywhere; when he was happy he bounded into tables and knocked things over; after he emerged from lake or ocean he shook himself dry in a way that wet everything around him, and made his hair fall every which way, so that he became an object of amusement in everybody's eyes. Deep down he liked the way he looked, he thought he was cute and "down home" with a kind of rumpled sexiness; there was something a little piss-elegant about the Afghans and Dalmatians that he had contempt for even as he longed to be them; rather, to be treated with the same seriousness and dignity as they were.

Now Lorraine and Jack were discussing something other than him. Jack had not heard his name mentioned in some time. He peed a little without their commenting; even snuck in a number two without their shoving a piece of paper under

his ass. In itself this was a pleasure, yet the relief was tinged with regret, reminding him for the umpteenth time of his lack of importance in their (especially *her*) life. All day long he thought about her, waited eagerly for her to come home from work, wagged his tail and jumped on her the second she walked in the door. The Girl, too, he had loved like that, until she had shown her utter indifference to him by refusing to walk him even when he was at the utter edge of torment, shutting the door on him so he could not sit by her as she listened to the noise machine, relegating her responsibilities concerning him first to the Woman With Dark Skin who came in the day, and then to the Man With His Name. And now that the Man With His Name was there, Lorraine barely found time to pet him when he ran to greet her at the door—unless she were with friends, when a fuss, almost unbearable in its phoniness, was made. It was almost worse than being ignored. Sometimes even a walk was worse than being ignored, Jack was so caught up in worry as to when it would end. If it were up to him, it would never end. He wanted to walk forever with Lorraine, off his leash, in the park, in a way that no longer happened.

For one day, just like that, the unspeakable had occurred. All his life, in the park, Jack had been allowed to run free and play with his friends. They would smell each other's sacred parts, to determine who was a male and who was a female, and who would try to mount whom, dancing the ancient dance of dominance and submission, with its rituals of barking and teeth-baring, so misunderstood by humans; they would run as fast as they could for a hundred feet, to show off their running skills, then lope slowly back, sometimes a bone or stick between their teeth. But one day when they reached the park and Jack had started to bound off (in the assumption Lorraine had released the leash from around his neck), he had been caught up short with a terrible yank. He pulled and pulled—but still, she wouldn't release him. He couldn't remember what he had done wrong. He lay down, paws crossed, and pleaded, he had jumped up on her and soiled her jacket with his paws, and—most oddly—she had not gotten angry. On the contrary, she had bent down and talked to him, in a soothing voice he knew was meant to be conciliatory and comforting, with sentences that used his name over and over. After a while Jack ceased to be angry; a part of him knew she was trying to console him for his still being on the leash in the park. He looked around; other dogs were on their leashes too. Great sadness there was in the park that day. Jack was still brought near and allowed to sniff other dogs, but the rituals of teeth-baring and attacking were almost instantly cut short; there was no running and demonstrating of hunting skills; worst of all, there was none of that camaraderie of dogs being off together as dogs, away and separate from humans. Lorraine's friends never brought dogs for Jack to play with when they came to the house (as they did little girl infants for Judy when she was young), nor did the masters Lorraine talked to in the park visit her in her house with their dogs, so this was almost his sole opportunity to enjoy the companionship of his own species. (Jezebel was there, of course, but this was almost more of an annoyance than a pleasure.) Why Lorraine's friends to this day brought Judy presents at a time when she had become so cold and unpleasant was something Jack couldn't comprehend, but such instances of neglect and thoughtfulness on the part of humans no longer surprised him; humans (unlike dogs but something like Jezebel) paid almost exclusive attention to themselves. It had become a part of doggy lore—an explanation of the apparent servility of the one species to the other. Not because humans were stronger, not because they were providers, had the wolves of more tender heart come in from the snow and cold to keep them company during long winter nights, but out of sympathy for human lack of stamina, their loneliness, their inability to run quickly, their difficulty in staying warm (they had to wrap themselves in the carcasses of dead animals), the weakness of their teeth and consequent persnicketiness of their eating habits (wolves just ripped an animal apart and ate it, without the necessity of dragging it back home, cutting it up, roasting it over a fire to make it tender), and even their incredible selfishness, which the wolves—out of embarrassment—pretended not to notice. It was clear that humans, to survive, needed the protection of the stronger, tougher, more savvy species.

And so an affinity had sprung up, one that existed to this very day, though humans did everything possible to eradicate the wolfy essence (the very soul!) from dogs: feeding them prekilled and precooked food that came in cans, putting them on leashes, transmuting primeval forests into parks with benches and fountains. But the ancient covenant, originated during a winter when breath was so cold it turned into snow in the air, would not be broken—at least by the wolves. Humans broke it all the time: by forced copulation of canine siblings so that swaybacks and other recessive abnormalities gained dominance; by eugenics that sculpted wolves so tiny their hearts beat as fast as a hummingbird's, or with jaws so large they necessitated caesarean births; there were even little crematoriums where unloved animals—both newborns and grown-ups—were housed and killed. Dogs forgave humans, for this cruelty was as inborn in humans as growling and barking and peeing with the hind leg raised were for dogs. They also had a secret and perverse admiration for humans for walking on two legs and for the males' not having to raise their hind legs as they peed.

Now it was time to leave the park. Jack pulled on Jack's neck so as to make him head out of the park; Jack, by habit, dug in his heels against the ground, fought back. As always, his heart sank; the walk had been long but it had not been long enough; it was never long enough when he was in the city, when he was on a leash. The call of the outdoors was not nearly so exciting to him in the country, when he was allowed to run free, as it was in the city, with a chain around his neck. In the country he never fantasized about running away, returning to his natural state; the coarseness of wolves revolted rather than delighted him. But in the city, he thought of a wolfy life with anticipated nostalgia—not for something he had done, but for something he would never do. Already, perhaps, he was too old and set in his habits to make the possibility real; and he would have to injure those he loved most in the world: Lorraine, the cruel Girl, even the Man Who Went Away.

When Jack and Lorraine and Jack returned to the house neither the dishes nor Judy's room were cleaned up, and she was on the phone with Saralee. Immediately Lorraine and Judy became locked in a fierce argument. They pretended it was about the nature of good and evil, but to Jack (the man), it sounded more like a discussion about what time Judy was to go to bed.

Jack sighed. He was sleepy too. Maybe it was boredom. He lay down on the living-room couch, flipped on the news. The argument subsided, and Lorraine disappeared with Judy into the bedroom. Jack lay there, listening to the litany of jetliners crashing, Arabs hijacking, dollars falling. He randomly punched the remote, but the same faces peered at him from each channel, as if out of the trillions of events that took place that day, only the same ten or fifteen were judged to be significant and real. What was real in Jack's life? What was significant? Was it lying on the couch watching television as the minutes slipped by; or was it the thirty minutes every few nights—an hour or two a week—he and Lorraine mingled their body fluids together; or the maybe six hours a week he stood pressed against others in a cold, dirty, smelly subway car; or the silent hours he endured each day in the presence of Aurelia (silent between them, though she played the radio or TV as she cooked and ironed); or perhaps it was that endless conversation he had with himself, even as he slept— the one that kept asking: is *this* what life is really like, can *this* be all there is, is it like this for everyone else? Was the "real" the dullness left over from his childhood, which surrounded him to this day, or the wild hope that sometimes still sprang into his breast, or the irony that did not so much exist in itself as approximate a golden mean between these two? The news ended, and a dark-haired detective and his blonde girlfriend ran across the screen. Counterpointed against their banter was the murmur of Lorraine's and Judy's voices in Judy's bedroom. Jack felt left out, jealous. He shut his eyes tight and emitted a wish they would call out for him. He waited five minutes, then swallowed his pride and walked into the room. Lorraine was lying in bed next to Judy telling her a story. The story was about the cats Jezebel and Marlene

and their great adventures in the big wide world—a saga that originated long ago as a bribe to help Judy go to sleep, but had now become a ritual in its own right. The overhead light was off, so the only light in the room came from the fifteen-watt bulb inside the huge Donald Duck lamp. It filled the room with a pinkish-orange glow that softened the otherwise cold white walls of the room.

"Once upon a time there were two beautiful alley cats. Their names were Jezebel and Marlene . . . ," began Lorraine. Quietly Jack sat down on the floor, leaned his head against the bed, shut his eyes. As Lorraine spoke he illustrated the adventures of the animals in his head—bright pastel washes splashed over black-inked outlines in a clever approximation of a child's scrawl. On the next present-giving occasion he will paint this for Judy. Perhaps it will cause an end to the war she feels obliged to wage against him; more than likely, however, she'll call him a sap.

In the middle of the story Lorraine fell asleep. "Mom," said Judy faintly. Jack shut off the Donald Duck light and began to improvise: "Outside there was a beautiful moon, runny and full of holes, like the ripest Brie . . ." Soon there were two distinct snores, Lorraine's and Judy's. It was a peaceful sound, like the ocean, or a train clicking against the rails, or a mother's heartbeat to her infant. "This is why I'm here," Jack thought. Too often, he forgot.

TWO

6

Carrying a fresh cup of nonfresh coffee brewed two hours earlier in the Krups automatic coffee-maker, Jack entered the living room. He sat down on a stool in front of a wall on which was tacked a sheet of canvas. He looked out the window at the sky. He was supposed to be painting the light reflected from objects (including those made of water vapor, like clouds) outside the window, to transfer what passed through the rectangle he taped on the window to the rectangle of his canvas. The ultimate effect of his paintings was a kind of imprecise, soft-edged, hyper-realism, but to associate his work with that esthetic movement would be incorrect, for his aim was not so much what was visible as what the visible could reveal of the unseen. On the floor he had placed a line of tape correlated to the placement of the tape on the window marking where he was to stand to get the proper angle of view. Jack stood behind this line, looked out the window, then sat down. His head hurt and his eyes kept drooping shut. Every once in a while he stuck his tongue in the coffee, where he lapped up a cold drop. When the coffee was gone he wandered into the kitchen, poured the remainder of the brewed coffee into his cup, then, after staring at it awhile, poured it down the sink without tasting it. He walked back to the living room and ripped the tape off the floor. He picked up a brush. The possibilities were endless. This was functionally equivalent to a state of no possibilities. A wave of fatigue knocked him onto the couch.

The slamming of the door knocked him awake. Within what seemed no more than thirty seconds "The Edge of Night" could be heard. Jack looked at his watch. Aurelia was almost half an hour late. He went into the kitchen. "I can't work when you have the television on," he told her, for maybe the fifteenth time. She didn't say anything. "Will you please turn the TV down?" he asked. Still, she didn't move. "Please turn down the TV," he repeated.

"I'm not deaf," she said.

Jack shut off the TV. It was the first time he had done this instead of waiting for her to do it. Searching for an excuse to wait in the kitchen to witness her reaction, he took the kettle from where it sat on the stove and stuck it under the faucet. As part of their unarticulated ideological battle, he decided to show her he could make himself a cup of coffee the old-fashioned way—without the assistance of $60 worth of white plastic. He sat there waiting for the water to boil as Aurelia emptied the dishwasher and finished cleaning up his and Lorraine's dishes from the night before. Then the kettle whistled, and he poured water into the filter. He waited for it to cool, watching Aurelia, a calm peace inside his head that thought would only disturb.

Aurelia went to the dryer, opened it, and began dumping laundry into the black plastic laundry basket. She carried the overflowing basket out of the kitchen. Feeling an odd sense of loss at her disappearance, Jack followed her into the bedroom on the pretext of needing a sweater. She was sitting on his and Lorraine's bed, in her hand a two-sided round bathroom mirror, the kind women use to check their pores and tweeze their eyebrows. She made no expression of any kind when she noticed Jack, but he blushed. More and more he's been realizing she's a woman. Not one that he's attracted to, but still, a woman, a human being. "Have you seen my blue sweater?" he asked. Aurelia didn't honor this with a response, and he didn't pursue it. He knew very well where the blue sweater was: in Judy's closet where she had put it after borrowing it (without permission).

Jack returned to the living room. He looked at his watch: 11:42. If Aurelia weren't there he would have crawled back into bed, pulled the sheet up over his head to form a sort of cave in which to hibernate, but he felt too embarrassed to do this in front of her. He had an irrational fear she would tell

Lorraine—though, when he tried to imagine it, there was no plausible way she could actually mention this. Warming his hands with his handmade cup of coffee, he looked at his blank canvas. What was he so frightened of? When he was a child and didn't know anything, the idea of painting never frightened him. He drew happily by the hour. He did not jump up constantly to get a Coke, or read a comic, or watch Dick Clark, or call up a friend.

"I found your sweater," Aurelia said. She threw it on the couch next to him, he imagined with a huge look of contempt. He felt compelled to put it on.

He made more coffee. He reread the *Times*. In approximately 200 minutes Judy will walk in the door. In 600 minutes it will be time to turn off the light and pray for an erection. In another 18,396,000 minutes he will have reached the age at which insurance companies think he will die. Jack grabbed his coat, sketch pad, and a collection of Paul Bowles' short stories, and headed for the subway. He took the local to Fifty-ninth Street, then switched to the D. He got off at Houston and First and headed to the East Village galleries. He spent at least two minutes apiece in Gracie Mansion, Piezo Electric, Semaphore East, Jus de Pomme, International With Monument, Zeus Trabia, and Fun galleries. His last stop was the Fast Money Gallery. Usually the work there was Neo-Post-Expressionist—childishly scrawled images in bright colors derived from mass culture, often having some connection to violence—but for a second Jack was pleasantly surprised: on the wall were a bunch of early Brice Mardens, all gray paint and wax. Then he saw, to his immense disgust, that these were the work of a duo of his former students: John and Robin Weird, "in conjunction with" esthetic consultant Murray Bottoms. No doubt it was a coincidence, but this was the same name as his former therapist. Jack checked the price list that sat on a wooden desk in the gallery; the paintings (all but two red-dotted) were in the $7500–10,000 price range—not just more than Jack's paintings sold for when he was their age, but more than his sold for *now*. These little punks make more than he does!

A young man with short hair and business suit walked out

of the office, saw Jack, and stuck out his hand. "Thanks for coming," he told Jack.

"Hi," said Jack.

"And what have *you* been doing?" the stranger asked.

"Painting. Teaching. And you?" Jack asked, playing for time.

"What do you think?" He looked around the gallery with pride, then noticed Jack's questioning expression. "You don't recognize me? I recognize *you.*"

The last time Jack had seen John Weird his hair had been dusted with a topping of blue; before that a mohawk. Now he looked like a young banker.

"My hair's the same," said Jack.

"A little less maybe."

"Yours too," said Jack, pretending to scrutinize it.

"Not less. Just reorganized."

They stared at each other. Jack found himself in a classic no-win situation. If he praised the show he'd make John Weird happy; if he insulted it John Weird would assume it was sour grapes. "Interesting show," said Jack, "interesting" being the current argot for awful.

"*We* think so," said John, without apparent irony.

"Why are you ripping off Brice Marden?" Jack couldn't help himself.

"Jack, as you very well know, we're not ripping off Brice Marden, we're *appropriating* Brice Marden."

"What precisely do you mean by that?"

"The same as everybody else means. We're bringing into question the notion of who owns an image, what it means to have a 'style,' what is the meaning of 'original,' and so on. We could have picked any artist—we could, for instance, have picked *you*—but we chose Brice Marden instead of you for three reasons: one, because people recognize his work, and, no insult, they don't recognize yours, which is important to the 'dialogue' created between the original and the replica; two, because they sell for a lot of money, which, irrelevant or not, helps enhance the market value of our work; and three, because he's easy to copy. Frankly, at this initial stage of my careeer I don't think I could have handled somebody like Matisse or de Kooning."

"In class when I gave you assignments to do drawings in the style of other artists, you attacked me for being old-fashioned, and refused to do the work," Jack complained.

"You didn't put it in the proper context, Jack. Frankly, I don't think you *intended* it in the proper context. Our aim is not technical virtuosity, but the metaphysical meaning of identicality, uniqueness, and so on."

"I think that's a crock, but even so, it's art criticism rather than art."

"Art today *is* art criticism. Nobody with a brain can possibly be interested in 'technique' or 'style,' so-called."

Jack felt like punching him. Three years ago this guy was painting giant roaches with mashed-up roach body blood. Two years ago he had a theory concerning the necessity of completing a painting without ever raising your brush from the surface of the canvas. "Don't give me this shit. You're just jumping on some bandwagon to get attention."

"Maybe yes, maybe no—buddy boy, who cares but you? I'm getting it, aren't I? *And you're not!* You don't invalidate van Gogh's pictures just because the guy was a loony, so why this great interest in whether I'm 'sincere'? As if there's any way of judging the validity of one's own intentions, let alone anybody else's. I don't believe in the unconscious."

"*I* do," said Jack.

"Of course. You're a product of the pseudo-idealistic notions of your time. You poor sucker. Do you know who we've sold paintings to in this show? Chase, Citibank, Christophe de Menil, and the Museum of Santa Barbara. We're in Documenta, the Venice Biennale, and the Philadephia Museum of Art. I own 5000 feet on the north side of Tompkins Square Park. I've got an indoor gym with three Nautilus machines, a rowing machine, a treadmill, and a 'spa' with Jacuzzi and steam. Come by and see it sometime. Here's my card. Now I got to go meet some krauts for lunch." He handed Jack his card and exited the gallery. The card read:

JOHN AND ROBIN WEIRD:
Art in the Age of Mechanical Reproduction

Not wanting to walk out with him, Jack stayed in the gallery. The paintings *did* look a lot like Brice Marden's early work, only, somehow, less interesting. But, in all honesty, were they really less interesting, or was it the knowledge that they were copies that made them *seem* less interesting; or was it that Jack would no longer find even the "real" early Mardens very interesting, either because they were never very interesting, or because he's already thought and experienced all there was to think and experience about them; or was it merely that a work's inherent "interest" was only what the spectator was willing to put into it? So he pondered, and paced, and before he knew it two hours had passed, a longer period of time than he had ever spent looking at the paintings in any of the real Brice Marden's shows.

Highly disgruntled, he walked out under a sky the same gray as the pseudo-Mardens, two doors down to Death Gallery, where an artist named "Andy Warhol," recently profiled in *Flash Art*, was showing Marilyn Monroe silkscreens. Of course it wasn't the "real" Andy Warhol but another (living) one. He had bleached white hair and sported a bullet-stained jacket, but he spelled his name differently: quote mark A-n-d-y W-a-r-h-o-l quote mark ("Andy Warhol"). The estate of the "real" Andy Warhol had sued to prevent "Andy Warhol" from using the name, but lost the case on the following grounds:

(1) That if an apostrophe can be used as part of the name "Macy's," quote marks can be used as part of the name " 'Warhol' "

(2) that "Andy Warhol" 's work was not a copy of Andy Warhol's work because

    (a) "Andy Warhol" 's work was about appropriation, which Andy Warhol's work (of course) was not, and

    (b) forgery was not an issue as long the works of Andy Warhol and "Andy Warhol" (no matter how superficially similar— even identical) were properly distinguished by a knowledge of their "initial conditions" and "continuity of motions" (the same method by which we tell one electron from another)—which, in the case of a work of art, is easily attested to by proper documentation of sales.

Complicating the issue was the fact that the photograph from which the original Marilyn Monroe silkscreen was made was in the public domain, and, since the technique of silkscreen-making was widely known, how were these any more of a "copy" than the original—an original that Andy Warhol himself in fact never made, since he hired other artists to do his art for him?

Irritated and restless, Jack headed toward the Jean Cocteau Cafe. "Cafe noir and triple creme Gorgonzola anti-pizza," he told the waitress. The cafe was decorated like a subway station, trompe l'oeil walls of dirty tiles spattered with graffiti and movie ads. A manifesto of the artwork's intent was stencilled on the walls.

"Art" is dead. But Art lives. It lives not in the Eyes but in the Head. You can recognize it by the headache that screams across your hemispheres. It lives not in galleries but in the locus of the Self. Not that the Self exists, but the concept of the Self exists, as necessary to capitalistic forms of social organization. BOREDOM is their means; UNCONSCIOUSNESS their intent; SUBJUGATION their aim. Do not SLEEP; in our dreams they enter us. . . .

A price list for the replication of this work, based on a complicated formula of decreasing dollars per square foot toward a maximum value of $50,000 per wall, followed. Jack felt such rage, spots rose behind his eyes. After blowing his nose, he realized a man at a nearby table was staring at him. He stared back a few seconds before realizing it was Jeremy.

His first impulse was to avert his eyes. Once they had been good friends. Then, as Jeremy had become a more and more successful art critic, and Jack's career had stagnated, they had pretty much fallen out of touch.

Jack was sure Jeremy wanted to avoid him. This became a reason for him to smile and nod hello. He was so depressed he wanted to torture Jeremy with guilt re his presence.

For a long time Jeremy had felt guilty about fallings-off of friendship such as had happened between him and those of his artist friends, like Jack, to whom success was coming slowly, if at all, until he had decided that the problem wasn't the snobbism he felt they attributed to him, but the combination of embarrassment, anger, and jealousy that they ex-

perienced in his presence. These were unplesant emotions—
for both the experiencer and the recipient of such feelings.

After nodding hello, Jack waited to see who would get up
and go to the other's table. It was up to Jeremy, as the successful one, to do this—and he did. But as he walked over
Jack remembered once again how Jeremy had not come to his
last show; a wave of fury ran through him, almost sexually
exciting in its intensity.

"Doing the galleries?" Jeremy asked.

Jack nodded. "Why I waste my time I'll never know. Those
John Weirds really burned me up. Less than two years ago
that guy was my student." Jack knew this was the kind of
comment that Jeremy particularly hated, not just on account
of its content but because it was phrased in deliberately phil-
istine fashion. He said it for this reason, and yet he felt irritated with himself for falling into Jeremy's expectations
concerning him so easily—just as he had done throughout
almost the entire course of their relationship, where this kind
of needling had provided the basis for so much of their inter-
action—at least once it had become clear that Jeremy would
become a critic instead of an artist and, in so doing, would
come down upon the side of "cerebrally justified" art (although the fact that such work was considered "cerebral"—
both by Jeremy and other critics and dealers—drove Jack absolutely crazy). Yet, on the other hand, what else had he to
say? Living with Lorraine had somehow destroyed the possibility of conversation for him.

"I enjoyed them. But of course, that's the kind of thing I'm
interested in."

"Of course," said Jack, imbuing the comment with as
much hostility as he could. On Jeremy's face was reflected
the same dislike that was probably on his own. "Well," said
Jeremy. He was about to move away. Normally in such a
situation he would utter some lie about "getting together
soon," but for once he was determined not to do it.

Jack sensed this. All of a sudden, instead of feeling angry,
he felt sad. As he remembered their old friendship his eyes
drifted up toward the left, as they often do when we recall
far-off things. Something relaxed inside him, as if he had just

come. Jeremy sensed this, changed his mind, and sat down. "I haven't seen you in ages. What's new?" he asked.

"Well, I've moved uptown, I'm living with this woman. And her kid. She's into fashion. . . ." Jack started off by rote, as if he were filling out a questionnaire, then the events behind the words came to have reality, and he began to put himself into his story.

As Jack talked, Jeremy realized that Jack did not love the woman he was living with in any profound sense—i.e., in the way Jack, when he was young, used to love women. This bothered him, that Jack had changed. But why shouldn't Jack have changed? And hadn't he, Jeremy, changed too, in ways of which Jack wasn't even aware? The fact that Jack, with whom he stayed up many nights till dawn in graduate school, did not now know so many things about him struck Jeremy as poignant, and he wondered how he could have so totally forgotten about their friendship as to have even thought of avoiding him when he saw him in the cafe. For the first time, he felt culpable about the loss of some of his old friendships. He felt that what they said was true, about old friends being best. In the light of this emotion, his newer relationships seemed superficial and unreal.

"Are you listening?" asked Jack, suspiciously.

"Of course."

"What was I saying?"

"You were saying your career was in a terrible state."

"Nobody seems to understand what I'm doing," Jack said, almost angry that he had been deprived of his fight. "My work is actually very complex, but since I go to this effort to make it appear simple, people think it *is* simple. Critics are so stupid—nothing personal." (Of course he meant it personally, but Jeremy accepted this without rancor.) "They don't respond to your work, but to what you *tell* them your work is about. I should develop a good rap, but, intellectually, I'm opposed to the necessity of doing this. Actually, all this is irrelevant right now, because I'm having trouble working. I thought when I moved uptown with Lorraine it would be good for my work, that's one reason I did it, perhaps the main one, but . . . I don't know. I just don't know what I should be doing any more. I mean, what's the point? There were some great paintings in my last show, but who cares? I'm in this gallery nobody goes to, I don't sell much, and when I do it's usually to unimportant people, hardly ever to corporations or banks. I don't know why; it's just the kind of stuff those kinds of people should like. But they don't like what they like, they like what they're *told* to like by people like you! I realize it sounds like sour grapes. So what? My students have contempt for me because I'm not rich or famous. They all think they're going to be like Basquiat or David Salle in another year or two. Remember how when we were young, people were grateful to have a painting in some group show at some Soho gallery during the summer? Not them; if they don't have a one-man show a year or two after graduation, they give up and become art consultants or free-lance curators or something. Half my former students have galleries in the East Village—they're making more at twenty-four than I do *now!* Their paintings are on the walls of the newest clubs, their photos are in *Interview* and *Vanity Fair....*"

As he listened to himself Jack wondered if he were making a mistake: you weren't supposed to express negativity in front of people who mattered to your career. But how could you help yourself when you were so unhappy? He decided it was okay, that Jeremy was more of a personal than a career friend. Perhaps this was the source of his failure, that in a pinch he always placed the former over the latter. He spoke as quickly as he could because he dreaded seeing that look of boredom come over Jeremy's face, the way it nearly always did when you described your miseries to other people. All his hopes and disappointments kept pouring out of him. Was he with Lorraine because her unhappiness in some way compensated for his?

"If it's any consolation," said Jeremy, when Jack took a breather, "the art market's due for a collapse."

"You think so?" Jack asked hopefully.

"Of course. These things are cyclical. Art represents capitalism at its purest extreme: a totally useless and arbitrarily priced product whose supply and price is utterly determined by demand—i.e., the temporary consensus of a fickle ruling class. Movements used to develop slowly, but already since the Second World War we've had First- and Second-Generation Abstract Expressionism, Color Field, Pop, Op, Minimalism, Conceptualism, Environmental Art, Pattern Painting, Neo-Expressionism, New Image, Middle-Age Image, Post-Conceptualism, Post Minimalism, Trompe l'Oeil, Appropriation, Dumb Art, Bad Art, Smart Art, Neo-Fascistic . . ." (As he spoke Jeremy flipped the fingers on his hand.) "In the last few years the demand for art has skyrocketed, but this is just a temporary readjustment of the market having more to do with tax laws, the high price of the dollar, and the application of leveraged buying principles to the art scene than to anything inherent in the art itself. Which means, once the investment climate changes, the bubble will burst. You don't really think the banks and corporations will keep on warehousing this stuff forever, do you? Naturally they have a stake in maintaining the value of their investments, but with tax deductions and depreciation, they really can't lose. . . ."

Jack's mind wandered, as it always did when Jeremy got political. Not that he ever found himself able to argue against him. Jack was not much of a capitalist, but when Jeremy got going, the most reactionary ideas always popped into his head. He began to pick at the remainder of his pizza with his fingers, rolling the cold sticky cheese up into little balls that he stared at with great interest.

"It's hard to believe," said Jack, "but in graduate school, we never even thought about money."

"Yes, that is hard to believe," said Jeremy.

7

After leaving Jack, Jeremy walked downtown to his loft, in a five-story cast-iron building on Greene between Broome and Grand, which he had bought for $15,000 fifteen years ago. If it were day he'd feel chilly but as it was evening his expectations (or perhaps his metabolism) were different, and he felt almost pleasantly warm.

He climbed up the metal steps to the loading platform in front of his building, took his key ring out of his pocket, unlocked a door of heavy, dark gray metal, then climbed up five flights of rotting wood stairs from which the paint was long gone, past puke-colored walls, to a glossy white enamel-sprayed door on the top floor. There he unlocked his two Medeco and one Fichet locks. He pushed the door open and stepped into the cleanest, whitest, emptiest space in all of New York City. He quickly reached behind a small painting on a wall near the entrance door, and within the allotted forty-five seconds disconnected the burglar alarm.

He sat himself on a white leather couch manufactured by Knoll, International from a design by Richard Meier, which rested on a highly polished bleached floor, over which hung a Unitondo four-way Italian track-lighting system, from which were suspended a variety of MR-16 low-voltage light fixtures, which threw varying spheres and cones of light on the white-on-white Robert Ryman and gray-on-gray Brice Marden and black-on-black Ad Reinhardt paintings that hung on his glossy walls. He picked up his $200 Italian wireless phone and called up Sandinista—a chic new Nicaraguan restaurant on Greene Street—to order the evening's take-out "security special"—in honor of people scared to leave their homes. He lit a brown—"brown, the new neutral"—Nat Sherman cigarette (which did not burn unless you inhaled it) as he waited for his meal to arrive. He mixed his nutrition supplements—Euga-Lein Topfer, Raw Stomach and Duodenum Substance, adrenal cortex extract and pancreatic stimuli—and swallowed them with the aid of apple juice and water. He picked up a book of poems by the famous Latin American poet and tried to read it. Instead, he felt fatigued, and dimmed three of his four tracks. Still, the room was not dark. Out the window the red lights on the transmission tower of the World Trade Center flashed love messages to the red and green LEDs inside his receiver, his TV monitors, his VCR, his smoke alarm, his burglar alarm, his microwave, and the burning red tip of his still-unfinished cigarette. It was almost like being in the command room of the starship *Enterprise*. The buzzer rang. The delivery boy used the daily-changing Sandinista password to let Jeremy know it was safe to buzz him in. Jeremy opened the glossy white door of his loft and waited as the delivery boy climbed the stairs. The ceilings were high and he listened to the steps a long time. The sound was comforting, like a heartbeat, a train, waves, interactively generated music. Jeremy paid for the meal via credit card, then placed the containers of food on a brushed steel tray that he carried to his specially made stainless steel dining table. On it were glasses and salt and pepper shakers and stainless steel dinnerware from D. F. Saunders, walnut oil and raspberry vinegar from Dean & DeLuca, pepper from Indonesia, salt crystals from the ocean. As he ate he listened first to John Zorn, then "Music on a Long Thin Wire" by Alvin Lucier, then gamelan music from Indonesia that, albeit ethnic, was acceptable, whereas American folk music, or Copland, for instance, was not. Any of his gestures could be witnessed by a stranger without embarrassment. When he was finished he put the remainder of his food in his stainless steel Sub-Zero refrigerator, prepared a cup of espresso in his Gaggia electric espresso maker, and carried the neo-deco espresso set designed by Aldo Rossi over to his Scott Burton faux marble coffee table and set it down. He placed the still-lit Nat Sherman cigarette in a trompe l'oeil ashtray that looked like a miniature toilet bowl. He turned up two of his four light tracks and glanced around the loft with apparent satisfaction. His walls were covered with glossy white enamel paint, the tiles in his kitchen were white, the industrial carpeting in his bathroom gray, his sweaters black. The only color in his entire loft was provided by paintings in the current Neo-Expressionist style, but these things were so clearly "historical artifact" (as opposed to "decoration") that they did not subtract from the formal purity of the design concept of the loft. His home has been profiled in *New York*, the *New York Times* Sunday magazine, and *Architectural Digest*. Only a wealthy person could duplicate his milieu, but Jeremy did it not with cash but with patience, good timing, foresight, obsession, market savvy, verbal facility, and an externalized projection of confidence. The work on his loft he did himself. The paintings and sculptures were presented to him by his artist friends in appreciation of his early and penetrating insights into the nature of their genius (in the form of critical articles in *Art Forum*, *Art News*, *Art in America*, *Flash Art*, etc.); some of these pieces he traded for work by older, even more famous artists. Of course, when he was first given these works, they had not possessed nearly the value they did today, but then Jeremy, more than any individual other than their dealers, was responsible for the subsequent increase in the value of these works.

To those in the art world and to his friends, Jeremy was an accurate barometer of the slightest change in the current visual atmosphere, one who was sure to eat at the right places before anybody else, who attended all the right parties, who had the correct opinions almost before it was correct to have them. But to himself?

He went to his study and called up a file marked with a special password no one knew but him. White letters glowed on a gray screen:

Thesis
"Object and Color Reductionism and/or Replacement" (aka "Minimalism")

What does the Sovet Union have that the United States does not have?

Space. Long dark nights in Siberia. Frozen wastelands of ice.

Aim
To set up insatiable yearnings for space, states of desire impossible to fulfill.

How?
Apotheosis of huge white lofts, the size of garages. Nothing in them except Marcel Breuer chairs and a row of telephones with answering machines.

Denigration of antiques and other expensive objects under guise of "clutter," resulting in discarding of both expensive historical objects and personal mementos. ("The wealthy class is definable only by its history.")

Wealthy move to factory lofts—causing destruction of Fifth Avenue as sacred neighborhood. (If the proletariat cannot become upper-class, let the upper class become proletariat!)

Creation of glass-enclosed bathtubs, transparent shower curtains. Elimination of walls, doors. Humans shit in public, like dogs (thereby contributing to the leveling of society).

Underlying strategy
Desecration of glamour by means of *style glut*, the production of new trends at ever-increasing rates resulting in visual, auditory, and olfactory burnout, as evidenced by alienation, depression, and indifference as to where one eats dinner.

Historical justification
When style replaces politics as the central concern of the populace, the mode of consumption supersedes that of production, resulting in (1) the elevation of the role of the critic, (2) replacement of *wealth* by *access* as the basis of power.

Tactics
Demoralization of the "A" list via constant and seemingly "irrational" revision of the weekly "A" list newsletter—which lists which restaurants, art galleries, clothing boutiques, and sporting events it is (a) mandatory (b) permissible (c) unacceptable for "A" list denizens (athletes, starlets, artists, rock stars, politicos, real estate magnates, museum heads, fashion mavens, heirs and heiresses, club owners, drug dealers, mafiosi, etc.) to attend that week.

Intended result
Schizophrenia, disillusionment, disenchantment, exhaustion with old notions and beliefs. In this mental vacuum can emerge a pre-revolutionary state of consciousness.

Purpose?
Destruction of capitalism.

Synthesis
A new and just world.
Permissible colors
White, black, gray.
Most unacceptable of all colors
Yellow: "the streets are paved with gold."

Jeremy sighed. He was tired. As the white of his paintings and his furniture and walls had begun to seep into his hair, so had "Object and Color Reductionism and/or Replacement" been replaced by newer art movements—which he had had to critique in such ways that they, too (though apparently opposite in intent to the old) ended up serving an identical function vis-à-vis the planned collapse of capitalism. And newer art movements even had followed *these,* until it seemed that the meaning of not just style—but the very politics it was meant to undermine—was not so much the thing itself, but this ever-accelerating rate of change, the sensual high imparted by an ever-changing succession of stimuli: an exhilaration that Jeremy, in his increasing disillusionment and exhaustion, was unable to share. Nonetheless, conscientious soldier that he was, having placed the newest Philip Glass in his new Sony CD player, having procured himself a glass of lime-tinted Perrier, he cleared the screen, gathered up the notes he had taken earlier that week, and began to type:

What is black and white and red all over? No, it is not a newspaper, nor a zebra caught in a Mixmaster, neither is it a card-carrying whale, but rather the newly renovated town house of Betsy Biminer III and her husband, oil baron and real estate magnate Abu Dabu Congo. . . .

Jeremy saved to disk, backed up, transmitted the copy over the modem to the newest lifestyle magazine, then, head on his polished steel desk top, watching the stars fade into the light of day, he fell asleep. In his dreams he's on a plane, it's landing in a place he knows he'll never reach.

8

Saturday morning Jack tried to explain his depression to Lorraine. As he talked he pushed two over-easy eggs back and forth on the plate. Like skaters they slid across the china. He picked up the bacon with his fingers, dipped it in the egg yellow, and swallowed it. Then he began to eat the bacon off Lorraine's plate.

" 'Appropriation.' In fashion we call that 'knock-offs,' " said Lorraine. "Like when Jack Mulqueen tries to rip off Calvin Klein."

Lorraine, somehow, always managed to find equivalents of every aspect of Jack's life in the fashion business. Lorraine, somehow, managed to find equivalents in the fashion business of absolutely anything that happened in the real world: starvation, war, sexual abstinence. . . . "It's different," Jack sighed. He saw the physical structure of the argument in his head, almost as if it were a path down which he were walking or, perhaps, had walked down before. But now he's too tired to do it. It's too complicated. He just got up, but already he felt like going back to sleep.

"*How*, Jack? Elucidate us. Not that I don't know that artists exist in an *entirely* different universe from the rest of us poor slobs. . . ."

"*Yeah*, Jack, *elucidate* us," echoed Judy.

"You don't even know what *elucidate* means," Jack told her.

"The fuck I don't! I'm tired of you always acting like I'm an idiot!" She jumped up from the table and ran to her room. "Like a Virgin" came blasting out from under her door.

"I don't think she should curse at me," said Jack.

"Adolescence," Lorraine shrugged.

Jack wasn't sure whether this fatalistic composure in the face of rampaging hormones was the correct approach. But at other times Lorraine cursed back at Judy, and Jack wasn't sure whether that was the correct approach either.

"If you don't do something about it, it's just going to get worse. She's only thirteen. Just think what's going to happen when she gets a little older."

"What am I supposed to do, Jack, *hit* her? If she doesn't like you, she doesn't like you. It's a free country. I can hardly punish her for that."

Jack dipped a piece of toast in the brilliant orange yolk. This was a beautiful color in the sky, at sunset, though, for some reason, always a little lurid and unconvincing on canvas. "You think it's okay for her to curse at me?"

"Put it this way. It doesn't bother me enough to scream at her and spoil my morning."

"You don't have to scream. It's a question of discipline. Just tell her calmly what's going to happen if she *doesn't* listen to you."

"Like what?"

"Like she can't listen to music for the rest of the day."

"Right! I'm gonna sit in her room all day to make sure she doesn't turn on the Walkman."

"Take away the Walkman. Or tell her she can't use the phone. Or go to the movies for the next two weeks. Anything."

"It's so stupid. I'm not into punishing her, Jack."

"You don't have to be *into* it. Being a parent isn't about being *into* it. It's about doing it, whether you feel like it or not."

"How do you know? You've never been a parent."

"Come on, Lorraine. If kids don't listen to you, you punish them."

"But I don't want to."

"You *ought* to want to."

"But I *don't*. This is a very difficult time for her. I'm sorry you can't see that. So either you *make* me want to, or you work it out with her in some way."

"How do I make you want to?" asked Jack.

Lorraine looked at him. "You know, Jack, you're one of the

most ineffectual people I've ever met. The only really clever thing you ever did was finagle yourself into this apartment."

"*Real* clever!" he said sarcastically. "Are you joking? I *hate* this apartment."

"Like I said, Jack, you're very ineffectual. Even when you manage to get what you want, it doesn't seem to make you happy."

Lorraine got up, carried her plate to the kitchen. Jack, who had been staring at the light reflecting on Lorraine's unpowdered nose, at the coagulating yolk on his plate, at the plant that has grown three inches from the last time he has looked —really *looked*—at it (what has he been looking at all the times he thought he was looking at it?), at a jam-encrusted crevice in the bleached wood table neither Aurelia nor Jack nor Lorraine has ever been able to clean, was unable to decide whether or not to finish his eggs. He kept lifting up his fork, carrying it to his mouth, putting it down.

Judy came out of her room and turned on the TV in the living room at what seemed a provocatively high decibel level. To Jack, who had been planning to work after breakfast, this was a declaration of war.

"What did your mother fix your TV for if you're not going to watch in your own room?"

"I have *no* idea. Why don't you ask her if you're so curious?"

Lorraine returned from the kitchen. "MOTHER, you SAID I could watch the cartoons in the living room! You said I could, you said I could!" shouted Judy.

"I *did* say she could," Lorraine said.

"*See?*" said Judy.

"Why did you tell her that?" Jack asked Lorraine. "You know that's where I work."

"Saturday morning cartoons. It's a family institution. You can't just come in here and change everything to suit yourself," said Lorraine.

"Who could paint with all that noise?"

"Saralee says Jack isn't even a good artist. Saralee's sister's boyfriend Mark's older brother, who's a famous artist, never even heard of him."

"What's this Mark guy's brother's name?" asked Jack.

"I dunno," said Judy. "But he's a household word."

"His name is 'Household'?"

"Ve-ry funny. You're just jealous."

"The fuck I am!"

"Don't you curse at my daughter!" shouted Lorraine.

"What are you *talking* about?" asked Jack. "She curses at me all the time!"

"You're thirty-five, and she's thirteen."

"Big fucking deal!"

"Jack! I'm warning you!"

" 'Jack, I'm warning you,' " mimicked Judy.

Jack laid his head down on his arms. Lorraine sat down next to him, moved his plate aside so he wouldn't get egg in his hair.

"Jack's crying, Jack's crying!" said Judy.

"I am *not!*" said Jack, raising his head briefly.

"Shh," said Lorraine. She put her hand on the back of Jack's neck.

"He's upset cause everybody hates him and he's a lousy artist."

"Tell her I'm not a lousy artist," Jack said, his face still muffled in his hands.

"Jack's not a lousy artist," Lorraine told Judy.

"Then how come Mark's brother never heard of him?"

"Judy," said Lorraine. "Jack is a wonderful painter, who will someday be well known and successful and wealthy. And if by any chance he isn't, this doesn't mean he's not a very good artist. Sometimes artists have a great deal of trouble being appreciated for what they are in the period they're living in. You've heard of the painter Vincent van Gogh, the artist who did those flower paintings I showed you on Channel Thirteen?"

"The weirdo who cut off his ear?"

"Yes. He died penniless, but he was a very great artist."

"He was a *ditz.*"

"No, Judy, he was not a ditz. In fact, there's a retrospective of his right now at the Met we're going to take you to if we can ever get tickets."

"Thanks but no thanks. *Arrivederci.*" She drifted back to the living room and turned up the TV even louder.

"Oh God!" moaned Jack.

Lorraine said to Judy: "Shut the TV off and go into your room."

"*No!* I hate him! I don't know why he's here!"

"Judy!" warned Lorraine. Judy flounced into her room. "Wait a sec," Lorraine said to Jack. She took her hand off his neck and got up. It was like a cool breeze departing. She turned off the TV and returned to him.

From out of Judy's room came the muffled sounds of Simple Minds. Then the sound got suddenly louder, as she opened the door. "I *hate* you!" she screamed. "I hate you ever since I saw you, and *all of my friends hate you too!*" She slammed the door again.

Jack waited for Lorraine to say, do something. She didn't. He stood up and leaned his head against the living-room window. It was pleasantly cool against his forehead. The sky was white, not as white as it was before, and yet not gray. It looked like it was going to rain. He could almost see the black behind the white, the black that would always be there if there were no air molecules for sunlight to bounce off from. For some reason this thought made him happy—happier than he had been all morning.

"Jack, *stop* it." (Lorraine said this just as she would to her dog.) "Why don't you call up your old shrink, what's his name? Morty?"

"Murray."

"Murray. He'll help you get started working, and then you'll feel better."

"I'm trying," said Jack.

"Don't try. *Do* it."

"Eat . . . *pudding.*" Her comments had truth in them. But they only served to paralyze Jack even further.

He went into the bedroom. He threw Jezebel off the bed and lay down. Jack the dog jumped up and put his front paws on the bed. He rolled his head around begging to be scratched behind the ears. Jack did this and Jack wagged his tail. He was so happy he made a high-pitched whine of happiness and began to drool. Jack the man *felt* like a dog, as if he had the same limited power as a dog. The only difference was, Jack the dog was happy, and Jack (the man) was not. He and Jack and Aurelia were the servants in the house. But the dog was on a higher level than Jack, as Jack was on a higher level than Aurelia, since Aurelia, on occasion, walks the dog, whereas Jack sometimes walks Aurelia, when it's very late and there's no traffic on the Drive, to West End Avenue to catch a cab.

A wave of tropical heat went through him. Tiny globules of sweat oozed out of his skin. To escape it, he rolled on his side. Out the window, on the corner across the street, there was a certified landmark building—a four-story stone building with round bay windows and wonderful south and west views that Jack envied. Shortly after Jack moved in with Lorraine wooden boards were taken off the windows of this building, and they were able to see inside. For a few weeks workmen brought in the apparatus of destruction and renovation: huge saws, lumber, tubs of plaster and caulk; then, when work had scarcely begun, they vanished, leaving the building as empty as before. Surely someone was paying a lot of money to maintain this unutilized space. Yet, sometimes at night, Jack was convinced he saw lights on in there. He was sure that whatever people were there were there illegally, and he thought of calling the cops. But what was there to steal—old moldings, a marble mantel? And even so, did he really care?

He decided to take a nap. He wished he were dead. Or on a spaceship, floating out into space. A clean white person with no worries.

A strange hollowness sucked through his insides, sending secretions of sour-tasting saliva to his mouth. He jumped up and ran to the bathroom. Kneeling on the floor, he extended his head over the open toilet. Violent waves went through him, totally beyond his control. When he was done vomiting, he stood up and turned on the right faucet with his right hand. He stuck his head under the faucet and filled his mouth with cold water. He twisted his head and spit out the water. He did this a number of times, then he brushed his teeth. He lowered the toilet seat and sat down on it. Through his pants he could feel its coolness against his skin, as he could feel, against the cool white of the sink, his hot head when he placed it down, sideways, on the porcelain. A glop of Crest was on the sink near his nose, and he could smell its clean, strong, pepperminty odor. It was strange how exquisitely happy he felt.

Jack, outside the door, hearing odd sounds, smelling odd smells, whined to get in. But Jack would not let him. Up and down he plopped his tail. Jezebel, stretching lazily on the windowsill, regarded Jack with a combination of pity and disgust. How dirty dogs were, how ungainly, how inelegant. Whereas nothing disturbed the calm equanimity of her life— except, of course, those rare moments when a dark brown bug scuttled out from under the fridge, or, as right now, a gray bird perched on the ledge outside the window. She would stand up on her hind legs and claw up in the air as if to swat him out of the sky. Meanwhile the bird sat there, seemingly oblivious, before swooping off into the empyrean. She could howl from frustration.

And yet what would she do when she had him? Crunch his head, bite into the neck so as to kill him, or play with him, dragging him around from room to room by the neck and then letting him go: merely to demonstrate her unlimited power?

When Jack was done in the bathroom, he staggered out and collapsed on the bed. He left the bathroom door open. Jack the dog ran in, placed his forepaws on the edge of the bowl, and lowered his head into the bowl. It was clean, yes (though humans did not drink out of this water, but from tall vessels made of the same hard invisible stuff as windows), but still, a smell lingered, as it always did, there in that secret room. He reached out his long red tongue to lick it.

Several days later Jack found himself in the elevator with a real estate agent and a client who were going to look at the vacant apartment above Lorraine's, and he asked if he might join them in looking at the property. He followed them into the empty apartment—once identical to Lorraine's, except it was approximately eleven feet closer to the sky. But if he had not known that before, he would never have guessed that now. He made his way around it like a blind man—a blind man with eyes, in a space he thought he knew—for the layout was unrecognizable, with its endless corridors and myriad smaller closets and rooms.

Apparently, when the apartment was renovated the old pantry was eliminated and the space absorbed into the enlarged and modernized kitchen; the wall that had bounded the fourth side of what had been the third bedroom was knocked down, integrating this space into the house as a second living room, and permitting light to stream into the kitchen and dining room—areas of the apartment that had formerly been forced to rely almost totally on artificial light. Other changes were also made—bathrooms modernized; recessed lighting installed in lowered ceilings; floors sanded, pickled, and polyurethaned; moldings knocked off walls and walls replastered and painted; small windows turned into large picture ones by knocking out nonstructural parts of exterior walls and replacing normal-sized panes by characterless square yards of glass; still, it was the structural renovation of the master bathroom (trebled in size by the addition of space once occupied by two closets and the small bathroom attached to the former middle bedroom), and the elimination of the third bedroom, that were most noticed by anyone who had seen the apartment in its original state. Oddly enough, the new apartment, for all its open spaces and loft-like appearance, gave the impression of being smaller than the more constricted and conventionally shaped apartment it had replaced.

The eliminated pantry was huge; Jack would have kept it as a breakfast room. The back walls of the master and third bedrooms ran the length of the apartment to the living room, and formed one side of a foyer that was large enough to have contained a bowling alley, a Ping-Pong table, or a "home entertainment center." Knocking it down had eliminated a small hall that had branched into Lorraine's bedroom and the

eliminated middle bedroom; as a consequence the entrance
to the master bedroom had been changed, necessitating the
destruction of the original closet and the building of new
ones, the latter of which had the unfortunate result of making the reconstructed master bedroom appear (if not actually
be) smaller than the one it had replaced—unless this was due
to the dwarfing effect of the large picture windows compared
to the more intimate original ones; this new entrance also
cut into the original living room, destroying its dimensions
and explaining to Jack why no one ever seemed to be able to
sit there. Lorraine's gigantic bathroom (with the whirlpool
that didn't whirl and the second-sink hookups that had never
been hooked up—installing the sink would have blocked the
bathroom entrance) had been made possible by the removal
of two hall closets—closets that could have been used to
store the stuff that now made the maid's room unusable. But
the real heartbreaker was the eliminated third bedroom (in
a better world Jack's studio), which was much larger than
Jack had realized, extending all the way to the wall of the
original foyer. It had its own bathroom (space Lorraine had
absorbed into the monster master bathroom), two normal-
sized windows, and a closet large enough to have held
most of Jack's painting materials. Its two virtually unin-
terrupted walls would have been perfect to tack his canvases on, and there would have been room for the thrift
shop chaise lounge and armchairs currently languishing in
his old apartment.

When Jack left the apartment he pushed the button on the
front door so that the door would remain unlocked; an hour
later, when he figured the realtor had gone, he returned and
sat down in front of the window of the third bedroom and
looked out at the slightly different view (because this apartment was higher) he would have been seeing had he lived
there: fewer trees, more Jersey, more sky. It was enough
to make a man weep—he could have been so happy! The
room, though not large, would have suited his work, even
as the old moldings framing portions of the old wall and
ceiling did, assuring one that the past still existed. Could

he not have painted there with equanimity—summers in the Hamptons, occasional trips to Europe—till his death? It was bad enough not having seen the "real" apartment, but now that he had—would he ever be able get the thought of it out of his mind?

After an hour or so he went downstairs. Something told him not to mention this clandestine visit to Lorraine. But that, perhaps, only made the unspoken image even more vivid in his mind. In future days he was haunted by visions of the astonishing paintings he could have painted had he only been able to work in that perfectly shaped and situated room, free from the eyes of Aurelia as she stood at the stove or ironing board, safe from the mockery of Judy and her friends, the snide (or even flattering) comments of the delivery boys and repairmen as they traipsed through the apartment on their way to the kitchen or bathrooms; these visions, accentuating as they did the huge gap between the Actual and the Ideal, paralyzed him until he became unable to work. The thought of the apartment (with civilized halls instead of "flow space" between rooms) made him want to scream with fury every time Judy turned the stereo to ear-splitting levels, or Aurelia dragged the vacuum cleaner through the house, or Jack's tail brushed against a still-wet painting. He lay in bed dreaming of the room, what his relationship with Lorraine might have been had he only been free to assert his independence after a fight by sleeping on a couch in his very own studio, instead of on the living room sofa, exposed to everybody's eyes.

One night, driven by the imp of perversity, he confessed to Lorraine that he had seen the apartment.

"Apartment?" Lorraine had just opened the predinner bottle of wine, and she suddenly stood still, eyes alert, neck stiff, like a hunting dog, a glass of St. Emilion halfway to her mouth.

"You know, the one upstairs."

She looked at him with hatred. "I don't want to talk about it."

"It seemed so much larger."

"I said, I don't want to talk about it."

"You don't have to get upset."

"Jack, when I say I don't want to talk about it, I mean *I don't want to talk about it.*"

"Could we rebuild the room?" he asked.

"Very funny."

"I mean it. Seriously."

Her eyes narrowed. "*Seriously,* you must be crazy."

"Crazy crazy crazy," said Judy, temporarily interrupting her phone conversation, twirling her forefinger in a circle around her head.

Lorraine left the kitchen and lay down on the couch. Jack followed her. He told her how all his life he had dreamt of the perfect studio. At last he had found it. Unlike dark cavernous lofts downtown, it was small, delicate, intimate—oddly fitting the image he had had of himself when he was young, wondering what it would be like to be grown up, standing in front of an easel with a paintbrush in his hand. A childish image maybe, but his. Very likely that was why he had become a painter: this vision of himself standing in a certain way in a certain place. He cried as if he were an orphan who'd searched all his life for a home—only to find when he found it, it was too late. Lorraine cradled him in her arms. She tried to think what was most important to her. Three years ago she and David had moved out of their comfortable eight-room apartment, spent a year paying double rents and living in a drafty and overpriced sublet while the contractors undertook the costly, time-consuming, and ultimately unsatisfactory renovations—all so that she could have a view of the river: not just when she was in her bedroom, but when she was in the kitchen, the entrance hall, the dining room, and on her way to and from the various bedrooms. During the disintegration of her marriage it had been the only thing (outside of her business and, on occasion, Judy) that made her feel life was worth living. She wished she could give it up; she wanted to give it up. If she had never had the view, or gone to all that trouble to get it, no doubt it would have been different, but she had—and could no more forget the misery of the past few years than Jack could the apartment he had seen upstairs.

So she had to tell Jack no. In Jack's mind, from this point on, although they continued to live together, their relationship seemed, in some sense, over.

9

The realtor and David sat in the realtor's Caddy: sunroof open, though it was night. "Why must I be a teenager in lo-o-ove?" the realtor sang.

"Nice car," David said, fingering the CB, automatic climate controls, automated sunroof. He hasn't been with a new male—a potential friend—in a long time. It's exciting, like when he first went to college, with that same odd mixture of anxiety and possibility as when he was going on a date. All his old friends were either alcoholics, married, or dead.

"Cost me plenty," said the realtor. He looked out the window; a Puerto Rican was staring at the car: with envy, hatred, indifference? A wave of love rushed over him and he flung open the door. "Come on, get in," he said. The Puerto Rican looked at him like he was crazy, then crossed the street.

"Are you crazy?" asked David.

"Just trying to be friendly," said the realtor. "Neighborhood make you nervous or something?"

"He coulda had a gun."

"Reagan coulda just stuck his finger on the button," said the realtor. "And I don't mean Nancy's button. Whoa!" He braked with a squeal in front of a building his grandmother would've moved out of fifty years ago, on the east side of Tompkins Square Park. "There's the building I'm fixing up. Supposed to be ready last month. Now they tell me next summer. Should have used the gooks. You wait a few months, though, I'll give you a good price on a nice new apartment. Up-and-coming neighborhood. You'll be able to tell that wife and that boyfriend of hers to go fuck themselves. Now over there is Dresden." He pointed east. "Village east of B, so-called in honor of the burnt-out buildings. In a few years that's gonna be hot too, in a different kind of way. Fucking gooks buying into it—that's always a sign. They own all the money in town. I'm not shitting you. They're buying the Bowery, Little Italy, the Empire State Building. In *cash!* You can't compete with um."

" 'Gooks'? The Vietnam boat people are buying New York?" asked David in confusion.

"*Chinks.* Generic gooks, slant eyes, slits, ding dong. Hong Kong, Red China, how they get the money to come here I never know, live ten in a room very un-American, sleep with their mother and father, work fifteen hours a day and before you know it they own the house you're living in. I'm Jewish, you understand, I know what it's like. But we *fought* sweat-shop conditions. These people *live* for work! I'm using them to fix up some of my buildings—sometimes I find them working *Sunday*—it's enough to make you sick!"

They did a high-five and the realtor went from zero to fifty in seven seconds. Then he slowed down and offered David a joint. David held it for a moment without smoking. "Cecilia hates me to get smashed," he said.

"The bitch who's throwing you out? Fuck her!" said the realtor. "We're going *fishing* tonight!" The joke was distaste-ful but David laughed. In spite of himself he was having a good time, listening to WBLS, feeling mellow in the big car. It was a different kind of night he was having—the kind of night he'd always thought having a mistress would bring him. But hadn't. The neighborhood was exciting in a way that vaguely seemed familiar, like from a long time ago. Be-fore he had money. Radios everywhere, kids in strange hair-cuts he wasn't sure were sexy or turnoffs, storefront doors that opened into galleries filled with paintings. People walked by, holding onto one another's huge tweed coats, laughing. Did Lorraine laugh? Does Cecilia laugh?

"Here she is," said the realtor. His use of the word *she* for a place reminded David of his father. In his mind he saw him with the eyes of a ten-year-old; about the same age as the realtor was now. David looked out the window. They were double-parked in front of what looked like a nondescript bar on the west side of Tompkins Square Park, except that your average nondescript bar didn't have a bunch of stretch limos parked on the street in front of it. "Pyramid," said the realtor, "art bar. Lots of weird chicks. You like weird chicks, don't you?"

"I suppose," said David, though he wasn't sure.

"Sure you do. It's a weird time for the world. They like old guys like us. Scared shitless of young good-looking guys."

"Why?"

"AIDS." The realtor looked at him like he was a nerd. Then he took out a little glass bottle, uncorked it, dipped a tiny spoon in it, and held the spoon under David's right nostril. David inhaled, couldn't get very much, and finally had to cover up his left nostril with his finger. Then he did it again.

The realtor gave a ten to one of the limo drivers to keep an eye on his car, then he led David over to where a velvet cable —the kind they had in movie theaters thirty years ago to separate the kids' section from the grown-ups'—was used to organize a line that formed outisde the bar on the street. The man at the door recognized the realtor and immediately let him and David in. David took out his wallet to pay the cover, but the realtor waved his hand and walked by. "I come here all the time," he explained. David felt confused, out of his element, in a way that paying the cover would have helped dissipate.

It was the exact opposite of the kinds of places David usually went to. Although uptown icons of money and beauty and prestige—fur coats, jewels, Armani suits—would have been absurdly out of place here, it wouldn't have been correct to say there was no style. It was just of a different kind: a combo of a hand-painted T-shirt with an antique jacket from the '40s with a thrift shop hat and fuck-me shoes. Almost with a pang David wondered whether Lorraine had ever been here: she would have loved it. The girls were young and sexy, if a little ugly, in their crewcuts, mohawks, spikes. But of course, "ugly" no longer meant what it used to. "Ugly" was now "style," which had replaced "beauty," which was now irrelevant. It wasn't exactly David's thing, but he decided he could get into it—at least if he could tell which of the girls

were boys, and vice versa. For instance, those two in sarongs
. . . When he smiled at them, one turned his head; David saw
the familiar three-day stubble. Then he realized he had forgotten how to breathe.

The coke was hitting, like a wave at the beach. David got
up and propelled himself to the john. He sat on the toilet to
catch his breath. He tried to read the graffiti but each letter
was in itself so interesting he never got around to finishing
the words in time to understand their meaning. When he
decided he could walk again he left the stall. He stood by the
urinals, pretending to comb his hair. Other people's stuck up
in ways that were now considered attractive, but his just sat
there. Guys entered the stalls two or three at a time; you
could hear them sniffing like a pack of hunting dogs. David
was scared to leave the john, but self-conscious about staying
there; what if they thought he was an old faggot and said
something weird about his dick? So he opened the door and
re-entered the club.

"Got any vodka?" he asked the bartender.

"Vodka? Oh no," said the bartender, with the utmost sar-
casm.

David turned his back to the bar and leaned back, survey-
ing the place as if to pick out a chick. Uptown he would have
known what to do, but here it was like a foreign country. He
worried about the fact that he still thought of chicks as
"chicks." Then he began to worry about the vodka—hadn't
he read that tequila was hip now, or was it rum—or maybe
it was gin again? Martinis. Then he told himself his real
problem was that he worried about such things, he should
stop thinking in that crazy, old-fashioned way. All his life
he's tried so hard to be with it; still he's never quite made it.

Finally David spotted the realtor. He weaved through the
crowd toward his table. He grabbed for an empty chair from
the next table, only to realize a vest made of dead paws sat
on it. He picked it up, looked around to see where to put it.

A tiny boy with pink hair and licorice skin looked
amusedly at him. "Your style?" he asked.

"No, I just want the chair." David blushed. "Is this yours?"
The boy nodded. "Where should I put it?"

"Round my shoulders, honey." The boy leaned forward.

Very awkwardly David put the coat around him. The boy
gave him a big smile. Again David blushed. He pulled the
chair over to the realtor's table.

"Thought I lost you. Hi," he said, to a woman—girl, really
—sitting next to the realtor. She sat there looking past them
both, as if she were seeing through the wall to the stars.

"This is Lydia," the realtor explained. The girl looked at
him with hatred, took a sip of her drink.

"You'll have to leave when my friends come." She
scowled.

"Lydia's an artist," the realtor explained. "A painter. We
were just discussing happiness."

"*You* were," said Lydia.

"Well, yes. I was just telling Lydia, I'm happier than I've
ever been in my life. Isn't that what I said?"

Lydia shrugged. "I don't remember."

"Sure you do," the realtor said genially. "Yesterday I was
unhappy. But today, like the book says, is another day."

"What book is that?" asked David.

"The book of happiness," said the realtor.

Lydia frowned, as if at the word *happiness*.

"I'm not happy either," said David, to make her feel better.
"Not that I necessarily give a shit." He began to giggle, from
the coke, he supposed. She looked at him as if he were a
worm.

"*I* give a shit," said the realtor. "In e.s.t. we like to share
things. I don't mean material goods, necessarily, but also
ideas."

"Gimme a break." Lydia shook her head.

"I know, you think I'm an asshole, but at least I'm a happy
asshole. Not everybody can say that. Can I buy you one of
what I'm drinking? I bet it's better than what you're drinking."

"What's that?" she asked sullenly.

"World's most expensive drink—Pear William."

She took a sniff of his. "All right."

The lights dimmed. An odd play about Chinese people,
which David was completely unable to follow, started. He

would have assumed it was insulting but the orientals in the
room seemed as amused by it as everybody else. As people
watched the play he looked around the room, to find someone he could talk to—rather, someone who might talk to
him. A girl was standing by the bar. At first he decided she
was ugly, then he decided she was acceptable, then he decided, maybe, she was beautiful.

He walked over next to her. He motioned to the bartender
for another vodka, then asked her if she wanted one. She
looked at him, shrugged, then pushed her glass forward.

"You're not the guy that owns Death, are you?" she asked.

"Owns Death?" David's heart skipped.

"Yeah, the gallery."

"Gallery?" A shooting gallery, where you did up coke and
heroin? Fear flooded through David, mucking up his digestive
system. Was she an undercover cop? Was she telling him she
thought he looked cool? Was there white powder stuck on
the hair in his nostrils?

Disappointment flickered across the girl's face. "You
know, the art gallery. On Eleventh Street."

"Oh, the *art* gallery," David said with relief. "Are you an
artist?"

She turned her back. The play ended. David clapped with
great enthusiasm. The girl walked away. David would have
liked to disappear, without saying goodbye to the realtor or
Lydia, only somehow that would have been even more embarrassing than staying.

He watched them get up from the table. Angrily, David
geared himself for their skipping out on him. To the disappointment of his anger, but the gratification of his loneliness,
they walked over to where he was standing. "Lydia's tired, so
I thought I'd give her a lift. You want to stick around or
what?" the realtor asked.

David shook his head, gulped down the rest of his drink.
Then he followed them out to the car. Somehow it was
just like in high school, tagging along with his best friend
Joey.

"It's the tiny Caddy," the realtor explained to Lydia. "Not
the ones with stretch marks. All my cars are virgins."

David blushed with embarrassment, but she laughed.

She directed him to Seventh between B and C, where she and her roommate were lucky enough to have found five renovated rooms for $750. David leaned against the back seat as Lydia and the realtor chatted in front. During the drive she played with the windows and the CB. David was alternately hot and cold as his window rose and fell. "Hot ass one," came a static-ridden voice over the realtor's CB. They stopped in front of an oasis of stone in a burnt-out world.

"How do you get a taxi around here?" David asked.

"You don't."

She got out of the car. The realtor hopped out after her, walked her to the door.

"You busy?" David heard him ask.

"When?"

"Now. Any time."

"Maybe."

David drummed his fingers on the window. He had a headache. The upper part of his body craved sex, but the lower part didn't.

Quietly, in case Cecilia was sleeping, David unlocked the door. The apartment was dark except for a bluish glow in the bedroom. Still in his coat, on an odd suspicion he walked there, super-softly, like a mime. Cecilia was lying on the bed, her eyes closed, pro Koss 4A headphones (the kind that eliminate external sounds) over her ears. The glow was from the tube, an old-fashioned b/w flick they must be showing on TBS.

Her hands were under the sheets. A pleasant hum came from there, like an electric shaver. Or lawn mower.

David stood watching her until she opened her eyes. Then she took off the headphones.

"How long have you been here?" she asked.

"Not very long."

"I know it's not very long. It doesn't take very long."

She placed the vibrator on the floor and with the remote control turned up the TV. She was not embarrassed, and

David was not aroused. He went into the bathroom and with the electric toothbrush brushed his teeth.

She was lying in the dark when he came out of the bathroom. She acted as if she were asleep, but something self-conscious about her mode of breathing made David think she was awake. He lay listening to her breathe, trying to fall asleep, but the drinks and the drugs still made his molecules dance. He did not so much feel like having sex as want to feel like having sex, so he could distract himself from the pounding. He tried to remember the last time he had actually wanted something—as opposed to wanting to want it—and drew a blank. No doubt it was the coke. He rolled toward Cecilia and whispered in her ear. "Are you awake?" he asked.

"What is it, David?" She yawned, opening her eyes, pretending to wake (or perhaps actually waking) up. She rolled toward him, but not to him.

"I did too much coke."

"You always do. I mean, when you do it."

"Come on. When do I ever do it?"

"You know. When you go out with that guy."

"Just cause you don't like him."

They were silent awhile. David took her hand, placed it on his heart. "I'm scared," he whispered.

"Of what?"

"Having a heart attack. Going crazy. Dying."

"Is that all?" She tried to joke, in a whisper, but it's hard to sound funny in a whisper.

"I feel like I don't know who I am any more. I don't know what I'm doing. I don't trust my mind. I mean, like in business, I don't think I'm really making the right decisions. But I don't know. And I don't know how to know I know. I don't know how I got where I am. I don't know why I married Lorraine, or why I'm here with you. Sometimes I don't even know who Judy is. I look at her and think: am I really her father? All of a sudden she's grown up. I don't remember it happening." He rubbed his fingers on his forehead, sniffed to see if there was sweat, or that weird smell that normal people emitted when they were paranoic—and paranoid-schizos emitted all the time.

"It's the coke, David. It always does this to you."

"You sure?" he asked, hopefully.

"Of course I'm sure. Why don't you try to get to sleep?"

"I can't." He was silent, then added, "You could help me, you know. " She didn't say anything. He took her hand and placed it on his cock. But she pulled away. "Come on," he said.

"No."

"Why not? It'll just take a minute."

"I can't. Please."

"What do you mean, you can't? You don't want to, is what you mean. If that's how it is, why don't you just say so, 'David, I don't want to, I know you're scared to death but I don't give a shit, I'm tired and that's more important to me, so go fuck yourself! Put your finger up your own asshole.' Go ahead and say it. Be honest at least." The more he talked the more David hated himself, but he couldn't stop.

"Okay." She sat up and turned on the light. "I wasn't planning to tell you this until tomorrow, but . . . I guess this is as good a time as any." David's heart began to pound, as it always did for bad—or even good—news. Bleary-eyed and tired, they looked at each other. "Well?" he demanded, as if he didn't know what was coming. He looked at the patterns the leaky shower upstairs had made on the as-yet-unrepaired wall as Cecilia told him how she had decided to go back to Michael. Michael: the most common name for newborn boys.

The stain was pretty, amorphous and subtle, like the paintings of the famous unhappy painter, the one who had killed himself a bunch of years ago.

From a distance, he heard Cecilia asking how he felt.

"A crock."

"What?"

"Crock of shit. 'Belong together.' Come on."

"I don't think so," said Cecilia, coldly.

"Please." David waved his hand, as much to indicate his disgust with her language as anything else.

"I'm sorry I had to tell you when you're feeling like this."

"Why does it matter when you tell me?" he demanded angrily.

"I don't know."

"If it's the truth, shouldn't you tell me as soon as possible?"

"I spose."

"So don't give me this horsespit. When are you moving back with him?"

"Tomorrow."

"Oh." David looked at her. The harsh light emphasized lines on her face he'd scarcely known were there, and the lack of makeup didn't help. Of course, in the wrong light, all women looked like this. Men too, no doubt. But with men, for some reason, it didn't matter.

"Are you upset?"

"What do you think?"

"I don't know."

"Of course I am. Who wouldn't be?"

"Yeah, who wouldn't be?" she echoed sarcastically.

"You sound like you want me to be. Is that why you're saying this, to make me even more upset?"

"You're the one who did the coke, not me."

"So what? Like I'm not the same person?" David felt numb, but also angry, as well as aware that the numbness somehow invalidated his anger, though that wasn't fair. Later on, when he would feel truly angry, who would be there to witness it? He was torn between showing her how wrong she was, for hurting him, and a desire to show that she was too insignificant for her to upset him. In a sick way he was also impressed with her capacity for sudden action—a capacity he hadn't realized was there, and that had made him underestimate her. Maybe if he hadn't, everything might have ended differently. Though he wasn't sure he cared. "I mean, for one thing, it seems kind of dumb for me to have moved out of Lorraine's."

"I see. I get blamed for the breakup of your marriage."

"I'm not saying . . . it's just . . . oh, fuck it."

"Yeah. Fuck it."

"Christ . . ."

"Come on, David. Be honest. Are you really in love with me?" A deep silence filled the room, broken only by the radio. What could he say? That in his panic he desperately needed someone? That she had wronged him by not falling in love with him, though he had not fallen in love with her. She put her hand on his arm. "You see . . ."

David shook it off. "All I see is it's not fair." To show her what he meant, he banged his hand against the wall. At first he intended to scare her by breaking it, then, at the last minute, he held up, the way Lorraine did, so that all he was left with was a gesture.

10

Monday afternoon Jack walked into the office of his old therapist, Murray Bottoms. Old therapist but new office, for Murray, who used to work out of a West Village apartment, had upgraded himself to two floors in a sturdy old red stone condo on lower Broadway. Jack complimented Murray on his new surroundings, then commenced the story of his current artistic stagnation. Murray listened in silence for several minutes before interrupting.

"There's two things I feel I must tell you, Jack. One is that as a consequence of my collecting Neo-Expressionist work in some volume, particularly that in which sections of the human body lie in a noncontiguous relationship to one another (that is to say, are disembodied), I've begun to function as 'esthetic consultant' to a number of artists, mainly in the realm of helping clarify esthetic stance, so *very* important nowadays. If you're at all interested, why don't you go to the Fast Money Gallery and check out what I'm doing? John Weird himself admits he would never have gotten into the Whitney Biennale without my assistance. With my specialist's insight on this matter, I hope you don't mind if I tell you frankly that you're (to put it bluntly) full of shit. There's no need to mime (or even *experience*) anger, for the second thing I must tell you is that the subtext of your argument clearly demonstrates the nonrelevancy of your manifest content. That is, your ideas are merely a symptom of your depression, and are hence irrelevant to your real malaise, as well as being (as I said before) *remplis de merde*. What you must do, in order to resume painting, is stop being depressed." He paused a moment, then stood up and shouted: "*Stop being depressed!*" Pleased with himself, he sat down.

"Is that supposed to help?" asked Jack.

"I don't know, Jack. Did it help?"

"No."

"That's too bad. In that case I suggest we start seeing each other again. Perhaps twice a week to begin with, then, when you've begun to work again, we'll switch one of the sessions to 'esthetic consultation.' My fee for that kind of service is substantially higher, but well worth it in terms of career advancement and material remuneration, as you'll soon find out. One of the more *outré* forms of Neo-Expressionism will suit you quite nicely, I'm sure. Now when I last saw you you were involved with a young dancer whom you were fighting with constantly, and had, as I remember, terrible sex. Tell me, are you still with her?"

"Of course not!"

"Good. Are you seeing someone now?"

"I'm sort of living with somebody. But that's not what I came here to talk about."

" 'Sort of living with.' Do I sense some resistance, Jack? Not just to me, but to this relationship."

"You're right, Murray. There *is* resistance," Jack admitted. "I resent the idea of having a therapist tell me what kind of paintings I should do."

"Not in my capacity as *therapist*, Jack, but as *esthetic consultant*. Normally I charge a flat sum per project—usually a show or series of shows—but since we've been friends for so long (I hope I can call you a friend, Jack) I'm willing to charge you per session, which usually comes out cheaper."

"When I first started going to shrinks, they wouldn't open their mouths, even if you were about to jump out the window. Now they won't shut up."

"Jack, baby, I'm trying to give you your money's worth. What's the point of paying somebody to listen to your thoughts, when that's what you do yourself all day long? The form of Freudianism to which you refer is as outmoded as the Abstract Expressionism which depended upon it for psychological validity. Psychiatrists no longer consider it necessary for an artist to *be*, or even to *have been*, an alcoholic or drug addict—even an unhappy childhood is no longer considered necessary, though on this admittedly touchy subject there is still some dispute. Being an extremist by temperament (the so-called middle is merely an average of two contradictory but wholly valid points of view), I no longer consider child-hood traumas of any relevance whatsoever; and if a patient persists in alluding to them, I refer them to some octogenarian more in sympathy with their views. I hope you did not come here to discuss your childhood, Jack."

"No. But I think some of my college experiences were relevant. Like when I was twenty I had a problem in painting very similar to that which I have now. First I abandoned imagery and began to concentrate on color—not the colored gestures of Abstract Expressionism, but mere color. Then I began to see that brush-strokes, of whatever anonymity and 'neutrality,' were nonetheless still 'contaminated' by personality, thus interfered with the direct apprehension of color, so I began to pour my paint directly on the canvas. As the gesso interfered with the union of paint and canvas and distorted its color in the direction of white, I eliminated the gesso. Then the colors themselves began to seem vulgar, so I began to discard hues first of red, then green, then yellow, until I was down to various shades of the hue blue, then one shade of the hue blue, until I realized it was the purest to eliminate hue entirely, and so I ended up using only white. For a while it seemed there was nowhere else to go, but then it occurred to me that paint itself was unnecessary, so I had only the plain stretched canvas, reflecting the shadows of the room. Then the stretcher began to seem redundant, so I got rid of *that*, and tacked the canvas directly on the wall. This looked uncomfortably similar to the way ordinary painters commenced their paintings, and I had a brainstorm: why not eliminate the canvas as well? I drew a line with a pencil on the wall where the 'picture' was; then, when I realized that a view could be of something in the middle of a room as well as on a wall I began to suspend simple metal frames from the ceilings, to outline rectangles of air. At first I placed masking tape where the spectators were to stand so that they would obtain the desired view; but then I realized, one, that the different heights and head shiftings of people made it impossible they would have identical views and, two, that it was arbitrary in any case to decide one view was quote preferable to another, so I eliminated the tape. Then I realized how absurd it was to pretend that we see through metal rectangles, so I substituted a less obtrusive sewing thread, then fishing line, until logic compelled me to admit that the fishing line was invisible, so I abandoned that too. I wrote paragraphs which I'd pin on the wall, instructing the audience (at Pratt this meant mostly students and professors) what they were to look at. When then this began to seem authoritarian, I eliminated the instructions. I sat all day long in a corner of the 'gallery' and stared, in an attempt to create an atmosphere of attention. By then my adviser decided I was off my rocker, and made an appointment for me with the school shrink, who told me that *functionally* I was no longer an artist. I decided this was okay, and for a while I ceased to attend class. One day, while glancing through a notebook of these 'viewing instructions,' I noticed, to my intense surprise and disgust, that some of the pages contained the impurity of doodles. This betrayal by my unconscious (for I certainly hadn't been scribbling *consciously*) disturbed me greatly, for at that point I no longer believed in an unconscious (at least *consciously* I didn't). Then I decided that my notion of a universe indifferent to man's desires contradicted this judgmental interpretation of my scribbling, and that the reflexes of my hand contained some self-evident metaphysical truth. What could this be—that perception could not exist without an object to be perceived? That in the realm of the senses there was no such thing as absolute purity? That as long as there was Mind there could be no emptiness? In search of the answer to this question I began to imitate the doodles, to see if the movements of my hand would re-create a muscle memory that would lead me to remember the content of my unconscious mind while I was making the doodle. Once line entered the picture, so did the whole kit and caboodle of color, shape, depth of field, until I was right back where I started from." He stopped to take a sip of water from the watering can.

"*Wrong!*" said Murray.

"Wrong?"

"You were not back right where you started from, you were *older*. If we were immortal, these peregrinations would have greater utility, but as it is . . . Hold your horses, have I got a surprise for you!" Murray got up, opened a closet, and picked out a cassette from a cassette rack. He stuck it in the cassette player on his desk, put on his earphones, and rewound and flash-forwarded till he found the spot on the tape he wanted. Then he took off the earphones and switched on Speaker:

"I abandoned imagery and began to concentrate on color—not the colored gestures of abstract expressionism, but mere color. Then I began to see that brush-strokes, of whatever anonym—"

Murray clicked it off. "Sound familar?" he asked.

"Yeah, you were just taping me, Murray. Thanks for asking my permission."

"*Wrong!* I made this little honey *three* years ago, Jack, during another of your esthetic crises. You don't believe me, let's flash-forward to"—he punched FF, Stop, then Play—"good body terrible sex," Jack heard in his own voice. "You don't believe me," said Murray, "play with it yourself." He handed Jack the deck. Jack REWed and FFed until he realized that the tape was not of very recent vintage.

"What's your point, Murray? That I'm boring? Too boring to see you maybe? Am I going to be shuffled off to some nonagenarian?"

"I'm paid to help you, not to be bored, though all too often that's an undesired by-product. Frankly, I don't see why my therapy sessions should not be as thought-provoking and exciting for me as the art of painting is for a happily functioning artist, or, for that matter, as such leisure-time activities as food, sex, squash, and sleep: after all, they consume more of my time. But this goes against the American grain—the more we earn, the more unpleasant and stress-inducing our jobs should be. You could have a great time in your life, Jack, if, instead of sitting around moping, you'd realize that ninety-nine percent of the people in the world would love to have your life: get up when you feel like it, paint when you want, talk for as long as you want about whatever you want to a bunch of kids twice a week. God, how I envy you!" Murray got up from the desk, and put his arm around Jack's shoulder. "So be a good boy, go home, pick up your paintbrush, and no matter what, don't stop until you paint at least nine square feet a day, no matter what. Doesn't matter how good it is, just that you do it. Okay?"

"Okay," said Jack reluctantly. "But I don't know what to paint."

"Doesn't matter, Jack. I'm just trying to get you back in the habit. You know, when you fall off a horse—"

"Yeah, Murray, but I still got to paint something."

"Paint yourself, paint your new lady friend—"

"I'm not into humans, I never have been."

Murray shook his head, "Tsk, tsk, very lucrative at the present moment, Jack, but it's your life. So paint your studio, try copying your old paintings. Try something different—performance art, graffiti, whatever. Got to get those muscles in gear. Hey hey." He punched Jack on the arm. "Gonna promise, old buddy, or what?"

"I think it's dumb, Murray, really dumb, but I'll try it."

"Promise?"

"Promise." They looked at each other with fatigue and satisfaction, as if they had just made love.

"Cuckoo, cuckoo," went a huge clock on Murray's wall.

"Nice, huh?" said Murray. "In the old days, when you looked at your watch to see if the session was over, patients always assumed it was cause you were bored. This way there's no confusion."

"If I know you, Murray, you got a little gadget in your pocket enables you to set off that clock any time you wish."

With a big smile, Murray pulled the gizmo out of his pocket and zapped a couple quick "cuckoos." "Sharp, Jack, but let's face it, we've said what we had to say."

"No, Murray, *you* said what *you* had to say."

"You're a mensch, Jack, I love you." Before Jack knew what was happening, Murray leaned over and kissed him on the lips. By the time Jack's lips realized these belonged to a man, they were halfway to kissing him back.

"Work hard, bring me slides, I'll see you next week."

As Jack went downtown to his old apartment to pick up his mail and, who knows, look at his old paintings, he felt strange, as if suddenly he did not know who he was, or who he might become. He had not thought about such matters in some time. A bum lay outside on an abandoned couch, newspaper over his head. He looked dead, but no doubt he was just sleeping. A few years ago it would have bothered Jack; now, with a hardened heart, he realized that even with broken springs it was a lot more comfortable than the places bums usually slept.

When he got upstairs Jack pulled out his old paintings from their wooden storage rack. Looking at them was like reading a journal of his mind. He remembered why he had made each brush-stroke, chosen each color, used which size brush. He could prove he's the smartest painter in the whole world. He could prove all of art history led up to him, that every one of his canvases is the greatest painting ever painted. Back in the days of his blank canvas, he could explain why his blank canvas was the greatest painting never painted. All you had to do was stare at it hard enough. A wall could be full of meaning, if you stared at it hard enough. He was looking at one now. It was a whitish beige, with cracks and missing chips, neo-baroque when looked at in a self-conscious light, but when deconstructed revealing blankness, the exhaustion of imagination, the decay of civilization. It's got marks of time's personality, hence is expressionistic; in its obdurateness and resistability to man it was pure Other; its conceptual quality resides in what it evokes in the spectator; as a Lower East Side artifact it's part of history; as his studio it's part of the environment that in an extended sense is his Work; as calling forth a multiplicity of interpretations it partakes of pure Being; as the explanations are meaningless, it signifies the pointlessness of explanation, hence thought, hence . . .

11

Lorraine was in trouble. If Jack ever paid attention to anything but himself he surely would have noticed this. Night after night she lay awake tossing and turning. Mornings she woke up exhausted, nervous, cold. Judy had to be dragged out of bed, gotten dressed, fed, sent off to school on time with bus pass, money, notebooks, arrayed with the proper degree of warmth, cool, hipness, good taste. Lorraine had to feed and clothe herself and read *WWD*. She had to go to the office and put on a bright face so that her partner Marianne, her employees, the bank factor, the union, and her customers wouldn't have the slightest idea that she was almost two hundred thousand on the wrong side of the ledger. She worried constantly (every minute of the day, during sex, before she fell asleep and the second she awoke) that the bank would call in its loans and put her out of business. She worried the union would demand its $45,000 in unpaid dues and put her out of business. She worried that her customers would smell panic and not place orders. She worried that Marianne was going to run out on her for a partner who had better backing—not that she hadn't spend months with high-priced lawyers working on a contract to forestall this very possibility. Weird pains went through her at odd moments like bolts of lightning, making her limbs quiver. Was she getting AIDS? Could you really be sure of whom a man had *not* slept with four years in the past? Didn't even the straightest of men possess odd dark corners of their psyches? Maybe it was not AIDS but a stroke and she'd have to lie paralyzed the rest of her life. She had no illusions in such a case that Jack would feed, clothe, bathe her. She tried to calm herself, tell herself it wasn't worth it, that she should sell the business, join a health club, become a vegetarian, learn to meditate, but she found herself unable to stop; the adrenaline in her blood was like an addiction. A sad mistake, for inside she was someone else entirely—not a grown-up with a failing business, a daughter, a car, a husband, a lover, a dog, a cat, but a five-year-old kid, someone who liked to cut up odd scraps of material and pin them on her dolls—someone younger, much younger, than Judy was now. Surely God had not intended her to stay up all night worrying about her high blood pressure. What had God intended her to do? Live in a small town upstate, milking cows.

At 7:30 Lorraine hugged Jack, rolled out of bed, staggered into the bathroom, peed, went into the kitchen to start preparing Judy's breakfast, into Judy's room to wake her up, back into the kitchen to feed Jack and Jezebel, back into Judy's room to make sure she was up, to the kitchen to finish making Judy's breakfast, to her own bathroom to take a shower and wash her hair, to Judy's room with a towel around her head to make sure she was finished dressing, discovered that she was not, whereupon she grabbed the patterned socks Judy was lost in thought trying to decide which to wear out of Judy's hands, picked out a pair and told her to put them on, ordered her to go eat her breakfast before it got cold, returned to her own bathroom to continue drying her hair, back to the kitchen to find Judy's breakfast still untouched, to Judy's bedroom to find her still futzing over the socks, whence in fury she emptied the drawer of socks on the floor, stalked to her own bedroom where she flipped through reams of pantyhose to find an untorn pair, back to the kitchen where Judy was playing with her cereal, insisted that she could not leave the house until she at least finished her banana, returned to her bathroom to finish applying her skin treatment, from which she was disturbed by Judy's hysteria concerning a lost bus pass, which she finally gave in and helped her search for, locating it in the pocket of the leather jacket Judy had worn yesterday, then (having finally gotten Judy out of the house), went back to her bathroom, finished the skin treatment, put on her makeup, came out to the kitchen to have a quiet cup of coffee and read the paper. As usual, her company was not mentioned in any of the columns or reviews. With a sudden burst of energy she tore the paper in half. She looked out the window at the sky. This was the only part of the day she really liked.

She grabbed her briefcase and headed for the subway, got off at the downtownmost Times Square exit, and walked to her office. At the top of a modern building, it had views of Bryant Park, the Hudson, and acres of sky filled with gray pigeons whom she often felt envious of. Could they not travel unencumbered, bed down in a new spot every night, sport gray and white, her favorite colors? After telephoning for some espresso and croissants (Bergdorf's was coming) she sat down at her desk. Meanwhile Marianne walked in, to complain yet again about the sudden success of Stephane, who used to cut patterns for her back when she first started selling to boutiques in and around Boston. Then Bob H called, then Tony, then the man from the union, then Tony again, Anne, Raggedy Andy from *Interview*, Bob H again, and so on.

As she half-listened to Marianne, Lorraine leafed through her mail. In it were the Italian and American *Vogue*, *W*, and *Rags*; cutoff notices from Con Ed and New York Telephone; warnings about bounced checks and Chase overdraws; invoices from fabric designers, cutters, pattern-makers; bills from her attorney; IRS inquiries about quarterly estimates and payroll taxes; appeals to buy tix for the Coty Awards, Metropolitan costume shows, Fashion Group breakfasts, etc. She fished in the back of the top drawer for Tylenol, grabbed three tablets, popped them in her mouth and let them dissolve without bothering to get water, swiveled in her chair, tilted it back by pushing her legs against the wall under the windowsill, and stared out the window at the pigeons. She fell forward, waking up just in time to push herself upright before her head hit the windowsill. She couldn't believe this wasn't all some strange nightmare; that any moment she wouldn't wake up into the existence that was really hers.

"God, those are gorgeous!" screamed Judy that afternoon in the Unique Clothing Warehouse, re a skintight pair of pink spotted leopard pants. "Can anybody lend me fifteen bucks?" she asked.

"They are *so* gross!" said Karen.

"Isn't he cute?" said Elissa re a stock boy who was straightening out a pile of jeans.

"Yuck!"

"Excuse me, sir, do you have the *total* time?" Saralee asked a man out in front.

"That lady gave you *such* a look," Judy said to Saralee outside.

"I fooled her," said Saralee, holding up a Day-Glo orange plastic watch she had slipped in her pocket.

"That's nice," said Judy.

"Here. You want it?" She gave it to Judy.

Elissa and Karen had put their names down at the Astor Place haircutters to have a haircut, so they went back to wait on line while Saralee and Judy headed for the Kiev, which they had heard of as kind of a punk luncheonette. "Two Cokes," Judy told the waitress. While they were waiting for the Cokes a young Puerto Rican boy asked if he could share their table. There were several Puerto Ricans in Judy and Saralee's school, but not many, so of course this became an interesting encounter to them. In truth, any unknown boy, of whatever nationality, would have provided an interesting encounter.

"What's your name?" demanded Judy.

"Julio," he said.

"I'm Saralee."

"I'm Judy," said Judy.

"They don't let you sit at a table if you come in by yourself. A coffee please," he told the waitress. He took out a book and started reading it.

"Actually, I'll have a coffee too," said Saralee.

"Me too," said Judy. They waited for the boy to speak but he continued reading. "What book is that?" Saralee asked.

"Just some computer stuff."

"We have computers in school," said Judy.

"Apples?"

"Yeah."

"We've got PCs," he boasted. I'm trying to disprove the red shift."

"What's that?" asked Saralee.

"It has to do with how fast the stars are moving away from earth. I don't think it's as fast as most scientists say. If this is true of course they're not as far away either, because time and distance are the same. The reason I think this has to do with what Einstein says in the theory of general relativity, that gravitation is indistinguishable from acceleration, which to me indicates that the red shift could be measuring not acceleration but the gravitational curve generated by a finite, curved universe. As Einstein said, if the universe is curved, you could send off a light beam from your eyes and it would eventually come back to the back of your head. So the star might look like it's coming from there" (he pointed north) "but it's coming from there" (he pointed south). "You follow?"

"Not exactly."

"Nobody does," he said. "My teachers tell me I'm a genius."

"Everybody in our school is geniuses," said Judy.

"Where's that?"

"Uptown," said Saralee, kicking Judy under the table.

"Do you go to public school?" Judy asked.

"Yeah, but I'm going to go to a good college. Not that it matters. Einstein didn't go to college."

"He did *too.*"

"He did *not.*"

"He did *too.*"

"No he *didn't.*"

"You want a refill, kids?" asked the waitress. They all bristled at the word "kids." Then they broke up laughing and Julio closed his book.

"A friend of mine's brother just got this VCR. You want to go there and watch a movie?"

"Where is it?" asked Saralee.

"Just down the block."

Saralee and Judy looked at each other. "Sure." They left the Kiev and started to walk up Second Avenue. Saralee chattered away but Judy was worried. She had never done any-thing like this in her life. She had heard of many young girls like herself who had been sold into slavery—by Turks, of course—but what if this dark-skinned boy's name wasn't Julio, but Ahmed or Mohammed? She walked along the street, her head down. Saralee nudged her in the ribs. She pulled herself up tall and straight—not "straight" as opposed to "gay," but "straight" the way girls from Nightingale-Bam-ford walked, an invisible shoebox filled with cocaine, which they must not drop, balanced on top of their heads. A stone lay on the sidewalk, but she did not kick it into the gutter, though she longed to.

The apartment was dark, with what looked like an old Indian bedspread covering the window. Saralee immediately plopped down on the floor as if she were at home. Judy was uncomfortable. She wandered into the john, then got a glass from the kitchen. When she returned to the living room Sar-alee and Julio were laughing together in a way that seemed to exclude her. A pang went through her—her first in this connection. But she saw it as iconic—it would always be like this, three people, with the other two liking each other and her out of it. That's what being an only child in a family was all about, wasn't it?

"Is *Back to the Future* okay?" asked Julio. It was a rhetori-cal question, as he and Saralee were already fast-forwarding to a favorite part. Once the movie started he went to a drawer and took out a plastic bag with what looked like oregano in it. "Oh good. Marijuana," Judy said, super-casually. Very carefully he rolled a joint. Judy had tried pot a couple of times at parties with ninth- and tenth-graders, but never alone in a room with a boy, even though the boy wasn't with her, but with Saralee. Saralee acted real cool, she held the cigarette like it was no big deal. Judy, impressed, decided to imitate her. She prayed she wouldn't cough, but she couldn't help herself. To her relief they didn't laugh at her, but probably that was because they weren't really interested in her, but in each other. She peeked through the bedspread covering the window to the street. Diagonally across was an old church, with some grass around it. This green, in the midst of these ugly old buildings, somehow seemed more interesting than all of Riverside Park, which she and her friends wouldn't play in after school any more because they were grown up and interested in different things. When she turned around, Julio was sitting with his arm around Saralee's waist, Saralee's head against his body. They looked happy, like a TV ad, like people she didn't know. In their bodies, somehow, was the secret of perfection. Judy knew she didn't have it, would never have it. It was unfair, but who was there to blame?

"What are you mooning at?" asked Saralee, giggling. She felt embarrassed, to be sitting there with this guy as Judy watched. She wondered what Judy would tell their friends. She wasn't sure if she really liked Julio, or was merely grateful he had chosen her over Judy.

"I'm *not*," said Judy. Despite herself, a petulant stubborn edge was in her voice. Whenever she heard herself sound like this she felt fat, like an old woman with a big red nose. Her voice sounded peculiar in her ears, as if she were hearing it in a different way than usual—through the bones in her body rather than through the air. Teeth make good antennas, she has read in some book. Or, at least, imagined she has read. The idea of teeth sticking out of the top of the World Trade Center made her giggle.

She sat down and tried to think normal thoughts. Julio's friend came in from across the hall. He was fifteen, taller and scarier than Julio. Just looking at him you could tell how cool he was. Actually, Judy liked Julio better; maybe because he seemed safer. The boy sat down next to her. "Where do you go to school?" he asked.

"Columbia Prep."

"What's that?"

"Oh. Just some school uptown."

He soon lost interest. He got a pillow from the couch and put it under his head. There was nothing Judy could think of to say to him. Meanwhile she watched Saralee and Julio kiss. They seemed to be doing it the way you saw in movies, with the mouth open.

"Okay," said the boy. He turned toward Judy, touched her arm. A chill went through her. Goose bumps rose on her skin.

"Do you have a sweater?" she asked.

The boy laughed, gently pulled her down to him, then kissed her softly on the lips. It was nothing like a spin-the-bottle-type kiss. Judy actually forgot about Saralee. She was both embarrassed and excited.

"Let's get some privacy," said the boy. When he got up and started down the hall to the bedroom Judy followed him. The last thing she wanted was to make a fuss. Obviously she was doing all right, better even than Saralee. He sat down on the bed, kicked off his shoes. Judy just stood there, staring at him.

"What are you waiting for?" asked the boy. Dutifully, Judy sat down on the bed and took off her shoes.

He put his arm around her shoulder. Instead of kissing her as she expected him to do he pulled her down on top of him. He smelled different from normal boys, almost sweet, as if he were wearing suntan lotion. She had no idea what she was supposed to do, or say, or not do or say. The last time she had been on a bed with a boy was when a bunch of kids were playing some stupid board game, back in elementary school. Since then they had gotten self-conscious and couldn't do things like that. His lips on her neck gave her more of the same kind of chill she had before. It was almost unbearable. He put his tongue in her mouth. It was fat and wet, kind of disgusting, though she wouldn't have admitted that to anybody. She tried to push it out with her tongue, but he pushed back with his. She got her tongue behind her teeth and clamped her jaws together so hard she began to get a head-ache. She could feel his tongue moving around her gums, a peculiar, almost ticklish feeling. She prayed he would stop. Then he rolled on top of her. He put his hand on her leg and pushed up her skirt. This felt so strange that to prevent it she opened her mouth in a trade-off; if she did this maybe he'd leave her leg alone.

He put his hand higher on her thigh. She couldn't help herself, she gave a little jump. He pressed down on her and she felt something hard against her leg. "Could you move your wallet?" she asked.

The boy laughed. Then he rolled onto his back. "How old are you?" he asked.

"What difference does that make?" asked Judy.

He laughed again. He leaned up on his elbows and opened the night-table drawer and pulled out a pack of cigarettes. He lit one with a blue transparent lighter, then leaned back on the bed. He looked like a god out of the movies. Matt Dillon, Sean Penn, somebody like that.

"What are you, in the eighth grade?" he asked.

"Yup."

"You go out with guys a lot?"

"Well, not all *that* much." She spoke as if she were embarrassed about the "not that much," when the truth was more like "not at all."

"I can tell," he said. "You call me up when you get older. Okay?"

"Okay." Judy would have loved to ask him what she did wrong, but the embarrassment of having to listen to the answer in his presence prevented her.

When he finished the cigarette he sat up and put his shoes on. Judy did the same and followed him into the living room. The VCR was on with the sound down. Saralee and Julio were listening to Simple Minds. Saralee gave Judy a look. "We gotta go," she said.

"Yeah," echoed Judy.

The boys didn't say anything as she and Saralee got themselves together. Judy wondered if she should remind the boy to give her the phone number.

"Bye," Saralee told Julio.

"Bye." They kissed. The boy Judy had been with was in the kitchen. "Hey, look, I don't remember your name," she told him, when she went in to say goodbye. She pretended to laugh.

"Paul," he said. Judy waited for him to ask her *her* name, but he didn't. She wanted to tell him her name was Judy but was embarrassed to do so without his asking. What if he said "What are you telling me that for? Do you think I give two shits?" She wanted to ask for his phone number, but was scared he wouldn't give it to her. She herself could (under)stand it if he did this, but what if he went out and said in front of Saralee and Julio something like "Do you believe it? This girl wants me to give her my phone number?" They'd all howl on the floor and laugh at her. "Come on," Saralee called.

"Well, we're going," said Judy. "Goodbye."

"See you around."

"Where?" Judy was on the verge of saying, but thank God didn't. She walked slowly out of the kitchen. He was emptying ice out of a plastic ice-cube tray into a plastic ice-cube holder. A dark god playing with ice.

Saralee and Judy were silent as they hopped down the stairs to the street. Outside, Judy turned around and looked at the number on the building.

"If you walk up three flights does that mean you're on the third or fourth floor?" she asked Saralee.

"What'djew do? Get laid in there?"

"Boy, are you dumb!" replied Judy. Actually, she wasn't too sure of the precise meaning of that word *laid*. People seemed to use it like "screwing," only the image she always got was of a hen, sitting on top of a bunch of eggs. "We just frenched a bit," she said.

"Us too. Then he wanted me to feel him down. Ugh!"

"Gross!" agreed Judy.

"Like, have you ever been so hungry?"

Judy realized that that feeling in her stomach was hunger. "Like . . . like . . . no."

"Pig-out time!" they shouted in unison. First they ate a pizza, then a souvlaki, then they got ice cream cones from the homemade ice cream place. They wandered into a record store that sold old records, mostly by groups they'd never heard of. When they came out they did not head to the subway, but still acted as if they did not want the afternoon to end.

"You want to see where Jack used to live?" asked Judy. "I came here once with my mom when he was moving some stuff."

"He's so weird. I don't know why your mom likes him."

"She *doesn't* like him. She's just mad at my father."

"She must like him, or he wouldn't be living there."

"She *doesn't*, I'm telling you!"

They walked downtown a few blocks. Then Judy stopped in front of a doorway. "This is it," she said, uncertainly.

"What a yucky building," said Saralee.

To make sure, they walked in, looked at the mailboxes. Jack's name wasn't there, so they went outside and tried the building next door. "Here it is," said Judy.

"Big deal. What do we do now?" asked Saralee.

"I don't know."

Judy pressed the buzzer. They giggled. The didn't hear anything. They pressed it again, holding it a long time. "He's hardly ever here," said Judy. "Just sometimes to pick up his mail."

Jack was roused out of his trance by the ringing of the buzzer. He buzzed back, then went to his door and opened it.

"Who is it?" he shouted down the stairs.

"Judy and Saralee!"

"Judy! What are you doing here?"

"I dunno."

"Do you want to come up?"

"*What?*"

"Come on up!"

Judy and Saralee stood inside the downstairs doorway. They looked at each other. "What do you think?" asked Judy.

"It's up to you," said Saralee, shrugging her shoulders.

"*Okay,*" Judy shouted. They started to climb the stairs. Several of the apartments had garbage bags sitting outside their doors, waiting to be brought downstairs. The steam was on and the bags smelled.

"Pee-yew!" said Judy.

"Gross!" said Saralee.

Jack waited for them by the open door. It was so hot he had his shirt off.

"God, Jack, you are so gross," said Judy.

"Spaz city," said Saralee.

Normally Jack hated surprises. But when he saw them his

heart, oddly, pumped with unexpected happiness. "Having a wild East Village afternoon, huh?" he asked.

"Don't be so uptight," said Saralee. She sprawled in the chair.

"Yeah, loosen up your anus," echoed Judy. She and Saralee began giggling hysterically. Jack's initial impulse was to be disapproving, then he thought, What the hell. He wasn't their father, after all.

"What were you doing before we came," asked Judy, grown-up conversational, "playing with yourself?"

Jack rolled his eyes, played literal. "In a manner of speaking, yes. I was looking at my old paintings, trying to work, not getting very far. I guess you could call that jerking off."

"Jerking off!" Great glee. "Don't let *us* stop you," said Saralee.

"Yeah, we wouldn't want to stop you from having *fun*." Judy and Saralee almost fell on the floor. Just as suddenly, they stopped. Judy got up and started walking around the apartment, picking up papers, putting them down, pulling books out of the bookcase. "God, what a dump. No wonder Mommy asked you to move in with her. Is this a lamp or what? Don't you ever make your bed? You got something to eat? We're famished."

"Maybe some ice cream," said Saralee.

"And a Coke."

"Cookies if you got any."

"Munchies, huh?" he asked.

"What's 'munchies'?"

"The intense hunger you get after smoking dope."

"The only *dope* we know about is *you*." Hysteria.

They followed Jack into the kitchen. He was both annoyed —that they've interrupted his work—and almost deliriously happy, that they thought about him when he wasn't with them—enough, even, to come visit him. Their good-natured insults washed off him like water.

"I'll have a beer," said Judy, sticking her head in the fridge.

"Yeah, that's just what your mother would love."

"Jack, you can't *possibly* take her seriously, she's such a stick."

Jack often felt this way himself, but it wasn't fair—for
Lorraine's sake—to admit this to Judy. Of course not admit-
ting this would impair (a little) his relationship with Judy,
because he wasn't being completely honest with her. On the
other hand, even to listen to this stuff, in unarticulated agree-
ment, he felt in a secret league with her. Two kids against
the big bad boring grown-up world.

"So how do you like being stoned?" he asked, super-casual.

"High on you, baby," said Judy. She grabbed him around
the waist. Jack got a hard-on, as he did on occasion with Judy.
Propinquity—he wasn't really attracted to her; at least he
was fairly sure he wasn't. Saralee was a different kettle of
fish. She was still a baby, but, let's face it, at five years old
Shirley Temple was sexy. When you're hot you're hot.

Jack popped open a beer, offered juice to the girls. Judy
reached for his can to take a sip. Finally, he gave it to her—
"just one sip." She gulped it down until he grabbed it away
from her. There wasn't much left so he offered the rest to
Saralee—not because he was attracted to her in this weird,
useless way (at least he hoped not), but in the spirit of fair-
ness. He opened the cupboard to see if there was something
to eat—nothing but stale crackers. They wolfed them down
hungrily, then stretched out on the floor, ignoring him.

"Stanley is such an asshole. He ran his finger down my
back to see if I wore a bra, and then he said—"

"He did the same thing to me yesterday!"

"God, I have a crush on Robbie."

"*Yuck!* You know who I think is hot? Alex."

"I can't believe it. He's such a geek."

"He's not a geek. I think he's really cool."

"He is *so.* Did you hear what he did to Diane? They went
to *The Breakfast Club* together last weekend."

"*The Breakfast Club.* Oooh!"

"I'm gonna take dance lessons."

"What kind?"

"I'm not sure. Jazz maybe."

"I may start gymnastics. Or ballet. I don't know."

"Robbie plays tennis."

"He's not so great."

"Compared to Alex he is."

"Like . . . like . . . bullfuck!"

"What do you know?"

"I know that Diane made up that story to get Casey jealous."

"That's what Alex says, of course."

"It's *true*, Diane told me."

"You believe her, you believe anything. She's such a slut."

"Yeah, what do you know?"

"You'll never guess who she let feel her up at the party last week?"

"You believe that story? You are *so* dumb."

"What do you know?"

"What do *you* know?"

"I know that Robbie is hot and Alex is not!"

"Alex is alive and Robbie is jive!"

"Hey!"

"Hey!"

They gave each other the high five. On and on they went. Jack lay back, listened, abandoned any idea of further work. Nothing could be more peaceful than this. He wished it could be like this for the rest of his life, listening happily as kids chattered inanely around him, then ran off to live their lives as he quietly stood in the room and painted.

At seven-fifteen he looked at his watch. "*Shit.* I forgot about the time." He jumped up, started putting his brushes away, ordered the kids to put on their coats.

"I'll call Mommy," said Judy, picking up the phone.

"No!"

"Why not?" she asked in surprise.

"I don't know." Jack took the phone out of her hand and hung it up.

"You're really frightened of her, aren't you?"

"Don't be ridiculous."

"Just because she has more money. Boy!" She gave him a vicious squinty stare. As he was about to defend himself she lost interest, and began flipping through records. " 'Living in the material world,' " she started to sing.

" 'I'm a material girl.' " Saralee joined her and they finished the chorus together.

Jack covered his paints with plastic, grabbed his coat from where he had left it on an old chair. A lightness was in his heart that it seemed hadn't been there in weeks, months, years.

Lorraine opened the door. She dropped her black rubber briefcase on the floor. She draped her black leather bag (cleverly designed as if it were made of plastic) over a chair. She walked into the kitchen and opened the drink fridge. It provided the only light in the apartment, a square of warmth that bounced off the tile floor and walls of her kitchen like moonlight on water. Out the window, also, as if the Hudson were thousands of pieces of broken mirror, was moonlight. She took out a bottle of seltzer and yesterday's half-finished bottle of Chablis. Since Aurelia still hadn't gotten the man to come fix the icemaker in the drink fridge she opened the regular freezer to get ice, but the light in the freezer was off. When she pulled out the ice tray it sloshed on her. She jabbed at a cardboard package with her forefinger; her finger punched into the meat. "Fuck." She took out the round roast and lamb chops. Wet. Soft. "Double fuck." She started to unwrap the roast to sniff it, thought better of the idea, put it back. Tears of frustration poured out of her eyes.

Foggy from the tears, she uncorked the Chablis, filled most of a large wine glass with it, added a little seltzer, then headed to her bedroom. She took off her suit jacket and pants and by feel, in the dark, carefully hung them up. Her blouse she left draped over the hamper for Aurelia to take care of the next day. She slipped on an old Adrienne Vittadini shirt and Norma Kamali sweatpants (her own designer refused to make comfortable gemütlichkeit clothing) and returned to the living room. Glass in hand, she sat down on the couch, leaned her head back, and stared out the window at the sliver of moon, the night sky. As her eyes grew accustomed to the dark, she was able to see the last fading bits of orange and violet in it. Or perhaps she was only imagining this. Why had she gone to all this trouble to renovate her apartment if not to be home in time to catch the sunset? She kicked off her shoes. She put her feet on the table Jack insisted on leaving his paints on. The house was the way she liked it best, devoid of human life.

It was perfectly silent—no music, no TV, no two of three fridges. Even the fridge that was still functioning soon clicked off, as if it too had stopped breathing. In the loud quiet the phone rang, once, twice, three times. She did not bother to answer it. She lay down on the couch and from that angle New Jersey and the trees of the park were no longer visible, only the sky, as if she were on an airplane, a spaceship. This was her favorite fantasy. No worrying about the union, the banks, customers, Judy, Jack, David, her sex life, her apartment—just staring into a black rectangle whose pinpricks of light were clues to giant seething worlds, where pinpricks of blackness might themselves conceal universes so twisted and intense no knowledge of their secrets could escape.

Were Lorraine not congenitally oriented toward unhappiness, she could have been happy at this unexpected quiet. Instead she was angry—at Aurelia, for leaving early, at Jack, who was supposed to be making dinner, at Judy—where was she? So after gazing at the sky, after sitting in darkness on her couch, watching shadows the streetlight threw onto the walls of the room, she stood up and with surprising intensity banged her fist into the wall. She went into the kitchen to get ice, remembered just as she was opening the door of the freezer that it was broken, and kicked it with her foot. She took two more Tylenol for the headache she had had since that morning, walked back out to the living room, lay down on the couch, and stared out the window at the streetlight. Her misery was so complete she was almost happy.

By seven-thirty Lorraine was insane, pacing like an animal. She was a mother, a boss, a wife, a person who by definition was never alone. The huge dark squares of the windows were beginning to frighten her. What if men were lurking in the park, staring into her windows, undressing her in their heads, divining the secrets of her mind from the way she walked, lit the cigarettes she pretended she didn't really smoke ("just

one or two a day, with my coffee"). She took refuge in the
kitchen, a room that had no window on the street. She turned
on the recessed ceiling lights, then the lights above the sinks
and stove and counters: twenty-seven bulbs in all, a huge
expenditure of electricity. Her hand (the one that she had
banged into the wall) hurt. Her foot (the one she had kicked
at the fridge) hurt. Her head (that thought these unpleasant
thoughts) hurt. She poured more wine. Thus fortified, she felt
able to leave the kitchen. She went into her bathroom and
aimed the shower nozzle at the whirlpool so she could calm
down in a bath. While she waited for the tub to fill (as much
as it was able to) she flung open the closet and pushed the
hangers on which her shirts and suits and skirts and jackets
hung back and forth. Worth thousands in retail, they looked
like junk. The second she got some money she'd get the
bathroom fixed. The second she got money she'd fire Aurelia
and hire a nice Swedish girl—oh no, Jack liked blondes. She
called up her friend Sally. NA. Caroline's number was busy.
Ellie's phone machine answered. Lorraine felt intimidated by
the over-enthusiastic message and hung up without saying
anything. She didn't want her weak, scared voice on that
machine. She's afraid, if she left her name, maybe Ellie
wouldn't return her call, and she'd never get to speak to her
again. It was possible they were no longer friends; she hasn't
seen her in over a year—and still she called her her best
friend. If she had left only her first name, would Ellie even
know who it was? Since she's started her business she's had
no time for leisure. Jack was almost the only person—other
than Marianne, employees, contractors, and other people associated with her business—with whom she talked. She no
longer was invited to dinner parties or to visit friends' country houses; she didn't meet people for drinks after work, or
buy presents for their children, or have them buy presents for
Judy. She no longer knew what a vacation was. Her hair was
almost entirely gray; every six weeks she paid somebody at
Bendel's $75 to color it, strand by strand. Oddly, Jack never
mentioned this, though he must notice her roots. Sometimes,
at night, if they're lying there not having sex, Lorraine can't
stop her mind from thinking: he's looking at my hair, he's

thinking I'm an old bag, he hates me. In her mind she replies: he's a lazy bum, a gigolo, he's using me for my money, he's immature, a mooch, a bad influence for Judy.

Lorraine knew these were simply stories in her head. But she would like to ask Jack about them—if only she could be sure he would tell her the truth, and that the truth would be something she wanted to hear.

Sometimes she thought it was a miracle he was here with her; the rest of the time she thought it was a miracle she hasn't already thrown him out.

It was so quiet she could hear the clock on the wall, the watch on her hand. The only interruption of this was the sink dripping—a broken washer Jack could fix in thirty seconds, if he so chose.

Finally, she caved in. She turned on the lights in her bedroom and bathroom, in the dining room, the two living rooms, Judy's bedroom and bathroom, even the maid's room. She walked back and forth looking at the rooms. They seemed strange to her, unfamiliar, menacing, filled with glare and shadows, like a movie from the '40s. She forced herself to resist the temptation to open closets to make sure strangers weren't lurking there, or to check under beds or inside Judy's or the maid's room bathtub. She turned on the kitchen radio, the living room tube, her TV, Judy's stereo. As the cacophony increased her irritation rose, but her anxiety level dropped. She gave catnip to Jezebel. She threw a plastic bone to Jack but he wasn't interested. As a bribe (for what, she wasn't quite sure) she gave him a cowhide chewy. He crawled under the bed to eat it.

In front of the mirror Judy had knocked a chunk off of while demonstrating somersaults to Lorraine, Lorraine tried to dance. Her movements looked spastic and unfamiliar. She realized she was doing the twist—a dance from more than two decades ago. In a few seconds she had to stop; there was a stitch in her side. She lay down on the bed and picked up a novel that she had been told was very interesting. The first paragraph was long—almost the length of the page—and despite her intentions her mind wandered before she managed to finish it. She flipped through the book, picking out sentences here and there, then turned to the last page. There were a few lines of dialogue and a short narrative paragraph that she managed quite nicely. No need to read the book now; she "got" it, whatever there was to "get." She listened to the noises Jack the dog made as he ate—the basic slurping, sucking noise as he rattled the cowhide around in his mouth, crackings of his teeth when he tried to bite into it. She got out of bed and went down on her knees in an attempt to coax Jack out from under the bed. He was contented and didn't want to move. She patted the bed. "Come on, Jack, you can sit on the bed"—a special treat—only he didn't understand, he thought she was hitting the bed out of anger, and slunk farther out of reach. She walked into the bathroom but the whirlpool had only gotten a few inches of water. She thought about whether she should sacrifice the time it took her, in her post-hemorrhoid era, to take a shit. She tried, got bored halfway through, and got up. She walked out into the living room. Any moment Jack or Judy could walk through the door; constantly she yelled at them about noise, TV, lights. She sat down by the window above the building's entrance, so she could look out for them. Soon, a man and a young girl could be seen getting out of a Checker cab. They were laughing. They looked happy and guilty, like adulterous lovers returning to their dull, normal life—the one in which they pretended to fight constantly with each other. It was Jack and Judy. What could they be laughing at but her? Lorraine ran quickly from room to room, turning off the radios and TVs, all the lights except the one in the dining room. She dumped the contents of her briefcase onto the dining-room table, took out her glasses, placed them over her eyes, picked up her black automatic Japanese pencil. By the time they entered the darkened apartment, she was deeply immersed in her work.

The quiet of the apartment wiped the smile off Jack and Judy's faces even before they opened the door. Inside everything was just as they had pictured it—Lorraine sitting with her papers in a silent, dark, apartment. Jack sighed. Life went

on everywhere but here. Judy extended her arms even as the
door was still closing behind her so that her jacket would
slide off her arms via the force of gravity without her having
to further exert herself. She left the jacket on the floor and
punched the dimmers so that lights in the main area of the
apartment flashed on and off in random patterns. She ran into
the living room to turn on the tube. Usually this instanta-
neous media blitz annoyed Jack, but for once he's on her side.
Grateful. Who's got the life around here, the pizazz?

He went into the dining room. Lorraine kept on working
as if she hadn't noticed him.

"Aren't you going to say hello?" he asked, sitting down
across from her.

"Have a nice day with my daughter?" she asked, head
down.

"Yeah. I was at my old place when she stopped by."

"Very cozy, very friendly," Lorraine said sarcastically.
"How was Murray?"

Jack shrugged. "Okay."

"Murray hurry furry worry," sang Judy to the tune of an ad
jingle that was on the tube.

"Jack," said Lorraine, finally putting down her pencil,
"why is she acting like she's stoned?"

"Maybe *she* is, you'll never know," Judy giggled.

"I'll know all right."

"What you don't know could fill a . . . a . . . a rhinoceros."
Judy giggled and went into her room. Lorraine sighed. It was
going to be one of those nights. She pulled herself up. She
turned off the living room TV, then walked to Judy's door
and pushed it open. "I'm not in the mood for talking to you,"
said Judy.

"I'm not in the mood for your moods," said Lorraine.

"Moo, moo," said Judy, "I'm a cow." Lorraine left the
room.

"Just exactly what have you been doing with my daughter?" Lorraine asked Jack, who was chewing a Pepperidge
Farm cappuccino cookie in the kitchen.

"What do you mean?"

"I don't know. She's acting weird."

"Sometimes she *is* pretty weird," agreed Jack.

Judy, who had come out of her bedroom to get a Coke, stared at them. "Mother, leave him alone, you're such a pill."

"*I'm* a pill? Since when do thirteen-year-olds go wandering around the East Village?"

"I'm a grown-up, Mother, for God's sake."

"Really? Since when?"

"For a *while*. Maybe if you thought about something other than work or *Jack* you'd notice."

"You haven't even gotten your period."

"Says who?" They eyeballed each other. The water dripped.

"I don't believe it."

"Well I *did*. So *there*."

"When?"

"A while ago. You said not to bother you with *unimportant* stuff."

Lorraine considered the possibility a moment, then rejected it. "I don't believe it. You would have told me."

"Oh yeah? I'll show you the blood."

"I haven't seen any Kotex in your bathroom."

"I don't use Kotex."

"What do you use then?"

"Well, I *almost* have my period. Saralee does. And Elissa. And Karen. Everybody except me."

Tears sprang to her eyes. She ran into her bedroom, slammed the door. Lorraine sighed, heaved herself off the kitchen stool, followed her back into her room and put her arms around her. "Darling, don't be upset. I got my period late too. I was almost fourteen."

"Fourteen! Jesus! Everybody else'll be married."

"I really don't think girls at Columbia Prep run off to be married when they're fourteen years old, do you?" She turned off the radio, then pushed her hand over Judy's brow, rubbing back her hair. Not that, in recent months, there was much to rub back; it mostly stood up in a long spiky pattern faintly reminiscent of Don Johnson's.

"I don't know. Maybe. Everything changes. Everybody's got a boyfriend, except me."

"Really? I didn't know that. Does Saralee have a boy-friend?"

"Oh, I don't know, Mother, leave me alone." Judy rolled over on the bed, hid her face in the pillow. "Turn on the radio please? I can't stand the silence. No wonder you're crazy."

"Judy. What's the matter? I know something's the matter."

"No, there's not," Judy sobbed.

Lorraine turned her over. "Come on. You can tell me."

Judy snuffled. "Only if you promise you won't get angry."

"That depends."

"I knew it. Forget it." She rolled away.

Lorraine sighed. "All right."

"Swear?"

"I promise. Not to get angry."

"Cross your heart and hope to die?"

Lorraine held up two fingers in a Cub Scouts salute. "Okay. Break it to me gently."

Judy took a deep breath. "Me and Saralee met these guys today, and we went to their house and made out with them."

"Saralee and I," said Lorraine. The grammatical correction was lost on Judy. " 'Made out' with them?"

"Yeah, you know Mother. *Frenched.* This guy put his hand on my leg. But . . . I made him stop." Although this wasn't exactly the way it had happened, she felt, in a deeper sense, it was true.

"Did you enjoy it?"

Judy shrugged. "It was okay, I guess, except when he put his tongue in my mouth." For a moment she grew pensive, then said, "Say Mom, can we buy *Back to the Future!* It's my favorite movie ever!"

On the whole, Lorraine felt relief. At almost the same age, in a less promiscuous time, she had gone further. "That's okay, sweetie. Don't be upset. I think you're a little too young. Maybe . . . "

"Mother, don't be such a bore! You don't understand any-thing. I knew I shouldn't've told you!" Judy sat up, jumped out of bed, went into the living room, turned on the TV, then sat down at the computer next to it and started playing Pac-Man.

Watching her, Lorraine realized Judy was not a human being in the traditional sense of the word. Nonetheless, she was her daughter, so she put her arms around her.

"Mother. *Pul-lease*," said Judy, pushing her away with the hand she wasn't playing Pac-Man with.

"Judy. I want to talk to you."

"*God.*" She slammed the joystick to the floor.

Lorraine sighed. Why was nothing easy? "Look, sweetie, what do you say we go out for dinner tomorrow night—just the two of us. Would you like that, to spend an evening with your old mom?"

"Without Jack?"

"Without Jack."

"What's the point?" For a second, Jack felt flattered.

"So we can get to know each other. I haven't been alone with you in such a long time."

"Why don't we go to the movies instead?"

"You can go to the movies with anybody. I want to spend time with you."

"We can spend time together on the way to the movie."

"I'll tell you what. We'll have dinner together, and *afterwards* we can go to the movie."

"Let's go to the movie first, and then have dinner."

"No, Judy."

"Why not? What's the difference?"

"I want you when you're fresh and don't have idiotic stimuli filling your head." Judy rolled her eyes. "Frankly, I think it's very insulting, that you'd rather go to a movie than have dinner with your mother."

"It's just, you're so *boring*, Mother. You don't talk about anything except stuff you don't like about me or Jack, or you complain because you don't have more money."

This was the closest Lorraine had ever come to understanding the way her child felt about her. It wasn't pleasant, but it was . . . interesting. She had been bored all throughout childhood, but it had never occurred to her to complain about it. "Thanks for *sharing* that with me, Judy," she forced herself to say. "We can discuss your opinion of me more tomorrow."

"If you're so interested in talking, why don't we talk now?"

said Judy. She turned off the computer, the stereo, the TV. Considering she always went to sleep with the Sleep button of her radio on, it was probably the least noise she'd heard while awake in years.

The room's quiet made Lorraine feel self-conscious, as if she were on a date. She stared at her daughter, who had lived inside her body for nine months, had her genes. Perforce, there was much they had in common. All she had to do was find the subject.

As he lay in bed that night Jack saw a light flicker in the empty building across the way, as if a match had been struck, or a lighter lit. Again he wondered who was living there, and why. He felt so easily it could be him instead of someone else. Everything that occurred in his life seemed to be an accident. Especially living with Lorraine. What was he to her, or she to him?

In his anxiety he began to sweat. He felt angry that Lorraine could so easily fall asleep and, in the pretext of turning over, half-intentionally kicked her. She turned toward him, crawled into his arms, and began to snore.

12

Cecilia ordered Michael which boxes to carry out to the U-Haul. David, working his way through a six-pack, alternated between watching Michael and watching the game on his tiny two-inch diagonal TV.

"You could help, you know," Cecilia, wrapping plates in newspapers, told him.

"Sure," said David. "Maybe you'd like to take my clothing too." Although Michael has plates, she won't leave any of hers for him. Until now, David had never realized what a bitch she was. Not that this realization totally disturbed him; on the contrary, it will help metamorphose her into a being he could not possibly have any desire of knowing. In the metaphysical (or perhaps the epistemological) sense, however, it was confusing. If he did not know her now, could it be said that he had ever really known her? If he had not known her, could it be said that he had ever truly known Lorraine? Had he ever in his life known anyone?

Cecilia crunched her lips and twisted her nose; her hair was straggling out from the ponytail she had tied it in for moving. She looked like a skinny, ugly insect. Repulsion rose up in David. She was so skinny, almost like a skeleton. She had never really enjoyed food; she couldn't tell good wine from bad. He wondered how he could ever have desired to sleep with her. When you looked at women closely, for what they were rather than what you desired them to be, so often they turned out to be disgusting.

"I feel weird about taking the bed," said Cecilia.

"Then leave it."

"I warned you. Come Saturday my stuff was gone."

"It's fine, Cecilia. I don't give a shit."

"Just cause your life is falling apart, don't take it out on me."

"Who said my life was falling apart?"

Depressed, David sank to the floor. The exercise mat on which he would now have to sleep was only a few feet away, but he was too lazy to roll onto it. He felt the floor only in certain places—back of his head, upper back, coccyx, heels. Knives flashed as Cecilia carefully packed them; he imagined lifting one and plunging it into her thin stomach. Carefully she wrapped a ceramic soap dish she had bought in a store that specialized in household items from the '50s.

"Here, I'll do that," said David. He stumbled to his feet, reached his hand out for the soap dish. Surprised, Cecilia handed it to him. He had intended to drop it accidentally on the floor, but, somehow, cowed by Michael, he wrapped it neatly enough, handed it back.

"I thought you hated that soap dish," said Cecilia.

"I do. It's only your generation that can think of the 'fifties with pleasure. I guess it's kind of like World War Two was for us." She looked at him as if he were crazy. "If you live through it, it's just life. But if you don't, it's interesting and exciting." It was impossible to tell whether she was listening. It was as if he had already ceased to exist for her. He felt like a dog, trying to perform tricks for her. She carefully packaged some Fiesta ware she had found in another shop. Although valuable, the memories they carried of the past depressed David, and he was glad to see them gone. Also, the idea of using used stuff, during the current Plague, despite Comet, Lysol, Clorox, was disturbing. Whenever he drank from a cup he had held it slightly over his lips, so that the liquid would pour into his throat without his having to touch his lips to the rim.

Cecilia began taking David's clothes off the wood hangers and piling them on a chair. She threw the hangers into a box. "I warned you," she said apologetically.

"I know."

"Don't look at me like that."

"Like what?"

"*You* know. You know, if you're not going back to Lorraine, you really should get some furniture."

" 'Going back to Lorraine,' " David echoed in confusion.

"Yeah, I always thought you guys were so good together."

"You did?"

"Conran's is great if you don't want to spend too much money." Then, because the chair was also going, she carried his suits to the bathroom and dumped them on the toilet seat. Like a dog, Michael followed her from room to room as she opened closets and kitchen cabinets to make sure nothing was left behind.

"Why are you following her?" David asked him.

"Don't answer him. Let's just leave," said Cecilia.

"You are a *dog*," David told Michael. "A *dog*."

Michael looked at Cecilia, cracked his knuckles. David sat down on the floor and began doing sit-ups. Cecilia opened her pocketbook to take out the keys. "Goodbye, David," she said. "Have a nice life."

Tears, unexpected, sprang to his eyes; any second they could bubble over his lower eyelids. To explain them, he said: "I miss my apartment. I miss my furniture. I miss my little girl." These things were not untrue, but the reason he was saying them at this moment was so Cecilia and Michael wouldn't pity him for Cecilia's having left him, so there was something false and misleading about it. Not that he *wouldn't* miss his little girl—even if his little girl had turned into a thirteen-year-old-bitch.

"I know how you feel," Michael said. Moved and embarrassed, he kneaded a fist into a palm as if he were imitating Marlon Brando at his most Method-y. "After Marnie went back to her husband, I missed Cecilia so much." He clenched and unclenched his fist. "I used to lie in bed and dream of killing you. I was gonna hire somebody to bash your kneecaps. Of course I wouldn't've. But even if I would've, I wouldn't've, cause I knew I deserved it. I was the one who started this thing with Marnie. Then I told myself, if Cecilia's happier with you, *really happier*, then I should be happy too."

"Were you?"

"No. Of course not."

"It's odd," replied David. "The way you felt about me is kind of the way I feel about Jack. I almost like him. He's such a little putz." As he spoke he imitated Michael's hand-clenching, in a way he wasn't sure was (or was not) humorous "quoting." Was it experience, fatigue, or sophistication that had turned all expressions of emotion into parody, or was it merely the movies?

"When I couldn't sleep I'd think, Are they making it now? And I'd try to tell myself, No, he's an alkie, he can't get it up. And then I'd think, That's stupid, of course they're making it, people who live together fuck," said Michael.

"Sometimes, sure, I have trouble. But who doesn't? It's got nothing to do with age. Look, I'm actually very grateful to you. I probably would never have left her, though I thought about it all the time. We had nothing in common, you know, even our taste in restaurants. I'm French and Italian nouvelle, whereas she's more . . . Cajun. So you saved me, both of you. And I thank you for it. And in honor of this I offer you . . . my very special old . . . old in honor of me . . . what's the word?—V.S.O.P. Hennessy's." He went to the kitchen, opened a cabinet. "I would, at least, if Cecilia had left me any glasses."

"Da-vid—" whined Cecilia. David pulled out the cork, took a swig from the bottle, then offered it to Cecilia, who declined, and Michael, who accepted. Then Cecilia changed her mind and joined the party.

"A toast," said David, when the bottle had come back to him. "First I toast to the end of our relationship." He nodded at Cecilia, then swallowed. "Then I toast to the beginning of my next relationship, with whomever it may be. Woman, girl, boy, horse." He took another swallow. "Lastly, I toast to the end of this next relationship."

"What David's really into is cheating. Everything was fine till Lorraine threw him out. Then he got depressed. It took all the fun out of it."

"Could be," David admitted. "You never know."

"You never do," said Cecilia. For a while David and Michael sat there in silence, waiting, each in a different way, for Cecilia to say the thing that would sum up the situation so that they would not have to think about it again in any serious way for the rest of their lives. Through the cardboard walls, in the next apartment, you could hear a door slam, then the faint beginnings of an argument. Cecilia yawned, brushed her hair out of her eyes, stood up.

"Well, David," she said. "I guess this is it." David and Michael stood up too. She reached out her hand to David. "I'll sure miss . . . your car." Then she kissed him on the cheek.

"So it's okay about the apartment?" David asked, not for the first time.

"Yes, David," Cecilia said, in an exaggeratedly patient tone, as to a not-very-bright child.

"If you don't want to bother each month about the checks, I could give you a bunch of postdated ones right now."

"Either way. Well, maybe you should give them to me. Then I can send them on to Margaret and be done with it."

"Margaret?"

"The person I'm subletting this apartment from."

"Subletting this apartment from!"

"Didn't I tell you?"

"No. You didn't." He couldn't believe it.

"Sorry, David, it must of slipped my mind."

"Slipped your mind! What are you talking about? I thought this place was *mine!*"

"Don't look at me like that! There's nothing to worry about. She hates New York, she's got this great job in Denver, she wouldn't move back for a million bucks!"

Dazed, David wrote out six checks and handed them to Cecilia. Michael extended his hand, and David shook it. It would have been symmetrical for him to kiss Cecilia at this point, but he had already done so, and he was also angry about Margaret. He walked them to the door, then stood by it as they waited for the elevator. At first they continued to make conversation with him, then, as the wait got longer, they gave up and talked softly to each other, occasionally glancing at him out of the corners of their eyes. They looked young, innocent. David felt overwhelmed by pathos, like the end of a bad movie. If he had had a million dollars he would have given it to them, just so he wouldn't have to imagine what life would be like for them when they got old. As they waited for the elevator, again he saw them through a magnifying glass of salinated H_2O—aka tears. He listened to the door shut after they got in, the clanky hum as it moved down, away, out of his life.

He went back into his apartment—Margaret's apartment. There was a footprint in the dust on the parquet floor. You could see where the furniture had been by the little squares of dust. Evidently Cecilia had never dusted under the couch. Of course, neither had he. He went to the broom closet but even the brooms and dustpans were gone. Fatigue hit him like a grand mal attack. He collapsed onto the floor. His eyes closed with a sigh. As he slept the city surrounded him with its millions of stories, some real, some made up. He dreamt he lived in a penthouse that looked out on the gray stone turrets and towers of a medieval city: castles with names like Tiffany, Dakota, Chrysler, Empire, each surrounded by its human and mechanical and electronic moats—doormen and elevators and locks and video intercoms—to fend off the barbarians outside. But eventually the barbarians will come. They always do; was not time on their side? Meanwhile the castles were aglow, with plain and colored incandescent bulbs, with fluorescent and Luminaire fixtures, with halogen and par-38 and low-voltage lighting, with the glowing red LEDs of stereo and phone machines, the blue of old black-and-white TVs, the green of envy. Inside each room was a rich and beautiful princess: virgins, each and every one of them in love with him. It was unnecessary to talk to them; intuitively they recognized his desires and serviced him to his complete satisfaction. His wife not only did not resent but encouraged this. She was blonde and beautiful and reminded him of Martina Navratilova's new girlfriend. In her hands were slippers. She handed them to him with a cocktail as he sank into the cushions on his couch. His apartment had so many rooms he couldn't remember all their names. Sunlight fell on wood floors so highly polished you could see the movements of your body in it as you had sex. The city was beautiful and empty, like the face of a model, the streets with hardly any cars, the way Moscow was to this day. It was safe. People went to visit other people, even at night; they didn't stay home to watch TV or their laser disks. But they were crazy about movie theaters and paid to sit in them several times a week. Popcorn was practically free and was covered with butter, not palm oil. There were no lines, and you could walk home at any hour without danger. Even the subways were safe, clean, and inexpensive. There was a war on but it was far away: far away and glorious. Everybody was happy fighting in it and reading about it; they listened to the news for hours. His ears grew like rabbit antennas. Soon he was able to hear the hum of electricity in a quiet room: it was the sound of the room breathing.

The phone rang. "Who is it?" David yawned. His back hurt and the sky was black.

"Realtor. I found a place for you. One bedroom eight ninety-five, a little terrace. . . ."

"No longer necessary. Turns out I can stay where I am. At least for a while."

"Something the matter, buddy? You don't sound so chipper."

"Problems with my partners. And then . . ." Tears sprang to David's eyes, not because he was so unhappy about Cecilia, but because there was only one person on earth he could tell this story to with any sympathy, and here he was, on the other end of the line, a stranger.

"My girlfriend split. Went back to her old boyfriend. Took everything except the toilet paper holder."

"That's too bad. Or is it? Look, you want to sell me those insider rights, you still can."

"I'll think about it," said David

"Up to you," said the realtor. "Say, why dontcha come on over? We'll have some chow, maybe call up Lydia . . ."

"Lydia?"

"You know. The chick we met that night."

"Maybe. All right." David yawned. "I was having this great dream about the future. A very spacey New York, lots of large, inexpensive apartments. Not much traffic."

"Sounds like before double-U double-U Two," said the realtor. "But it's your dream, you oughta know."

David stood up, yawned, tottered into the bathroom. With relief he noted the medicine cabinet and shower curtain still in place. He turned on the shower and crawled in with his clothing on. He stepped out of his clothing, leaving it on the floor of the shower, and reached for the soap.

No soap.

No razor. Cecilia took that, too, by mistake, in the spirit of obsessive vindictiveness as she was emptying out the medicine cabinet.

David dried himself with some Bounty towels, draped the Walkman over his ears, picked out something from the pile of clothing on the floor to wear. Whistling in the same carefree way as when he used to go on dates, he got dressed and ready to roll. World War Two, he thought, on the way to the realtor's. He doesn't so much remember it as know it secondhand from the stories his mother told him, and the movies.

He thought of buying flowers, picked up vodka instead.

13

In front of Lydia's building, David switched off the motor. The silence was overwhelming. He had no idea why the realtor had invited him along, but the strange passivity that had taken hold of him lately seemed to be carrying him places he could not reach by conscious intention. He worried about having his car stolen but decided not to mention it for fear of not looking cool—or whatever word denoted "cool" these days.

He smelled cabbage, urine (dog, cat, or human, he couldn't tell), rotting food that must have spilled out of wet brown paper bags being carried down to the street (older people used plastic garbage bags only when they got them free from the supermarket), behind which specific odors was the common smell endemic to old brownstones: a generalized mustiness that arose from either the building itself (too many years of cooking odors emanating into the same hallways), or perhaps the inhabitants: despair, the consciousness of age, infirmity, unrealized dreams. The three flights bothered him; he wondered how old people managed to do it. Thank God he belonged to a gym and could climb them without stopping. He faked a little run near the top, to show he found it easy, but his heart was pounding as they entered what fifteen years ago would have been called Lydia's "pad." David was unsure what to call it now, though he had a suspicion "apartment" wouldn't do.

It was much nicer than David had anticipated on the way up. The floors had been sanded and stained; the walls were smooth (no paint peeling down like torn paper from walls and ceiling), painted in pale "blush" shades of pastels of varying hue but identical intensity and brightness; the furniture "consciously ironic" pieces from the '50s. Her sound system astonished him; there was equipment there he didn't even know what it did. She asked him and the realtor what they wanted to listen to. David strained to recall the names of rock groups Judy listened to, came up blank. Did he not know or was he too nervous to remember? For a long while he couldn't think of anything except "Michael Jackson"—only that was ages ago. Then "Madonna" floated into his brain.

"*Jesus*," said Lydia.

"What about some Bruce Springsteen?"

Lydia rolled her eyes.

"Actually, some of my friends just came out with a pretty good record. You want to hear it?"

"What's their moniker?" asked the realtor.

"The Rim Jobs. But they may change it. Because of AIDS."

All rock music has sounded the same to David for the past ten years. The realtor could differentiate normal records but he had trouble with what was called "art," or "downtown," rock, which was what Lydia was playing. He searched in his pocket for his security blanket. "You want to do some coke?" he asked.

"Sure," said David.

"Nah, I'm trying ta cool out," said Lydia.

The realtor took out his little glass bottle and placed it on the coffee table but, wanting to be on the same wavelength as Lydia, didn't do any. David, having just said he wanted to do some, felt obligated to do a few lines. He felt the realtor and Lydia were looking at him, criticizing the way he knocked the coke out of the little bottle and separated it into lines, or rolled a dollar bill to suck it up through his nostrils. When he was done he began to worry about whether there was powder visible on either the end of his nose or the hairs inside his nose. He would have liked to go to the bathroom to check this in the mirror but he was worried they would say horrible things about him behind his back. Or what if they were planning some sadistic trick on him? Now that he thought of it, he didn't even understand why he and the real-tor were friends: they didn't have anything in common—

except, of course, the fact that they lived alone, were middle-aged, and kind of on the prowl. Was that enough? But if the realtor were on the prowl, why had he invited David up here with him and Lydia? Unless that was Lydia's idea, and the realtor was odd man out. Or maybe the realtor had particular tastes, and had invited David up so that David could fuck Lydia while the realtor sat by the side of the bed and jerked off. The more David thought about it the murkier it got, and the more confused he became as to what—if anything—he was supposed to do. If he's supposed to come on to Lydia and doesn't, they'll think him a creep. But if he's not supposed to and does, they'll also think him a creep. Perhaps it was just in his mind that this thing was about sex. Probably the realtor was just being friendly; it was only David's sick mind that saw everything through a veil of innuendo and illusion. Did people ever *have* sex any more? The music wasn't sexy either, quite the reverse. Then the coke began to hit, and he decided that this lack of romanticism *was* the New Romanticism. It was the kind of remark Lorraine would have appreciated, but he didn't feel up to sharing it here.

"You don't do drugs any more?" David asked Lydia, mostly to reassure himself by the sound of his own voice.

"Not lately. I'm trying to get my life together. All my friends are in AA or NA or something. It really freaks me out."

"Because they're so fucked up?"

"Because they're so straight. They're all making a mint, and I still don't know what to do with my life."

"You want to come work in my office, I can arrange it," offered the realtor.

"Nah, I'm not into money. I mean, I'm into money, but I want to get it by selling my work. Not that I'm in a gallery or anything."

"That's a hard life," the realtor flattered her.

"Oh, I know. But actually, a lot of my friends make a lot of money out of it," she said, somewhat wistfully.

"But not you?"

"I don't have the business side of it together. I was doing nuclear war stuff ages ago, before it became popular, but I didn't show it in time. Now that's over. Then I started using cartoon figures, but I was too late, and now I'm doing cat paintings. Camels and polar bears were really big a few years ago, but would you believe, so far nobody's done cats? I'm just waiting till I have a few more done to take them around. They're really good. I can show them to you if you want."

"Sure," said David and the realtor simultaneously, but nobody moved.

Lydia yawned and leaned her head back against the couch. "It's kind of hard to stay awake without drugs, isn't it?"

"Sometimes. What did you used to do?"

"The usual. Coke, heroin, uppers, downers. You know, everything but pot. It weirds me out."

"Really? I still like it," said David. "I always carry some with me, just in case." For some reason he felt he sounded like a liar, so he pulled out a little silver cigarette case and opened it. Inside it were five neatly rolled joints. He had started buying marijuana again when he first started seeing Cecilia—kind of to show her how hip he was—only it turned out she and her friends had long ago stopped using the stuff.

"Regular supermarket, huh? Go ahead."

"Sure you don't want any?"

"Yeah. It makes me paranoid and self-conscious."

David lit a joint, took a hit, offered it by habit to Lydia, who waved it away, then to the realtor. Ditto. David took a few more hits, then put it down. He didn't know why he had mentioned it; smoking made him paranoid and self-conscious too. Some part of him was still back in the '60s or early '70s, when marijuana was the "in" drug, and not passé, as it was now. Of course then he'd been into liquor. Would there ever be a time he'd be in sync? Again he felt sorry that he had come upstairs, and wondered how long he should wait before leaving. Lydia did nothing to help the conversation. She leaned back with her eyes shut, presumably listening to the music.

"What do you like to do?" asked the realtor.

"Right now? Nothing, I told you," said Lydia.

"No, I mean in bed." Rather than try to disguise the embarrassing aspect of what he was saying, he emphasized it.

David admired the realtor's nerve, but thought it a dumb thing to do. Lydia blushed. But the realtor asked the question, not so much to find out what she liked, but because experience had taught him that the question was a turn-on for a lot of women.

"Oh. You know . . . ."

She shut her eyes, not looking at either of them. A weird passivity floated out. It could just be fatigue, or laziness. But maybe not, the realtor decided.

"You got any vodka?" he asked.

Lydia went to the kitchen and returned with a bottle of Stolichnaya, several glasses, and a glass bowl with ice cubes in it. Inspired by the drugs, David got entranced by the ice in the bowl. He experienced Lydia from the inside as a visually oriented person, one who has thought about the proper way to display things such as ice cubes. Not that he had previously consciously thought of her as being a liar in regards to her claim of being an artist, but unconsciously he had.

"You fixed this place up pretty nice," David complimented her. After he spoke he heard the surprise in his voice, but luckily Lydia didn't seem to notice this.

"Yeah." She drank a little vodka. "Actually it was my old boyfriend who did it. The walls and floors were a mess when I moved in. When he got it through his thick skull I wasn't going to live with him he began working on it so he could stand it when he slept over. He's very fastidious. He refinished everything, even the doorknobs."

"He must have liked you pretty well," said the realtor.

"Oh yeah. He's crazy about me. Still is. Sometimes I think he's just crazy." Pause. "He really makes me nervous."

"Why?"

"I don't know. He likes me too much. That's always kind of creepy, don't you think?"

Lydia turned toward the realtor and leaned back, her lips slightly open, as if she were trying to imitate Marilyn Monroe. If he were younger, her mention of her former boyfriend might have disturbed his ego, interfered with the possibility of sex, but at his age he was happy to use anything he could. "You don't have to worry about that with me," he said.

They sat quietly for a while, then the realtor suddenly stood up. "Come on," he said, extending her his hand.

"Huh?" Lydia said.

"Come on, babes, let's go to it, we don't got all night you know. Scuse us, David. You can hang out if you wish."

"What are you talking about?" she asked.

"You know. Why we got together tonight. Let's hit it."

"You got to be crazy. I'm not gonna make love to you. I don't know you from Adam."

"Don't worry. I've got condoms. Where's the bedroom?"

"Kristina's gonna walk in and—"

"Come on. I'm too old for this kind of game." For a moment David wondered if the realtor was going to try to rape her and, if he tried, what he would do. What he *should* do.

"What if I don't want to?" asked Lydia.

"What if you're a liar?"

"What if I'm not?"

"We'll see."

"What do you mean?"

The realtor considered picking her up and carrying her into the bedroom. But it was maybe a little too self-consciously romantic, in a '40s kind of way, plus it could fuck up his back. So he stuck out his hand and said: "Like I said, *we'll see.*" But the words sounded a bit off, too "Dragnet"-y. To wipe them from memory he decided to risk his back. He bent down, picked her up, carried her to the bedroom, and lay down on top of her. Usually he tried to keep his weight off his women with his elbows, but now he pressed down.

"You're hurting me," she told him.

"Tough." He took her hands, put them over her head, held them down.

"Come *on,*" she whined.

To do what she wanted while not appearing to do so he turned on his side so his pants could be removed. He unbuckled his belt. The open end with the holes dangled like some weird two-dimensional dick. He waited for her to unbutton and unzip them. Then he raised himself up so she could pull them down past his knees. She tugged off his shoes. At this point it was no longer sexy so he took over, kicked off his pants and socks. She was about to take off her skirt when he stopped her, pushed up her skirt, and got on top of her. He reached for the box of condoms in his pants pocket, ripped open the little gold package with his teeth, and slipped one on. It was difficult to get his penis in, partially because the skirt acted as a bondage element around her legs, and partly because he had difficulty maintaining his erection. He kept having to jerk at himself. Lydia squirmed as if to get away, but he continued to hold her down.

"Stop it," she said. "You're acting weird. What about David?"

"What *about* David? You want company?"

"I don't know."

"Hey David, come join the party," the realtor called.

David heard them call him, but he couldn't believe it. "David, oh David," the realtor repeated in a musical voice. Meanwhile he had slipped out. David took the glass of vodka and walked down the hall to the bedroom. He felt like he was in a movie. Lydia lay there half-dressed, her skirt pushed up near her thighs, her blouse open and messed up, like the photographs they stick outside porno theaters. Unwillingly, he also saw the realtor's hairy belly, his semi-flaccid cock with the tip of the condom hanging down. It was disgusting, but, somehow, not quite as disgusting as he would have thought he would have thought.

"Come on, have a seat." The realtor patted the bed.

"Well, just for a moment. Having a good time?" David didn't know what to say.

"It's no fun sitting out there all alone, is it?" the realtor asked.

David shrugged. "It's okay." He finished his glass, put it on the floor. As he straightened up he saw the realtor put his hand under Lydia's skirt. In his head he pretended something else entirely was going on. He couldn't really believe they'd invite him in of their own free accord. "I should leave," said David, as he stood up.

"Something wrong with her body?" asked the realtor.

"No."

"So look at her." David looked at her. "Sit down." He sat

down. The middle part of her body undulated so that her breast seemed to follow the realtor's hand. For her size it was surprisingly large. "I thought you told me you were horny and lonely," said the realtor.

"Yeah," David admitted grudgingly, "in a way."

" 'In a way' ? " The realtor hooted, stuck out his hand to touch David's cock through his pants. David jumped. "Does that seem 'in a way' to you?" the realtor asked Lydia.

Lydia touched it also, then she unzipped David's pants. He sat there like a statue, breathing as shallowly as he could, afraid that this would end if he made his presence any more visible than it was. "A *big* way," she giggled.

"Come on. Get undressed," the realtor said. "We don't got all night."

David blushed. Why *didn't* they have all night? Too embarrassed to say he was embarrassed, he took off his shoes, his pants, his tie.

"He's embarrassed," said Lydia. "Me too."

"Fuck," said the realtor, entering her again. "You like it."

"I'm horny, that's all. People don't have sex any more. Maybe it would be better if both of you would go." But she started moving with him.

"The younger generation," the realtor sneered. He kissed her. "They don't know what they want."

"You sure?" David asked.

"*Bullfuck.* She loves it. Can't you see?"

The realtor pulled out and told David to come up behind her. He handed him the package of condoms. But for some reason David wasn't as hard as he'd been when they'd touched him a few minutes before. It was confusing to have a long-term fantasy realized—almost disappointing. Perhaps it was just the condoms. In his mind they were still associated with prostitutes. Lydia tried to move, but the realtor held her hands down to remind her she couldn't get away. Finally David, half-hard, rolled off. What he would have really liked to do was kiss her, suck her breasts, fall asleep. He thought of Cecilia, Lorraine, frat parties of the distant past. In a weird way the fact that the girls were so drunk back then that they didn't know what was happening made the whole thing more bearable. Now Lydia was as sober as he was. More so. He couldn't decide which was better or worse. He joined in a little, more than happy to get the realtor's "drippings," too embarrassed to even aspire to "center stage." Really, it was what he liked to do best, look on from the side.

Except, of course, he was lying. He didn't trust his impulses—even the seemingly benign ones. Underneath the desire to leave no doubt was the impulse to stay—vaster and sicker than the realtor's. David didn't want to know any more about this. He rolled away to the side of the bed.

"You got any more coke?" Lydia asked.

"I thought you didn't like it."

"Not for me, silly. *You.*"

"Me!" For some reason he was astonished. "Why?"

She looked at him strangely. "Cause I want you to have a good time."

The thoughtfulness overwhelmed him. "You do? *Why?*"

She looked at him as if he were crazy. "Cause I like you."

"You do?"

"Oh course. Why do you think you're here?"

"I don't know. I thought maybe he paid you or something."

Lydia looked at him oddly, as if she were going to get angry, then she began to laugh. The realtor joined her. "Listen to this guy," the realtor said hysterically. "What a *putz.* You forget how to have a good time, David?"

"I guess so." They looked at him as if he were a being from another world. "Sit on his face," the realtor commanded Lydia. She pushed David down and did as commanded. "Open your mouth," she told him. Meanwhile the realtor removed David's condom and started to stroke his penis. The revulsion of it made David incredibly hard. He tried to push Lydia off, but she leaned forward, pressed down on him. He couldn't sit up to get enough leverage to push the realtor away. He had to maneuver his nose to get enough air to breathe.

After a final try, he relaxed, gave in. Telling himself none of this was his fault, he came in the realtor's hand. It was like coming with himself, only more so. In a haze, David drifted off: he was young, lying on pillows, relaxed in front of a warm, glowing fire.

He woke up when Lydia crawled off him and went to the bathroom. The realtor placed David's hand on his cock. "Now me," he said.

"Wha-a-a-t?" said David. He pulled his hand away.

"Come on." The realtor grabbed it and replaced it on his penis.

"I don't know what to do," said David. Again he pulled his hand away.

The realtor laughed. "Like you haven't been yanking on it all your life?" He put David's hand back on his penis and held it there. It was like touching himself except he couldn't feel anything, as if he had a shot of novocaine down there. To make it bearable he pretended it *was* himself, himself jerking himself off with a shot of novocaine in his penis so he couldn't feel anything. He shut his eyes tight until he saw purple and red dots. He was lying in the sun, in a race car, on a spaceship flying through the stars—anywhere but here. Then Lydia came back into the room. Guiltily David pulled his hand away, then blushed; the guilt would make it look like it was something he really had wanted to do. "I wasn't . . . " he began to say, then stopped. Excuses only made it worse. Again, Lydia laughed at him.

The sky was turning gray by the time they conked out. The realtor's tie was around Lydia's neck (he used it to pull her around with) as if she were strangled; her ass had a lot of tiny red marks on it; the next day they'd turn blue. David pulled the sheet up around her. He could smell the odors on his hand as he put his hand over his face to shield the light from his eyes—on her mouth, too, when he kissed her good night, with that strange soft moistness that comes from oral sex, a slight rubbery taste from the condom. Lydia breathed, waited awhile, breathed again, as if in slow motion. The realtor breathed loudly, halfway to a snore. David listened to this as long as he could stand it, then covered his head with a pillow to muffle the sound. He turned so his back faced the realtor. He was petrified the realtor would roll over and touch him.

Despite his fatigue, he couldn't quite sleep. He would have

left if he could have done it without anybody waking up, but he had an odd dread of being caught. What could he say, if they caught him creeping out? He dreaded being noticeable in any way. No longer being part of a couple somehow magnified his movements and slowed them down. His heart pounded as if he'd done a ton of coffee. He wondered if he'd have the heart attack here, in a smelly bed in a crummy part of town, with these weird people, instead of in a nice clean apartment uptown. He wondered why it would matter.

He felt like he'd been a good boy all his life—at least, no worse than anybody else. Yet where had it gotten him? Forty-six years old, he lived in a one-bedroom, without furniture or friends or dog or cat, as if he were just out of college. So inhibited, despite outward appearances, that on a night like this somehow he couldn't be sure whether or not he'd had a good time. In a way he wished he'd stayed home. He lay next to the wall—not the one in his head separating him from the feelings in his body, but the wall against which one side of the bed was propped. In the middle was the realtor. David tried to move, so that he could get to the other side of the bed, but whenever he did the realtor would start moving around, and David would stop, afraid to wake him up. He remembered a story Lorraine had told him, how once she was with a guy she hated, who lay on top of her all night long so she could hardly breathe, and yet she wouldn't push him off, because she didn't want him to wake up and have him start in all over again.

Finally, David began to get sleepy. A vague fantasy filled his mind, and he started playing with himself. Only at a certain point he realized it wasn't himself he was playing with. In his sleepiness the disgust didn't affect him as much. This was not real life, but a porno movie starring himself. None of it counted. And yet what could be more important? What were all the tedious days of his life about if not to support occasional nights like this?

An image filled his mind, one left over from his childhood. Slowly he inched himself down among the sheets, until the soft, warm, dark cave utterly surrounded him. It smelled like bears, as if sweaty, smelly animals were in there with him.

He felt like an infant with its mother. He opened his mouth and began to suck. He did not feel sexual so much as peaceful, as if all the sex acts of his life had been a substitute for this sucking: a breast, a bottle. . . . The word "AIDS" popped into his mind, but instead of getting a condom, he repeated it over and over in a singsong accompaniment to his sucking, until it had no more meaning than the clicking of a train wheel over the track.

A few hours later the realtor woke up. Immediately he began to talk, oblivious to the fact that Lydia and David were still sleeping. "That was super." He stood up and began to stretch. "Up and at 'em." He didn't seem the least bit repentant about waking everybody up, or self-conscious about his doing stretches and sit-ups in front of them. Lydia sat up bleary-eyed as she searched for slippers and robe, but surprisingly cheerful. "Yeah, it was fun," she said. David had expected her to be embarrassed, either hostile or clinging, but her tone was what she might have used about an exercise class. Chicks were certainly different from what they used to be, which was ironic; he was more like they used to be now than they were now like their former selves. (Of course, you weren't supposed to call them "chicks" any more.) His eyeballs ached, the vodka was killing his gut, he would have liked to lie there in bed all day. But it was not his home, and though he'd spent the night in the same bed as Lydia, he didn't feel in any way that she was his lover. She wasn't the realtor's lover either, but he acted as if she were, and by this action she would probably become so. David wondered why he couldn't act that way, so she would become his lover instead of the realtor's. He used to be able to, but somehow lately he had lost his nerve. He rolled over to the edge of the bed and swung his feet to the floor. Normally he did exercises in the morning too, but if he did them now it would look like he was copying the realtor. He stared out the window, opening and shutting his fists. Lydia went into the bathroom, swinging the door shut but not really closing it. He heard the toilet flush, the shower come on. A fog of warm moist air seeped out the narrow opening, moved across the hall, making it easier to breathe. It warmed David who, from the fatigue and drugs, was shivering. He wished he could be unselfconscious enough to jump in the shower with Lydia, but he felt shy, that it was somehow up to the realtor to initiate something like that. Not knowing what to do with himself, he wandered down the hall to the kitchen.

He looked for the kettle to make coffee, didn't find one, finally put water in a two-quart pot. Waiting for the water to boil he discovered the studio where Lydia painted. On the wall were large paintings of cats. They seemed awful, so he decided they must be good; Lorraine had always told him his taste in art stunk.

"Don't you want to take a shower?" Lydia asked him. She stood at the kitchen entrance carrying a towel. There was something both sweet and formal about her manner. She led David to the bathroom. The realtor was shaving in front of an old-fashioned mirror with patterned gilt edges that hung on the wall above the sink. The glass was slightly wavy and it further flattened the realtor's already somewhat pudgy face. Instead of a standard medicine cabinet there was an old wooden pharmacy chest with glass doors, and on the wall above that some wooden shelves. The bathroom was the most luxurious room in the apartment: a painted turquoise tub with claw feet, a thick glass shower stall with a seat large enough for two inside it, a beautiful marble sink, a bidet. The floor was carpeted with industrial-quality carpeting. "Fags lived here," Lydia explained. "I was lucky I didn't have to pay a huge key fee."

"How come?" asked David.

"You don't want to know."

"I don't?"

"The guy's lover died of AIDS. He was trying to sell the place but when people found out the story they didn't want to buy it. Then he decided it was bad karma to sell it and moved back to Ohio."

"Gosh!" It was a word David probably hadn't used in over twenty years. But for some reason he felt like he was in high school.

"I told you you didn't want to know."

Only the towels were old, unmatched in color, straggling threads hanging from them. "They're yours, aren't they?" he asked.

"Yeah, but, you don't know who used them before you did, do you?" David felt sick. "Just joking," said Lydia.

"Why are you trying to upset us?" the realtor asked.

"*Revenge.*" She turned her back toward him, lifted up her robe to show him her ass.

The realtor lightly ran his hand over it, pulled back as if to whack it, caressed it instead. David would have liked to kiss it, not because it was especially beautiful, but out of some weird kind of homage. Of course, he was too self-conscious to.

The realtor went into the shower. David would have preferred a shower to a bath but he was afraid Lydia or the realtor might make him join the realtor if he mentioned this, so he turned on the bath. When he was done and stepped out the realtor slapped him with his wet towel, like frat guys did in college. They were careful not to touch each other. Lydia watched in her robe.

"You guys act like . . . brothers," she said.

David blushed. He had been expecting something else. "You want to come down and get some chow?" the realtor asked Lydia, when they were dressed.

"Nah. I need to be alone for a while. Otherwise I can't get into my work."

"You sure?"

"Yeah."

"I hope my car's okay," said David. "If I'd have known I was going to stay all night I would've looked for a garage."

"Garage! Ha!" laughed Lydia. "The neighborhood's not as bad as you think."

"Yeah, but, it's not exactly the safest place in the world either."

"It's healthy for you to visit the real world sometime," she said.

"What makes you think this is any more real than where I live?" David asked.

"Gimme a break," said Lydia. "That's why you're here."

"I don't know why I'm here," said David.

"Your car's fine," the realtor assured him. "I spend half my life in neighborhoods like this. Or worse. Nobody fucks with my car, and it's a Caddy too. Bigger than yours."

"Says who?" said David. The realtor reached out as if to grab his crotch.

"Jesus," said Lydia. "You guys are too much." But she said it as if it were a compliment.

The realtor stuck his tongue in Lydia's mouth as he kissed her goodbye. She seemed irritated, but responded anyway. David bent down to do the same thing, but for some reason ended up kissing her cheek.

"Take care, David," Lydia said, as he started down the stairs.

"You too."

On the way down the stairs David felt sad. Somehow he was out and the realtor was in. It did not seem inevitable. Looking back, it seemed as if any moment it could have gone the other way. But wasn't this true of most of the moments of his life? Did he have particularly bad luck or was this just the way life was? Then he burst out of the urine- and cabbage-smell-filled building and into the clear blue of a chilly morning. The sun was so bright it glinted off broken glass in the street, off chrome handles and car mirrors, and into his eyes. A radio was playing Spanish music; somehow this reminded him of summer, so it seemed odd it was so cold.

They crossed the street. In the midst of the rubble, the burnt-out buildings, the dealers, the junkies, the cruising cops, neighborhood women walking to the grocery, the supers on the stoops, the old cars, dead trees, roaches, rats, pigeons, garbage cans, sat David's silver-gray '85 Caddy. Eighty-five, the last good year. The car was safe and sound— nothing missing, not even a hubcap. An absurb happiness flooded his heart.

After the realtor and David had gone, Lydia got back into bed and lay staring out the window at the soft brown stone wall on which the sun was falling. The cup of coffee first grew cold, then warm when sunlight entered the room and fell on it. She picked up a book, held it up to her face, put it down. She lay there all day, watching the sun move slowly across the sky (more accurately, charting the progress of the sun by the light that slid across her room), illuminating at various times a mirror, a TV antenna, a radio knob, a pen, a telephone, an old typewriter case, magazines lying on the floor, the rug, her phone book, a glass of water that for a few moments became a prism, creating a tiny rainbow on the night table where its sat. Then the sun sank behind the buildings to the west of her, and finally the huge curve of the earth, dragging the white out of the blue, which got darker and darker until it became violet, then purple, then a velvet black with stars. She witnessed this without consciousness of effort, without turning on the TV or the VCR or the stereo or the clock radio or the Walkman. It wasn't much of a day by most people's standards, but, in fact, Lydia was happy—happier than anybody else in this book on this particular day: David, Jack, Lorraine, Judy, the realtor, Jeremy, Cecilia, Michael, Aurelia, the realtor's wife, Jack the dog, Jezebel, Saralee, Saralee's sister, the Puerto Rican janitor, his nephew, John Weird, "Andy Warhol," Murray, Jack's students, Judy's classmates, the woman in the whirlpool and the Moroccan at the food counter at David's health club, the waiter who served David breakfast at the corner luncheonette, the superintendents of the buildings he searched for apartments in, the mailmen who delivered his mail, Koreans who operated his vegetable stands, Italians who sold him his meat, Russian and Haitian taxi drivers, Jamaican elevator men, reporters of all colors and nationalities who researched the stories he read, photographers who took the photos that illustrated these stories, printers who typeset the words, truckers who transported the papers to news vendors, vendors who sold them, sanitation men who cleaned the streets in front of the vendors, mechanics who serviced the sanitation men's trucks, launderers who washed the mechanics' uniforms, bank officers who approved loans to start these businesses, businessmen and individuals who deposited the money to be loaned, tellers who typed these transactions into computers, programmers who wrote the programs that recorded these transactions, manufacturers who produced these computers, computer geniuses from MIT who designed them, and so on, until the entire universe revealed itself as a gigantic spider web in which wherever one was was the center, a huge pond in which the tiniest ripple did not stop till it reached the farthest shore, a trampoline so delicate the movements of a single electron a billion light-years away could make it vibrate forever. . . .

14

When Lorraine entered the apartment Jack was sitting on the couch, staring out at a black rectangle, the window. A pencil was in his hand, but he wasn't using it. Earlier that day a moving van had parked in front of the house. A Japanese-American couple had stood downstairs, talking and gesturing with their hands to the movers: huge cardboard and wood cartons and pieces of furniture began to appear on the sidewalk. Later in the afternoon a grand piano had sailed past his head; its legs dangled obscenely in the air above him. All day he had heard the sounds of banging and scraping on the ceiling. Thinking of the missing room—the room that should have been his—he had become unable to move.

Oblivious, Lorraine sat down on the couch next to Jack and resumed the monologue she had commenced on the phone with him earlier that day: " 'So Tony,' I told him—there's a lot of Tonys in this business—'personally I think you're a very nice guy. And if I could afford to pay you what you wanted nobody would be happier than me, I believe in the unions even though I personally think their time is past.'

" 'There's people from Vietnam working for two dollars an hour sewing shirts in Queens,' he said. 'Did you know that? They work twelve hours a day and some of them are four-teen-, sixteen-year-olds, they don't go to school, how are they ever gonna get a good job?'

" 'If you want to talk knock-offs that's another thing, Tony, but designer clothing is a different ballgame, our girls always got good money, I was paying my people union wages before you guys ever forced me to sign that contract and you wonder why people resent you, if I go out of business it's gonna be your fault and who's it gonna hurt but your people whom I employ? You make it too expensive to hire you, why do you think Calvin gets his stuff made in Korea? You don't find me doing that. But you got to let me get my foot in the door. . . . ' " Eventually, however, she noticed that Jack wasn't paying attention.

"Is something the matter?" she asked, not without hostility. As was usually the case when she came home, she felt irritated at what she perceived as the indifference of Jack's welcome. She kept waiting for him to manifest his immense gratitude for being allowed to live here with her, in her apartment—so much bigger and more luxurious than any he had ever lived in before. Jack, sensing her desire for this, naturally refused to give it.

That afternoon Jack had decided he would not mention the new Japanese couple. But he could not help himself, so his tone was deliberately unconvincing when he said: "No, not really."

Lorraine sighed. She did not want to be drawn into this. But she could not help herself either. "Come on, what is it?" she asked.

"Oh, you know. . . . " He waved his hand vaguely at the window. They sat there silently, looking at the purple sky, the purple water, purple Jersey, until, just as Lorraine was about to heave herself up to go into her bedroom, Jack said: "This couple moved into the apartment upstairs today. Japanese. Young. Very . . . you know . . . *upscale*." Tears for Fears blasted into the silence.

"Here we go," said Lorraine. But the coming anger energized her, and she felt better than she had a moment before. "Do they have any kids?"

"I don't know. Maybe."

"Judy could start babysitting."

Jack picked up the pencil again and began doodling. Lorraine watched him for a while, then got up and walked into the kitchen. "Some wine?" she called.

"I spose."

But instead of opening a bottle, she sat down at the kitchen counter. Jack followed her in there, curled his legs around the legs of the stool.

"David called this afternoon," Lorraine offered. "He wants

to have dinner with me. I have this weird feeling he wants to get back together."

"His girlfriend leave him?"

"What's that got to do with it?" Lorraine didn't appreciate the unflattering implication. "It would be good for Judy, you know."

"Maybe."

"What do you mean, *maybe*? He's her father."

"I don't know."

They looked at each other. Each of them wished the other would say or do something they seemed to be consciously avoiding saying or doing. "What are you thinking?" asked Lorraine.

"His girlfriend left him, he's lonely, he doesn't like the expense of separate apartments, he's having trouble with his partners—sure, he wants to get back together."

"Not that. *You*. What do *you* think? What do *you* want?"

"The truth?"

"Of course."

"A new life," said Jack. "To start over." A long silence. The ticking of a clock, the beating of a heart, his own.

"That doesn't make me feel very good. This was supposed to be your new life."

"I know." More silence. Tears for Fears ended. Judy put on a new David Bowie, almost immediately took it off, and switched to an early Beatles. "Revolver." The '60s were back. "It's the missing room," said Jack. "I can't stop thinking about it."

"*Jack.*"

"It's been haunting me ever since I saw it. Every time I try to paint, I wish I were working in it. That's what I think about, instead of what I'm supposed to be painting." He walked over to the window, looked out. He saw himself standing in the missing room, working as the family slept, not lonely for once in the dead of night. "Walls are nothing. And we could build another entrance to your bathroom through the wall."

"Through the wall is the shower and the whirlpool."

"Through the wall there's a shower and a huge useless basin that would be a whirlpool if it were ever fixed."

Lorraine banged her fist into the plasterboard, so hard her ring made a dent in it. This so enraged her she punched it again. "I hate this apartment! I hate the way you make me feel about it. I wish I'd never seen it! It destroyed my marriage, and now it's destroying my relationship with you! You know when I was happiest? When I was living in a tiny little fourth-floor walk-up in the Village, before I got married, and I could do whatever I wanted! People feel sorry for poor people, I don't know why—they're the only people who can do what they want!"

"Please."

"Jack, suppose you'd met me and I was living in some tiny apartment. Or you hadn't seen the apartment upstairs. We wouldn't have had to go through all this."

"Maybe not. But you live in this large apartment and I've seen the apartment upstairs—"

"No, Jack. *Don't* think of this apartment as the one upstairs. Think of it as some other, *different* apartment."

"I've tried to, Lorraine. I can't." He sighed, walked to the window, looked out above the glaring streetlight into the blackness overhead. "Look, we both know this isn't any good. It would be better for both of us if I just split."

"You've said this a thousand times before."

"This time it's *true.*"

Lorraine looked at him, thought of walking over to put her arms around him, changed her mind and went to the fridge instead. "Come on, let's make dinner." She opened the fridge, began pulling out peppers, radishes, red-leaf and romaine lettuce, arugula, onions, a cut-up fryer. "Potatoes or rice?"

Jack shrugged. "Either. Spaghetti."

"Okay."

He opened the cabinet next to the sink to get out the pasta pot and the old black frying pan. The top hinge broke off, so the door hung on to the cabinet only by its lower hinge. "Christ!" Did nothing in the whole apartment work? In his anger he kicked the door. It fell off completely. "Jesus!" He sat down on a stool. In the background, accompanying "Penny Lane," was the sound of dripping water.

Lorraine shook her head, sat down next to him. "I love you," she said.

"I know." They listened to the water dripping.

"You could change the washer."

"I've been meaning to."

"So why don't you?" Jack shrugged. "I don't understand you. Somehow you act like you don't live here."

"I don't *feel* like I live here."

"Why not?"

"You know why." Larger than the moon, the room hung over their heads.

"You'll never be satisfied. No matter what."

"You're right."

"It would be one thing if you loved me. . . . "

" 'Love. . . . ' "

Lorraine looked at him in disgust, and left the kitchen. A few minutes later Jack followed her into the bedroom. She was lying on the lower half of the bed, her legs dangling off the end, her eyes closed, listening to the water from the shower splash into the tub. Jack stood on a chair to reach the old, dirty nylon suitcase he'd stored high up in the closet, and threw it onto the floor. Then he pulled out the wire drawer where his Jockey shorts and T-shirts were—part of the hideous and inefficient "closet system" the architects had installed. As often happened when he jerked too hard, the basket came off its runners, tilted, and sent a bunch of his Jockey shorts onto the beige carpet. Lying there—mostly old-fashioned and yellowing, a few colored Calvin Kleins Lorraine had bought him among them—they looked like a bunch of wilted bouquets. He felt ashamed of them, as if they revealed something horrible about his psyche. He gathered them up and dropped them back in the wire basket. Then he sat down on the bed next to Lorraine. He brushed the hair off her forehead. As if he cared.

"I *do* love you," Lorraine repeated. "You know that."

"What good does it do? *I'm* miserable. *You're* miserable."

"I'm not miserable." Nonetheless, tears started out of her eyes.

"See?"

"My period, that's all."

"No it's not."

"How would you know?" she asked angrily.

Jack tried to remember the last time they had made love, couldn't. He put his hand out, touched her shoulder.

"I can't stand it. I'm so tired."

The venetian blind slats had broken in a permanent open position, so they were able to see the sky. Oddly, it was now lighter, a black-tinged pink.

"Rain," said Jack. "I'm tired too."

"Can't you have an original thought?"

"I had the thought, I just didn't say it." When Lorraine sighed she sounded exactly like the dog. She got up, went into the bathroom, turned off the water, came back.

"You're putting on weight," she told Jack.

"No, I'm not. I weigh exactly the same."

"You feel different."

"It's my mind. It used to be able to control everything, even my stomach muscles. Now I'm too tired."

Lorraine rolled on top of him. They kissed. In the back of Jack's mind was the thought that at any second Judy could open the door and walk in. He supposed it must be in the back of Lorraine's mind also, but neither did anything about it. Mechanically Jack moved his lips, his tongue, his arms. They felt tired, as if he'd just been doing Nautilus.

The dream of a home, of course, was this: to curl up on a bed or a corner of a couch, one with high arms you could use as a pillow, as you lay there and read, or watched the sun traverse the sky. . . . In this spot were your memories, which you could recover by going back there; they adhered to the significant form of the shadow of the bed or couch against the wall, appeared as familiar streets you didn't quite remember in dreams. All your adult life was spent escaping from this childhood spot; then you grew old, and used the excuse of age to return to it. . . .

Lying there, they fell half-asleep. During his half-dream Jack became aware of a pain in his side. When the pain became greater than his fatigue, he woke up enough to remove Lorraine's elbow from pressing into his stomach. Then Lorraine woke up. They were rumpled, as if they had slept a long time, although it was probably only a few minutes. "Good day / Sunshine," they heard, faintly, disconcertingly. The room was cold, as it often was, for the contractors had replaced the efficient old radiators with new wall units that didn't retain heat. Jack got up and went into the bathroom. He put his hand into the tub water. It, too, had cooled off, was almost cold. He opened the drain, then turned on the hot water nozzle of the shower. He sat on the edge of the tub, watching the stream of water fall on the receding water in the tub, like rain on a pond.

Lorraine came into the bathroom and started getting undressed. Jack has seen photographs of her that show that once she was genuinely beautiful, but this is no longer the case. Age and anxiety have attacked her skin, her eyes, her posture. Secretly he pities her for this, and wonders how she can stand it. Of course he's not perfect either, but until this year he used to think he was—even though nobody else did. He hadn't known her when she was young, but he used the documentation of her early beauty to console him, to in some way justify his being with her.

"Don't stare at me like that," said Lorraine. "I know you hate me. But I wish you'd hide it."

"I don't hate you."

"You do, but it's not personal, so I can stand it."

Comments like this almost made Jack feel understood. "If I hated you, why would I be here?"

"Because you're getting old, and scared no one will ever fuck you again."

"People downtown don't care about fucking any more. You ought to know that by now."

"I know it. Someday my designer will know it, and then we'll make a million bucks."

They climbed up onto the tub and into maybe twelve inches of bath water—all they had the patience to wait for. The water was so hot they got the same unpleasant shock as if it were freezing. They danced from one foot to the other until they got used to it, even as the chill that emanated from the huge nonthermal window that looked out on the street gave the upper part of their body goosebumps. The blind was broken but steam fogged the window—the streetlight glowed softly through it as though it were London. In life Jack hated London, but in his head he liked it.

"We've got to hurry," said Lorraine. "Judy must be starving."

"Not with what she eats after school."

"So *that's* what happens to the Pepperidge Farm." Lorraine stood up to leave the bath, which made the water level fall even further. Jack curled as much of his body as he could under the water. When the water was a dull filmy gray like the top of old chicken soup he got out, reached for Lorraine's damp towel and dried himself. There was a clean white one on the towel rack next to the door but he'd have to walk naked across the cold tiles to get to it. He put on a clean flannel shirt, the same corduroy pants he was wearing before, and headed to the kitchen. Water was boiling and the smell of garlic and the sound of rock music filled the air.

David Bowie on the tape, Judy on the phone, Jack lounging around hinting for food, the kitchen fan buzzing, the dishwasher washing, clothes tumbling in the washer, clothes spinning in the dryer, water running in the sink, the splash of water on lettuce in the salad spinner, an argument between Lorraine and Judy as to whether Judy should continue her conversation with Saralee on a phone in another room, the banging of the refrigerator door, Jack slurping water, molecules of air banging into each other billions of times per second, a plane outside, a bicycle making circles on the kitchen floor upstairs, an unexplained but somehow nonthreatening cry from who knows where, the elevator man picking up the garbage outside the kitchen door, a car honking, a kid shouting, the opening of a cabinet in search of a glass, the weatherman on the radio announcing the possibility of a dusting of snow . . . this was Jack's life now, his family, and who was to say it was any worse than any other? When he lived alone he had to make all the noise himself; surely this was easier. He drank some cranberry juice, rinsed out the glass, and poured in some of the Cabernet Sauvignon Lorraine opened to keep her amused and warm as she chopped anise, red onion, and yellow peppers for the salad. The spaghetti water boiled, fogging the cracked mirror and the kitchen window; occasionally the fryer crackled some oil into the air. Jack curled his feet on the base of the black steel stool on the opposite side of the kitchen counter from Lorraine, not clearing his throat even when he felt he might choke, because was not one of the great pleasures of life being invisible? Thus he forbore from asking her why she was sticking cauliflower in the tomato sauce for the spaghetti even though by now she must know he hates it, or why she was using hard red tomatoes instead of plum ones, and by this silent compact he hoped not only to avoid a fight, but to avoid having to help with the dinner. For this moment he could sit here watching her forever. Only the cauliflower, or rather the signification of it as a hostile gesture, bothered him (as a revenge for his bringing up the missing room?), then he decided that it wasn't hostile after all, but a metaphor for "home." After all, was it not reassuring sometimes to have to eat a food one doesn't like —for in this manner was not one forcibly reminded of the existence of other people?

Sensing it was a mistake, he nonetheless explained his thought processes to Lorraine.

"You're crazy, Jack, you interpret everything as some kind of weird gesture against you. Here, why don't you help with the dressing or something, instead of just sitting there?"

Jack hopped off the stool, got the oil and vinegar from the pantry. Despite his best intentions he heard himself say, "Maybe someday we'll get the Cuisinart fixed."

"May be," sang Lorraine.

"Maybe someday you'll remember how much I hate cauliflower," Jack sang back.

"May be."

"Unless you buy it on purpose?"

"Jack, you're warped. Do you *really* think that every time I'm in the supermarket I ask myself about *every* item whether you like it or not?"

"Not consciously, no, but unconsciously, the way you do for Judy."

"But I'm her mother. And although you'd like me to be your mother, I'm not."

An argument ensued, mostly Jack's fault. He wondered

what psychic purpose it fulfilled. Surely it must, or he wouldn't have so many. A reminder of childhood? A Jewish compulsion to destroy perfection, lest undue satisfaction bring down curses? To mimic a network tube family, whose tiny misunderstandings concealed unspeakable fears?

Or was it merely the artist's fear of boredom?

Jack the dog was excited. Usually at night Lorraine or Jack took him on a short walk around the block, but now, following loud words, they headed down to the park. Due to the tension between them they were paying more attention to him than usual. Happily he dragged them from tree to tree until they finally gave up and let him off the leash, as they sometimes did at night. He bounded over to a group of dogs and sniffed their rears. He tried to mount a collie, but she turned toward him and barked angrily. He leapt away. He bared his teeth at a male Akita, but the Akita was huge, and growled back, and Jack ran behind a tree. When the Akita loped away Jack rejoined the group. After the collie's owner took her away, Jack picked up a stick that he carried to Lorraine and the Man With His Name. He stood there panting, in front of them, stick in his mouth. After a while, seeing they weren't going to try to grab it out of his mouth (which he would happily resist—for a while), he dropped it on the ground in front of them. But they were engrossed in making human sounds and showed no interest in it. When he tried to jump on them, they pushed him down. He ran back to where the other members of his species were, but found only two weimaraners and an Old English sheepdog, all on leashes. Then he ran back to Lorraine and the man, and lay down panting on his paws.

Again they ignored him. Their voices were loud and unpleasant, in a way that made Jack feel like running away and hiding himself in the forest. They put the leash on him and started walking back toward the street. They fell silent in the strange little room that did odd things to his stomach ("elevator"), but as soon as they entered the apartment their voices grew even louder than before, in a way that usually preceded the slammings of doors and throwings of plates and glasses. The Girl peeked her head out of her room, then shut the door. Soon the music coming from there was even louder. Lorraine's face was drawn, her voice hoarse. She stalked back and forth. The man sat on the couch watching her. Jack hid under the piano. Then Lorraine picked up a stick with black hair at the end of it—the thing the man used to put colors on the paper tacked to the wall—and jabbed at the paper with it. The man jumped up, shouted something, ran over to Lorraine, pulled back his arm as if to—

Jack ran out from under the piano. He jumped against the man's chest and knocked him down. He went over to Lorraine, out of whose eyes water was pouring, and licked her face: to see if she was all right and to tell her he loved her. The water had that funny acidy taste it always did when it came from human eyes. The man got up, grabbed the thing he put on his back when he went outside, opened the door, shouted something, slammed it shut. Almost as if she were imitating him, Lorraine ran to the door, opened it, shouted something after him, slammed it shut. Then she fell against it, banging her fists against it, water pouring out of her eyes and nose. She stumbled to the couch. Again Jack tried to lick her face and neck; every once in a while she let him. "Good dog, good dog," she said, absentmindedly petting him. When she pushed him away he rubbed against her leg in a way that let her know he wanted her to scratch him behind the ears. She held a piece of white cloth over her nose into which she exhaled violently. She began to pet Jack in a rhythmic fashion. "There, there," she said in the singsong voice in which she always spoke these syllables, *"that's* a good boy, *that's* all right." Jack yearned to tell her how much he loved her, that she should never cry, that he would kill anyone who tried to harm the slightest hair on her head, that it was okay if they lived alone, just him and her (and, okay, the Girl), without either of the men who caused all the door slammings and water drippings. For once she didn't yell at Jack for getting his dirty paws on her blouse, though she kept turning her head so his tongue wouldn't touch her lips.

When Lorraine calmed down she went into the white tiled

room where she did number one and number two, took off her clothes, and stepped inside the little area where there was indoor rain. Jack watched for a while, then, when she lifted up the toilet bowl (she cruelly kept it closed so Jack couldn't drink water out of it), she shoved him out and shut the door in his face.

After the excitement and eroticism of these moments, Jack was exhausted. As he waited for Lorraine by the foot of her bed, now happily empty of competing humans, he fell asleep. First he dreamed he was the man Jack being attacked by the dog Jack, then he was a dog again, himself, walking out of the falling room onto a street where all the humans were on leashes. Lorraine was there, on a leash held by him. Try as she might to escape toward the Man With His Name, Jack dragged her belly and legs along the rough bumpy pavement, away from her love. Although he knew this was cruel, she belonged to him and this didn't bother him one bit.

THREE

||||||||||||||||||||||||||||||||||||||||||||||||||

15

With his clothing, his paints, and his dreams, Jack returned to his old apartment. At Lorraine's he'd thought of it with longing, a place where he could work all night and sleep all day if he pleased, consume pints of Häagen-Dazs unchastised, play music of his own choosing uncontested, but now that he was here, it seemed less like a comforting cave than a prison: tiny, dark, cold. During the day he would stare at the sunlight on the brick wall opposite his window the way he imagined convicts did in prison, with a desire almost that it not be there, tormenting him with unfulfillable desires.

The trouble he used to have sleeping alone, which, oddly, he had forgotten about, recurred. Just as he was about to fall asleep, a twitch would jerk him up and awake. He'd lie sweating under the blankets, yet his forehead felt like ice. Or was it his hand that felt like ice? How could you tell? His teeth chattered as his armpits secreted sticky, smelly substances. Sometimes the smell was like the acrid odor of the paranoid-schizophrenic. If he tried to get up and work, the combination of cold air and sweat would make his nose run, his eyes squint with tears, tears that he interpreted as emotional correlatives of his misery. Old age and death seemed just around the corner: already his body parts were growing recalcitrant, stiff; if he didn't stretch properly after working out he'd feel it for days. His dreams were horrible, continuities of daily thought that provided no relief. He opened his phone book and flipped through, searching for the 213 and 415 area codes, where people whom he used to call friends were still awake. After a few rings, he hung up. What could he say? That life was miserable and he was a failure, alone and frightened, on the verge of killing himself? Exhausted, he would open the window and exhale into the cool air, daring strep, pneumonia, suicide. Sweating, chilled, he would listen to the sounds in the street: radios, brakes, doors opening and closing, a startlingly close voice of a boy asking a girl a question. If he stood as close as he could to the window and gazed straight up, he could occasionally, if he were lucky, spot a star or two, shining in the air shaft between his building and the one next door. Whereas at Lorriane's, there was nothing between him and the stars but the light from streetlights, the reflecting river, and New Jersey. As for work: not only could he not force himself to paint, he had forgotten why he had become an artist in the first place. Self-expression? Ideas about color and form? The very notion made him laugh.

"Nothing's helping," Jack told Murray the next week. "Not only don't I know who I am, I don't know who I *was*. I wish I were somebody else. Like a cowboy. Or movie star. Or Jeff Koons. Sometimes I think I should just run off and . . . become a truck driver, or short-order cook. Or start a business—in some place nobody knows me."

"What kind of business?"

"You got me." Jack stared glumly at the carpet, brown flecked with maroon. It was a male-type carpet, almost aggressively so. Jack wondered how Murray's homosexual clients must feel, staring at this carpet. He realized how rarely he actually thought of things *inside* from a homosexual's point of view—or a black's—or a woman's. "You know, I really resent having to pay to tell you this, instead of having a friend to complain to for free." Murray pushed back against the back of his ergonomic chair. Then he clasped his fingers together, pushed his palms out and over his head in a big stretch, and yawned. "Must you work out as I talk to you?" Jack asked.

"You can't stand anybody else to be happy or feel good— even for a few seconds. Have you thought about the implications of that?"

"It doesn't bother me when most people have a good time. I just resent your doing it while I'm paying you to help me so that someday I can afford to live in a loft maybe half as large as yours."

"Are you interested in becoming a therapist, Jack?"

"Are you kidding?"

"So *shut up!* Who's responsible for the state you're in—you or me?"

"That doesn't make me feel better, it makes me feel worse."

"*Good.*"

" 'Good,' you smug sonofabitch?"

"Yeah, *good.* Why don't you get mad and beat me up? I mean, not that you could, but why don't you try?" Jack stood up. "Go ahead, you wimp, do it. Don't stand there, wasting both our times, *do it!*" Jack took a halfhearted punch, but Murray parried the swing, and, with a judo-like motion, flipped Jack onto the floor. It was carpeted, so he wasn't really hurt, though the carpet rubbed, somewhat unpleasantly, into his cheek. "Jesus Christ, you *stink,*" said Murray.

Jack stood up. He saw himself, a fool in front of a desk, manipulated into starting a fight, the way bullies made him do in grade school, so they would have an excuse to beat him up. Instead, he picked up a glass apple—he hoped a Steuben one—and threw it against the wall. But it bounced from wall to carpet harmlessly. Murray bent down, picked up the apple, and replaced it on his desk. He got Jack's coat off his $600 Memphis coat rack and threw it on Jack's lap.

"Can't take the heat, huh?" sneered Jack, standing up.

"Not at all," said Murray, pleasantly. "We're taking a walk. I'm through for the day, so we've got time." He opened the closet and got out his own coat.

"A walk. Where?"

"You'll see."

"Your time or mine?"

"It depends on which way you look at it, Jack. In a way it's your time, since you're giving me your work in exchange for these sessions. On the other hand, at the moment your work is worth virtually nil, so in a way it's *my* time. Let's think of it as a gamble—my time against your future. I help you, the value of your work—and my property—goes up."

This was capitalistic logic, and fair, yet Jack resented it. Around Murray he always felt sulky, unappreciated. He had a suspicion Murray despised him.

They walked east, past the the Bowery to Second Avenue, First, A, to Tompkins Square Park. Murray stopped by a bench and sat down. Except for a few bums, the park was empty.

The air was moist, with a raw dampness that bothered Jack more than colder, drier weather. Even his gloved hands were cold. Unconsciously, Jack crossed his arms and slipped them under his armpits.

"Take off your gloves," said Murray. Jack took off his gloves.

"How do you feel?" asked Murray.

"Cold," said Jack. "I could do with a cup of coffee."

"Ever been in India, Jack?"

"No."

"Africa?"

"On what salary?"

"Then this will have to do," said Murray. He stood up. Jack started to follow, but Murray pushed him down. "You're staying."

"What?"

"All night. See what it's like."

"I know what it's like, Murray," said Jack. "Nineteen sixty-seven. Concerts, camping out in the park. 'Summer of Love.' I was young. You think I forget?" A time that seemed impossibly far away.

"Nineteen eighty-seven, Jack. Great Depression, part two. See how the other half lives."

"Other half?" Jack sneered. "You think I never had to wait half an hour on a subway station in the winter?"

"Yeah, Jack, that's *just* what it's like."

Jack laughed. "Okay, Murray," he said, standing up. "I get the point."

Murray pushed him back. "No you don't." He started to walk away, then stopped, came back. "Promise?"

"Why the fuck should I?"

"If you don't I won't see you any more."

" 'Esthetic consultant' Murray Bottoms. A man of many hats," said Jack.

"No more than I can wear."

Jack promised. He intended to leave as soon as Murray was out of sight, but then, as a kind of macho test, he decided to see if he could stick it out.

At first, it was his hands that got to him. They turned red, raw. Soon, his nose and the cartilage of his ears were numb; he couldn't feel them when he touched them. Or was it his fingers that had no sensation? How could you tell? His body shook, yet he knew it wasn't that cold. It probably wasn't even freezing. There were many nights twenty or thirty degrees colder than this throughout the winter. Yet he began to shiver uncontrollably. He told himself to be calm, inhale very slowly through his nostrils, hold the breath as long as he could, then exhale slowly as he counted to ten. He became more relaxed and calmer when he was able to concentrate on his breathing, though, paradoxically, his body seemed more open to the weather. But when his thoughts wandered, and he thought about something other than his breathing, he found himself shivering again.

He told himself to concentrate on the subtle beauty of the darkening sky, a subtle (seemingly dull) sky without sunset, the pattern of the bare branches and the buildings surrounding the park against the grayish purple. But he kept being distracted by the cold, the danger, the boredom, the movements of his mind meditating on itself.

"Motherfucker. Look at this."

Jack opened his eyes. He realized he had fallen into a dreamy, perhaps dangerously dreamy, state in the cold. It was inside rather than outside of him, so that he didn't perceive it as an external unpleasantness, but as something inherently part of himself. Cold. Dead. A black man wearing torn pants was talking to a garbage can—not the nice old-fashioned wire kind but a new one made of brown plastic, with a little roof to shield the garbage from the weather. "Whatchoo looking at?" the man asked Jack.

"Nothing."

Jack stood up. In the night, in the cold, his promise to Murray seemed a joke. He would rather have avoided the man, but he didn't want to seem (either in the man's eyes or his own) like he was avoiding a confrontation by taking another route, so he forced himself to walk past him.

The bum grabbed his arm. "Look at this."

"What do you mean?"

"What's in there?"

"I don't know," said Jack.

"That's what I mean. How are you supposed to know what's in there when they've got it covered?"

"I don't know. I never thought about it till now."

"I'll bet you didn't."

"You've got a point. It must be hard to find what you're looking for." Hoping the man was mollified, Jack tried to move off. But the guy held onto his arm.

"Damn right it is. Now some guy before threw a pizza in here. See if you can find it."

"No."

"Come on." With surprising strength he forced Jack's arm into the bin.

"*No!*"

"Why not? Scared of dirtying yourself? Strong, ain't I?" he asked. "Try to find that pizza." Jack surrendered, grasped something slimy, wet. He pulled it out: a shit-laden newspaper from a conscientious dog-walker. It barely touched his hand but he dropped it on the path; his stomach began to turn and he broke out in sweat. "See that?" the bum asked. "New fucking cans so you people don't have to see garbage, and you don't have to *see* people picking up garbage. But the garbage is still there. Only you can't get what you want no more. You know what I look forward to?"

"What?" Jack frantically rubbed his hands, first on the cleaner part of the newspaper, then on his pants.

"The day when assholes like you are on the street with me.

Motherfucker, you see this?" He pulled out a knife, held it up to Jack's throat. "What's to prevent me from making a little sacrifice with your throat?"

Jack stared, thought: This can't be happening to me—not to *me!*

"Come on, man, answer me."

The knife was at his throat. *"Don't."* said Jack.

"That's no answer."

"You don't want to go to jail."

"I'm a loony. Even if they catch me I don't go to jail." Pause. "So tell me. One good reason I don't do whatever I goddam feel like doing to you. *One good reason.*"

"Most of the things I want to do I don't get to do either."

"That's your problem, ain't it?"

"Yeah, but—*I'm just like you!*" Tears came to Jack's eyes: not so much in anger as in poignancy.

"Motherfucker, you are *not!*"

"I *am,*" said Jack. "In my own way I've suffered too. I understand. I've been there." His voice sounded like he was lying. And yet he *had* suffered, was suffering.

"You understand *what?* You've been *where?*" The man spit. "Do you know where *I've* been? Come on, tell me, where have I been?" Jack shook his head. "You don't know everything, do you, motherfucker? Well, motherfucker." He shook Jack.

"No," said Jack.

"Somehow I didn't think so. You know who I am motherfucker?"

"No . . . ."

"That's right, motherfucker, you don't. But you think you do. You hear voices, they lock you up, they pass a law, they let you out, you live on the streets, they fucking interview you for the news." Again he spit. "You *understand.* Try spending one night out here . . . ."

"I *have.* I *am.*"

"You think I crawled out of my mother like this? You put you and me together back then, and nobody could tell the difference between us—except of course our skin. 'There but for the grace of God,' you heard of that, ain't you?"

"Of course."

"You believe it, don't you?"

"Sure."

"You wouldn't patronize me, would you?"

"No."

"*Liar*. Why the fuck you let me talk to you like this? Don't you have any self-respect?"

"Fuck you, Murray!" Jack shouted.

"Murray? Hey, *faggot*, he your lover?"

"*Shrink*. He made me come here. *Fucker!*" Behind his anger, Jack was conscious of the need to garner the man's sympathy and curiosity. This made him feel phony, his anger unconvincing—even though it was real. Meanwhile the man danced around Jack's neck with his knife, touching the point very gently every once in a while to Jack's skin. Chilled, waiting for this touch, the excitement was almost sexual.

"What for?"

"To make me stop feeling sorry for myself."

"That's a good one!" The bum laughed. "You got to pay this guy?"

"Sure."

"You on SSI?"

"No." What perverse impulse had caused Jack to tell the truth? Sweat poured down his pants.

"Murray!" screamed Jack.

"He ain't gonna help you now, motherfucker."

"Go ahead, kill me. Kill me!" Jack suddenly shouted. "See if I care!"

"Man, you're nuts."

"That's right, buddy, just like you." He cackled.

"Really, motherfucker? Want to change places?"

"No."

"*See?*"

"Cause I'm not you. And you can bear being where you are. But I couldn't take it. I'd kill myself if I were you."

"Tell me about it. You couldn't hack it."

"You know something else? You'd kill yourself if you were *me!* You think it's easy to get out of bed in the morning and drag yourself in the subways and be frightened to death of people like yourself, who look terrible and smell terrible, who at any second might kill you—not for any reason, but just because they *feel* like it—and they won't even go to jail if they do cause they're too fucking loony? You think it's not a fucking *huge* effort to go to the bank and try to be polite to those schmucks who won't raise my credit line or okay a mortgage so I can buy a loft, when they keep refinancing loans to these fucking bankrupt dictatorships? You know why they do this?—if they told the truth and wrote the loans off the whole fucking banking system would collapse! Do you think the people you see on the fucking subways wearing their suits and ties are not aware of this stuff?—it drives us absolutely crazy! Do you think that every second all of us out there are not struggling to keep ourselves sane and not kill each other? You think we hate you, and have contempt for you, and don't want to give you food or a place to live— but you know why that is?—it's cause we *envy* you. Yeah— *envy!* You got two fucking worries—where you gonna eat and where you gonna sleep. You don't have to clean up the place you sleep in, you don't have to worry about phone or rent or Con Ed bills, and you don't have to shop or cook your food. You don't believe me? Hey! Watch this!" In a weird euphoria Jack stuck his hand back in the garbage can. "See? It don't bother me." He came up with the pizza.

"Okay. Eat it."

"Eat it?"

"Yeah, eat it."

"No. . . ."

The man put the knife to Jack's Adam's apple. It stuck out huge, a lump in his throat it was almost impossible to swallow around. *"Eat it."*

Jack started to retch. "My hand . . ." It still smelled of shit —that damn pooper-scooper law. He dropped the pizza.

"If it's good enough for me, it's good enough for you. Grace of God and all that."

"But—"

"Pick it up and eat it."

Jack wiped his hand on his pants, trying to get off the shit. Then he bent down to pick up the pizza. But he couldn't bring himself to stick it in his mouth.

"Okay, asshole, shut your eyes."

Jack shut his eyes. His bowels slipped, and he could feel the warm stuff in his underpants. As if he were an infant. Under his breath, automatically, through the velvet blackness, he heard *"B'ruch atah Adonai . . ."* Like a mantra, over and over he repeated it. Then the blackness parted, and he realized there were maroon and orange little clouds there, lighter spots that grew, and some tiny smaller white dots, almost exploding as if they were little stars, pulsating in and out like fireballs under his lids.

He heard running feet, laughter. Cautiously, gratefully, he opened his eyes. Saw the moon, no, a streetlight, a bunch of streetlights, a tree, a bench, asphalt path. He walked slowly, trying to maintain a minimum of sway, so that the shit wouldn't slide out the Jockey shorts and down his leg. In a weird way it felt good, comfortingly warm and mushy. The bottom part of his pants felt wet, too, damp with condensed sweat that made it stick to his legs. He was alive. Gratuitously, absurdly alive. As he might have been gratuitously, absurdly dead. It was all an accident. And not just this, but everything in his entire life, from being born to the parents to whom he was born, in the city in which he was born, in the country in which he was born, in the universe in which he was born, to wanting to be an artist, to meeting Lorraine, to breaking up with her—and not just her, but all the women he had ever met (or had not met) before her—to all the cars that had not hit him, all the bricks that had not fallen off buildings on top of him, all the bullets that had not gone into his body—or the bodies of everybody living (or not living) on this (or other) planet(s). Nothing was guaranteed; each moment was more fragile than a faded flower. In his head, without conscious intention, the words kept repeating, *"B'ruch atah Adonai . . ."* Then he hailed a cab, got in, opened the window, and gave the man five dollars for the short ride home.

•

Obsessively he washed his hands, then he took off his
Jockey shorts and threw them away. He removed the dish
drainer and jars with silverware from the wooden board that
sat on top of the tub in the kitchen and lifted off the board
and propped it against the wall. Only on rare occasions did
he bother; usually he just took a shower. In the hot water he
lay a long time, a bottle of wine on the floor beside him,
slightly high, listening to the stereo. It felt great to be inside,
with a little lamp shedding an orange glow: old-fashioned,
the very image of "home." Finally he got out and lay down
on his bed. He felt like calling up Lorraine and telling her
that if she did not come down to get him this very instant he
would die. She would come—or, rather, tell him to come on
up to her—but of course if that were all he wanted why had
he not stayed there in the first place? Why was nothing
enough? Would anything ever be enough? What did he want?

Supposing he had been killed tonight? What would people
have said about him? "Tragic Death of Artist . . . Unfulfilled
Dreams . . . Mediocre. . . . " Blah blah. Without conscious intention, he sat up and with all his force "pulled a Lorraine":
that is, he punched his fist into the wall. He screamed with
the pain, then ran to the fridge and dumped some ice cubes
in the sink, put in the stopper, and filled the basin with cold
water. For as long as he could stand it he kept his hand in the
freezing water, sobbing.

He had to face it. He had achieved none of his dreams. He
was not a great painter. Not only wasn't he a great painter,
but he didn't have any of the perks that made not being a
great painter bearable: money, fame, the sucking-up of the
triple Cs—critics, curators, collectors. But if you didn't have
the perks, and you didn't have the greatness, how the hell
could you keep on going?

16

You could blame it on the collapse of OPEC, David supposed, and its pyramid effect on the Texas oil industry, that the big development David had forced his reluctant partners into financing (on account of a passionate affair with a Houston waitress he needed an excuse to escape New York for) went bankrupt. In the expectation that Reagan's huge deficits would cause a further increase in inflation, thereby further depressing the stock market, he had sold short in an attempt to make good some of his losses. But inflation hit twenty-year lows, and the stock market began to climb. In a last-ditch gamble, he had used whatever capital he could scrounge up to buy options in a company involved in the projection of crop futures from information gathered from space satellites. Then *Challenger* blew up, and with it David's dreams. Over and over he watched that oddly beautiful explosion, the rocket and plume falling in a slow and elegant parabola off the screen.

Now, for the last time, he stood in his office, forty-four floors above the city, looking out a huge beige-tinted window down onto the Statue of Liberty, immobilized far below like a masochist in her steel cocoon. Even if he squashed his nose against the window and looked straight down, he was too high up to see the pavement. Tears came to his eyes as he threw whatever personal belongings were still in his desk into his briefcase. Then he said goodbye to the receptionist, and waited for the elevator to carry him down into his new life.

When he got off the elevator, he automatically bought *The
Wall Street Journal* at the newsstand in the lobby of his building and tucked it under his arm. But on the street he realized
there was no longer any reason for him to buy it: interest
rates, tax abatements, SEC regulations, fall of the dollar, no
longer had significance for him. So what if NBC relocated to
New Jersey; so what if the price of oil went up due to troubles
in the Persian Gulf? He stuffed the paper in one of those new
brown garbage cans and bought some hot chestnuts. The
briefcase was vestigial; it was all he could do not to throw it
away, too. But he remembered it had cost over $800. While
the streets were jammed with people rushing to get to lunch,
health clubs, discount stores, and quickie brothels, David, for
once at leisure, meandered lazily amongst the tall and narrow
buildings of the financial district as if they were pedestrians
to avoid. It was sunny up there in the sky, cold and dark
down here in the canyons. He stopped to look at a Dubuffet
statue whose absence he would have noticed had it been
removed, yet until now he could not have said what it looked
like. He stood there, trying to describe it to himself in words
so he could remember it. Then he headed south, toward light,
open water. Soon the Upper Bay was spread out before him,
cold and clear, the Lady surrounded by crutches, old and tired
now. He tried to imagine what it had been like a hundred
years ago, when she was the only belle on the block—a long-
necked beauty in a world where skyscrapers were still a
nightmare undreamt. On the ground were some huge pieces
of rusted metal—not junk, no, but sculptures, *art*—paid for
by guys like him. He spit. Through his skin he heard his
stomach growl. He bought a hot dog with mustard and sauer-
kraut. He bought another. He watched the boats crisscrossing
the white-capped waves and imagined another life. It was too
far away now to get there from here, but he entered the ter-
minal anyway and slipped a quarter in the turnstile. Waiting
for the ferry to start loading, he bought caramel popcorn, an
apple, a beer. When the light flashed, he got on board for
lovely ride on beautiful New York Harbor to Staten Island on

convenient and economical Staten Island ferry. Millions of
foreigners did this every year. Statue of Liberty, get inspira-
tion; Ellis, healthy happy Americans make money.

As he stood there by the railing, a woman came up to him.
In front of her she rolled a metal shopping cart filled with her
belongings. In it was clothing, books: *Remembrance of
Things Past* (revised edition), *Real Estate Investing Under
Late Capitalism*, poems by someone he never heard of.
"Don't I know you?" she asked.

"Of course not!" said David, disgusted.

"I'll read you something. . . . 'What is this desire for expla-
nation/but the desire for yet another paraphrase?/There is
nothing to learn/It is all here, you, me, the sky/If I were a
bird, watching the clouds form the dream of Russia/Could I
be happier than this?/In the sunlight I watch the water in
the glass magnify your fat fingers . . .' "

When he considered her suitably engrossed he walked
away, took the metal stairs to another deck. He leaned over
the rail. Threw a cigarette, hoping to see it land in the water,
swirl around, disappear. "That's illegal, ain't it? Littering?
Loitering," she giggled. Without turning around he recognized the woman's voice. "Saturday afternoons my father
used to take me to play in the park. We had a game where he
would hide and I would have to find him. But if I passed by
where he was and didn't see him he could jump out at me
and grab me. One day he kept my hand in his and put it inside
his pants. I told him I'd tell my mother and he said, 'All right,
but then she won't let us come to the park.' So I didn't say
anything but it continued to bother me. We didn't do it in
the park any more but in the house, when my mother wasn't
home. Finally I told him I wanted to stop, it was wrong. He
said who the hell did I think I was, I started it and had no
right to stop in the middle, he was my father. He beat me up.
After that I went along with him until I had a boyfriend who
got me to stop. Later I found out my mother had known about
it all along, but was scared to do anything."

"Um-hum . . . that's interesting," David interjected from
time to time. He half-listened, half-hummed an old song. To
avoid paying attention to her words—lies or not, he didn't
care—he tried to remember the names of buildings that grew

smaller as he watched them. The cold air hit his eyeballs, exercising them, a kind of massage. When he got tired of this he put on his shades. The boat hit S.I., emptied, refilled. He didn't get off. The woman stuck by him, continuing her story. "For years I hated men, though now I don't. I like them very much." She sidled closer to David. To his disgust he had a hard-on. "You want to suck my pussy?" she asked.

"No!"

"Then what do you like?"

"NOYB."

"What's that?"

"None of your business. Leave me alone."

"Faggot, huh?" the woman said loudly. People on nearby benches turned to look at them. To escape their stares David went inside to the snack bar. Hot dogs were on the grill so he ordered another.

"Look at the fag eat the hot dog!" the woman shouted. "You know how many hot dogs he's had today?" Everybody moved away from them, as if it were some kind of family quarrel, an assault on their privacy rather than on his.

"I don't know her," David told the world in general.

"The fuck he don't!" screamed the woman. They looked at her in pity, but at him in disgust.

"Women!" He shrugged, attempting insouciance, at the boy selling the food, to show this didn't affect him. The boy whistled, looked away, started to clean the grill.

David carried the cardboard cup of coffee back outside. He decided it was dumb to get upset. All this was within his control. If he paid serious attention to her it would be disturbing; if you paid serious attention to almost anything nowadays you'd kill yourself for sure. On the way back the buildings of downtown Manhattan—now a postcard in the distance—grew larger until they towered over the ferry. You'd think the sudden increase in size would scare small children, but it doesn't—just previously blind people who can suddenly see. Then the ferry gently bumped the wooden pilings that caressed the boat like pillows.

The woman followed him off the ferry.

"Buy me a drink," she demanded.

"No."

"Come on. This is the nicest conversation I've had in years."

"Are you kidding or what?"

"You're not so hot-looking either," she said, eying him up and down. He walked away. "Wait." David walked to a nearby bar and ordered a whiskey. She tried to follow him inside but they wouldn't let her enter. Through the window he saw her waiting patiently for him, her nose pushed against the glass so it looked like the snout of a pig. To spite her he ordered another, although all it did was make the pain that was lately always inside his stomach sharper. When the drink was nearly done he looked up to find her gone. He felt a strange sense of loss.

But she reappeared beside him when he left the bar and followed him to the car. "Who do you think Gorbachev is, but Ronald Reagan's twin brother? He looks younger but that's because of the face-lift. Nancy went to school with his wife, and sends her clothing from Neiman-Marcus, that's why she's so well dressed." When David got in the driver's side she managed to open the passenger door but the man from the garage pulled her away until David could lock it. David rolled down the window and gave the man a buck. Of course the woman could use it more, but he refused to give her any.

As he started uptown a painful rumbling went through his intestines. He pulled over. Suddenly the coffee and liquor and dogs got to him; he needed to pee real bad, maybe something else too. He looked around for a coffee shop, but at this hour the neighborhood was dead. He turned down a little street and looked for a phone booth, the old-fashioned enclosed kind. He took out a quarter and, pretending to make a phone call, managed to unzip his pants and pee. He got back in the car. Then he realized he really *did* have to make a phone call, so he got out of the car and went back to the booth. "Lydia?" he asked. "Are you there?" As usual, he got her machine. He could smell the urine there, his urine, see the dark stain on the ground. It didn't bother him, though anybody else's would have.

17

Jack stood in front of the mirror, studying the image of himself. He was wearing black jeans and Reeboks, a black leather jacket over a white T-shirt. The liberal use of gel made his hair stand straight up so that he looked like a young punk. He put his hands in his pockets, scowled, pulled out a gun.

"Stick 'em up," he said to his image.
"Come on, mister, hand it over.
"This is a gun. And this is a robbery.
"One word and I'll blast your face.
"Take off that watch.
"Gimme your wallet and everything will be all right.
"Come on, I don't got all day.
"You feel something cold on the side of your head?
"You feel something sticking into your back?
"*Now*, motherfucker, or I'll blow you away.
"Shut your eyes and count to ten."

A middle-aged German dressed in a muted gray Giorgio Armani suit and a Claude Montana topcoat walked out of his gallery on West Broadway and headed toward the parking lot near Grand. During his walk he stopped to talk first to a woman from Belgium who was an acquaintance of his wife, then to two Japanese men. As he approached his gray Mercedes he began to jiggle the keys in his pocket.

"Hold it," said Jack, a ski mask over his face, gun in hand, approaching the man.

"What do you want?" the man asked.

"What do you think, schmuck?" asked Jack.

"*Fuck.* Here's my wallet," The man took it out and threw it on the ground. "Would you mind leaving me my credit cards? You can't use them and it will only cause my wife trouble. She's leaving for Rome Tuesday and—"

"*Asshole,*" said Jack. "You don't give a shit about me! Why the fuck should I give a shit about your fucking wife and your fucking kid and your fucking car? Now kneel down and shut your eyes."

"What for?"

"Shut up, *Nazi,* and do what I say."

"I'm no Nazi," the man said. "I was five years old."

"*Shut up,*" said Jack, and kicked him. The man knelt down. "Now tell me, what do you sell that garbage in your gallery for?"

"The art in my gallery?" the man was confused.

"Art," Jack spit. "Fifteen thousand for a neon sculpture anybody could copy at a hardware store! Give me a break!"

"Capitalism, don't blame me."

"Start talking," Jack shoved the pistol in the man's back. "And when you're done, I want to hear you begging for your life."

As the man talked, he began sobbing hysterically. He slumped to the ground. Only when he got up did he notice a sheet of paper lying on the pavement next to him.

Manifesto #1

This is not a robbery; this is a performance piece! Thank you for participating with me in this interactive work of art. Yes, *art*—or don't you recognize art when you see it, Mr. Gallery Dealer? Now let's get clear about our terms. By art I do *not* mean those meaningless yards of canvas filled with representational images that no longer shock, or abstracts with all the stimulation of a tie-dyed T-shirt—stuff you coerce yuppies and curators and banks into buying to support your upscale lifestyle! By art I do *not* mean what banks buy to deduct as business expenses so they can avoid paying taxes; by art I do *not* mean the museums you drag your kids to on Sundays to help make them "respectable" members of society. "Respectable members of society"—that's a good one; do anything to get out of paying taxes that you can—rob the government of hundreds of times more dough than someone like me could ever get from someone like you. You make me sick, with your tax-deductible trips to Europe and your pretentious bullshit rap about "hegemony of the picture plane" or "disenjoined signifier" or whatever critical theory you're currently spouting to sell your latest crap. Jeff Koons could cast his shit in bronze and you wouldn't miss a beat: "an ironic commentary on the ultimate, irreducible product, a symbol not just of personal excrescence (and excess) but society's as well, in a post-modern context that sends up the very idea of sculpture even as it creates, in its cool irony, an object that is, once divorced from its signifier, possessed of an odd, but indisputable, beauty. But perhaps this disjunction is the very point, a kind of paradoxical signaling of the. . . ." Can't you just hear it? And you pretend that crap like this is "political," a critique of the status quo—such a critique that the fucking banks buy it and the government gives the artists grants! Who are you kidding, asshole? Art that's truly provocative doesn't sell to banks! Art that's provocative isn't supported by the government! Art that's provocative isn't adored by professionals; it's ignored, insulted, walked out on, cursed. How could it be otherwise, for, let's face it, the only thing that really means anything to anybody in the twentieth century is *money*, and *violence*, and *power* to fuck over other human beings . . .

Jack ran across Grand to Mott, up Mott to Spring, across Spring to the Bowery, then north to Houston. He realized he wasn't being followed, but in his exuberance he continued further east, to the river. The gun—a starter pistol, actually—banging against him in its shoulder holster, should have slowed him down, but he felt he was running on a little carpet of air, a hydrofoil boat flying over the asphalt and grass. A barge was on the river; he passed it. A cloud scudded across the sky, creating a milky halo around the moon; he raced it across the park. The sweat on his face felt like a glow of happiness; it fell in his eyes, creating a tiny rainbow around the lamps in the park. The moon shone so brightly on the river he could distinctly see the ridges formed by the shadows of the waves, the beam seemingly so substantial he felt he could have walked across it into a different universe. But why leave the wonderful one he was in? He was afraid of nothing and no one. Sweaty, his heart pounding, gasping for breath, he sat down on a bench. When the sweat evaporated he realized he was cold. He stood up and began jogging again, more slowly this time, and didn't stop till he saw his building, glowing with an eerie beauty in the yellow light from the streetlamp and the whiter light from the moon.

When Jack walked in his door he extended his arms, let his jacket drop on the floor, stumbled to the john, took his pulse, splashed cold water on his face, turned on the shower. He didn't immediately get into it, but stood there breathing the steam. His lungs were bigger than ever before. He felt he could dive to the bottom of the ocean, drag a lobster out of a cave, have plenty of time to float back to the surface. Through the fog of the steam he looked in the mirror, at the face of this new man, this stranger he was creating. Then he picked up the phone and called Jeremy.

> *New York Post*, "Page Six"
> We thought we'd heard of just about everything, but this about takes the cake. Seems there's this guy downtown who looks like he's robbing people, only he stops in the middle and says "just kidding; it's only art." Soho folks may be amused, but not Captain Julio Brownstein of the 6th Precinct, who says that the perpetrator may be insane, perhaps violently so, and to report all suspicious circumstances to the following special number: 670-H-E-L-P. The identity of the Lone Ranger? Don't be fooled by those shadowy mug shots on the "Wanted" posters about town; rumor has it this is none other than the Silver Shadow himself, come back from the dead. . . .

Jack stood in front of the mirror, studying the image of himself. He was wearing oversized pants he had found in a thrift shop, deliberately torn and made filthy, shoes whose soles were becoming detached from their uppers, a frayed old jacket of his own. His hair was filthy and matted, his face and hands dirty—the very image of a homeless man. He headed uptown to the fabulously expensive new French fish restaurant, from which exited a young couple in their mid-thirties who had just bought two prix-fixe dinners for $85 apiece—not including wine, tax, and tip.

Jack followed them a few blocks, then ran up and tapped the guy on the shoulder. "Spare five bucks for dinner?" he asked.

"Five bucks for dinner! Buddy, that's a good one," the man replied, pushing Jack away with one hand as he hustled the woman past him with the other. "Can you beat that?" Jack heard him say. "Wait till the guys at the club hear that one."

"Alan, I can't stand it, give him something."

"All right." The man stopped, turned around. "Hey, *you*," he shouted at Jack. "Here's a quarter."

Jack took and examined it as if it were an ancient Roman coin. "A quarter, huh. Tell me what the fuck am I supposed to do with it?"

The man looked puzzled. "Do with it? I don't know. Get a drink or something," he said uneasily.

"A drink? You want to tell me where I can get a drink for a *quarter!*" The man tried to move past but Jack pulled out his pistol. "I like your sense of humor, mister, *five bucks for dinner*, yeah, that's a real laugh riot, all right, for the guys at the club. How much you pay for the club, mister? And now that we're being so conversational, when was the last time you spent five bucks for dinner? Let's see that dinner receipt, mister—I know you got a receipt because you're so smart you probably manage to deduct your condoms, ain't I right?"

"You're crazy," the man said.

"You live in a country that spends three hundred billion a year on defense, and when we invade Grenada the navy's got to use an ordinary AT&T telephone to coordinate the attack with the army—because the army and navy don't have radios that can talk to each other—and you think *I'm* crazy? Now where's that dinner receipt?" The man flipped through his wallet for the receipt and handed it to Jack. "Yeah, *I'm* crazy, all right—and *you're* the one who spent three hundred twelve dollars to stuff food in your mouth. *That's* the laugh! Hey, lady," Jack said, turning to the woman, "who's crazier, me or that husband of yours? I know I look like scum, but don't you think I'm worth maybe one sixtieth of your dinner? Maybe I'm not, but what percentage of your dinner do you think I'm worth—or maybe I should just starve to death on the streets and not eat at all? Hey, I don't mean to offend you. Maybe you're not married to this schmuck. You're not wearing a ring. Hasn't Mr. Generosity here proposed? Or does he want to go spreading that AIDS virus around a little more? What business are you in, mister?" The man said nothing. Jack nudged him with the pistol. "I said, what business are you in?"

"Securities."

"*Securities.* I like that word. Secure from whom? I wonder. Not from a little insider info, I'm sure. —Or a crash. Hey, whatsa matter, mister?" Jack punched the guy on the arm. "Don't you got a sense of humor?" Sweat poured out of the man's forehead; he turned white and started to retch.

Manifesto #2
You know what I like? I'll tell you what I like? *To see schmucks like you start sweating!* Because that's what schmucks like you make guys like us feel all the time. Most of us don't got doormen and buzzers and intercoms, we ride the subway instead of limos, our neighborhoods suck—hey, you buy the *Post*, you know the story. So I thought I'd bring a little bit of downtown up to you, guerrilla art, you know, I'm an artist; yeah, buddy, this was all a joke, a "performance piece" as we call it downtown. I hope you dug it, got your thrills, maybe even rev up the sex a bit tonight. Now what I'm curious is, are you going to complain to the cops? Cause after all, what the fuck did I do but harangue you on the street with a starter pistol in my hand? Sorry, schmuck, you could have been a hero! *But you weren't, were you!* No, you just stood there and took it in front of the lady; you would have let me rape her too, wouldn't you've? Wonder what she thinks of you now—hey, like, no balls? Probably she'd rather do it with me. You know how it is, uptown chicks think us artists cool. . . . And now you hate me, cause I "violated" you, made you frightened, shit in your pants maybe? But think about it, buddy, what is violation? what is terror? what is privacy? You who have enough bombs and mis-

siles floating over your head to exterminate you and everyone you
love fifty times over, who live in a country where the per capita
ownership of handguns is equivalent to that of the population,
who walk streets surrounded by madmen carrying not just starter
pistols as I do but semi-automatics, whose homes are barricaded
by locks, and doormen, who interrogate all visitors by intercom,
whose steering wheels are fitted with special locks to make them
safe from thieves, whose every financial transaction is recorded
electronically to eliminate forever any notions of privacy....
That is the violation, *that* is the terror—yet who will you be
angry at tonight and tomorrow and the day after?—*me!*

Jack stood in front of the mirror, studying the image of
himself—a young punk with hair goop and torn jeans.

A middle-aged man got out of a taxi on East Seventy-fifth
Street between Second and Third and fumbled for the key to
his building. He was drunk and he swayed a little.

"Hey, there," said Jack, his hand menacingly in his pocket.

"Don't kill me, please," the man begged. "I'll do anything
you want."

"Do anything I want? Now, what would you think I'd want
you to do for me? Now go down on your knees and tell me
what an asshole you are."

"What an asshole I am?"

"Yeah. You are, aren't you?" Jack nudged the man.

"Of course."

"So—"

The man sank to his knees. "I cheat on my wife with my
girlfriend. I lie to my girlfriend I'll marry her. Sometimes
when I used to get real drunk I'd suck off guys in the Mine
Shaft—suppose I got AIDS? I lie on my taxes . . . I got credit
cards in phony names I never pay. . . ."

Manifesto #3
The intention of this work of art is to bring into consciousness
the utter centrality of terror in your daily life, so that you may
realize how the avoidance of potentially dangerous neighborhoods, the necessity of curtailing movements during the night,
the daily reports of murders and muggings and sexual violence
affect not just your physical activities but penetrate into the very

depths of your psyches. . . . Surely you would not have been frightened had you known I was only "performing a piece," i.e., "pretending." But what *is* reality? what *is* pretense? Do you feel that even though I'm not robbing or physically harming you I should be prosecuted under the law? Under which law? Why does this performance anger you more than if I wrote a lousy play you wasted $47.50 to see on Broadway?—this is a free performance and I'm doing it just for you! Why are you angrier at me than you would be if I inadvertently plowed my car into your car, thereby depriving you of its use for a month? Why is five minutes of fear worse than staring at the graffiti you detest all the combined weeks and—yes—*months* of your life you've spent crammed against other human beings in the subway—any one of whom could go crazy at any second and stab you? Would I be more acceptable if I took your money instead of making a fool and coward of you? Why do you hate me more than Reagan, who's fucking up the country forever? Point to my crime, where is it? I haven't stolen your property, harmed your body, or forcibly removed it to another location. My gun can't kill you, it's got no bullets. Why aren't you angry at this society that does nothing to protect its people, whose victims pay for their own medical care while the criminal gets his paperback royalty millions? Why aren't public officials jailed for their stupidity, and held reponsible for the consequences of their actions—shouldn't this be a logical risk for assuming a position of power and financial remuneration? Did you know that you, the Victim, have a greater chance of being mugged than I, the Perpetrator, have of being arrested, for doing this to you? . . ."

In Jack's typewriter were notes for the "documentation" he hoped to sell when the performances were done. He was tired. His back hurt. His head hurt. It was two in the morning. He drank a beer, then another. The music was turned up as loud as it could go. He tried to reread his notes, but the words danced in his head. He went into the john to take a shower.

In the mirror he saw a man he did not recognize.

This man was wearing black. He had stubble on his face. If it was not him, who was it?

The face looked dangerous. But surely there was a dreamy sadness in those eyes? . . .

Could one forget who one was, what one believed in and cared about, how one was supposed to behave? What could it mean to "lose" one's "character"? What did it mean to be a person? How were we connected with the person we were years ago, when all the cells from that time were dead?

Could he really change who he was? And if so, who would he choose to be?

18

With one person less in the apartment, Lorraine had expected an improvement in Aurelia's housekeeping (for example, cleaning of bathroom walls, washing of windows, silver-polishing), tasks whose neglect she was willing (at least in retrospect) to attribute to the burden of an additional human being living in the house. And not just improvement, but Aurelia's assumption of one or two duties she had never before performed: such as on occasion venturing to Zabar's to pick up some gourmet specialty, or maybe even walking the dog.

This turned out not to be the case. Were Lorraine too specific in her requests (e.g., smoked sturgeon, wild rice with porcini mushrooms, smoked goose breast), Aurelia would report either that such an item had been sold out, or was not on the menu for that day. Given greater leeway, with unerring instinct she would bring home just the similar item that Lorraine could not stand: whitefish, rice pilaf, barbecued wings. As for walking Jack, though she would swear she had done so, Lorraine would often find that, when she didn't do this herself (or coerce Judy into doing it) there was a good possibility that sometime before the evening walk she might find a puddle—or worse—in the vicinity of the front door. When taken to task, Aurelia would assert that Jack, despite a lengthy perambulation, had refused to perform his business on the street. "I be thinking he hates me," she would assert, "he be not going on purpose." Jack didn't like Aurelia, but whether this was a cause or a result of some deficiency as to being walked (or otherwise), Lorraine couldn't be sure. She assigned Judy this task, but Judy asserted she would rather give Jack away than be responsible for walking him every day.

"Who'll adopt an eleven-year-old mutt? The pound will take him, and you know what they'll do to him."

"Daddy will take him. He's always complaining how lonely he is."

"No, he won't. His building forbids dogs. I've already asked him." Silence. "I'll give you one more week. Then I take him to the pound."

"You won't," said Judy. "You couldn't stand the idea of anyone knowing you'd done that."

Judy was right in her prediction as to what Lorraine would(n't) do, but the basis of her belief indicated a terribly grim view of human motivation. Lorraine wondered if this was but another manifestation of the female adolescent's necessary rebellion against the mother, or an indication of some more profound (hence—oddly—more treatable) disillusionment with human behavior in general. Whatever it was, somehow the absence of a man in her life, for the first time in almost twenty years, made it harder for Lorraine to deal with her. It was one thing to run a business, another to deal with a recalcitrant thirteen-year-old. Perhaps if she did not have to deal with the former, she might have been able to handle the latter. But she had to deal with the former, and she was conscious of being more tired at the end of the day than she had been in the past—even if this fatigue were not truly fatigue, but only "depression." Even before Jack and David had "abandoned" her (as Lorraine described it to herself), she had felt herself growing old, tired, undesirable. The idea of a new relationship with a man—let alone falling in love with someone new—seemed inconceivable. Wasn't a woman over forty more likely to be struck by lightning than to get married? The concept of happiness was so far away that although she could visualize such moments, as if scenes from a movie viewed in childhood, she could not re-create them so as to experience them from the inside. She missed Jack, but what did she remember?—the back of his neck as he half-knelt on the floor of an art gallery bathroom trying to wipe a red stain from a white dress, falling asleep as he lay in bed reading next to her. She was forced to admit that, in the future battles between her and Judy, if Judy held out long enough, she would win most of them—or rather, whether

Lorraine won the battles or not, surely Judy would win the war; if only due to this fatigue, the normal attritions of age.

Lorraine could not remember what she had expected of her life, but certainly it was not to go through these battles alone. Whether she was more angry at Jack, David, or herself for creating this unpleasant state of affairs, she wasn't sure. She tried to take consolation in her unobstructed view, through the bare trees, to New Jersey.

The phone rang. It was Judy. "Where have you been?" demanded Lorraine.

"At Saralee's. She's loaning me something for the party tomorrow night."

"How come you didn't call? It's almost seven."

"I tried you at work, Mom, but the line was busy."

"Judy—" Such a palpable lie—such an *insult*—demanded some response, but, in her frailty, Lorraine felt she needed her daughter on her side, and she had trouble finding the words.

"Mom, I got to go. I'll be home soon. Bye."

"Judy—"

The dial tone buzzed in her ear.

For as long as Jack could stand it (which wasn't very long) he lay quietly on the floor near Lorraine's feet, his head half nuzzling one of her shoes, then he got up and placed a paw on Lorraine's knee. Reprimanded (to Jezebel's delight), he took refuge under the dining-room table, then almost instantly returned to the living room. Ordered by Lorraine to sit, he did, for a few moments, then wandered into the bedroom and crawled under the bed. There he found the remains of an old plastic bone. Its shape and the act of biting it reminded him of former, greater pleasures. Not knowing language, and therefore not possessing what we call consciousness, nonetheless somewhere in the gray cells of his brain was manifested the image of a cowhide chewy, and he moaned. Absently, discontentedly, he gnawed the plastic, waiting for—what?

•

Jezebel lay on the couch. All day she had listened to the fridge going on and off, the water dripping from the washer neither David nor Jack nor Lorraine had ever replaced, the roar of the vacuum cleaner, the noise of the TV and radio Aurelia listened to (sometimes simultaneously) as she worked, her voice on the telephone as she talked to her friends, the occasional ringing of the phone or doorbell, the elevator opening and closing, the wind rustling the venetian blinds; she had heard the clank of Jack's collar as he ran to the door when Lorraine came home (Jezebel disdained such fawning tactics); she heard Lorraine saying hello to Jack, the pads of his paws thumping and the click of his nails as he tried to jump up on her; she heard the shutting of the door, the placement of Lorraine's huge black leather handbag (the one cleverly designed to resemble plastic) on the dining-room table, the opening of the hall closet, the hanging-up of her coat, the opening and shutting of the fridge, the clank of ice and the splash of liquid in the glass, the shuffling of feet to the couch, the kicking-off of her shoes, the slight sigh as the air went out of the cushions as Lorraine lowered her body onto them. Only now did she raise her head, reach out her paws, and permit herself to be scratched behind the ears. When she got tired of this, she stood up, performed the yoga stretch known as "cat back," yawned, and ambled off to another, more private chair.

Consoling herself with the view out the window, a glass of wine in her hand, Lorraine gathered her resources for the rest of the evening. She should cook, of course, but an intense consciousness of the meaninglessness of this task suddenly overwhelmed her. Judy would walk in, drop her coat on the floor, turn on the stereo, the TV, reach for the kitchen phone. As Lorraine chopped, sautéed, washed lettuce—for a meal she didn't even feel like eating—she would be forced to listen to each word of Judy's half of the tedious conversation and, in the obsessive way the mind works, would find herself, despite conscious intentions, struggling to piece together the meaning of the bits and pieces of the words she was overhearing. When the meal was finally ready, she would order

Judy off the phone to the table, where (having just gulped
down cookies, potato chips, juice, soda—whatever instantly
available food was most guaranteed to destroy her appetite)
Judy would ungraciously allow herself to be coerced into
swallowing a few bites before excusing herself—so she could
spend the next few hours talking on the phone to the very
same kids she'd sat next to all day in class, gone out with
after school to some place or other, and chatted on the phone
with before dinner. Threats were of no avail to make Judy
help clean up, for she'd assert she'd sooner go without dinner
than carry dishes into the kitchen. She would run off, leaving
Lorraine sitting alone with her half-full plate, the crumpled
napkin, the wine glass, the empty walls. Where was the satisfaction in this?

For the first time in she couldn't remember when, Lorraine
asked herself what she really felt like doing.

What she really felt like doing was lying in bed, listening
to WNCN, the classical music radio station, reading a book.
And so, with a feeling of immense satisfaction, she went into
her bedroom, kicked off her shoes, and did just that.

She was half-sitting up, leaning on a pillow propped against
the wall, a book lying face down on her chest, in the dark,
when the doorbell rang. Lorraine started to get out of bed to
open the door, then it occurred to her, for perhaps the first
time in her life, that it was unreasonable of Judy to expect
her to do this. For years now Judy had had her own key: it
wasn't Lorraine's fault she often forgot to take it with her in
the morning. Lorraine lay back down, though it took all her
willpower to prevent herself from jumping up and running to
the door. For a long time the bell continued to ring—a few
quick rings, a pause, several long ones, one monstrously long
one, a bunch of quick toots like a train whistle. Then the
banging began, first of a fist, then what sounded like the
kicking of a shoe. Then it stopped, and Lorraine heard (or at
least imagined she heard) the sound of the elevator door opening and closing. After a few moments of quiet the banging
and bell-ringing briefly resumed, then there was the sound of
a lock being turned.

"Thanks loads!" Lorraine heard Judy say, followed by the slam of the front door. Then: lights (punched on), action (dropping of book bag on floor), camera (the TV)—she could see it as clearly as if she had been standing in the living room.

"Mom! Mom!" Judy shrieked. She dashed into the bedroom and turned on the overhead light. Lorraine squinted. "Mom, what's the matter? Are you all right?" The concern in her voice touched Lorraine.

"I think so. A little tired maybe."

"Then why are you lying here like this?" Judy turned on the bedside lamp. "Isn't that better?"

"Not really," said Lorraine, shading her eyes.

"Gosh, Mom, you're really weird! Ohmigod, it's almost eight!" Before Lorraine could reply to this, she dashed out of the room. Lorraine could hear her fumbling with the VCR, then, when the sound came on, she ran back to the bedroom.

"Guess what's on, Mom? *Ghostbusters!*"

"For only the tenth time. How exciting!"

"You sure you're okay?" Judy sat down next to her, and felt her brow.

"A little depressed, I guess."

"In the dark like that, who wouldn't be? Say, what's for dinner?"

"Nothing."

"Nothing?" Judy looked at her in amazement.

"Nothing." Lorraine would have thought she'd feel guilt at this admission. Instead, a warm feeling of pleasure rippled through her body.

"Nothing? You mean you didn't make dinner?"

"No."

"What are you going to eat?"

"Nothing. I'm not hungry. I'll just read a little, then go to sleep."

"You *must* be sick."

"Maybe," Lorraine shrugged. "There's some eggs in the fridge, if you want to make an omelette. Or the leftover chicken from last night. Or heat up some frozen pizza."

"Mom!"

"Judy, I'm not your servant. If you're hungry, you're perfectly capable of making something yourself."

"Mom, look—why don't we call up for Chinese food? Wouldn't you like some nice hot-and-sour soup? I'll get the menu."

"No," said Lorraine.

"No?" Judy widened her eyes in incredulity as she said this, as if she were auditioning for the school play.

"*No!* With the tip and everything, it was almost thirty dollars the last time we did that."

"*So?*"

"I can't afford it. I'm on my own now, without your father or Jack."

"Whose fault is that?" She picked up the phone. "Could you give me the number for Mr. Chang's on Columbus Avenue?" she demanded.

"*Judy*—I said *no.*"

"799-7997." Judy started to dial.

"Hang up the phone."

"Mo-ther! I don't know what's gotten into you."

"You don't call till almost seven, you lie to me, then you expect me to have dinner waiting!"

"I didn't lie to you! Your line *was* busy."

"I don't want to discuss it. I'm going to sleep."

"That's fine for you, but I have to eat!"

"I told you. There's plenty of leftover chicken. Heat up some soup if you want."

"What I want is Chinese food."

"I don't object a bit, Judy, as long as you pay for it yourself."

"God! I'm gonna call Daddy. He'll take me out."

"Go right ahead. I'm going to sleep now. Please shut the door when you leave."

Lorraine reached up, turned out the light, and rolled on her side away from Judy. In apparent disbelief Judy remained sitting on the bed. Lorraine felt so uncomfortable until she left the room that it was all she could do to prevent herself from sitting up and screaming. Even when Judy had gone, and she was able to relax, paradoxically, to the sound of the TV and the stereo, she was still unable to fall asleep, but found herself in that deep fatigue in which dream images appear, where

the events of the day, slowly and without affect, parade before one's eyes. She was so tired she felt almost paralyzed,
though she was convinced she could lift her arm to prove she
wasn't—if only she were interested in lifting her arm. As she
lay there she listened to the sounds of the apartment as it
was when she was not in it: TV, cabinet bangings in the
kitchen, giggles, phone calls, hang-ups, phone ringings, the
opening and shutting of her door as Judy checked up on her.

It was like being an invalid. It was as if she were a child, or
a very old woman. It was pleasant.

Sometime later she heard the front door open, the sound of
David's voice. Then he knocked on her door and came into
the room. For a while she kept her eyes shut, trying to get
back to where she had been, then she sat up suddenly and
turned on the light. "What do you want?" she asked irritatedly.

"Judy called. She said you wouldn't give her anything to
eat."

"David, you know this house. Go check the fridges. Do
you really think it likely there's nothing to eat?"

"She wanted Chinese food."

"She wanted to cause trouble."

David sat down on the edge of the bed. Her senses sharp
from sleep, Lorraine could smell the vodka. "We've really
made a mess of it, haven't we?" said David. He opened and
shut his hands. They were red, puffy, disgusting. She had an
impulse to reach out and touch them.

"I've been meaning to talk to you," he said. "I've got problems. My partners ditched me."

She nodded. "I know."

"You know?" he asked in surprise.

"I ran into Andy. He wanted to know if you were okay."

"He's a fine one to ask," David gave a bitter laugh. "I lost
money in the market too. I'm wiped out. But in a weird way
I don't give a shit."

"What are you talking about?"

"I don't know. It all seems so arbitrary—success, failure. If it weren't happening to me, I'd laugh about it." He paused, examined his knuckles. "Come on, don't tell me you don't feel that way sometimes too."

"I do. Sometimes. But—"

"But what?"

"Oh, she sighed. "I don't know."

She fell silent. The moment was right, but he still wasn't sure he wanted to go through with it. "Look, Lorraine, I've been thinking . . ." He stopped, waiting for her to ask him what.

"What?" Though she was almost sure she knew.

"Maybe we should get back together. I mean, look at the phone call tonight. Judy misses me. I miss her." Pause. "I miss *you*."

For a while he just sat there, then, realizing the implications of what he had said, he put his hand on her leg. It felt strange, as if he were in a movie. He tried to kiss her, but she turned her head so his lips landed on the slight fuzz above and slightly to the left of her lip. When he looked at her, he could see the hair in her nostrils.

Lorraine had often wondered how she would feel if David wanted to come back. A wave of gratification washed over her—as satisfying as an orgasm, and disappearing almost as quickly. For the first time in years, she felt no anger toward him. But there was no desire there either.

"What are you thinking?"

"Nothing. I just feel a little sad, that's all."

"Me too. That's why I think we should get back together. So we can get rid of the sadness."

"I would find this a lot more convincing if you had brought it up before Cecilia left you."

"You're gonna mess up our lives on account of a little timing. Christ!"

"Who messed up whose lives?" Lorraine demanded angrily.

"At least I'm trying to repair the damage. And you accuse me of being insincere."

"Not exactly insincere. But I don't believe you love me. You're lonely, you're broke, you don't like where you're living, so when you walk in the door naturally you get a bit sentimental."

"What about Judy? You don't believe I miss her?"

"I do, David. It's *me* I don't believe you miss."

"But I do. I *do*." He banged the mattress. He could feel tears inside his eyes. He tried to make himself feel sadder, so they would well up and roll down his face. Lorraine patted his arm.

"You don't, David. You just miss . . . something."

"How do you know?"

"I know. I feel it too. I keep thinking, maybe one day Jack will figure out what it is he wants, and it will turn out to be me."

David began to feel angry: where was his reward for coming over and condescending to deliver what amounted to an apology? Maybe she couldn't be expected to leap immediately into his arms, but his words should evoke at least some emotion in her about *him*—rather than about some other man. "Come on, you know that's not gonna work out. You know what these artists are like. Self-indulgent, self-destructive, immature. What has he ever done in life except try to coerce people into supporting his little works of 'self-expression?'" David put as much contempt into this word as he could muster. "He's never really lived with anybody. What does he know about relationships? What does he know about . . . *duration!* And then, he's never had kids of his own, he's gonna want children. What are you, forty-one, forty-two? Don't tell me you're gonna—"

Lorraine started crying. Nothing David was saying was something she hadn't told herself any number of times, but hearing it out of his mouth somehow made it more official. Watching the tears roll down her face, David was able, for a moment, to see her as a human being separate from himself. How many years has it been since he has done this? "Look. I know how you feel. Cecilia . . . I'm not saying this out of jealousy, believe me. I *like* him. But he's . . . not *it*. I really think—"

They fell silent. Lorraine, staring at the glowing dials of the clock radio, seemed lost in thought. The clock ticked; a car, which had been stopped by a light, started up. The pipes in the bathroom gurgled. The familiar routine overwhelmed David with emotion. How could this ever have bored him?

Wasn't the beauty of the world inherent in this? What had ever possessed him to leave?

"Really, Lorraine, I *do* love you." He lifted his head, put his mouth on hers, stuck his tongue inside. This time she didn't resist, but she didn't help either. Without enthusiasm on her part he couldn't go on. He didn't feel anything either. But he *wanted* to. It was so unfair. He banged his palm on the mattress. Then he really started to cry.

She patted his hand. "You'll feel better when you find a new girlfriend," she said.

"A new girlfriend? Lorraine, *look at me.*" She looked. On her bed lay a man in his upper forties, red-eyed, red-faced, sweating. His shirt was dirty, and a smell of alcohol and tobacco emanated from his body and his jacket. David stood up. "I'm getting something to drink."

Lorraine got out of bed and followed him to the kitchen. With relief she saw several plates out on the counter, ends of bread encrusted with dried peanut butter and jelly: Judy had gotten herself something to eat. She closed the bread bag with the fastener and put it, the peanut butter, and jelly back in the fridge. Meanwhile David had gotten out vodka and ice. "You want some?" he asked. She shrugged.

"You should cut down on your drinking," she told him.

"There's a thousand things I should do." He waved the hand with the glass in it at the kitchen tiles, wavy because the contractors had not bothered to first straighten the walls.

"You couldn't try to get back with your partners?"

"Ha! Those fuckers!"

Lorraine rinsed Judy's dishes in the sink, then brought them to the dishwasher. It was full of clean, still-warm dishes. She began wiping off the counter, then, seeing the automatic coffee-maker was turned to On, she shut it off and rinsed the sludge out of the pot. "Aurelia." She shook her head. Remembering how she always complained how terrible he was around the house, David thought of helping her, but feared it would look phony, as if he were trying to butter her up. He poured some more vodka. He realized he was quite warm, and took off his jacket. "I want you to promise me you'll think about what I said," he said.

"I will. But—" she sat down next to him—"don't count on anything."

"Why not?"

"It's too late, David. Too much has happened."

"Happened? What's happened? To late for *what?* Come on, we've still got half our lives!" He was swaying in his drunkenness, and the stool tipped. He landed on the tiles. The coolness felt good against his warm body. He decided to take advantage of his position by going on his knees, the way guys supposedly did in the old days when they proposed. "Look, Lorraine, I love you, I've never stopped loving you."

"David. *Please.*"

"Even when I moved out, I always felt we'd get back together again, sometime or other. I was just playing out the string. You still love me. I know you do. I can see it in your eyes." He stared at her without blinking, as people did when they tried to convey their sincerity.

"I'm sorry, David. I really don't. Sometimes I don't even know whether I *like* you." Pause. "Sometimes I think I never liked you."

"Don't be ridiculous. You were crazy to marry me."

"I wonder. I think I married you because I was living with you, and all my friends were getting married." David's heart skipped; could what she was saying possibly be true? For almost twenty years he had congratulated himself on the great favor he had done her by marrying her. "Come on. There's no point in going over all this. You're just talking like this because you're tired and drunk. You'll feel better when you get a good night's sleep."

"Don't patronize me—you shit!" David stood up. Lorraine began emptying the dishwasher. David wanted to shout at her how much he hated her. He also wanted her to take him back. Walking carefully over to the dishwasher to cover his drunkenness, he lifted a serving bowl out of the dishwasher: a blue flower design on the outside, Lorraine's favorite.

"You *really* don't want to get back together?" he asked.

"As you said, David, look at yourself."

Against the glass of the cabinets he saw his face reflected: the face of a man who would not be served any more meals out of this bowl—a bowl that probably was a wedding gift. He thought of pot-au-feu, *pasta e fagioli,* chicken with forty cloves of garlic. Would he ever eat so well again? He watched his arms heave the bowl, saw the turquoise and white crash into the shiny white tiles of the wall, fall down in tiny pieces onto the dull white tiles on the floor.

Judy rushed out of her room. "Mom, Dad, what is *with* you?" she demanded.

"Your father dropped something," said Lorraine.

"You're mother's a bitch," said David.

"I *hate* you!" Judy screamed. Both Lorraine and David felt this comment was directed specifically at them. Then she ran back to her room.

"I'd like you to leave now," Lorraine told David.

"No!" David shouted. He reached into the dishwasher, grabbed another dish, and threw that too. Almost immediately, the music coming out of Judy's room got even louder. David hated everything he was saying and doing, but could not stop himself. If only he could go back, even five minutes in time, to undo what he had said and done. But he couldn't. So he kept trying to correct things. But he just kept making things worse.

Lorraine shook her head. She bent down to clean up the mess David had made. David knew he should have done it, but he felt too embarrassed to move. He was emotionally exhausted. He tried to recall an emotionally gratifying experience. For a long while his mind was blank, then the image coalesced: popcorn in hand, watching *Bus Stop* with his best buddy Joey. At the pizza parlor afterward they ran into two girls in their class. Joey flirted with one of the girls and David with the other. He didn't really know how but he copied Joey. He was used to copying Joey in lots of things. Then it was time for the girls to go home. They walked the girls to Joey's girl's house. A big white house with a porch on a corner, lots of grass. David wondered whether he was supposed to kiss the girl good night; uncertain, he decided to wait and see what Joey did. But by then, somehow, it was too late, so David didn't do anything. He and his girl just stood awkwardly around watching Joey kiss his girl. Then the girls went inside. He and Joey listened to them laughing as the

door closed. Outside a streetlamp shone on the lawn, same color as the moon. He smelled cut grass, honeysuckle, tasted a piece of red pepper caught under his tooth. In the twilight he walked Joey back home. "You can spend the night at my place if you want," Joey told him. David wanted, but for some reason he lied and said no, he'd promised his mother he'd be home that night. David watched the door close as Joey went inside. He watched a light go on upstairs in Joey's dark room, then a dim sound of the radio, mournful and nostalgic, filled the air. For maybe a half hour David sat on the lawn, hidden by the shadows of a tree, watching Joey's room. Why he did this he didn't know, then or now. All of a sudden, feeling deeply embarrassed, he had stood up. The back of his pants was wet—dew. He felt petrified someone would see it and think he had done something in his pants. He got up and started to walk, not home but just walk. The sky got darker and the streetlamps no longer looked like the moon, but still, he tramped for hours among the lighted houses, alone in the universe, his body on fire with strange desires.

David grabbed his jacket. "Say goodbye to Judy for me, wouldja?" he asked. "I can't face her now." Lorraine nodded. "I'm sorry," said David. "I'm just not myself lately."

"You need help."

"I know."

"If for nothing else, you owe it to Judy."

But instead of heading toward the door, he walked into the living room and whistled for Jack. Under the piano, Jack, caught in dreams, gave a muted growl, then stood up and staggered over to David. David began to play with him, not so much because he really felt like it as because he thought that maybe this evidence of his sentimentality might impress Lorraine. He waited until she emerged from the kitchen, then, as if suddenly exhausted, plopped down on the couch, leaned his head back, and shut his eyes. "Look, would you mind if I stayed over, just for the night? I'm so tired I can sleep right here."

"David, you know that wouldn't work." She opened the
door and rang for the elevator. As they waited for it he swayed
back and forth. "You don't want to give me a blow job, do
you?" Lorraine looked away in disgust. When the elevator
man came Lorraine gave him five dollars to help David into
a taxi. With relief she closed, locked, and chained the door.

David leaned his head against the cool glass of the front
door of the building as the doorman went down to the Drive
to whistle him a cab. Somehow the furniture of the lobby
was reflected in the glass of the door so that it became super-
imposed on the pavement outside, the kind of perception you
noticed only when you were drunk or stoned and which
seemed a justification for such states. Across the street, in
the building nobody's lived in for years, David thought he
saw a light flicker on, off. He wondered if the owners had
finally sold it, or if they were starting to renovate it for themselves. He felt himself start to retch. He tried to get out of
the building, but in his drunkenness he couldn't grasp the
doorknob properly. He vomited on the marble floor right inside the entrance, then managed to get the door open and
step outside into the cold. The doorman helped him into the
cab. He knew he should tell him about the mess on the lobby
floor, but he didn't have the guts.

At least I gave it a shot, David told himself, re Lorraine, as
he rode home in the taxi. Yet he knew, somewhere inside,
this was a lie. Not only had the attempt been a failure, he
had known it would be a failure; in some weird way he'd
wanted it to be a failure. Even in his misery, the totality of
his failures was in some way gratifying. It seemed clean, even
pure, to eliminate everything from the past, so that wherever
he was going, nobody would know, and nobody would care.
Especially him.

When he was gone Lorraine went into Judy's room. "Daddy
said good night. He wasn't feeling well," she said.

"He wants to get back with you, doesn't he, Mom?" Judy
asked.

"Yes."

"Will you do it, Mom? Oh pretty please! Say *yes.*" Excited, she sat up in bed, very much a child.

"I don't think so, honey."

"Oh, Mom! Just cause he got a little angry."

"It's not that, honey. I'll think about it. But I don't think it will happen."

"Because of Jack? He's such a creep. I hate him!"

"Judy!"

"I *do.*"

"It's got nothing to do with Jack. Here, let me tell you a story."

"*No!*" Judy turned her back toward Lorraine. Lorraine tried to stroke her, but Judy pushed her hand away.

"Good night, sleep tight, don't let the bedbugs bite," said Lorraine.

Lorraine went into her room, lay down on her bed. Rationally, getting back with David made sense. But in the flesh? The thought of his red face, fleshy body, alcoholic breath, nauseated her. She picked up the phone and began to dial Jack's number—an act she had forced herself to refrain from innumerable times. Half-hoping he wasn't going to pick up (as she did not entirely trust the impulse that had led her to this call), she listened to the ring.

And yet, when it became clear he wasn't home, she grew desperate, and hung up and dialed again. Then again. Now that she had finally given in and called him, it did not seem possible he was not there. Could it be possible his brain waves were so unreceptive to hers? She began to sob. The saner part of her realized it was probably a good thing he wasn't there to witness this late-night craziness, yet still she held onto the phone, praying he would pick it up. Eventually she placed the receiver next to her ear on the pillow, and used the repetition of the rings as a mantra to lull her to sleep.

19

David tossed and turned. Not since college had he not had someone there—usually more than just one someone. He'd tried some Valium, but with the coke the realtor had given him these had trouble working. The fatigue was there, but he was scared to let go enough to sink into the boredom sleep required; it seemed more fatiguing than action itself. The worst minutes of his day were those spent ripping off his clothes and washing his face alone, in front of a mirror that echoed no one but him, no one to knead his shoulders and make sure he continued breathing as he slipped into unconsciousness.

He got up and began walking around the apartment, picking up ashtrays, looking out the window, bending back his fingers just to feel the reality of pain. He turned the volume of both his radio and TV up as loud as they could go—a bombardment of conflicting stimuli that would hopefully cancel each other out into peaceful nothingness. When that didn't work he turned off the sound, lay down again. Shutting his eyes he heard a hum, like the residual noise of the Big Bang, which those guys over at Bell Labs discovered. Only it was the sound of the city itself: TVs, fridges, computers, toasters, phone machines, phones, gas lines, subways, cars, taxis, airplanes, tugboats, fire engines, cop cars, humming, glowing as the city slept.

He looked at his watch—3:45:01. He picked his toe, rubbed his nose, tried to pick what felt like little scabs off his scalp. He felt wet, brought his fingers in front of his face, smelt blood. He held his finger up to the light, thought he saw some. Not much, just a streak, thin and brown, as if you killed a roach with your bare hand. He sucked it off his finger, then dried his finger on his pants. He checked the time again, 3:46:57. He took out the pocket knife that was useful for so many things, cleaned his nails. He threw it hard against the floor to see if he could get it to go in enough to stand up. It didn't. He tried it again, with more power. At an angle, it stuck. Without conscious intention he found himself putting on his coat, taking the elevator down to the garage.

He got in the Caddy and flipped on Radio Bullshit, WBLS. The fact that he couldn't remember the words didn't stop him from singing. His voice reverberated nicely in the closed metal space, picking up resonance and echo. For a second he felt totally happy—as happy as he'd ever been—though he knew this wasn't true. He'd been just as happy earlier that very evening, shoveling a bunch of snow up his nose. He drove down the FDR, took the Brooklyn Bridge to the BQE, then out to Sheepshead Bay. It's an area he's been meaning to check out; just by looking at the cars parked in the driveways you could find an awful lot out about a neighborhood. Maybe he should try and scrounge up some money to buy some property there.

But he got lost, found himself at the water. Dark, but the stars were disappearing. Other things were on their way. Lights, action, camera: the day. He got out of the car, began to walk on the sand. It quickly got in his shoes: soggy, wet, cold. He remembered a movie he saw, a decade ago maybe, mass murderer on the lam with his girl, dancing in the headlights on a lonely road to nowhere. He walked back to the car, untied his shoes, emptied the sand out of them, turned off the radio to see what it was like without aural stimuli. Quiet. Interesting. Scary. He went whole hog and clicked off the light, so he was alone in the cold and dark. After a while he went back onto the beach. Barefoot, he started to walk. He felt a little spooked—by contradictory things: being mugged by a stranger, having a heart attack and dying alone. But was it really better to die with somebody than alone, or was that just a sentimental notion put forward by those who pretended to believe in families? At that time you were alone anyway, weren't you? Advancing slowly toward a white smiling mist . . .

He reached in his pocket for a different kind of white. He

sat down on the sand and did the last of what the realtor had given him. He didn't really need it, he was just trying to make his heart and eyes happy. A glow was upon the water and the sky, very pretty. You could almost see the white behind the black. Soon it would be dawn. He got up and started to walk east, to where that bit of light was, the light in his head advancing to meet the light of the world. There was the cold sand between his toes. He imagined he could feel each separate grain against each ridge that formed the pattern of his toes, that marked his toes as distinguishable from all other toes. In the sand his toes spread out, like an animal's, not confined by shoes, which modified his gait so that he consciously pressed his heels into the sand before rolling forward onto the balls of his feet and then pushing off from his toes. Blood rushed into parts of his feet not used to so much blood; muscles worked that hadn't in years. He felt it in his calves, his ass. That was the good part. The bad part was the wet sand crusting on the bottom of his pants. It was unpleasant, disturbing, almost disgusting for some reason, the way shit in his diapers must have been once, long ago.

When the coke slowed down David headed back to the car. He turned on the radio and waited for sunrise. It never came, just an ugly white mist that would burn off later in the day. When he looked in the car mirror he saw a white man with no color. An ugly white man with no color. Then he gunned the motor.

He cruised till a coffee shop called out to him. Men were breakfasting here, Toyota and Datsun and Ford pickups parked outside, as they did in small towns across America where guys didn't want to face their wives in the morning. He ordered eggs over easy, English, coffee. He poured milk in the black coffee, watching the white wash into the black, making it brown, then tan, then beige, then octoroon. The light reflected downward into the sugar by the metal top of the sugar canister made the sugar look like a slope of clean fresh Utah powder—though on a smaller scale, of course. After the fourth coffee refill the waitress lingered by his side.

She was in her upper thirties, thin, a little lined, but not bad,

long hair, like a hippie, but clean. Ex-hippie. Smoked too
much. One-third owner of the coffee shop. She told him
about the man and woman who owned the place with her.
They all lived together in a big house—the big house the
coffee shop was in. They owned two more houses, in worse
neighborhoods, neighborhoods you wouldn't want to live in,
which they fixed up in their spare time. You wouldn't believe
how some people left their property. Disgrace. Hurt the value
too, but some people just don't care. It was watching the "No
Money Down" real estate man on cable at 4 a.m. when they
had trouble sleeping that taught them to do this. Every week
they spent one day doing nothing but driving around, check-
ing out properties, getting the lay. Sheepshead was getting
hot right now—well, on the verge of being hot—but unfortunately they couldn't take a profit on their house, they lived
and worked there. On the other hand, they've got their dream
—in ten years they're going to retire to Florida, millionaires,
live on their income or maybe open a little fishing shop down
in the Keys. Why do you have to wait until you're half-dead
and can't fuck any more to retire to Florida?

"No reason," said David.

"Course it ain't as easy as it looks. Not all that hard but
not as easy as it looks."

"I know," said David. "I used to be into all that. Shopping
centers, developments, big stuff like that."

"What happened?"

"Money troubles. Then the wife fucked me over."

"Looking for a place out here?" asked the waitress. David
shrugged, tilted his head back as he finished the cup.

"Boy, you can really hump that coffee."

"Not just coffee." He leered at her.

"Mister, I'm not your ticket."

"Figures. Isn't three a crowd, though?"

"Three's everything. Try and name something you can't
do."

"Yeah." Tears came to David's eyes. He felt like moving in
with her and her friends, changing his name, living with
them the rest of his life in a new, ready-made, surely more

perfect family. He left his card for the waitress, just in case, along with a five-dollar tip. Outside, he checked his face in the reflection of the coffee-shop window. The whiteness of his skin was blurred by a kind of shadow. Every day, summer or winter, spring or fall, life went on, pushing its way to the surface of his skin, wanting to cover his face with its plot of black stubble. He liked the rough feel, the smart on his hand when he rubbed it across his cheek. Nonetheless, he looked for a barbershop; he needed to be touched by something human—even for a few minutes, even if it were only by the indifferent hands of a stranger.

He had barely gotten into his apartment when the intercom rang. Post office with a registered letter needing David's signature.

Against his better judgment, knowing it was disaster, David buzzed the man in. He took the pen and signed the receipt with a gigantic flourish, then leaned against the door watching the mailman shift impatiently from foot to foot as he waited for the elevator. Uncomfortable under David's gaze, he began to make funny noises with his lips, then started bobbing an invisible ball up and down in his hand. Who knows what he would have done had the elevator not come.

David let the door of the apartment close. Slowly he made his way over to the exercise mat. Almost fondly he caressed the envelope.

Dear David,

I hope this won't inconvenience you too much, but I've been offered a job in NY I just can't refuse . . . so please consider this an official notification to vacate. You've got two months though, so I'm sure you'll be able to find *something!* Sorry!

Best,
Margaret

P.S. We've never met, but I feel I know you from Cecilia. Let's catch a drink sometime!

David fell back on the mat. The sunlight was moving from the second toe of his right foot over to his big toe. For a long time he lay there watching it. He wiped sweat off his fore-head with his fingers, then brought the fingers in front of his nose and sniffed. He liked the smell.

Could it really be that less than a year ago he had had a wife, a mistress, a career, a home? Now his designer suits hung useless in his closet, his socks lay a cornucopia of color on the storage shelf in the closet, his sweaters collected dust on the closet floor. His mink-lined car coat was his blanket, his pillow a pillow case filled with dirty laundry. How had his normal life gone so awry?

He closed his eyes as tight as he could, hoping somehow he would wake up in the past, to discover that what he had thought his life was was just one long, vivid nightmare. If only he could push Rewind: six months, a year, five years, start college all over. Why couldn't Lorraine have understood, his "affairs" no more interfered with his relationship with her and Judy than his high school dates interfered with his relationship with his parents?

He tried calling Lydia. As usual, her machine. The realtor: NA. He reached for the vodka—empty.

"Dear God," sobbed David, "why are you doing this to me?" He thought of calling Lorraine, but when she picked up, overwhelmed by his sense of failure, he hung up the phone. Exhausted finally, he fell asleep, as he used to some-times in the midst of fights he'd had with the women in his life—until he had become accustomed to their virulence, fre-quency, and lack of consequence. In his dream the words of the old song (from the '50s, when he was just a kid), ran through his head: "Since you've gone/ The moon, the stars/ No longer shine/The dream is gone/I thought was mine. . . ."

Waking up, his eyes still shut, he was happy: in a moment he would get up and meet his best pal, Joey, baseball mitt in hand, for the Saturday morning game. Then he opened his eyes.

Sweating, he stumbled to the john. He cupped his hand and blew in it; his breath was bad. In the fluorescent light his skin—gray, red, crisscrossed with tiny lines, endless bumps, black dots like pencil stabs, grayish black stubble—scared him: who would ever want to touch it?

In despair he returned to his bed, unzipped his pants. For a long time he worked at it, thinking first of Lydia, then Cecilia, at last Lorraine. Zip. He turned on the light, started flipping through old sections of the *Times*. There were glossy advertising insets from Macy's, Bloomie's, Radio Shack. In them were the glories of Western civilization: computers, tubes, VCRs, CD players, tape decks, movie cameras, projectors, microwaves, toaster ovens, coffee-makers, juicers, electric frying pans, gas grills, can openers, knife sharpeners, pasta-makers, food processors, electric juicers, hair dryers, humidifiers, Dustbusters, vacuums, carpet cleaners, air ionizers, wireless phones, magic thermostats, submersible radios, depth-diving cameras, inflatable typewriters, answering machines that responded like dogs to the sound of your voice. . . .

SITE-SPECIFIC ART:
THE GALLERY AND THE STREET

... but by far the most fascinating examples of New Wave street art are the "proto muggings" by the artist the papers have dubbed the Lone Ranger. These audacious and cunning performance pieces both evoke our most intimate fears and desires as well as initiating serious reflection on such questions as the nature of perception and reality, sanity ("paranoia as a nonparanoic response"), our conception of justice and its relation to the legal system. Pirandello, Brecht, Dada, Beckett, Vito Acconci, and the Red Army are the most obvious influences on these extraordinary performances—which are terminated at various stages of progression, some just short of actual physical (but perhaps not psychic) harm. Captain Julio Brownstein of the 6th Precinct assures me that authorities are *not* amused.

"Malefactors will be prosecuted to the full extent of the law, regardless of whatever art critics describe as the 'subtext' of the event." As for the elderly woman who was reported to have suffered a heart attack during a "fake" or "proto" rape, it turns out that the alleged rape was in fact real, but that the perpetrator was not (as previously thought) the Lone Ranger, but a black dropout from Flushing High.

"I'm not trying to destroy the social contract, rather to examine it," says the Lone Ranger, who agreed to be interviewed only under conditions of total anonymity. "Street crime is both the ultimate existential encounter as well as *the* exemplary (in the religious sense) contemporary experience. For instance, consider the extreme nature of our response to such violations, in contrast to our relative tolerance of far more serious events such as chemical disasters, pollution of the environment, the expenditure of billions on useless rocket parts." As for the artist himself, a white male Caucasian whose more conventional work has been exhibited for years to no special acclaim, he can be seen—courtesy of the workings of the mysterious "A-list" newsletter—nightly at Palladium, Siberia, Don Corleone's and other places where the fashionable take their food and water. Let me add simply that this represents an extraordinary career twist for an artist stuck in the midcareer doldrums, and proves that yes, Virginia, there is life apart from Mary Boone.

What's next in line for this young genius? "Possibly fake kidnappings and hijackings. I want to throw a monkey wrench into our false assumptions of comfort and safety, that psychic division that says there is a difference between the streets of New York and those of Belfast, Beirut, or Rome." Forgive the exaggeration, folks, for, as far as I know, there ain't no Dean & DeLuca in Beirut. But who can blame a poor boy for talking up his 15 minutes in the sun?

Jeremy saved the file, sent it via modem to *Vanity Fair*, then sat down to eat a well-deserved late lunch of smoked tuna, roasted peppers, hot Russian mustard on sourdough bread. He threw the remains of his lunch in the garbage, placed the plate in the dishwasher, and lit a Havana cigar. He reached for his cup of coffee—already his fourth of the day. It was almost all gone, but he tilted the mug way back so the sludge at the bottom of the cup drifted slowly toward his mouth. It tasted muddy, gritty, sweet. But it did not help his fatigue, the fatigue that lately was always there.

Judy and Saralee were sitting across from each other on Judy's bed. Their blouses were on but their underpants were on the floor beside them. On the VCR was *Sixteen Candles* (which they had seen often enough to make into accompaniment rather than the main event), on the stereo was Cyndi Lauper. If Lorraine had walked in at that moment she might have been upset, but what they were actually doing was conducting a scientific investigation to discover if, indeed, they each had that tiny penis-like thing inside of them called a "clitoris."

Not likely, they had decided, searching through memory; on the other hand, there was that book Lorraine had given

Judy last year with the diagrams and pictures. Also on the
bed was the round double-sided mirror whose magnifying lens was useful for pimple-popping, eyebrow-plucking, and the detection (on Lorraine) of gray hairs. Judy held the mirror while Saralee searched, and vice versa.

It was hard to see anything up there. "God, this is really gross!" said Judy, to cover her embarrassment, as she pulled apart her lips to see what was hidden inside.

"Ga-ag me with a spoon," said Saralee, with ironic reflection, to show she was using a Valley Girl-ism solely as parody.

"Fuck me with a fork!" replied Judy.

They laughed hysterically, then proceeded through the vast parade of similar such phrases: "neck me with a napkin," "feel me with a frying pan," "screw me with a doorknob," "blow me with a whistle," etc. A movie on the tube, a song on the stereo, Pepperidge Farm in the mouth, they were happy: who wouldn't be?

Since Jack had left Lorraine almost welcomed the sounds of music and TV in her apartment; it reassured her that life was progressing in normal fashion. On the other hand, it was late, and the kids should be asleep. She thought of saying something, but instead simply took out her wallet and gave Aurelia her cab fare home. Aurelia didn't get up, but just sat there, apparently waiting for the end of the show. Suddenly furious, Lorraine leaned forward and shut off the TV. The quiet imparted by the sudden cessation of noise served only to reveal further cacophonies of sound (stereo, TV, giggling) emanating from Judy's room. Aurelia sighed, then slowly stood up and made her way to the door.

When Judy had heard Lorraine's voice she had grabbed the underpants, slipped them under the sheets, and quickly pulled on her jeans. Saralee pulled down her skirt. By the time Lorraine opened the door they were intently working on their math problems. "How are my little girls?" she asked.

"Fine."

"Kids, it's a school night. Shouldn't you be getting to sleep?"

"We're studying for a test."

"To Madonna?"

"Mom, that's Cyndi Lauper. You just hum the song and you remember everything."

"Oh." This sounded familiar. Was it familiar because it was true, or because it was the same lie Lorraine fed her own mother years ago? In any case, she didn't have the strength to fight. "Okay. Don't go to sleep too late, though."

"We won't," said Saralee.

"Hey, Mom?"

"What?"

"How do you tell the difference between an intraveneous needle and a dick?" Giggle giggle.

"I don't know."

"I'm sure glad you're not my doctor!" Hysteria. "Here's another. How do you tell the difference between a banana and a dick?"

Lorraine left the room, shut the door, went into the living room that she had refused to let Jack convert into a studio, and sat down on the couch. Even Cyndi Lauper did not so much intrude as assure, a pleasant and predictable heartbeat of life. The only thing worse than having a kid would be not having one. She was, after all, lucky. She had a home, a business, a child and animals who if they did not love at least tolerated her. As for the rest—it would come. Someday, surely, she'll see Europe again. Someday, surely, she'll join a health club. Someday, surely, she'll have lunch with Ellie. She looked out the black square of window to the streetlight, the park, the river, New Jersey, the stars that wound their way across the universe. She sat this way for another ten minutes, then, quite inexplicably, started to cry.

She got up and went into her bedroom, kicked off her shoes, and stretched out on the bed. The room was cold, the new (unaptly named) radiators failing to radiate any heat. The thought of getting undressed in the cold bathroom, slipping on the cold silk of her nightgown, sliding under the cold sheets, with no one next to her to warm them up, with nothing to think about as she got undressed but her own loneliness, was so depressing that, removing only her skirt and shoes, she crawled into the bed as she was: blouse, pantyhose, and underpants still on, unpleasant taste still in her mouth from the wine she had drunk and the cigarettes she had smoked over dinner with Marianne and the two buyers from Bergdorf's. On such occasions she always drank too much, in the hope of creating a personality. Oddly, she usually succeeded. But it never felt like her, and, once the exhilaration of the (to her always surprising) social success had worn off (usually when the effects of the wine and vodka did), she became exhausted, weak, a defenseless animal crawling into its lair.

Lorraine used to hate it when David or Jack turned on the TV in the bedroom. But since Jack's departure silence had acquired a new and more unpleasant connotation, and she had found herself getting in the habit of turning on the news to lull her asleep. Terrorist attacks, unrest in the Philippines, arrests in South Africa, starvation in the Sudan, an acrimonious ending to high-level disarmament talks—in and of themselves these events were not soothing, but, oddly, en masse, they were.

MARA BREZHNEV
*(from "Eyewitness News," interviewing people
outside Penn Station)*
You thought the Lone Ranger was a cowboy who roamed the wild and wooly West with his buddy Tonto? Well, maybe he did, but now he's on the prowl again, only this time it's not just West, but East and North and South— Manhattan, that is. At least, that's what they're calling the young man who's been terrorizing the streets of Manhattan with his "fake" robberies and muggings. Yes, folks, art in the twentieth century has certainly liberated itself from the easel. Sir—

She stops a man entering the station.

MARA
Have you heard of the Lone Ranger?

MAN #1
Which one? The cowboy or the nut?

> MARA

The nut.

> MAN #1

Sure.

> *(holds up* **New York Post** *with headline:* THE
> LONE RANGER RIDES AGAIN*)*

What do you think, I'm dead?

> MARA
> *(laughs)*

You don't look dead to me.

> MAN #1

I'm not. But if I had my way, this fellow would be.

> MARA

Would you rather be mugged by him or a real mugger?

> MAN #1

A real mugger any day.

> MARA

Why's that?

> MAN #1

At least a real mugger is doing an honest day's work. It just shows you what this country is coming to. . . .

CUT TO:
Mara talking to a young woman wearing warm-ups and carrying a large canvas bag.

> DANCER
> *(laughing)*

Pretty weird, huh? But that's why I moved to New York. I wouldn't live anywhere else. I love it!

CUT TO:
Mara talking to another man.

> MARA

Sir, what do you think of the Lone Ranger?

> MAN #2

The Lone Ranger? You mean—

> MARA

The fellow who's terrorizing the city with his fake muggings.

MAN #2

Nothing. I don't think anything.

MARA

Nothing?

MAN #2

Nope. *Nada. Niente.*

MARA
(still trying)

It doesn't surprise you?

MAN #2

You (bleep)ing me? Nothing in New York surprises me. Well, one thing might. You know what that is?

MARA

What?

MAN #2

Winning the lottery.

CUT TO:
Mara talking to a group of black teenagers.

BLACK TEENAGER #1
(grabbing mike)

If he were black, he'd be a dead man. But he's white, so it's cool.

TEENAGER #2

I'm gonna be an artist when I grow up. It's the biggest scam in the world, everybody knows that.

CUT TO:
Mara stopping a man carrying a briefcase and *The Wall Street Journal*.

MARA

Sir, what do you think of the Lone Ranger?

MAN #3

Who?

MARA

The Lone Ranger. The artist that's been doing those fake muggings. He calls them "performance pieces."

MAN #3

Art, huh?

(chuckles)

God, that's a good one.
(disappearing into station)

CUT TO:

MAN #4
(middle-aged, well-dressed, carrying expensive briefcase)
Ed Koch can't control the city, so what else is new?

CUT TO:

SCARSDALE MATRON
(carrying packages from Bloomie's)
I'm flying to Anguilla tomorrow. Hopefully he'll be caught by the time I get back.

CUT TO:

MAN #5
If this doesn't show that we need the death penalty, I don't know what does.

CUT TO:

SECRETARY
It's better than a real mugging, that's for sure.

CUT TO:

MAN #6
(getting out of cab)
I've lived in Lebanon and I've lived in Italy. As far as I'm concerned, New York is the safest city in the world.

CUT TO:

YUPPIE
He's just trying to make an honest buck like everybody else.

CUT TO:

COLUMBIA STUDENT
(drably dressed, carrying books)
All he's saying is that society's a joke. And it is.

CUT TO:

MARA
You sir, what do you think?
(sticking microphone in his face)

I've been a member of the New York City police force for the last fifteen years.

(opening coat, revealing shoulder holster and .45 Magnum)

Come on, fella, find me. Make my day!

MARA

This is Mara Brezhnev of the Channel Seven news team, hoping that all your muggings be fake!

"What crap!" thought Lorraine, as she turned off the set. Why was it that items like this, of no import whatsoever, were personally far more irritating than reports of wars, tragic deaths, incurable diseases?

A train was crushing her chest. People were standing around, talking and reading the newspaper. She tried to shout for help, but her lips wouldn't move. Was this the way she would die, in the midst of people who could not see she needed to be helped? Finally she managed to pronounce the word—but so softly nobody heard it. She did it again, louder. Then even more loudly.

The sound of her own voice—shouting "help"—woke her up. In the dark she looked at the glowing green numbers of the clock radio: 3:45. A sound of feet outside the door; Judy came into the room. "Mom?" she asked, "are you okay?"

"I was having a nightmare," said Lorraine.

"Gosh, you scared us! We thought somebody was in the house!"

"My brave little girl!" Lorraine hugged her. "Coming in to help out your old mom."

"Well, we didn't *really* think somebody was here. Hey, you're still dressed."

"I fell asleep watching TV. I think I drank a little too much wine."

"Mo-*ther*, you *always* do when you go out with Marianne."

"It's not Marianne, honey, but the buyers. You're right. I get scared they won't like our line." Amidst the sarcastic coldness of adolescence, these unpredictable moments of seeming insight and caring were all the sweeter. Tears of gratitude filled her eyes. "You've got school tomorrow. Get back in bed, and I'll bring you some hot milk."

"Ooooh!"

"Only if you get back in your own bed."

Lorraine went into the kitchen to heat up some milk. Carefully she carried the two hot cups of milk (a pat of butter floating on top of each) into Judy's bedroom. Saralee had fallen back asleep, so Lorraine drank hers. She held Judy's cup up to her mouth for her to drink, as she had when she was just a child. When Judy was done, Lorraine lay down beside her on the bed. In the day Judy could barely tolerate Lorraine's kissing her, but at night she became another person. Lorraine watched her daughter until she fell asleep, breathing in unison with Saralee the deep, not unpleasant semisnore of children. Somehow she had managed to wrap part of the sheet around her legs. Her face was flushed, as kids' faces often are when they sleep. Lorraine felt moved and reassured. The fluorescent stars Judy pasted on the ceiling last year in the shapes of her favorite constellations glowed in the dark. The Big Dipper, Orion, the Pleiades, places where Lorraine would like to go. Judy turned, almost into Lorraine's arms, the way she would do in a year or two or three with some fourteen- or fifteen- or sixteen-year-old boy she has still to meet. She looked and acted like a child, but no doubt Lorraine had too, back when she was thirteen and in love with Sammy Kato, who told all the boys in school what he had persuaded Lorraine to do with him. Almost thirty years later, the memory of this still rankled. Would it ever entirely disappear? Did any pain, ever, entirely disappear, or when she was eighty would it still be gnawing at some corner of her mind, drift with her into senility? Never since had she suffered so much about anything. How could she?—with a business, a car, an apartment, a dog, a cat, three fridges, a dishwasher, clothes washer and dryer, three TVs, a VCR, a video camera (broken), an 8-mm movie camera, a projector (also broken), seven still cameras (Cannon AE-1, Minolta mini, waterproof diving camera, an old Leica, Polaroid Sun

Camera, Polaroid SL-70, Kodak disk), eight radios not including stereo tuners or receivers (clock radios for her and Judy and the kitchen, two Sony Walkmans, a waterproof beach radio, a huge old multi-band and a ghetto-blaster), two stereos (Judy's and living room) complete with cassette decks and speakers, six clocks, four irons (two regular, one cordless, one traveling), three hair dryers (hers, Judy, one traveling), an Atari computer, HR-1 printer, SCM electric portable, an old manual Royal, an electric pencil sharpener, knife sharpener, can opener, microwave, coffee grinder, coffee-maker, juicer, Osterizer, Cuisinart. . . .

How could you tell a thirteen-year-old with just the beginning of breasts some of her greatest moments of suffering might be six months down the road?

If you didn't, how did you forgive yourself if some new Sammy Kato came along to mess up her life?

She went back to her bedroom and stared at the pattern cast by the streetlight through the venetian blinds onto the ceiling. When she was young and unable to sleep she had stared at similar patterns for hours, only then they were cast by the branches (and, in the summer, leaves) outside her window. One night in seventh grade, so nervous her hands began picking at herself, she had discovered a sure-fire insomnia cure.

Now she was lazy. It was the electronic age. With a sigh she got up and went to the underwear drawer where she hid her vibrator. Shuffling through the Fernando Sanchez slips and nightgowns she found a note: "Hi Mom," it says. "And you complain about me using the word FUCK!" Lorraine tore up the note, plugged the vibrator into the socket by the bed. Who's counting? but in 149 seconds she came, she hoped in spite and not because of the image she had in her mind of her daughter, restless, insomniac, trying to find a way to sleep. Should she tell her, or would this warp her for life? or did she already know? But for once, even this sure-fire cure didn't work. Hot, sweaty, and very much awake, Lorraine threw off the covers and tried again. In the graying light, it sounded less like a lawn mower or electric razor and more like the drone of a dentist's drill. No matter where she put it, over the sheet, on top of the blanket, on top of the doubled-over blanket, the vibrations were too intense; her teeth were set on edge. She told herself to relax, breathe slowly, let her mind wander, but she sweated, shivered, finally gave up.

What she wanted, of course, was to call Jack. All the ordinary reasons she brought forth against doing this every time she thought of calling him came to mind, plus others specific to this moment: her headache, her earlier drunkenness, the lateness of the hour and the desperation this implied. Against this there was only the suddenly irresistible desire. Even as she dialed she knew it was not just not the optimum time to call, but perhaps the *worst possible* time to call. But when else was one driven to call, except at the very worst time?

Four rings and Lorraine began to feel herself saved. Then she heard a click as the phone was picked up. "Hi. This is Jack. Sorry I'm not home right now. Leave your name and phone number and I'll get back to you as soon as I can." Disconcerted by the machine (when had Jack bought it?), Lorraine waited silently for the phone to disconnect. But her heart pounded from hearing even this electronic reconstruction of Jack's voice.

She wondered whether she should call again and leave her name. Perhaps he had been sleeping and should pick up. But if she called back, he would assume that it was she who had hung up on him earlier, which would be embarrassing. And what if someone was with him in his bed? Surely someone was in his bed, or he was in someone else's bed. The only other place he could be at this hour was a club—and Jack did not like clubs.

Or did he? It struck her she knew almost nothing about what he was like when he was not with her. When they had gone to art openings at clubs usually they had not danced— or maybe only for a few minutes. But perhaps this was not because Jack hadn't liked dancing, but because they had to leave early so Lorraine could get up in time to go to work, or because the extreme self-consciousness that afflicted her in discos (of being so much older than most of those around her, very much the mother of a teenage child) had destroyed Jack's pleasure in dancing with her. Perhaps Jack loved to dance, or perhaps he didn't love it but did it anyway, as a way to meet women. Or would he be more likely to offer to buy someone a drink? (But how could he afford five-dollar drinks on his salary?) And hadn't Marianne said clubs were the very worst places in all the world to meet people? (But surely this couldn't be true; otherwise what were people doing in them till four in the morning, now that the age of drugs was over?) The more Lorraine thought about it the more she realized how little she actually knew about the habits of this person she had lived with. Did he usually have dinner with his friends, or did he eat alone? In an apartment or a restaurant? Would he cook or pick up something from a Korean grocery or Chinese takeout? Did he read or watch TV or listen to music as he fell asleep? Go to movies by himself? Talk much on the phone?

She turned on the radio. A booming symphony on WNCN disturbed rather than soothed her: why didn't they confine themselves to sonatas and trios during the fragile hours? When she tried to read her eyes closed, but instead of sleep she found herself stuck with images from the preceding day jumbled together in strange juxtapositions as if there were something to be learned from them. But there wasn't. There was nothing to be learned from anything: you were born alone, into a world without meaning, full of violence and indifference, then you died.

There was nothing particularly awful in any of this, nothing that was more true for her than for anyone else, but the hangover and fatigue and loneliness intensified these thoughts until she began to panic at the thought of years made up of days and nights like this. Was this all there was? If these were the good times, what were the bad? She began to have trouble breathing. Her pulse was the normal 72, but perhaps this was not normal for one who had been lying in bed for hours. Again she turned on the vibrator, but the sound made her crazy. She yanked it out of the wall and stood on the chair to hide it high in the closet, so she would not be tempted to use it again. She went to the bathroom to look for

Valium or some sleeping pills. She couldn't find any; either she had finished them, or someone had stolen them, probably David or Aurelia. . . . If it were Aurelia she should fire her, but how could she find out? Suppose Aurelia were stealing her jewelry; she was so disorganized she might not realize it for years. She filled the sink with cold water and stuck her wrists in it, then soaked a washcloth and held it over her temples and the back of her neck.

Still, she was not breathing. Rather, she was breathing, but she couldn't get enough air. Probably it was because she was having a heart attack and the blood wasn't pumping any oxygen. She would pass out, and Judy would find her in the morning: cold, stiff; what a trauma! And yet she did not wake up Judy, or dial 911, or even ring the elevator to talk to the doorman; after all, she had felt this way many times before, and nothing had been the matter. But suppose this time there was, and it was not all in her mind, and she were dying? Who knew how many people died every day from embarrassment, or laziness, or from fear of asking others for favors? She decided she would try to hold out until Judy and Saralee had gone to school—three more hours. She was exhausted. She didn't see how she could go in to her business, but if she didn't, who could deal with the man who wanted to rep the line in Dallas?

Again she picked up the phone. "Jack, are you there? If you are, could you please pick up the phone? I've got to talk to you."

"Lorraine?" said Jack in a sleepy voice. "Is something wrong?"

"Did I wake you up? I'm sorry."

"Is something the matter?"

"No."

"Oh." He almost sounded disappointed. "Is Judy all right?"

"Fine. She sends her love."

"Bullshit. She hates me."

"She doesn't hate you. You know kids."

"Do I? You always told me I didn't. Well"—silence—"I guess I better get back to sleep."

"Why? Am I disturbing you? Is someone there?"

"I really don't think that's any of your business."

"*Jack.*"

"All right, I'm alone. Does that make you happy?"

"In a way, yes, it does." They fell silent. Lorraine realized she could breathe again, but this meant her excuse for calling him was gone; perhaps she had only had the breathing spell as an excuse to call him. "I've been having trouble sleeping. I was out with some buyers, so of course I drank too much, then I saw this stuff on TV about that crazy artist who goes around pretending to mug people—"

"The Lone Ranger."

"Yes, and I felt, oh, you know, that everything was stupid, and pointless, and that the art world was full of shit, so naturally I thought about you, and how you were doing, and then I fell asleep, and then I had this nightmare, and then when I woke up—"

"The art world is no more full of shit than the fashion world."

"That's not the point, Jack. It doesn't *pretend* to be any better. But I didn't call you up to argue." (Nonetheless, she felt herself starting to get angry.) "I just wanted to hear your voice."

"And now you have."

"What's the matter?"

"Nothing."

"Come on. I know you. Something's the matter."

"Maybe you *don't* know me."

"*Jack.* What are you talking about?"

"I don't know if I should tell you."

"*Jack!*"

"You can't keep a secret."

"Of course I can. What about the time—"

And so he told her.

Lorraine was so mad she couldn't stay in bed. She turned on the shower and aimed the nozzle into the tub. While it was filling she went out into the kitchen to turn on the Krups. She was mentally exhausted, but physically she felt that she could run around the block. As she waited for the coffee she sat at the dining-room table with her calculator, playing around with some numbers. Then she poured a cup and carried it back to the tub. Her heart was pounding again, but this time from anger. She punched the water with her fist as if it were Jack. "You fucking asshole!" she kept repeating. If he had been there she would have clawed him.

By noon her anger was supplanted by a feeling of shock and betrayal—as if she had found out that David had gone out dressed in women's clothing one night each week the whole time they were married. Nor could she relieve her mind by discussing it with anybody. Marianne would have been perfect, but people in fashion had such big mouths, they couldn't control themselves. She could almost hear her saying: "Fabulous! Can we tie it into the spring showing?" Just imagining Marianne's presumed reaction made Lorraine feel as irritated with her as if this conversation had actually occurred, and she found herself screaming at her about the shape of some buttons. She brought herself to apologize, but throughout the rest of the day the glib talk of the buyers and salespeople continued to alienate her. She thought of her apartment with longing, and couldn't wait to be home and in bed. Her business seemed to have nothing to do with her: a monster she had created that had taken off on its own. Was this not true of Judy, her marriage, Jack, everything in life?

And yet, disturbed as she was, after a few days Lorraine noticed she was beginning to think of Jack in a way she never had before. The lazy, exasperating, semi-failure had, out of the blue, in a remarkably short period of time, somehow transmogrified himself into an ambitious, successful media star. The method was deplorable, but she could not but help admire the results. She realized she had thought of him something like a dog: a friendly, safe, pettable animal whom in some sense she did not have to take utterly seriously. Now he had burst out of his cage and done something nobody had in ages: surprise her. She had never really respected him before, but she did now. *The shit.*

21

Not just were the streets empty, but they were so quiet. The cars were old and boxy-topped, the men wore hats and the women bright red lipstick. Some of the women's hats had veils that were almost invisible, like screens over a window. People stood outside the candy store listening to baseball over the radio. The score was 6 to 2, top of the seventh. Then he was in his apartment, 6 to 5, bottom of the ninth, the Dodgers trying to tie it up. The door opened, the police entered. With them was a woman from the IRS. "What are you doing here?" she asked.

David opened his eyes. A woman wearing a Ralph Lauren jacket and tall brown boots was looking down at him, a look of extreme distaste across her face. On the floor behind her was a set of matching leather-trimmed nylon suitcases. "What are you doing here?" she repeated.

"Margaret?" asked David. There was an empty bottle of vodka on the floor next to the exercise mat. He hoped she didn't see it. But he saw her glancing from it to him.

"I tried calling you for days. I assumed you'd already moved out. You're supposed to be out of here."

"*Next* month, I thought."

"Didn't you get my letter?"

"You said *next* month."

"The *second* letter."

"Ohh." David glanced at the kitchen drawer where he'd been stuffing his mail. "I kind of got behind on my mail."

"Mmm." For a while she just stood there, staring down at him. Being naked, David couldn't move. Finally she went over to the kitchen area. She opened a cabinet, no clean glasses. She took a dirty one from the sink, turned on the water, then looked—uselessly—for a sponge and soap with which to wash it.

"There's Bounty in the bathroom," said David.

"My things should be here tomorrow. I came early to make sure the place was cleaned up and ready."

"I guess you want me to get my stuff out."

"I'm sorry. But I'm not responsible for you not opening your mail."

"I know. It's my fault."

"It is. It really is."

He reached for his shirt and put it on. "No problem," he lied. "I found a place. I was just a little confused about the date, that's all. What time are the movers coming?"

"I'm not sure. But the sooner you're out of here, the better."

He stuffed his Gucci overnight bag with as much as he could fit into it, moved the rest of his stuff into a pile, stuck it in a corner of the room, then took the elevator down to the street. In spite of his anger at Margaret, he felt a certain relief; nothing had gone right since he had moved into that apartment.

Meanwhile, he had nothing to do, nowhere to go. It was odd, like being a teenager. He went to a pizza parlor and ordered a slice with pepperoni, then one with mushroom and anchovy. He tried the realtor, but he wasn't home or in the office. He walked to Loew's 86th. *Top Gun* had just started so he bought a ticket. When it was over he crossed the street for *Peggy Sue Got Married.* Then he was hungry again, so he went to a nearby luncheonette and ordered a burger and fries with Coke. Once more he tried the realtor: NA. By then it was time for *The Color of Money,* so he walked back to the movie theater. But there was a long line and he decided the hell with it. He walked to one of the famous singles bars on Second Avenue where he ordered a St. Pauli Girl. Then another. At a certain point he remembered he had no place to spend the night, and he looked around the bar—as he might have twenty years ago, when he was in his twenties and the hippie era was just beginning. Of course he had not been a hippie then, and the women he had found it so easy to pick up in those days had not been hippies either, but that looser

spirit had pervaded the city in a way that, at least in retrospect, seemed warm, generous, romantic.

The women in the bar now were the same age he had been then. But how cold and suspicious they looked. No doubt it had much to do with diseases, but even more, perhaps, to do with money. David used to sneer at the hippies; he had not believed them when they pretended not to care about money. But at last he was getting the point. Not that he didn't want money, but having had it had not especially brought him happiness. He tried to catch the eyes of a woman, but they continued to move past him as if he were no more alive than the poster on the wall. On the rare occasions he actually got someone to look at him, contempt flickered, then immediately she looked away, as if he were too disgusting to contemplate.

The longer he looked at them, the more he realized how much he hated them. Secretaries, salespeople, insurance claims adjusters—all with the makeup, hairstyles, and attitude of movie stars. With their stupid jobs, tiny apartments on which they spent half their salaries, the way they came to bars like this to meet men like him—men who hated them —how could they be so smug? He wanted to make love to them to show them how much contempt he had for them— except you couldn't go over to somebody and ask them to spend the night with you just so you could show them how much you hated them. He couldn't even blame them for not looking at him; why should they sleep with someone who felt like that about them? At least Lydia, for all her faults (the primary one being she didn't return his phone calls) had imagination and daring, a certain quality of living on the edge.

He had told himself she was a dead issue, but after a few more beers, the idea of surprising her with a visit occurred to him. Surely the spontaneity of the gesture would eradicate any notion of hers that he was too old or middle-class for her. You never really knew the reason people didn't call you back; just as likely she was scared of liking him too much as not wanting to see him at all. Hadn't he himself sometimes avoided responding immediately to the very woman he liked most, out of a weird desire to prolong the moment of expectation and fantasy?

He got into his car and headed downtown. It took him a while to locate her building, which was farther east than he had remembered. He started to get out of the car, then sat back down. The closer he had come to her apartment the more he had felt he should call, but if he called almost surely he would reach her machine, and if she refused to pick up, what excuse could he have for barging in on her? He opened the half-pint of Absolut he had bought before heading downtown and had a shot to help him make up his mind. There was a phone booth on the corner. He made his deal with God: if it wasn't broken he would call. There was a dial tone. So he took out his quarter. Halfway through, he hung up. According to the deal he should call, but then he decided there was no reason that his earlier decision to use the phone should be any more valid than his decision now *not* to call. Surely the gesture itself—of dropping in on her—would carry him through, if only he were in the right spirit to carry it through. But was he in the right spirit? After drinking a little more vodka he decided he was—at least as much so as he was going to be this night. He was probably more spontaneous now than he had been back in his bell-bottom days. Probably he should just bring his overnight bag up the stairs, plunk it inside her open door, and announce: "I'm moving in." Just like that. Bet she'd like it.

If she didn't? Then, obviously, she wasn't for him.

Comforted by this logic, he grabbed his Gucci bag, walked inside the building, and rang Lydia's bell.

She buzzed him in—a propitious omen, unless of course she was expecting a date.

"Kristina?" he heard her call, above him. He looked up, couldn't see her.

"David," he shouted, with false heartiness.

"David?"

He didn't want to shout up the stairwell which David he was, so he said nothing until he reached her floor. She was standing in front of her door. No particular expression crossed her face when she saw him—not even surprise.

"You remember me, don't you?" David asked, suddenly
not at all sure. He had no idea what her life was like. Maybe
she brought men home all the time.

"Of course."

"I mean . . . I didn't mean . . . you're not offended, are
you?"

She looked at him strangely. "Should I be?"

"No." Still she offered no sign of recognition. He began to
wish he weren't carrying the overnight bag. In spite of the
vodka, his confidence was wearing off. "A funny thing happened on the way to . . . the Lower East Side," he tried to
joke. "I got evicted." He held up the Gucci bag by way of
explanation. But she didn't move out of the doorway to let
him in, as he had hoped.

"That's too bad."

"I was in the neighborhood. You mind if I come in for a
little while?" He had never been a good liar, and he felt his
face turn red. He started forward. Even now, she didn't move
out of the way.

"Actually, it's not a very good time."

"Oh. Someone's there, huh?" He shook his head. "Just my
luck. Bad timing, in everything I do. It's not Ed, is it? I've
been trying to reach him for days. Ed? Hey, Ed?" He tried to
stick his head in the door.

"Ed?"

"The realtor. You met us at the Pyramid. You *do* remember
me, don't you?"

"Of course. But Ed's not here. Why should he be?"

"No reason. I just thought—"

"You know, this is not a good time for me to talk. When
you rang the buzzer I thought it was my roommate Kristina.
Sometimes she forgets her key." Without thinking, David
took out the Absolut, twisted off the cap, and started to drink
right out of the bottle. He saw the distaste on her face, and
recapped it without drinking any and put the bottle back in
his pocket. Then he felt even stupider. "You should have
called before you came down. I could have saved you the
trouble."

"No trouble. I had to come down here anyway." He felt

compelled to back up the original lie by another, though he knew she didn't believe him. "Would you like some?" he asked, offering the vodka to her.

"Some other time. Look. I've got to go." She went inside and shut the door.

"Sure. Some other time!" David shouted after her. He waited, hoping she would change her mind and open it. After a few minutes, he rang the bell. She didn't answer. He rang again. Then he held it a long time. He could hear the sound ringing through the door, but that was all: no footsteps, no music. The more he rang the more embarrassed he became, and the more necessary it became for her to answer the door to remove his embarrassment. He began to hate her for not doing this. "You shit," he said. "You *shit.*" Soon he began to shout it. One of the doors across the hall opened. A little old man stood there, looking at him. David pretended not to see him. He began to talk to the door as if Lydia were there behind it, as if she were his girlfriend and they had had the ordinary fight. "Come on, honey, let me in, wouldja? I'm sorry." The man shut the door. David rang the bell again, then he began banging on the door with his fists. Still she didn't come. "FUCKER!" he shouted at the top of his lungs. It seemed outrageous that someone would let you abuse their body any way you pleased, and then, when you needed them, not even let you spend the night on the floor. She wouldn't treat her fucking cat like that! By now, even if she had opened the door he wouldn't have spent the night with her—but he wanted to tell her this, to let her know exactly what a scumbag he thought she was, what an absolute piece of shit. To this end he hurled himself against the door. "You shit! YOU PIECE OF SHIT!" he screamed.

He was still outside her door when the police came. "Come on, buddy," said one, "leave the lady alone."

"Leave the lady alone?" said David. "What do you mean? I'm not even in the same room as the lady! The lady can't even see me!"

"Come on, buddy, let's go."

"But she saw me once—didn't she?—the slut!"

•

The cops escorted David down to the street, then, after
warning him he'd be arrested if he bothered Lydia again, let
him go. He knew he should be grateful, but it was all he could
do not to curse at them and tell them exactly how he felt for
their interference in his personal life. He walked slowly over
to his Caddy, as if it were not his car, but one he was maybe
thinking of stealing. He could feel them looking at him suspiciously. Playing the moment for drama, he waited as long
as he could before taking the key out of his pocket and opening the door. The cops laughed, then got into their squad
car.

In his nervousness he couldn't tell if the lights in his rear-
view mirror were the police following him or not. What if
they tried to arrest him for drunken driving? He drove like a
model citizen, not thinking about anything except getting
out of this neighborhood into an area of more expensive
buildings where he'd feel safer. He was sweating a lot. He
turned on the radio: WHN, your country music station.
"Take me back to yesterday / When the line between right
and wrong / Didn't seem so hazy. / Lovers really fall in love
to stay / Stand beside each other come what may / Promises
really something people really kept / Not just something
they would say. / Families really bowed their heads to pray /
Daddies really never go away / Grandpa, tell me about the
good old days." Tears distorted his vision, all he saw were red
and green and white lines. He pulled over, then realized he
was in the middle of a parkway. Trees were there, the river.
It was the West Side Highway, as if, when he'd turned the
ignition, his car had become a horse with a memory for
home.

He slowed, rolled up over the little concrete ridge onto the
grass, took out his handkerchief and blew his nose. He
opened the window and let the breeze dry the water from his
face. It was invigorating. He liked the sounds of the cars—
"whoosh," "whoosh"—moving past him.

When he felt better he got back on the road. He exited at
Seventy-second Street and drove up a few blocks until he
found a space across from his old building. Through the wind-
shield he stared up at his apartment. The blinds still had not
been fixed, and a faint glow was visible, probably from a light

still on in the kitchen. Something moved on the window. He almost jumped, then realized it was Jezebel.

They had to take him in, didn't they? Home was where you went when there was no place else. He felt for his keys, grabbed the bag, and got out of the car. Tomorrow he could rent a U-Haul and bring the rest of the stuff back from Margaret's. He crossed the street and reached for the lobby door. It was locked. He looked at his watch: past two. He would have to ring the bell for the doorman.

Then he remembered the vomit on the lobby floor.

A fine mist was falling, one that enveloped the street in a soft light and, oddly, made the night seem warmer than it was. The muscles in his legs ached. He decided to take a walk before confronting the doorman; oddly, the idea of facing him was more disturbing even than having to deal with Lorraine. He descended the stone steps into the park, then, taking the route he and Lorraine used to take when they'd first moved into the apartment, before Judy was born, followed the path down a second set of stone stairs to the boat basin. How many years has it been since he's taken the time to walk down here? Minuscule little water drops floated in the air: was this mist or extremely light rain or just the wind gathering up water molecules as it swept across the river? For once, the park was empty of dog-walkers. The houseboats in the basin were dark; only the pier light was lit. The dark and the mist gave him a rather pleasant feeling of danger. In his current state would he even care what happened to him? Sitting on the wooden bench, he felt like someone who lived on the edge—maybe a guy who liked jazz, who played his trumpet on the fire escape of his tenement building on a summer's evening. He fell into a dreamy state in which Lorraine took him back, Andy worked out a deal with his old partners, and the apartment was fixed up with all the splendors they had planned.

Then he began to remember all that had happened to him this evening, and all that still lay before him. A taste of bile rose in his mouth, almost pleasant in its acidity. He fished in his pockets for a Lifesaver, then stood up and began to walk back the way he had come.

The sound was familiar—a pleasant muffled sound that was both erratic and essentially predictable, and somehow out of the past. It reminded him of his first car: an old Pontiac he and Joey had fixed up; they had driven it to all the games. *The games.* Of course: it was the sound of a basketball bouncing on an outdoor court. You could see the backboards from his old living room in winter when the leaves were gone from the trees.

He walked over to the chain link fence surrounding the playground and pressed his face against it. Between the shadows of the trees, the shadows cast by the backboards and the links of the fence, and the general darkness of the night, it took him a while to locate the guy. At first he found him by the sound of the bounce, the glint of streetlight on the zipper of his jacket as he took the ball out, dribbled, faked, spun, and shot, but then he was able to see a black man, neither especially fast nor tall but with a nice touch, go up in the air past the invisible guard and lay it in. Over and over he dribbled out, faked, spun, and shot. Between the bounces David could hear him pant. He shut his eyes, and it seemed that the sound of the sneakers skimming and pounding on the asphalt, the bounces of the ball on the ground, the deader sound off the backboard, the pant of the player, told him as much as his eyes could about what was going on on the court.

The metal was cold against his nose and cheeks. He went over to a wooden bench across from the playground. He could have sat there all night, listening to the game. When had he last felt this happy? He took a slug of the vodka and began to hum, then sing, out loud: "See the pyramids along the Nile / Watch the sunrise on a tropic isle / Just remember, darling, all the while / You belong to me. / See the marketplace in old Algiers / Send me photographs and souvenirs / Just remember when a dream appears / You belong to me. . . ."

On the last verse, someone began to sing along with him, the harmony to David's melody: "Fly the ocean in a silver plane / See the jungle when it's wet with rain/Just remember till you're home again / You-oo, be-loo-oong, to me-e-e. . . ."

When it was over they hesitated a moment, then the man started in again with the bridge: "I'll be so lonely without you . . ."

David joined him ("Maybe you'll be lonely too / And blue") and they ran through it again. When it was over, David thought of starting a third time, but didn't. Neither did the unknown singer. The night was suddenly very quiet, and David realized he was no longer hearing the basketball.

The player emerged from behind the fence. "Hi," said David.

"Hi," said the man. He sat down next to David. Up close, David realized he was not as young as he'd looked.

"Nice workout," said David.

"You look like you've had one yourself," the man told him.

"Long day," said David. "Longer night." They sat in silence awhile. "You know something?" said David, turning around and pointing, "that place on the second floor, the one with the lights and no shades, I used to live there."

"Yeah?" the man said. It did not sound as if he believed him.

David started to get angry, then realized, considering how he looked—unshaven, drunk, manhandled by the cops—why should anyone believe him? "It's the truth. It's my old apartment. That pink glow—that's my daughter's bedroom. When she was younger, she used to leave the light on before going to sleep. She stopped, but she must have started again. She must be scared. Not that I blame her," David added.

"Uh huh."

"You don't believe me. Come on, I'll introduce you to the doorman."

"Forget it, man."

"Really. I'll show you." He took out his wallet and showed the man his license, his credit cards—now all canceled and useless. David began to sob. The man didn't say anything, but just sat there watching him. For some reason, perhaps because the man was black, it did not embarrass him.

When he had calmed down the man stood up. "You gonna be all right?" he asked.

"Sure."

The man walked away a few steps, then stopped. "You got some place to stay?"

"Yeah. I mean, I was gonna try my old apartment."

"If you want, you can stay there with us." He motioned to the uninhabited building across from David's.

"You live there?" David asked in astonishment.

"In a manner of speaking," the man laughed. "The owners don't seem to know, and somehow we don't get around to telling them. You coming or not?"

"Maybe."

David followed the man out of the park, across the street, up the soft stone steps of the turreted brownstone no one had lived in for years. It was Victorian, with oddly placed cornices and gables, a rounded tower at the corner with bay windows. Lorraine had always made fun of it, but it seemed charming, cozy, comfortable. David remembered the house he had grown up in, with its attics and basements and hidden corners to hide out in.

When they had shut the door the man flipped on a lighter. David could see they were in an entrance hall. Very faintly he heard music. They began to climb the stairs. At the second floor the man pushed open a door that led into a small hallway with two doors; the construction workers must have started dividing the building into apartments. They entered the one on the left. By the light from the streetlamp David could see a fireplace stuffed with pieces of wood and the round bay window visible from the street; this must have been the living room of the original house. You could still smell the sawdust; his feet slid softly and comfortably over it. A skinny white man with a matted beard was leaning against the wall next to the fireplace, a red-and-white box of Kentucky Fried Chicken and a radio on the floor beside him. He looked at David without interest.

"Come on, I'll show you around," the black man said. He led David through the apartment. There was a tub, toilet, sink. In the bedroom were cartons of clothing, sleeping bags. "Not bad, huh?" said the man. "Almost a hotel. Toilets work, by the way. And the sink—but no hot water. Tub's not hooked up either."

"You got a towel by any chance?" asked David.

The man laughed, then went into the room with the sleeping bag and shut the door. David watched as a faint light came from under the door.

He walked back into the living room. With the bay window, marble fireplace, and curlicued moldings, it was the perfect, dream living room; he could almost see the stuffed sofas, the grand piano, a huge rug. He walked over to the bay window and sat down on the sill. The view of the river and park was almost identical to that from his old apartment, except that whereas from his old living room and bedroom he could see into this building, from this building he could see into his old living room and bedroom. He lit a cigarette. The red at the end of his cigarette was the same red as that on top of the two tall apartment buildings David could see across the Hudson in New Jersey, or inside his old apartment on the living room stereo that no one ever turned off.

The cigarette was knocked from his hand, and he was dragged off the sill. He started to scream, but the man with matted hair jammed his hand in his mouth. "You crazy? You want the cops to spot us? Anybody can see you up there!"

"Sorry." The man continued to stare at him. It made David nervous. "You been here long?" he asked.

The man shrugged. "Long enough. It's pretty good. Better than the shelters, that's for sure."

More to alleviate his self-consciousness than for purposes of communication David pointed to his old apartment. "I used to live there," he said.

"Sure."

"I did. That pink glow is from my daughter's bedroom. She must be having insomnia."

They sat in silence awhile, then David remembered the bottle in his pocket. He took it out and offered it to the man. The man reached out and took a long swallow, then handed the bottle back to David. David realized he was expected to drink some himself. But who knows what the man had—

hepatitis, herpes, AIDS? Almost surely he was a drug addict.

David wiped the rim of the bottle off on his jacket, then held
the bottle a little above his mouth as he let a few drops fall
down his throat. "Here, you can have the rest," he said.

The man looked at him in contempt, as if he knew what
he was thinking, then took the bottle. All of a sudden David
began yawning uncontrollably. "Do you mind if I lie down?"
he asked. "I'm awfully tired."

Despite knowing it was a dead giveaway, David patted his
pants pocket, then lay down on the side where his wallet
was. It pressed into his body, hurting him. But he was scared
to shift to the other side, where the man could steal it as he
slept.

Someone moved behind him, and he felt something brush
against him. David grabbed for his wallet. But it was only a
sleeping bag. "Don't be scared," the man said. The sleeping
bag smelled of sweat and dust but the building had no heat
and, dirty as it was, David was glad to curl himself up in it as
he fell asleep.

He woke up just as it was starting to get light. His back
hurt, and his breath was terrible from the vodka and beer.
His eyes stung with ash and dirt. He lifted his upper eyelids
over the lower, to get out the specks, but this only made it
worse. The man with the beard was sleeping in the corner,
rolled up in some old clothes. For some reason, David found
the sight of him comforting.

Friends who had been to India had told David that the
poverty there, though far more widespread than that in New
York, was in a way less disturbing, because the people in
India lived a normal life, cooking and bathing and defecating
on the street with their families and others in similar circumstances, whereas the people one saw on the street in New
York were isolated, alone, cut off from all community.

For the next two days David stayed inside the apartment.
He thought of leaving to call Margaret to arrange about the

stuff he had left there, then realized he didn't give a shit; she could throw it away for all he cared. He thought of taking a walk, but the idea of possibly bumping into Judy or Lorraine stopped him. Mostly he lay on the floor, half-asleep, watching the people who lived in the building pass in and out, listening to them talk or listen to the radio. He gave the black man the rest of his money to buy food. He tried to wash himself, but with no hot water or heat, he quickly abandoned any attempt at even a sponge bath. He was glad when night came, and he was able to sit in the bay window and stare at his old apartment without fear of being seen. It was strange, watching the lights come on, almost hearing the TV as he saw Judy flick the remote, almost smelling the food as he looked past the living room into the dining room to find Lorraine and Judy staring silently at each other across the table, seeing the dining-room lights dim as Judy went into her bedroom and Lorraine went into the kitchen to clean up. He could almost predict the moment when Lorraine would leave the bedroom to yell at Judy to turn out her light; he could see Judy sneaking into the kitchen when Lorraine was asleep. During the day he had to be more discreet, but during his quick peeks he often saw Aurelia sitting in front of the TV, a phone in her hand, a plate on the sofa beside her. Unfortunately he would never be able to tell Lorraine any of this, for this watching of the silent movie of her life, one he knew so well he could almost have recited the dialogue, was too creepy to ever share with her.

His third night in the building, he saw the pink glow in Judy's room again. Insomnia. She must have woken up in the middle of the night. Scared, trying to fall asleep. Perhaps she was listening to the radio, or reading a book. If he were there he could tell her a story, like he used to do—oh, so long ago. He wished he could reach out and tell her that it was all right, not to cry. Of course it was not all right, but it was permissible to lie to children. If you did not lie to children, what would ever make them wish to become adults?

Again, he found himself crying. He realized the doorman no longer mattered. It was time to go home.

"You all right?" asked the man with the matted beard, as David began gathering his stuff. The voice shocked him. He had grown so comfortable around him that he had almost forgotten him, as if he were a piece of furniture, or an old, familiar lover.

"Yes. Goodbye. And thank you."

"Good luck," said the man.

"You too." David started to leave, then he thought of something and walked over to the man. He took off his jacket and placed it around the man's shoulders. "I don't need this any more," he said.

The man fingered the material. "What's this made of?" he asked.

"Cashmere mix."

"That's expensive, isn't it?"

"The best."

The man reached out to shake his hand. They had scarcely talked, and yet a feeling almost of sadness came over David at the thought of leaving him.

"Who is it?" he heard a sleepy voice ask.

"It's David."

Lorraine opened the door. "David, what are you doing here?"

He shook his head. "It's a long story."

"You look terrible."

"I know."

"You smell terrible too."

"I haven't bathed in days. Can I come in?"

"David!"

"It's my home too. I could've sold the insider rights. But I didn't."

She sighed. "All right. I guess you can sleep in the maid's room."

Judy ran out of her room. "Daddy, Daddy," she cried. She flung herself into his arms. The smell didn't seem to bother her at all.

•

"You sure you don't want company?" David asked Lorraine, after he had showered. He was in his old Armani robe, the one Lorraine had given him one Christmas before he had gone to Texas and they had had lots of money.

"Oh David," she said, shaking her head.

David, lying on the little bed in the maid's room, was unable to sleep. He thought of Lorraine, lying all alone in the king-sized bed, and Jack, lying beside her on the floor—not next to him—and for the first time the full tragedy of what he had wrought came upon him.

MARA BREZHNEV
*(holding a blue margarita outside
Cafe Death on Leonard and West
Broadway.)*
This is the second of two Eyewitness News
reports on the Lone Ranger, the young artist
who calls the fake muggings he performs "performance pieces." Where else to find out what
the art crowd thinks about him than here at
the Cafe Death in Tribeca, where New York's
hottest artists can be found sipping blue margaritas? Sir,
(grabbing YOUNG MAN)
Are you an artist?

YOUNG MAN
Yes I am.

MARA
Are you famous?

YOUNG MAN
Not yet but I will be soon. I'm having my first show next
month at the C.O.D. gallery on East Fifth.

MARA
That's very nice.
(turning to person on other side of her)
Sir, what do you think of the Lone Ranger?

MIDDLE-AGED PAINTER
(bitterly)
I was doing work like that four years ago. Where the (bleep)
were you then?

CUT TO:
Mara grabbing waitress holding tray full of tapas.

MARA
What's your opinion of the Lone Ranger?

WAITRESS
(carrying tray of tapas)

I don't know. I'm too busy making money to worry about art.

CUT TO:
Mara standing with mike over table of yuppies. The table is littered with dirty dishes, cigarettes, beer glasses.

YOUNG MAN

Stuff like this is why my parents wouldn't send me to art school.

MARA

Do you regret it?

YOUNG MAN

No. I'm a Manny Hanny guy now and I love it.

MARA
(to young woman)

What do you think of the Lone Ranger? How would you feel about meeting him in a dark alley late one night?

WOMAN

I'd love it!

MARA
(surprised)

You would? Why?

WOMAN

I'm a grad student at the Columbia School of Journalism. It'd be the scoop of my life.

CUT TO:
Mara talking to waiter.

MARA

If a man came in and you knew he was the Lone Ranger, would you give him a table?

WAITER

Why not?

MARA

A good table or a bad table?

Shot of waiter thinking.

WAITER

Somewhere between Eric Fischl and Julian Schnabel.

CUT TO:
Mara to man at bar.

MARA

Sir, are you an artist?

MAN

No.

MARA

But you like artists. Is that why you're here?

MAN

No, I'm an alcoholic.

CUT TO:
Mara's face.

MAN

Just joking.

CUT TO:

FEMALE GALLERY OWNER

By the time you people latch on to something it's yesterday's news. The really hot thing right now is miniature biological sculpture.

MARA

"Miniature biological sculpture." What's that?

GALLERY OWNER

You combine various bacteriological life forms on a slide, and freeze-dry them. All the work is done via miniature tools under a microscope, and involves an incredible amount of skill and precision. A number of the best artists in this area have medical degrees.

MARA

Really?

GALLERY OWNER

Oh yes. They find it much more challenging than medicine. After all, you're not just dealing with people, you're creating whole new life forms.

CUT TO:

MARA
(to café owner)
Is the Lone Ranger good for business?

OWNER
*(laughing as he looks around at packed
restaurant)*

Business is always good. This is the hottest restaurant in
New York City.

CUT TO:
Mara talking to man in his thirties seated in front of the bar.

MARA

Someone over there told me you were the Lone Ranger?
Are you?

MAN
(laughing)

No, but I wish I were!

MARA

Why?

MAN

Because if I were, you'd let me buy you a blue margarita.

MARA

You can buy me one anyway.

**Mara sitting at the bar next to man. Bartender places a blue margarita in
front of her. She takes a sip.**

Hmm, not bad. Folks, this is Mara Brezhnev of the Channel
Seven "Eyewitness News" team saying *"hasta la vista"*
from the Cafe Death in Tribeca, hoping that all your margaritas be blue.

Jeremy chuckled, turned down the TV, continued typing.

. . . oddly, the Post-Modernist investigations into the notions of
artifice "posed" by the artist known as the Lone Ranger have
managed to outrage the very segment of the art world that one
would think would be most receptive to this new form of theater.
The hypocrisy of much of the avant-garde stance is made clear by
such reactions, asserting as they do a false division between the
Private and the Public . . . .

Midsentence, he quit. It was too easy. Now that he had the
language and the point of view, his fingers danced on almost
by themselves. Was there nothing in the world—the message

on a Hallmark card, the threads in a dollar bill, a change in
Afghanistani grammar, the switch of a football team from
one city to another, the stripes of a zebra, the lines on a
phonograph record—he couldn't deconstruct any way he
pleased?

He got up, went over to his Sony CDP-302B, and placed the
newest LaMonte Young on it. Pure electronic tones filled the
room. Under this, or perhaps encapsulated by this, was the
sadness that never left, that filled his heart sometimes to
bursting, and other times left it empty, angry, drained. What
if it was the sadness of his unrequited passions to which he
was addicted, rather than the passions themselves? For if he
achieved his dreams, and they disappointed him, what then?
If he could, would he go to his utopian Moscow, the ultimate
Minimalist city, or has he stayed too long in the corrupted
and corrupting city, an Anthony Blunt so captivated by dec-
adence he no longer even desired to leave? Was it possible he
no longer even desires to change it? Does he not in fact prefer
to dream of it the long winter nights (as Jews at Passover
dream of "next year in Jerusalem"), as snow drifts over New
York garbage cans and streets, deadening automobile sounds
for an hour or two before tire tracks and white salt pockmark
the snow, thus temporarily bringing the sounds and smells of
his dream world to him, a madeleine of the ever-postponed
future.

He cleared the screen, removed the disk, then switched the
modem to the Receive mode, in case somebody from his network wanted to share their hopes, desires, sexual fantasies
with a stranger who knew them as Flash, Gonzo Ga, The
Word, Pure Mind, whatever alias the flickering white dots
proclaimed them for this night to be. Nowhere Idaho, Wintersnow Nebraska, Further Utah—out of the night the voices
came as he sat there in a dark alleviated only by the gray
glow of a monitor, solo occupant of a spaceship hurtling
through the void, in touch with the world only through this
dance of vibrating electrons. The melancholy of these strangers' stories moved him more than the events of his own life;
in return he made up stories about himself that, though not
true in this world, were perhaps true in others. This made-up

life seemed as real as his "real" one; or, perhaps, his "real" life seemed as made-up as this. Or was reality not the point, but something else entirely—something that often seemed inconsequential, and other times quivered with meaning? He sat there listening and dreaming, as in lofts around him families cleaned the dishes, put the kids to bed, and thought of yet another reason to avoid making love, and as he listened he kept straining to hear the only voice that mattered: not the one from Nowhere Idaho or Wintersnow Nebraska, but the one from his magic kingdom, that gray capital where Anna Karenina is forever walking off a train into a new life, where Natasha dances, Pierre dreams, and Raskolnikov stabs an old lady for no reason. Did they know the stuff of his dreams? Will he ever get there? Does it matter?

The phone rang, four times, then the sound of his own voice, announcing to the world he was not there.

At the party at Don Corleone's in honor of the Lone Ranger, tape loops of the "Eyewitness News" feature played over and over on the video screens that surrounded the bar and dance floor. In honor of the occasion the bartenders and bouncers wore black jeans, Reeboks, leather jackets, ski masks, shoulder holsters with guns. Some of the customers also wore "mugging outfits"; others dressed in standard downtown garb—similar to the above, but with slightly more glitter. With their weird hairdos and makeup they looked crazed, as if they were drug addicts, but their eyes were clear, constantly scanning the room to see if anybody "important" had come in; most of them would get up early the next morning for their jobs on Wall Street, PR agencies, and "lifestyle" magazines.

"Enjoying yourself?" Jeremy asked.

Jack shook his head. "Are you kidding? I can't take too many more nights of this. It's worse than a job." Every night, courtesy the mysterious "A-list" newsletter, there were openings, dinners, parties at clubs, then parties after the parties at the houses of famous people Jack had only read about in magazines. By the time he got home he was so exhausted he couldn't sleep; the music rang in his ears for hours after it stopped. He couldn't stay awake without alcohol or drugs, but the more he did these, the less he felt like himself. And yet, no matter how exhausted or bored he was, it was almost impossible to stop himself from taking advantage of each invitation. Who could?

"It *is* a job," said Jeremy. "Didn't you know that? How about another beer?"

Jack shrugged. "Sure. No. I don't know." He sat down at the bar and picked his way through the fluorescent-dyed popcorn.

"To your fifteen minutes of fame," toasted Jeremy, when the beers arrived.

"To your exclusive stories," said Jack. They clicked glasses.

A chic young model with hair colored like a rainbow sidled over to Jack. "Someone told me you're the Lone Ranger," she purred.

"If I were, would I tell you?" asked Jack.

"It's not going to do you any good if you don't tell *somebody*. My name is Clear," she said. "Dawn Clear. If you *are*, call up my answering machine and say hello. Or you can reach me through Elite's. If you're not, don't bother." She handed a card to Jack, then walked away. Jack stuck the card in his pocket without looking.

"If she knows, how come the cops haven't caught on yet?"

"They will. Which is why you gotta come clean before they do. Look. This was your idea. It's dumb not to take advantage of it."

"And go to jail for the next ten years? They're already accusing me of half the crimes in the city. Did you know the crime rate's up by seventeen percent in the last month? If I were as energetic as they claim, I'd have been famous long ago."

"Who goes to jail, Jack, in America? By then you'll have your book. You'll make a mint. Your students will respect you."

"Gimme a break!"

"All you need is a good lawyer. Everybody wants to interview you," continued Jeremy. "Donahue, David Letterman; you name it. You sell the rights to some publisher for a mint; we can write it together—or write it yourself if you want. You wait too long, somebody's going to appropriate *you* and steal all the credit. It's easy. All they have to do is start mugging people themselves."

"They already have. Muggers claim to be me, the victims feel safe, they don't resist, I'm making it easy for these creeps!"

"So schedule a press conference. If you'll do it at Palladium they'll give you a top-notch party: four-color invites, Mike Todd room, the works."

"Just what we need—another night in the Mike Todd room."

"Hey you, stick 'em up," a man dressed as the Lone Ranger said to a woman standing near them at the bar.

"Very funny," she said.

"Funny my ass. Give me your money." He pulled the gun out of his holster and stuck it in front of her face.

"Okay, I get it," she said, pushing the gun away, "A performance."

He fired at the ceiling. The band stopped playing and the crowd became quiet. Then someone applauded, whistled. The music started again.

Again the guy stuck the gun in the woman's face. "Look, you made your point, it's part of the show," she said.

"The hell it is." The guy pushed her off her stool, grabbed her pocketbook and ran toward the door.

"Hey, you, stop! Stop him!" cried the woman. She tried to chase him, but couldn't make her way through the jostling crowd.

"You fuckers!" she screamed. "Let me through. I had nearly five hundred dollars in there!"

"Five hundred dollars—I would've stolen that myself!" said one wise guy.

The woman kicked him on the shins as hard as she could. As he was falling he grabbed for her and pulled her down onto the floor. A man who'd been standing nearby jumped on top of the guy. Other people joined in; some because they thought it was part of the show, others because they were mean from liquor or drugs. Meanwhile the woman had gotten up and was trying to chase the mugger. The crowd coming through the door pushed her back and she began to get hysterical. Then she took off her shoes and with the spiked heels began to hit people to get them to move aside.

A whistle blew, the revolving light of a patrol car flashed through the room, the music and disco lights stopped as policemen ran through the room. Shots rang out. People screamed and dove under tables. All the lights but the red EXIT ones went out.

"What the fuck?" Jack asked Jeremy. "Is this part of the show?"

"Shit if I know," Jeremy grabbed Jack's wrist and began leading him to the door. Suddenly the lights came on. As if caught in a strobe, people became paralyzed. In the eerie silence the lead singer of the Psychic Terrors (a band whose songs chronicled the Lone Ranger's doings) jumped on the stage. "Hey, lady, here's your purse." He threw the purse at the woman. Then the band ran screaming through the club, jumped up on stage, picked up their guitars, and started playing. The music released people from their trance, and they began talking and dancing again.

"Sick fucks!" the woman screamed. Her dress was torn and her face was bloody.

"What's the matter, honey, can't you take a joke?"

Immediately afterward, a videotape of this "performance mugging" replaced the tapes of Mara on the TV sets over the bar. Cursing and crying, the woman made her way out of the club.

"*Jesus*," said Jack.

"Imitation is the sincerest form of flattery," said Jeremy.

"I'm splitting," said Jack. "I can't take any more of this."

"Don't tell me you're copping out on the party *after* the party. The one at the house of the ex-wife of the very famous rock star?"

"Nah, I'm beat. You go if you want to."

"Are you kidding? I've been doing this for years. Should we take the limo?"

"Let's walk. Cold air'll do us some good."

At the door Jack stopped, and turned around to look at the slides of the composite police drawing of his face flashing in syncopated rhythm to the music everywhere in the club. The dancers' faces were silhouetted against it on the walls, their shoes stomped over it on the dance floor, it hung above them like the moon.

They walked uptown a few blocks, then sat down on a bench in Tompkins Square Park, very near the one Murray had brought Jack to only a few months before. "You think I'm a sellout, don't you?" asked Jack.

"I think you're the only person in New York who would still ask that question."

"And you're not answering it." Jeremy remained silent. "Maybe I am. I don't know. But I'd reached this dead end. I couldn't paint any more. I didn't know what the fuck to do. Of course this doesn't feel like 'me,' but you know, lately, I don't know if I even give a shit any more what 'me' is. I mean, it seems so egotistical. Who the fuck gives a shit about my so-called vision? At least this stirs people up. That's a good sign, isn't it?"

"Did I criticize you, Jack?"

"No. But I *know* you. Deep down you think it's a crock. Why? I'd have thought this would be right up your alley. 'Questioning the very bases of society,' and so forth."

"Right up Vito Acconci's alley, maybe, Jack, but not yours."

"But you *like* Vito Acconci's alley—and you don't like mine."

"Oh, who knows what I like any more," sighed Jeremy. "Anyway, even if I did, who gives a shit?" He bent down, picked up a stick, and threw it at a tree.

"Don't give me this. You're got everything you've every wanted."

Jeremy laughed. "Good old Jack. You'll never change." He stood up and punched Jack lightly on the arm before saying good night.

Jack, who had changed, remained seated. He opened his mouth wide, moved his jaw back and forth, put his fingers above the bridge of his nose to the pressure point that sometimes helped ease his by now almost constant headache. He shut his eyes and massaged the back of his neck and shoulders and tried to breathe slowly. But music and bits of overheard sentences continued to meander through his mind. Behind his eyes were exploding orange flowers, erupting volcanos of color.

A man was sitting on the bench across the path, under a streetlamp. He was wearing an old suit jacket. At first Jack decided he was one of the bums who slept in the pavilion where the park toilets were, then he decided that he was an artist who'd bought the jacket at Crazy Jack's or someplace like that. Actually, it was impossible to tell: people's strangeness seemed to increase the longer you looked at them, so that after a while even the most ordinary person began to look weird.

He wondered what the man would think if he told him about the performance muggings. If he was an artist he'd love it. If he was a bum, he'd think he was an asshole. So how was one to determine the truth about this event?

Whenever the man caught Jack looking at him, Jack would look away in embarrassment. Then he realized the man might think he was looking away because he was frightened of him, so he forced himself to look at him. Then it occurred to him the man might think he was cruising him, so again he looked away. But the energy involved in this avoidance of the man was as great as if Jack had continued to look at him, so that his self-consciousness began to create the very relationship he was ostensibly trying to avoid. Then Jack began to wonder how much the man was conscious of what was going on in his (Jack's) head. It seemed impossible he could not be aware, and yet, if he was as conscious of Jack as Jack was of him, why didn't one of them just get up and say hello to the other, instead of just sitting there in silence thinking about each other? Jack could not figure out if this particular man exuded a particular vividness, or whether it was not merely some element of the circumstances—the conversation with Jeremy, the party at Don Corleone's, his fatigue—that was responsible for the intensity (at least in his own mind) of this encounter.

If all encounters were this intense, it would be impossible to walk the streets without being overcome by the most terrible self-consciousness and anxiety.

The man stood up. "Good night," he said, to Jack, before walking out of the park.

"Night," Jack replied, relieved at this evidence that the enounter had occurred inside the man's head also. He watched him as he walked out of the park, and decided he was not a bum, but an artist. He had an impulse to get up and follow him, to grab a late-night bite with him in one of the chic restaurants on the west side of the park. They could drink wine and confide their problems to each other and discuss what they had thought about each other in the cold.

Of course, if he were a bum and not an artist, Jack would not be interested in grabbing a bite with him—even though, if the man were a bum, he could certainly use a free meal.

But the same shyness—or, perhaps, the conventions of shyness—that prevented Jack from talking to attractive women who walked past him on the street or stood near him in the subway prevented him from speaking to the man. For what kind of confusion would result if any human being were available to us at any moment of the day, if we only put our minds to it? What if every woman Jack watched reading a book or newspaper on the subway wasn't reading a book or newspaper at all, but was secretly conscious of Jack's gaze, his hands on the overhead metal bar, the zipper of his pants almost level with their eyes? What if the stories we made up all day long in our heads about other people were echoed by similar stories they made up about us inside their heads—and not just when we were with them, but at other times too? What if we were not so alone and crazy as we thought?

•

Once the man was far enough away so that it would not seem like Jack was following him, Jack stood up and left the park. He bought a *Post* at Gem Spa, then walked to the Kiev, where he ordered French toast and coffee. As he waited for it, he tried to make up his mind about this Lone Ranger business. If he were going to cash in on it, now was the time; much longer, either he'd be caught, or the novelty would be gone. Unable to deal with his ambivalence, he opened his *Post* and began to read about the Rangers and the Knicks. As usual, the Rangers were giving the Flyers fits; as usual, the Knicks were terrible. Yet surely the Rangers would find some way to lose, and the Knicks would refuse to get some decent guards. The French toast came; made with challah, it was remarkably good. He looked out the window at the people and cars passing, and he felt that nothing in the whole world could have suited him better than sitting here, eating breakfast, at night, reading about basketball and hockey. You'd think it would be boring, but in fact the predictability covered each season with a nostalgic glow: you could count on the Rangers to be not quite good enough, and you could count on the Knicks to be awful, and what could be more reassuring than this? The little pond of butter melting slowly on the thick challah, mingling with the larger pond (lake, really) of maple syrup flooding over the toast, the deep black of coffee melting into tan as the milk flooded it, the people in their weird downtown costumes passing in front of the window, the garbage lying in what seemed like random patterns on the pavement and in the gutter (but really, was the habitual and personalized sculptural expression of the person who had discarded it), the reflections of himself and his coffee in the glass of the window, his walk in the park and silent communication with the man, all seemed remarkably harmonious and beautiful. Beautiful, as things had been in graduate school, not so much by virtue of the grace of the inherent form, as his vision that had made it so. Looked at in the proper light, the people at the tables around him in the Kiev stopped being ugly freaks and turned into interesting shapes and planes and angles, beings that were interesting to look at. And draw. The table, the smudged floor, the fingerprints on the creamer, all interesting, hence . . . if you looked at it in a certain light—the proper light—beautiful. It was beautiful, and he was happy—just sitting here by himself, looking quietly at ordinary things, he was happy—much happier than when he was at Don Corleone's, or the Palladium, or 1018, or Siberia.

Unconsciously, Jack's hand reached out, grabbed a pencil out of his pocket, started to doodle on a napkin. He did it without thinking, a muscle memory from long ago.

He looked down, saw outlines of a garbage can, a man, a table. Soon the whole table was littered with his drawings. He drank cup after cup of coffee. And with every stroke of his pencil, he felt himself becoming more and more like himself, the person he used to be, whoever that was.

Slowly he climbed the stairs to his apartment. His old paintings, the ones he had looked at in disgust not so long ago, were still piled against the wall. He spread them around the room, to see what he would think of them now. He sat there a long time, just looking. They did not seem so awful. The early work, particularly, he liked; that is, he liked the person who had done them, the vision he'd been trying to express. Maybe the paintings were not "showable," but there was something sweet and touching about them, almost the way the work of a child was "touching." Then the work became more "mature," "better"—in the sense that that word was normally used. That is, whatever the paintings were trying to express was expressed more clearly on the canvas, so that the work, in accomplishing what it set out to do, was "successful." But "success," as was so often the case, had its drawbacks, for as the work got "mature" it also became narrower, less allusive, less interesting. Was that because he had changed what he was trying to express, or because the unexpressed was more interesting than the expressed, or because when you formally came to know what it was you were doing, the energy disappeared from your work?

In high school, Jack had drawn and painted in his bedroom, the living room, on the dining-room table, the kitchen table, and on the margins of all his notebooks in whatever classroom he was sitting. In college he had painted in class, in the cafeteria, in his girlfriend's room, a car, a subway, a park bench, a kitchen table . . . anyplace would do. In those days he could think of no better way to spend an afternoon than to sit alone in his room, humming along with the radio as he drew or painted, his mind wandering where it would, with no one to tell him that what he was thinking or doing was weird or strange. Was the reason painting had gone dead on him because he had become too interested in the finished product, rather than in the movements of his mind as he worked? Could he stop being a grown-up, and go back to being a child?

He looked up at his bulletin board, where clippings concerning the Lone Ranger were posted. In the lower left-hand drawer of his desk, the starter pistol sat. Opposite this was the wooden table with his old, half-used tubes of paint.

He could see it all clearly. First he would perform in New York clubs, then in performance spaces across the country; finally he would be invited to travel to Germany and Japan. And as he traveled and performed, and the rooms got bigger and the crowds more demanding, slowly he would evolve from a person who did performances, to a person who utilized video cameras, and lighting effects, and music. Technical people would travel with him, and help evolve his projects with him, and much of his time would be spent having lunches and dinners with foundation heads, coercing money out of people and institutions he despised. He would get invitations to chic performances and dance concerts and parties, to openings and dinners, and people he had never heard of would want to meet him: rich people with money, who thought artists were chic. He would lecture on campuses for gobs of money, grants would pour in, and if he played his cards right, it could go on forever.

He got out a beer, put on an old Grateful Dead record, lay down on a pillow on the floor. From this angle he could see the sky. It was a cloudy night, pink, no stars, a bit of mist. On nights like this, the streetlight outside Lorraine's window would glow through the haze, an eerie light that always made him glad to be safe inside. If he could make a wish and by magic be instantly transported wherever he wanted, he would be uptown staring at it now—at the bars of light cast by the venetian blinds on the ceiling—instead of at his own cracked and gouged water-stained walls.

White walls, large closets, windows that closed, a maid to iron his shirts, leftovers in the icebox, bottles of cranberry juice that did not have to be carried up four flights of stairs, sheets that tucked themselves into the bed, floors that licked themselves clean, bathtubs that made their own bubbles, refrigerators that did their own shopping, ovens that did their own cooking, clothing that washed itself, towels that enfolded you like a diaper when you emerged shivering from the shower . . . had that really been so terrible? Surely the void that he had found even there, lurking amidst the business, the furniture, the husband, the child, the dog, the cat— a disappointment strong enough to drive him away—was one he would find everywhere. If one was to lie awake, tortured and miserable in the night, wasn't it better to do this next to someone, than to do it alone?

It was not a glamorous image, but it seemed to be his. When he got right down to it, what he really wanted was not to be famous, but to lie in bed next to someone, complaining —rather happily—about not being famous.

He looked at his watch: 5:40. Soon the heat would come on in Lorraine's apartment, rattling the radiators, waking her up. He could almost see her yawning, turning over, sticking out an arm to reach for him, an arm that would not find him. Then she would get up and stumble to the cold bathroom. On tiptoe she'd run back to bed, wrapping the top sheet around her as if she were a mummy. He wondered if she'd manage to fall back asleep, or, as often happened, she'd miss the moment, and lie there tossing and turning as Jezebel licked her face, trying to make her get up to give her some food. Was she awake now, and if she was, was she thinking about her business, or Jezebel, or Judy, or was she by chance thinking about him? And if by chance she was, what was she thinking? Was she still angry? Did she miss him? And if she was thinking about him now, what about when he had lived with her? Was it possible that, beyond the fog of the days and nights through which they had drifted, physically together but mentally separate, there had been something entirely different going on: a congruent, silent telling of stories about a world far more complicated and interesting than the one in which each had thought the other had lived?

He picked up the phone, dialed a familar number, heard a familiar sleepy voice saying hello. A deep breath escaped him. It felt like he'd been holding it inside forever.

"Lorraine," said Jack. "It's Jack."

"Jack! Why are you calling?" Jack knew, but for some reason he couldn't bring himself to say it. With Lorraine, for some reason, he never could. "Do you want to get together and talk?"

"I suppose." As if he were doing her a favor.

"Dinner tomorrow?"

"Sure."

"Pick me up at the office around seven? Oh. *Shit.*"

"What's the matter?"

"Macy's, California. Marianne and I are taking them to the Water Club." Jack sighed; here it was, the same old story. Already, almost, he was bored. "Look, we'll be through early. Do you want to come over around eleven? Or we can do it the night after?"

"Tomorrow's fine," said Jack.

23

A long wet tongue and a cold black nose greeted Jack the next evening before he was halfway through the door. "Jack, you old thing," he said, scratching behind the ears, allowing himself to be licked.

"Am I next in line?" asked Lorraine.

"Jack!" shouted Judy, running out of the bathroom. She jumped up on him with her legs around his waist, hopped off, and jumped up and down in front of him. "Guess *what!*"

"What?"

"I've got my first boyfriend. Whe-ee!" She did a cartwheel over the sofa. "He's really cute. Do you want to see his picture?"

"Of course."

"Come on." She dragged him into her room.

"*Plus ça change, plus c'est la même chose,*" said Jack, following her.

"Isn't he adorable?" asked Judy.

"Very cute," said Jack, holding the photograph. "But why is he wearing a dress?"

"*What?*" She grabbed the picture. "That's Annie, stoopid. He's over there. Oh, you're joking. Ha ha. So funny I forgot to laugh. I had the third-biggest part of everybody in my grade and when this person I was singing this song with got a sore throat I got to sing it all by myself—"

"Okey-dokey," said Lorraine, "enough's enough. You promised you'd go to sleep after Jack got here."

"Mo-ther, you're such a bore. Come on, tell me a story, please please please."

"Judy, Jack and I haven't seen each other in—"

"So whose fault is that? Not mine. Come on. One short

story. Otherwise I'll never be able to get to sleep. You wouldn't want me running in and out of your room all night, would you?"

Jack and Lorraine looked at each other, then laughed. "Adolescence," said Jack. Lorraine sat down on the bed, tucked Judy in, turned off the overhead lamp so the only light in the room was from the fifteen-watt bulb inside the huge Donald Duck lamp. "Once upon a time there were two beautiful alley cats, Jezebel and Marlene, and they had been best friends ever since they could remember. One winter afternoon, a day so cold you could hear their paws crinkle as they broke through the crust that lay on top of the frozen white snow . . ."

As Lorraine spoke Jack, sitting on the floor, leaned his back against the mattress, looked up at the fluorescent stars shining brightly on the ceiling, shut his eyes.

Lying in bed with Lorraine that night, he heard the front door open, a person stumble and fall. "What's that?" he asked, sitting up with a jerk, starting to get out of bed.

"David."

"David? What's he doing here?"

"Is this a visit, Jack, or do you think you're here for good?"

Jack felt that old familiar constricting chill around his heart, but he had determined not to pay attention to it. Live with somebody, or alone, it would probably be there for the rest of his life. "For good, I guess. Why?"

"He's been staying in the maid's room. If you're really moving out of your old apartment, he could use a place to live."

New York Post, "Page Six"

We *really* thought we'd heard of everything, but this is positively un-American. The Lone Ranger, the chic post-Marxist who had the art world in such a tizzy but a few short weeks ago

(not to mention suburban matrons,
whom, it is rumored, ostentatiously
sported gold chains around their
necks in the East Village in hopes of
luring the debonair revolutionary),
has apparently taken a permanent
powder from the American version of
success. In an exclusive phone interview given only to squelch rumors
that some "Dirty Harry" cop gave
him the permanent deep-six, the
Lone Ranger reveals that he's alive
and happy and well, hoping to get
back to his first love: painting. It was
great fun but it was just one of those
things. *Requiescat in pace.*

The secrets of the universe lay in the realtor's hands. They
were white and crystalline and glistened in the morning sun
like the promise of youth. He held the little glass bottle up
to the light. In it were mountains and valleys, front and back
bowls of gleaming snow down which he could ski as the wind
whipped past his face. He put his hand in his pocket, took
hold of a little silver spoon, and dipped it into the tiny glass
jar. Huge avalanches slid down the face of mountains, dis-
rupting all geography, burning his eyes with the light. The
faintest of rainbows was on the snow, a prism born of the
curved glass of the bottle. He moved the bottle away from his
face; a tiny object in the landscape of the room. He held the
spoon up to his nose, held the second finger of his left hand
against his left nostril, inhaled with his right. A power went
through him, he was God, he was Man, he was Woman, he
was Beyond Gender, he was Total Possibility, he was as tiny
and unpredictable as a quark, as huge and sluggish as the
slothful grinding of the continents against each other. He was
mountain snow, a sandy beach, pebbles in a brook in Idaho,
a catfish on a lazy bayou, a giant mammal who dragged his
clumsy body from dull unyielding land back to the salt water
from which he'd come, a starfish, a book, a killer whale. He

was a lamb who lay with a lion, a lion who killed the coyote, a hyena of tragic vision whose only recourse was an eternity of laughter. Far away the little bottle was nothing, but up close, in the center of his hand, it was everything.

David looked around Jack's apartment: at his old records and books, his clothing, the paintings he still hadn't moved uptown. Yellowing Jockey shorts—Jockey shorts, for chrissakes!—still lay on the floor of the closet; blackened pots with gunk burned into them were messily stacked in the old cupboards; spatulas whose plastic coating had melted and recongealed like the dried yellow of egg yolks filled kitchen drawers. The gray paint Jack had painted over the uneven floorboards had half worn off; the ceiling and walls were a disaster area of bumps, cracks, and missing chunks—a map of the new world David suddenly found himself living in. If you could call it living.

There was a human being out there he knew he should care about—Judy—but he felt a helpless bystander to her bright adolescent chatter, increasingly awkward and embarrassed and useless. What could he say to her that would be helpful, cheerful, interesting, that could in any way enhance her life? His truths had become too repugnant to share with anybody, and he no longer had the energy to hide them.

He picked up an empty bottle of vodka lying on the floor beside him, and threw it as hard as he could across the room. It hit a framed drawing—a tedious abstract in muted grays and blues, with a yellow slash across the middle—and smashed the glass frame.

David walked over and picked up the drawing. The broken glass had cut into it, and he finished the job by tearing it in half. Then he tried to smash his knee through a small maroon-colored painting that had been hanging over the bed. The canvas stretched, but did not break. He took the painting into the kitchen and stabbed a hole in it with a knife. After this, it was easy to rip. The sound was peculiarly satisfying, and he did not stop until the painting was in long, thin strips.

He destroyed the remaining paintings and drawings Jack

had left hanging on the walls, then he carried a chair over to the storage rack Jack had built to hold his work and tossed the rolled-up canvases onto the floor. He ripped the canvases apart, then tore the drawings up in little pieces and flushed them down the toilet. As he did this he drank vodka and listened to early Stones, and he was as happy as he had been in a long time.

When this was done he started on Jack's clothing. The cloth was softer than the canvas; sometimes he didn't even have to make a slash with the scissors. Then he took Jack's records out of their sleeves and smashed them against the floor and walls. He dumped the books from the bookshelves, but ripping them apart took too much time, so he threw as many as he could in the bathtub, poured a can of turpentine over them, and lit a match.

Exhausted, he turned the light off and flopped down on the bed. But the alcohol continued to burn in his blood, and he had a horrible taste in his mouth. In a mode that was either listening or feeling—he could not determine which—he began to count the beats of his heart pounding in his chest. When he reached 3,000, he took the last of his Valium. At 4,500, the ice entered his body and began to take effect. It wasn't that he didn't feel the pain any more, but it was somehow far away, and he didn't care, and behind the pain was happiness—a happiness he could get to if he only tried. Then music, slow and beautiful, began to play inside his head, so low at first he couldn't be sure whether it was real, or merely the sound of his own blood. When he placed his ear against the wall to hear it better, the hum of the building and the city entered his bones, spinning electrons and protons and quarks of electrical and phone and TV cable lines and plumbing pipes, whirling atoms from people long dead, white men and Indians and Eskimos and the dinosaurs and fish before them, ferns and amoebas and X-rays and neutrinos from the birth and death of far-off stars. The beauty of it made him start to cry, and a halo began to form around the objects in the room, as they gradually began to take shape with the advent of yet another day.

Another day—surely no better than the one that had come

before, and perhaps no worse than the one that would come after. He looked around the apartment, as messy as if a tiny ticker-tape parade had taken place inside. It would take forever to clean it up. But then, why should he bother? It was not his home. What did he care about Jack, or Lorraine—or even himself?

He stood up, fumbled beneath the confettied canvases for his coat, then made his way to the door. Where he was going he did not know, but slowly he made his way downstairs. West was still dark, but there was a pink rim rising from the east, so he turned his face toward the new day, the blackened shells of buildings in the far East Village, the decay of the city.

Jeremy printed out the letter, then turned off his computer for the last time. He addressed the envelope by hand, then walked slowly up to the Prince Street post office. No real reason to go there, but he wanted a last look at the trucks unloading their merchandise; at the gallery dealers making final pitches to their customers; at the wealthy young real estate lawyer buying yet another $600 sweater at Dianne B.'s; at the artist's wife carrying arugula, prosciutto, and twelve-dollar bottles of olive oil and five-dollar pints of ice cream home from Dean & DeLuca's; at the gridlock attacking cars all the way down Broadway to Canal; at the sky turning an ever-deeper blue as it spun away from (and toward) the sun, causing lights to come on in renovated lofts and rehearsal spaces and co-ops and condos, thereby illuminating the middle-aged wife of the once-successful painter preparing pesto sauce in the kitchen, the Japanese artist practicing t'ai chi, the young girl riding her tricycle around in a circle in her loft, her older brother taping her with his new video camera, and Jeremy, sitting in the dusk on a couch, watching this. Feeling quite sure that no one in the history of the world had ever felt as alone as he did now, he took a last look at his white Robert Ryman, his gray Brice Marden, and his black Ad Reinhardt paintings, his Scott Burton coffee table, the stainless steel dining table and refrigerator, the microwave and the espresso maker, the low-voltage light fixtures and burglar alarm, the VCR and CD disk player. Out the window he could see the World Trade Center with its gleaming red LED, tirelessly filling the city with its electronic dreams. "Object and Color Reductionism and/or Replacement"—he had had his dreams too. He opened the window, stood on the windowsill, and gazed down at the street below. It was pleasantly gray, like the dining table and the refrigerator and the sky. He breathed the cool evening air and then made his last, impossible gesture, hurtling toward earth at thirty-two feet per second per second. In at least one of his possible lives, he is traveling to his magic kingdom, the home of Pierre and Raskolnikov, Natasha and Trotsky, Mayakovsky and Malevich, where Anna Karenina is forever getting on a train, and Vronsky will forever break her heart.

Lorraine yawned, opened her eyes to find Jezebel rubbing her fur against her face, pestering her to get up and give her breakfast. Jezebel's long hair made this feel like the caress of a luxurious fur muff. Then Jezebel rather solemnly lowered her head toward Lorraine, as if she were humbling herself, but really it was so Lorraine would scratch her behind her ears. When Jezebel got bored with this she lay down with her head on Lorraine's arm, almost as if she were a lover, then she suddenly jumped up over Lorraine's face and onto the windowsill.

Six-forty-five. With a sigh Lorraine got up, grabbed her robe, and went into the kitchen. Out of the broken cabinet they still hadn't bothered to fix she got out a can of Nine Lives cat food, opened the can, dumped half of it into Jezebel's glass bowl. She placed the bowl on top of the counter so that Jack (the dog) couldn't get at it, then covered the can with Handi-Wrap and put it in the fridge. Meanwhile Jezebel, feigning indifference, curled herself up on top of the dining-room table—a forbidden area. Jack growled at her for this, then jumped up on a dining-room chair. "Jack!" warned Lorraine. Jack jumped off the chair, then slinked into the kitchen to slurp up water from his bowl. A few minutes later Jezebel followed him into the kitchen. After jumping up on the counter, she slowly circled the food before lying down on the counter with her head on her paws. She stared at the bowl a long time, then, sighing, got up and leaned her long supple body over the bowl. Her apparent disappointment fascinated Lorraine: mice, birds, roaches—what was she yearning for? Lorraine watched as she picked at her food with her paws and tongue, then, the bowl scarcely touched, jumped off the counter and lay down in a corner to lick her paws. Later she'll jump back up on the counter to continue this meal.

Lorraine initially assumed Jezebel adopted this fastidious reluctance for show—as a kind of objective demonstration of the power relations concerning food presentation and choice of brand between them—but, having spied on her on more than one occasion, she had learned this was not the case. Unlike Jack (the dog), as well as most of the people she knows, Jezebel acted the same whether or not Lorraine was there. It was a trait Lorraine very much admired.

She drank some coffee, glanced at *WWD* to find out about the recent showings, and went over some bills. When it was seven-thirty she went into Judy's room and woke her up. Then she went into the bathroom to turn on her shower, being careful to make just enough noise so that Jack would wake up—but not enough so that he could ever be entirely sure she had done this on purpose. She supposed, for better or worse, she had woken up into the existence that was truly hers.

"Once there was a scuba diver, so beloved by the fish that not even the hungry shark dared go near her. One day as she was sticking her hand under a rock to grab a lobster for dinner, God, who had taken the form of a lobster, grabbed her with his big claw and said: 'O daughter, you whom the fish love, why do you disobey my commandments and consume shellfish, which I have expressly forbidden you to eat?'

"The scuba diver was frightened and tried to withdraw her hand. But God would not let her go until she had answered the question to his satisfaction.

" 'I love clams and mussels and oysters and the hard- and soft-shelled crab, but most of all I love lobster and crawfish and prawns—things that crawl upon the bottom of the sea. And if I do not eat them, O Lord, for no other reason than my love for you—then out of this irrationality will I separate myself from those I love, who long ago have forsaken the strict path of food and dress the better to resemble their neighbors. And if I follow thy commands, I will lead a lonely path in this world, separated from those I love forever.'

" 'That, my daughter, is why I have given this commandment, so that thy love for me is proven above all others.'

"When the lobster let go of her hand the scuba diver opened her net, letting loose all the lobster and crab she had gathered. Then she followed her bubbles to the surface, saying goodbye to the shellfish she had loved, for she knew her path would take her far from them."

When the woman was done the two men said nothing, though the black man did get up and add a chair leg to the fire they had built in a makeshift brick fireplace in the midst of the burnt-out building. The only sound was the burning of the paper of their cigarettes as they inhaled, the crackling of the fire, and the rain falling gently outside.

A while later the white man spoke: "There was a German who went around the world trying to do good, to atone for the evil his country had done.

"And his parents said to him: 'We didn't know Jews were being killed, and thus we are absolved of responsibility. Why should you, who were unborn, have to atone for the destruction of these people, whom we did not ask to move here in the first place, who came to us, unbidden, from Spain?'

"And he said: 'If I do not atone, who will, for you, who were alive at the time, will not? In what other manner can evil be expunged, both from our souls and the memory of the world, than by using it to lead directly to some otherwise unattainable good? Thus we integrate evil into the ultimate moral thrust toward goodness of this world, by which it thereby ceases to be a random, horrific, unassimilable event productive only of despair, and becomes, instead, one of regeneration and salvation. For how else can we erase the terrible blot we have put on the world, other than by becoming a nation of saints, to create a heaven on earth?' And he went on wandering, trying to do goodly deeds, speak righteous words, and have purity in his heart.

"One day he arrived in Beirut in Lebanon. Tiny pieces of metal were being catapulted all around him, and bombs were falling from huge metal birds in the sky. Nonetheless he walked unscathed through the flames and bullets until he reached the commander of the Jewish forces. And he said to him: 'General, what are you and your men doing here, so far from home, on the eve of Yom Kippur, the holy of Holies?'

"The commander said to him: 'I am fighting a just war to preserve the pride of my heart, my daughter Israel, and to avenge the terrorist murders of my sisters and brothers.'

" ' "Vengeance is mine," saith the Lord, did He not?'

"Then the commander began to weep, for he knew that what the man had said was true, and he smote himself upon the breast: 'O God, tell me thy will, for I have lost my way,' and he lay down and prayed to God.

"And God said: 'Rise up. Do you not miss your children and your wife, your son who is being bar-mitzvahed, and the apple orchard you planted when you were nine?'

"The commander said: 'There is nothing I would like more than to go home, and yet I cannot betray my country, my beloved and afflicted Israel.'

" 'Yet you betray me, the creator and destroyer of nations, I who gave Israel its name?' And God waxed terrible in His wrath.

"Then the commander resigned his position and went home, and somebody else was assigned to take his place. Having been warned about the holy German who had sown dissatisfaction and grief in his predecessor's heart, the new commander refused to grant an interview with him. But one day when he was out walking, a mine exploded nearby, killing all his guards and temporarily knocking him out. As he came to he heard a voice: 'Why do you not listen to my messenger, when I send him to speak to you?'

" 'But Lord, how could you send a German to speak to me, he who murdered one-third of my people?'

" 'What can atone for horrendous evil but magnificent good? Is it better I should condemn a people forever, or use them to do my will?' The commander promised he would receive the German, and soon, he, too, resigned his commission and went home to tend his olive trees.

"Finally a third commander was appointed. He, too, refused to see the German, and when the German continued to press his suit, ordered him locked up on suspicion of treason. That very afternoon he was out walking when a shell from weapons the Syrians had bought from the Americans landed near him, killing all those around him, and knocking him out. As he lay there unmoving on the ground, wondering whether he would ever see his beloved again, he heard a voice saying: 'Rise up, evil man, and confess your sins to the Lord.'

" 'There's no Lord,' the man told himself, for he was an atheist. 'The war must be getting to me.' He drew his automatic and sat up, but no one was around him except a goat, so he went over to slay the goat.

" 'A goat is nothing without atonement,' said the voice.

" 'There is nothing I need atone for,' said the man. 'And besides, you do not exist, and I am not feeling very well.' Then he looked up, and saw an old Palestinian woman, and he took out his gun and shot her.

" 'Kneel down and confess thy sins,' said the voice. It came from a nearby olive tree that had suddenly burst into flames. The commander tried to extinguish the fire but could not, and soon the whole orchard was engulfed in flames. 'Must I destroy the whole world to have you acknowledge me?' asked the voice in a thunderous tone, as He caused the heavens to flood and put out the fire.

" 'I'm going crazy,' said the man. 'These voices will not stop.' So he pulled out his automatic and placed it to the side of his head.

" 'What I have created, I will destroy, and no one else,' cried out the voice of God.

" 'There is no God, but you are the spirit of insanity, and in such a world I cannot live. If you would have me live, be silent; if not, I will die, and then my blood will be on your shoulders.'

" 'Sun and blood are on my shoulders, and you will live in the world I have created, for there is none other. Wherever and whatever you are, living or dead, a human encased in the illusion of your own skin or a myriad of molecules dispersed to all the corners of the earth, you will not be able to escape my voice.'

"Unwilling to go on living, the commander pulled the trigger. A hundred thousand thoughts were brushed by metal, and he lived the possible lives stored in his brain. In some of them he was an insect, in others a tree, a canoe, a piece of chalk, a record player, a fire, in others a lion, a bird, a female of ancient races, a Palestinian, a German. In all these lives God appeared, sometimes as a starfish, sometimes as the wind, and in others He was nothing more than the little voice inside the television set.

"The man died smiling. After this the Israelis knew they were snakebit, and slowly began to pull their troops out of Lebanon."

The woman sighed, said good night. The white man smoked the last of his cigarette, then stretched himself out on the cold floor beside the woman. His arm was around her as the black man began to sing: "Sweet dreams . . ." As he was falling asleep David realized, for the first time in his life, he was happy.

Jack was standing by the sink, holding a coldish cup of coffee (for Lorraine had pushed the automatic coffee-maker to Off), when Aurelia handed him Jeremy's letter.

Dear Jack,

Answered prayers, they say, are the worst, so perhaps I should be grateful mine are unrequited. Of course it has been clear to me for years that the gray city of which I dreamed was in fact merely that—a chimera driving men to madness with the temptations of the unachievable. Naive, you say, to imagine a world far better than the one we live in, but my need for this is—or should I say *was?*—as great as yours is . . . oh, for success, or security, or whatever it is you intend by that word *love*. Alas, it turns out to be a desire far worse than the craving for lust or money, for it is vast and hungry as the sky—being as it requires nothing less than the utter transformation of the world! Hubris—you say? Of course. In your heart of hearts, are you not a little god before your canvas?

In any case, I am tired. Once I was tired only of reality, but now I find I'm tired of my dreams as well. So I will end them—or, who knows? go on to others as yet unknown. No need for pity—for at last, as my molecules dissolve into earth and sky, I will become at least in some sense part of that great ecosystem which is the closest to Community I will ever know: breathed in and out of the nostrils of every living being, living simultaneously in a multitude of universes, in some of which I am Hadrian, in some of which I am Lenin, in some of which I am (alas!) Hitler—and in some of which, for all we know, I am your chair, your pencil, your paintbrush, your tooth, your cup of coffee. . . .

When Jack was done, he poured the remainder of his coffee down the sink, then rinsed the cup off under the water. The glass was wet, and the letter slipped out of his hand. It fell into the sink, into the cold soapy gray water in which the pots from last night's pot-au-feu were soaking. He watched as the ink began to run, then vanished almost entirely off the page. Then the paper itself began to disintegrate, until it became part of the gray soapy water that will soon flow from that sink down to the sewage treatment center of the city, thence into the ocean, from whence its molecules will fly and dip and whirl until they, too, become part, not just of the ocean and the sky and the air, but of the desk on which I am writing, the chair on which you are sitting, and the book you hold here in your hands.

"Another World" came on as Aurelia prepared to do her ironing. Unwilling to have yet another confrontation about the TV, Jack poured the rest of the cold coffee in his cup and left the kitchen.

Jack the dog was groaning. Behind his eyelids was a vision of an Irish setter with hair that glowed like sunset. Over the fields of Riverside Drive they loped, without I.D. tags, licenses, collars, dancing the ancient dance of dominance and submission. Growing small in the distance were Lorraine and

Judy and the Man With His Name and the other man, the one who first lived with Lorraine, who now came to walk Judy once a week. As if in unison, the two men unzipped their pants and, in full sight of Lorraine and Judy and everyone in the park, lifted their right legs and peed. Jack and the Irish setter, having outpaced servile Afghans, Lhasa apsos, Akitas, lay down panting on their paws. Soon it will be night, time to search for food—not pre-killed and pre-cooked food out of a can, but that which they have to track and rip apart for themselves. In the winter their urine will make frozen yellow tracks through the snow; the crystals on their shaggy coats will catch the sun as if glass dust were sprinkled on their fur. In the rain they'll smell like old wool coats. Burrs will stick to their fur, and they'll be cold, flea-ridden, chased by cars. And one day, one day, just for fun, Jack will stand up on his two hind legs and pee.

Jezebel, dreaming of a big gray pigeon, reached out and swatted Jack on the nose. Jack, discombobulated, jumped up, yawned, then slouched into the kitchen for some water.

Apparently, when the apartment was renovated the old pantry was eliminated and the space absorbed into the enlarged and modernized kitchen; the wall that had bounded the fourth side of what had been the third bedroom was knocked down, integrating this space into the house as a second living room, and permitting light to stream in the kitchen and dining room—areas of the apartment that had formerly been forced to rely almost totally on artificial light. Other changes were also made—bathrooms modernized; recessed lighting installed in lowered ceilings; floors sanded, pickled, and polyurethaned; moldings knocked off walls and walls replastered and painted; small windows turned into large picture ones by knocking out nonstructural parts of exterior walls and replacing normal-sized panes by characterless square yards of glass; still, it was the structural renovation of the master bathroom (trebled in size by the addition of space once occupied by two closets and the small bathroom attached to the former middle bedroom), and the elimination of the third bedroom, that were most noticed by anyone who had seen the apartment in its original state.

Now, in his perfectly shaped and situated studio, safe from the glance of Aurelia as she stood at the stove or ironing board, the mockery of Judy and her friends, the snide (or even flattering) comments of the delivery boys and repairmen as they traipsed through the apartment on their way to the kitchen or bathrooms, the careless swipe of Jack's or Jezebel's tail, Jack stood in front of a blank canvas in the center of the missing, rebuilt room—the very image he had had of himself when he was young. Unwitnessed, he looked out on trees, a basketball court, the ice-blue river, clouds of dark gray smoke that a burning pier a mile and a half away sent into the sky. Behind him was a storage rack for his paintings, shelves for his pastels and inks and tubes of paint, drawers for his papers and prints, a steel table piled with brushes, palette knives, and the paper cups he used to mix his colors. His old couch was there, the one on which he and Lorraine used to have so much fun, and a chair whose stuffing was falling out. On the wall in front of him was tacked a four-by-six-foot Belgian linen canvas, newly gessoed white, ready to receive whatever image he chose. He opened a tube of BLOCKX cobalt blue paint, squeezed some onto his palette, picked up a three-inch bristle brush, and started to paint.